Praise for *Distant Echoes*

"Colleen Coble has concocted a tangy *whodunit* and spiced it up with just the right amount of romance, intrigue, inspiration, and a generous splash of spine-tingling suspense. Sit back, put your feet up, and try to sip it slowly—if you can! Aloha!"

—Kathy Herman, author of the Baxter Series and *Poor Mrs. Rigsby*

"This story of restoration steeped in Hawaiian tradition and culture will make you want to pack you bags and head for the islands. Aloha, baby!"

—Stephanie Grace Whitson, author of *A Garden In Paris*

"In *Distant Echoes*, Colleen Coble paints a picture of Hawaii that is as real as the characters she breathes to life. Rich detail, realistic romance, and you'll-never-guess suspense make this a story you won't want to put down until the last page. This story will echo in my mind for a long time."

—Denise Hunter, author of *Saving Grace*

"Colleen Coble soars and delivers with *Distant Echoes*. If romance, suspense, and action, blended with a strong Christian message are what you're looking for, *Distant Echoes* is it. From the first word I was hooked."

—William Kritlow, author of *Driving Lessons*
and the Lake Champlain Mystery Series

"Colleen Coble is the master of romantic suspense. Whether we're tracking villians, swimming with dolphins, or enjoying a luau, *Distant Echoes* delivers the best in suspense, action, romance, and family drama. I love a book that takes me someplace I've never been and Colleen's Aloha Reef Series does that wonderfully! I can't wait to come back and visit again."

—Kathryn Mackel, author of *The Surrogate* and *The Departed*

"No one does romantic suspense like Colleen Coble: Tightly-plotted, deeply-drawn characters and, as always, a fascinating setting! Colleen only gets better and I highly recommend *Distant Echoes* for an exciting adventure vacation without ever leaving home!"

—Kristin Billerbeck, author of *What a Girl Wants*
and *She's Out of Control*

"*Distant Echoes,* the first of The Aloha Reef Series, is another of the quality novels we have all grown to expect from Colleen Coble. The fast-paced suspense, well-crafted romance, vivid descriptions, deep spiritual insights and fascinating glimpses into Hawaiian culture will keep you reading until the very last page. And of course, there are the heart-tugging animal scenes, with Nani the dolphin a very worthy successor to Samson, everyone's favorite Search and Rescue canine. It is easy to see why Colleen is a RITA finalist."

—Hannah Alexander, author of *Last Resort* and *Note of Peril*

"In *Distant Echoes,* Colleen Coble sets her suspense in glorious Hawaii. Her heroine, Kaia, seeks to communicate with her special friend, a dolphin, but the past swirls in with the tropical tide. Not just Kaia's past, but many dangerous currents sweep in threatening lives and futures."

—Lyn Cote, author of The Women of Ivy Manor series

"*Distant Echoes* is a well-crafted story filled with page-turning intrigue and suspense. I loved the details of Hawaiian culture sprinkled throughout. A fun, yet moving read. Highly recommended!"

—Marlo Schalesky, author of *Only the Wind Remembers*

DISTANT
ECHOES

ALSO BY COLLEEN COBLE

DISTANT ECHOES

COLLEEN COBLE

THOMAS NELSON
Since 1798

NASHVILLE   MEXICO CITY   RIO DE JANEIRO

Published in Nashville, Tennessee, by Thomas Nelson. Thomas Nelson is a registered trademark of Thomas Nelson, Inc.

Thomas Nelson, Inc., titles may be purchased in bulk for educational, business, fund-raising, or sales promotional use. For information, please e-mail SpecialMarkets@ThomasNelson.com.

Publisher's Note: This novel is a work of fiction. Names, characters, places, and incidents are either products of the author's imagination or used fictitiously. All characters are fictional, and any similarity to people living or dead is purely coincidental.

Scripture references are from the HOLY BIBLE, NEW INTERNATIONAL VERSION ®. Copyright © 1973, 1978, 1984 by International Bible Society. Used by permission of Zondervan Publishing House. All rights reserved.

ISBN 978-1-4016-9003-8 (RPK)

Library of Congress Cataloging-in-Publication Data

Coble, Colleen.
    Distant echoes / Colleen Coble.
      p. cm.- (The Aloha Reef series ; bk. 1)
    ISBN 0-7852-6042-0 (trade paper)
    I. Title.
    PS3553.O2285D577 2005
    813'.6—dc22

2004022254

Printed in the United States of America

HB 07.16.2018

For my perfect, wonderful children
who bring me joy every day
David Coble Jr.
Kara Coble

A pronunciation guide for the Hawaiian language
is included as a resource in the back of the book.

Do you not know?
  Have you not heard?
The LORD is the everlasting God,
  the Creator of the ends of the earth.
He will not grow tired or weary,
  and his understanding no one can fathom.
                              —Isaiah 40:28

ONE

The turquoise water surrounded Kaia Oana in a warm, wet blanket of delight. She angled her body like a torpedo and zipped through the lagoon beside Nani. The Pacific bottle-nosed dolphin spiraled like a top then burst through the waves above Kaia's head in a jump of pure joy.

Kaia felt like doing the same. She arched her back and moved her hands through the water in the flowing hula movements she loved. The movement felt like a prayer, and in many ways, it was. She smiled and kicked her fins, shooting to the top of the water with Nani.

Her head broke the surface three feet from her boat, *Porpoise II*, as it rocked gently in the small swells off the island. She blinked salt water out of her eyes then waved at her brothers before turning her gaze to the Na Pali coastline. It soared some four thousand feet and touched clouds that covered the peaks with mist. If she squinted her eyes just right, one rock looked like a brontosaurus straight out of *Jurassic Park*.

The music from the CD player she'd brought echoed on the wind. Amy Hanaiali`i Gilliom sang "Palehua," a song about the way Hawaii's mountains call to the soul. Today Kaia felt that pull strongly. She swam to the boat and slipped off her fins then climbed into the *Porpoise II*. The Hawaiian trade winds brought more than mere salt-laden breezes today, a sure sign that the perfect day with her two brothers was about to end.

Bane sat in the bow with his fishing pole over the side. He saw Kaia and nodded toward the clouds. "*Auê*! You didn't check the weather again, did you?" Her brother's tone was gentle and held only a hint of reproach. Mano looked up at the sky and then into the fish bucket, which held only a couple of small snapper.

Kaia grabbed a towel and grinned at her brothers. "Why check? It hardly ever changes." She would relish this time with them. They were so often separated these days.

Nani rose on her tail and moved backward through the water. The dolphin gave a chirp then sank beneath the waves and chased brightly colored fish beneath Kaia's boat. Two other dolphins, eager to play with Nani, jumped in front of the boat in perfect unison then swam away.

They gave their pod's characteristic "call," a signature whistle that had been imprinted by their mother in the hours after birth. Nani had been only a few months old when Kaia found her as an orphaned calf, but when Kaia released her into the wild, she'd quickly joined this pod of six bottle-nosed dolphins. Nani never forgot Kaia was her "mother" though, and the two had formed a bond that had fueled Kaia's obsession with dolphin research.

Kaia laughed at their contagious joy then noticed a man along the shore staring out to sea through binoculars. A tourist probably. She watched him a bit longer. There was a curious intent in the way he stood, and a touch of unease stirred in her stomach. Her smile faded. She shook her head. Her imagination had a tendency to run wild.

She turned to watch the dolphins again, never tiring of their grace. Nani chattered and swam to the boat. She pushed her nose against Kaia, and Kaia ran her hand over the dolphin's sleek head. It felt like a warm inner tube. Nani butted her again, and Kaia laid her head against the dolphin. Nani seemed to sense her moods with an almost uncanny ability.

Several warm drops of rain pattered onto the sea. Kaia lifted her face into the mist and watched the clouds swoop lower. Her brothers would want to get in, but she loved to be part of the elements, to smell the moisture and to experience the boat rolling along the waves.

"Storm's coming pretty quick now," Mano said, putting away his gear.

Kaia glanced at the sky. "We'd better get to shore." She yanked on the boat's anchor. As she bent over the boat and tugged at the rope, a vibration seemed to come out of nowhere. Kaia looked up and saw something pass overhead with a shriek that caused her to clap her hands to her ears.

"Look out!" Mano shouted. He grabbed Kaia's arm and forced her to sit down.

The high-pitched sound surrounded Kaia and made her want to scream herself. The vibration intensified then rocked their vessel. She dropped her hands from her ears and grabbed the side of the boat. The vibration grew from a steady hum into thunder, ending in an explosion that seemed to fill the world. Bane reached over and steadied her or she would have toppled off her seat and into the water.

Still holding her brother's hand, Kaia stared in the direction of the blast. Thick, black smoke roiled up from the water to her east, nearer to shore. The echoes of shouts and screams rose above the sound of the waves and wind. She tore her gaze from the sight and turned to find Nani. Only the dolphin's nostrum protruded from the water like a beak as she quivered at the commotion. She rolled to the side, exposing one eye that blinked with concern.

"I think it's a tourist boat!" Mano leaned forward with a pair of binoculars.

Dread coiled in the pit of Kaia's stomach. She squinted. "Can you see the boat's name?"

"Yeah, it's the *Squid.*"

"Laban's boat!" She stared at her brothers and saw the same stricken expression she knew must be on her own face. Their cousin had only operated the tourist sightseeing catamaran a little over a year.

New urgency fueled them. Bane pulled in the anchor. Mano started the motor.

"Come, Nani!" Kaia shouted over the roar of the engine as the boat picked up speed. Mano turned the boat toward the disaster. Kaia leaned into the wind, frantically scanning the sea for people. The fresh scent of salt water mixed with an oily odor that clung to her nose and throat.

The dolphin kept up with the *Porpoise II* as it slammed against the waves, the swells building now from the impending storm. As they drew nearer, she could see a sixty-foot catamaran on fire with at least a dozen people in the water.

"I'll call it in!" Mano turned and grabbed the radio mic.

"Help me!" a woman screamed as she caught sight of Kaia.

Kaia turned to seize a flotation cushion, but Bane beat her to it and tossed the cushion to the woman. A boy of about fourteen, his face blackened by smoke, swam toward the boat and reached out his hand. Bane hauled him in.

The boy landed on the deck. "My mom!" he panted. He scrambled to all fours and pointed to another woman floating face- down in the water.

The woman wasn't moving. Kaia dove overboard. The mounting waves tossed her about as she swam to the woman. She rolled the boy's mother over. The woman's eyes were closed, and she didn't appear to be breathing. Kaia fought the whitecaps and towed the woman to the boat then pushed her into Bane's arms. He pulled the limp figure over the edge.

"I know CPR," the boy panted. "Please find my sister. She's out there somewhere." He bent over his mother.

Bane hesitated then nodded and jumped in the water with Kaia.

Kaia wanted to search for Laban, but victims bobbed all around her. She struck out toward a man ten feet away, but the dolphin got there first. Nani nudged him until he grabbed hold of her dorsal fin, then she towed him toward the *Porpoise II.*

Mano soon joined them. He struck off toward the burning catamaran. Kaia propelled herself through the waves toward another victim. The thick, oily smoke hung low over the choppy seas and burned her eyes and throat. Her muscles ached, and she lost count of how many people she and her brothers hauled to her boat. At least ten, she was sure.

Looking around her craft, she saw people lying on the small deck. The boat rode low in the water, and she knew they'd have to stop soon or the rough seas would swamp the small craft. But not yet. Laban was still out here somewhere.

Praying for strength, she plunged back into the mounting waves.

THE BLACK SMOKE TOLD LIEUTENANT COMMANDER JESSE Matthews where to aim his boat. He stood in the bow of his vessel as it sped toward the catastrophe. For catastrophe it surely was. He felt physically sick. What could have caused the missile to veer off course that way? Every stage of the new missile defense system tests had gone perfectly up to now.

This new missile defense system was capable of distinguishing between decoys and true incoming missiles, a feature no previous missile defense system had possessed. The navy had a lot of money riding on it, and even more pressure from Washington. Tests so far had been promising: the exoatmospheric kill vehicle had managed to separate from the interceptor and the booster rocket, the interceptor had worked, and the infrared signals had performed flawlessly.

Until today. For no explainable reason, the test missile had turned north five miles off course and then plunged. He prayed no one had been killed.

Another long night lay ahead. He'd already been on the job nearly eighteen hours, investigating a security breach at the base that had resulted in a fatality. But an adrenaline surge now pushed away his earlier fatigue. The boat's bow slammed against the waves, and the salt spray drenched him. Jesse put binoculars to his eyes. The horrific scene jumped into focus: bodies everywhere in the water, and what remained of a tourist catamaran was quickly being swamped by the swells. Another boat loaded with victims rode precariously low in the water. He lowered the binoculars as he drew near. The vessel slowed, and the engines throbbed as the craft fought the seas to maintain its position alongside the sinking boat.

For a moment, the horror of knowing people had been hurt paralyzed him. Would he ever be able to avoid this kind of loss? He got control of himself and began to bark out orders. The crew scurried to rescue as many as possible.

Jesse blinked the salty spray from his eyes and then blinked again at the sight of a young woman battling the high seas. Her exhausted face was surrounded by long black hair that floated behind her. The girl seized a dolphin's dorsal fin with one hand and grasped a female victim with the other. The dolphin nimbly managed the waves and had the women alongside Jesse's boat in moments.

Jesse shook off his shock at the unusual rescue and reached down to help. He tried to pull the injured woman onto the deck, and a medic rushed to care for her. But the young woman clung to the dolphin, and her gaze met Jesse's. He saw exhaustion in her eyes.

"I think you're done for," he said. "We'll take over now." He held out his hand to help her aboard.

Her face was strained with fatigue, but she gave a stubborn shake of her head. "There are still people out there. My cousin—" Her eyes filled with tears, and she turned to paddle back out. A wave rolled over her head, and she came up sputtering.

"It will do them no good if you drown in the process of trying to get them. My men will haul in all they can find." He wished he could reassure her about her cousin, but the death count today was likely to be high. He set his lips in a determined line. "Give me your hand," he told the young woman.

Another man surfaced next to the woman. Hawaiian like her, he flung his wet hair back from his face. "Kaia needs to get out of the water," he gasped. He grabbed the young woman's arm and pushed her toward Jesse.

The mermaid—for that's what she looked like—shook her head and started to push away from the boat again. There was no time to argue with her. Her olive skin was paler now. Jesse reached down and grabbed her arm. The man in the water pushed her toward him, and Jesse easily lifted her into the boat.

She struggled briefly then sagged. "I'll just rest a minute," she muttered. "Bane and Mano need to rest too. They've been in the water as long as I have."

"I'll get them too," Jesse promised her. He helped her sit on the deck and went back to grab the man in the water, but one of the boat's crew had already helped him aboard.

Dressed in dripping shorts and a T-shirt, the man squeezed water out of his thick black hair. "Lucky for us you got here. I don't think I would have been able to get Kaia out of the water until we'd gotten all the victims out." He turned and looked across the water. "Stay there, Mano!"

Kaia. Pronounced the Hawaiian way as "kigh-yah," meaning "the sea." How appropriate of this Hawaiian who had thrown herself into the sea with no thought for her own safety. The island spirit of aloha meant uninhibited love and affection freely given. She'd certainly shown that today, as had the two men.

Jesse heard a shout and turned back to the ocean. A man in the boat loaded with victims waved toward the one who'd insisted Kaia get out of the water. Jesse wondered if one of them was her husband. He ordered some of his own men to go help the overloaded boat.

He crouched beside the water nymph. "You okay?"

Kaia struggled to sit up. "Bane, what about Laban . . ." she began.

"No sign of him," Bane said. He turned and scanned the water. "Your dolphin is having a fit. She's not letting this boat out of her sight. Whistle to her so she knows you're all right."

Obviously still shaky, Kaia wobbled to the port side of the

boat. Nani chattered from the storm swells. Kaia pulled the whistle
dangling from a chain around her neck up to her mouth and blew
a series of short and long blasts. The dolphin chattered again then
turned to slowly circle the boat in a calmer manner.

"You can talk to them?" Jesse asked, pulling a chair forward
for her.

Kaia sank into it. "I'm working on it. I'm studying mammal intelligence at Seaworthy Labs. Nani is the best I've ever worked with."

"She's phenomenal," Bane put in. "I've never seen anything
like the bond between Nani and my sister. They're soul mates. Kaia
found Nani as an orphaned calf. She doesn't belong to Seaworthy."

So these two were related, not married. Jesse turned and checked
the progress of his men. Most of the victims were now out of the
water. "We'll have everyone to shore soon," he said.

As THE BOAT RODE THE WAVES TO BARKING SANDS NAVAL BASE,
Jesse's gaze wandered to the dolphin that followed them. He'd never
seen a dolphin act that way.

Maybe it was his fatigue or maybe it was truly inspired, but a
thought began to take shape in Jesse's head. This missile system was
important to national security. They had to get it right. With one
man already dead from the security breach last night, he couldn't
afford another problem.

He knew the navy sometimes used dolphins and sea lions to
patrol offshore for divers who were threatening national security.
Sea lions were trained to carry a clamp in their mouths. They would
approach an intruder from behind and attach the clamp, which
was connected to a rope, to the swimmer's leg. With the person
restrained and tagged, sailors aboard ships could pull the swimmer
out of the water. Would something like that work here with Nani?

"How many dolphins do you work with?" he asked slowly.

"Three," Kaia said. "But only Nani is this responsive." She pushed her wet hair out of her eyes.

Bane put his hand on her shoulder. Jesse could tell they were both done in. His aide, Ensign Will Masters, motioned to him, and Jesse went to join him. "What's the death toll so far, Ensign?"

Masters grimaced. "Five dead so far, sir. I don't know about missing yet. But we've got another problem, Commander."

"What is it?"

"Headquarters just radioed. Television news cameras are waiting for us."

Great, just great. As if he didn't have enough to worry about, now the media would be swarming the base gate and trying to point a finger at what went wrong. "I'll take care of it." It was all he could do to suppress a sigh.

"One of the survivors is asking to talk to you, sir."

"Which one?"

The ensign pointed out a white-haired man leaning against the railing. Jesse made his way through the survivors. He paused frequently to offer reassurance to those crowding together before he finally reached the man. "Ensign Masters said you needed to talk to me?"

The elderly man blinked bleary hazel eyes and straightened. "Been years since I was on a navy ship," he said. "This is the first time I've been to the islands since World War II, and I get fired on again. That missile came right at us like it was aimed, my boy. I think the navy has a big problem."

Jesse pressed his lips together. Could the missile have been tampered with? Security was already so tight a crab couldn't scuttle across the sand, though an approach by sea was still a possibility. He wasn't sure how to tighten it, but he was going to have to find a way before the next test.

By the time they arrived at the base, the storm had passed.

When Jesse got to shore, he headed off to talk to Captain Lawton, who was in charge of the testing. He found the captain pacing his office. Nearly sixty, Captain Jim Lawton had the vigor and drive of a thirty-year-old.

Lawton stopped wearing a path through his carpet. "How many dead?"

"Five."

Lawton's expression didn't change. "The next trial is in two weeks. I don't want to miss that date."

Jesse nodded. "Sir, one witness, a World War II veteran, said it looked like the missile had targeted the catamaran."

The captain scowled. "That's not possible, Jesse. I was right there watching the trial. It was a computer malfunction. The guidance system, most likely."

"I don't think we should do any more trials until we investigate. What if it was more than the malfunction it seems?"

Lawton jabbed his finger in Jesse's chest. "Security is your baby, Commander, not missile design. I've waited my whole life for this moment. Nothing is going to stop this test. I'll get my engineers on it. It was a simple computer problem and I'll fix it. You just do your part and make sure the public doesn't panic. There's nothing to fear."

"What about the possibility of terrorist interference?"

The captain stared hard at Jesse. "Are you saying you suspect a terrorist plot?" His lips lifted in a smile that didn't reach his eyes. "Don't mention such a harebrained idea to the press. You just keep everyone off my back until I get the real problem corrected."

"Sir, last night's security breach. It could be related." Jesse could hear the captain's teeth grinding. Sometimes he wondered if Captain Lawton had it all together.

Lawton's teeth grinding grew louder before he spoke again. "I'm not going to stop our military exercises on a vague feeling from an old man. It's not going to happen. We have this under control. You're dismissed."

Jesse didn't understand the captain's stubborn position. The World War II veteran wasn't some crackpot. This was more serious than the captain wanted to admit. Jesse had to figure it out somehow. But first he had to deal with the media.

He could hear the buzz of voices as he approached the gate to the base. A young man with a shock of red hair was the first to reach Jesse.

"What happened, Commander? A terrorist attack?"

Other reporters joined them, and Jesse took a reflexive step back from the mics reaching toward him. He held up his hand. "A computer malfunction is suspected at this time. We're conducting a full investigation, but we don't believe the accident was terrorist related." He just hoped the captain was right.

"What about more live testing? We don't want a missile coming down on our heads because the navy can't get their computer to work." The young woman asking the question thrust a mic into his face.

He pushed it away. "There will be no more live testing until we are sure the problem won't reoccur." Lawton had his theories, and Jesse had his. Jesse only hoped his own would prove false before the next test was scheduled.

Two

A successful trial of our new weapon," he said. He leaned back in his leather chair and propped his feet on his desk. The bank of windows behind him looked out on the Pacific Ocean, a grand view at this height that reduced the surfers to antlike figures riding the waves. He'd been one of the ants all his life, but that was about to change. He just wished his dad were still alive to see this success.

He glanced up. "Make sure you reward our man on the ground for a job well done."

"I already did." His right-hand man handed him a can of Red Bull.

He took it and popped the top. The immediate caffeine jolt would make this moment sweeter. "You're sure they won't realize this failure was deliberate?"

His assistant shook his head. "They're blaming the guidance mechanism."

"How many casualties?" Not that he cared about the lives lost. This would be just a handful compared to what he had planned for the next launch. A stab of guilt startled him. He'd thought he had successfully discharged feelings like that when he first planned this. He focused on what his assistant was saying.

"Mixed reports so far. Some say ten dead and twenty injured; other reports say only five dead." His assistant never showed much emotion. A tall blond man in his forties, his bland expression never changed.

The man scowled at the remorse that kept rearing its head. He had to eradicate it now. "I'd hoped for more." The more dead bodies, the more the media would sit up and take notice.

"A woman and her dolphin showed up and saved many of them."

"A dolphin?" He waved his hand to indicate how unimportant it was.

His assistant nodded. "Part of the Seaworthy Lab research."

"Interesting." He glanced at the fish in the huge tank behind his desk. If only his piranha wasn't a freshwater fish, and so small. But the sea mammal was unlikely to interfere.

This was his one shot at success. In one brilliant move, he could gain the respect he'd lost—no, the respect that had been stolen from him. Nothing could be allowed to go wrong. And he certainly couldn't afford to let pity or guilt distract him from his purpose.

JESSE RUBBED HIS EYES. HIS VISION WAS BLURRY, AND HE KNEW his eyes had to be as red as this morning's sunrise. He couldn't remember when he'd slept last. It would be hours before his head hit the pillow today as well. The night had been a blur of interviews and questions.

His cell phone rang and he clicked it on. "Matthews."

"Same here," a familiar voice said.

"Kade?" Jesse hadn't heard from his cousin in several months.

"You got it on the first try." Kade's voice was cheerful. "I'm going to be on the island in a couple weeks for some training. Can we get together?"

"You bet. Just you and Bree?"

"And Lauri, Davy, and Samson. Thought we'd make a family vacation of it. Our first official getaway."

Jesse chuckled. "Wonder dog too?"

"You know he won't let Davy out of his sight. And since he's a service dog, he can travel on the plane with us."

"We'll get together for dinner," Jesse promised. "Give me a call when you get to town." They chatted a little longer, then he said good-bye. It was going to be good to see his cousin. They tried to get together once a year, but he and Kade had both been so busy, it had to have been eighteen months or so since they'd seen one another.

He grabbed a cup of coffee on his way to the control room. He added a bit of water so it was cool enough to gulp down quickly. The shot of caffeine revived him, and he stepped into the room filled with banks of computers with more spring in his step. The servicemen and women were too busy with their computers to notice him as he stood and gazed around, hoping to catch one of them taking a break and willing to answer a few questions.

He caught the eye of Ensign Donna Parker. She quirked an eyebrow, and he joined her at her desk.

"I wasn't expecting to see you today, Commander," she said.

Her red hair just skirted her shoulders in a sleek regulation bob, and the flirtation in her aqua eyes was subdued but obvious. Jesse had been aware of her interest since he'd arrived, but he hadn't encouraged it, though he'd been flattered.

He smiled but made sure it was impersonal. "Good morning. I was wondering if you were on duty yesterday when the missile veered off course?"

Donna grimaced, her smile fading. "Sure was. We had to watch while that thing took a nosedive."

"Any idea what happened?"

She shook her head. "Not yet, but I'm looking into the GPS system or the gyros. The system performed perfectly until it veered off course. It didn't seem to hear any of our commands. I've never seen a test go so haywire."

"You think it could have been deliberate?"

She frowned. "Deliberate? It would have had to be someone on our own team, and no one I know here would send a missile into a boatload of tourists."

"We've had some break-ins. Could someone have accessed the missile controls?"

She shook her head. "No. Only our computers can do it, and

they're all here. There has been no break-in to this room. And it can't be one of our own. We're all together. Someone would have noticed. It was a malfunction."

"You're sure?"

"I'm positive. The bigwigs are going over the missile scraps right now, but I'm sure they'll find it was in the navigational system."

Jesse nodded in feigned agreement. He still wasn't convinced. The WWII veteran's words wouldn't go away, no matter how much he wanted them to.

KAIA DROVE HER MAZDA PICKUP ALONG THE NARROW HIGHWAY. A flock of chickens squawked and ran for the ditch when she turned into her driveway. She slammed the brake to avoid hitting the last straggler. Wild chickens had once roamed freely on all the Hawaiian islands, but the introduction of the mongoose to all except Kaua'i and Lana'i had decimated the wild chicken population on the islands where they'd been imported. The chicken situation on Kaua'i had grown worse when Hurricane 'Iniki roared through the island in 1992 and freed most of the domestic chickens. The island had slowly recovered from the big blow, but capturing the chickens had been the least of the islanders' concerns.

Bane clung to his door handle as the truck jerked to a stop. "Where did you learn to drive?" he demanded.

As an oceanographer for the Coast Guard, he was taller and slimmer than Mano, and his long limbs could glide through the water like Nani herself.

She stuck out her tongue at Bane. "You taught me," she said. She rubbed her eyes. They'd been at the Lihu'e hospital all night, and the sun was already halfway up the horizon now. She glanced at her watch. Nearly nine o'clock. Her gaze met her brother's. "They never found Laban."

"I know."

Kaia wanted to comfort Bane. She hadn't known their cousin well—he'd spent most of his life in California and had only recently come back to the islands—but Laban and Bane had grown close in the past year. Thankfully, Laban hadn't left a wife or children.

The media had accosted them when they'd gone ashore, and she was sure reports of the disaster had been on TV this morning. After disappearing for a time, the handsome lieutenant commander had returned to take charge of the reporters with the same aplomb he'd demonstrated on the water. The self-sufficient type always made her feel inadequate.

Bane got out of the truck and went to the porch of Kaia's bungalow. The neat green shutters framed windows that overlooked the blue waters of the Pacific from the house's perch atop a cliff. A set of steps that had been cut into the face of the rock led to Echo Lagoon, a tiny smile of beach on the leeward side of the island. Square and squat with a roof that looked like thatch but wasn't, the house had been in the Kohala family, her mother's ancestors, for nearly a hundred years. Her brothers had opted to let her have it, and she hadn't refused. A brightly colored rooster crowed and hopped off the step as Bane neared. "You'd better run or you'll be dinner," he said. He held open the door for her.

"He knows he has nothing to fear," she told him. "No one in their right mind would try to eat one of them." The local joke was that if you put on two pans to boil and put a chicken in one and some lava rock in the other, the chicken would be ready when you could stick a fork in the lava rock.

Bane laughed, but his eyes were grim. She pushed open the door, and her brother followed her inside.

"This place looks like 'Iniki just came through again." He looked around with obvious disfavor.

Kaia tried to look at it through his eyes. Her cat had knocked last night's popcorn bowl onto the floor, and unpopped kernels littered the carpet. The laundry she'd sorted on the living room floor was still there. "I haven't been home much lately," she said. "Besides, I'll never be Suzy Homemaker."

"Yeah, but not even the *Clean Sweep* crew would be willing to take this on. Don't you believe in organization?" He picked up her discarded shorts and top that she'd changed out of on her way to work a week earlier and dropped them in the first laundry pile.

"Sure, I believe in it. I'm just not obsessed with it like you are. It's not that bad. Besides, no one sees it but me." The message light on her answering machine was blinking. She punched it, and her grandfather's deep voice came on. Twice. The second time he sounded worried. "Sounds like *Tûtû kâne* thinks we might have gone down with the ship." She cleared the messages and walked toward the kitchen. She'd go visit her grandfather in a little while. His fears wouldn't be allayed until he saw her. She wondered if he'd heard about Laban. Maybe the news hadn't announced the name of the catamaran involved.

Her stomach rumbled, but nothing sounded good. She was too tired. She knew she had to eat something though. It had been eighteen hours since her last meal. "Want an omelet?"

"I'm not hungry."

"Me neither, but we haven't eaten since noon yesterday."

Bane shrugged, and Kaia grabbed the eggs and ham from the refrigerator. She chopped pineapple to toss in as well, and its aroma filled the kitchen. She handed her brother a plate heaped with his omelet and taro hash browns then joined him at the table.

"I need to call *Tûtû kâne*." Kaia suppressed a shudder at the thought of explaining to her grandfather about his great-nephew.

"Mano has probably already told him about Laban. He was heading there from the hospital."

"You know *Tûtû kâne* though. He won't rest easy until he knows all his *keikis* are safe and sound." Kaia finished her breakfast then grabbed the toothbrush she left near the kitchen sink. There was another one in her bathroom, and one more in her purse.

She brushed her teeth vigorously. She could feel Bane's gaze on her.

"None of us will love you less if you forget to brush."

Kaia didn't answer. She and Bane had been over this ground many times before.

Her tabby cat, Hiwa, had come out from under the couch to investigate. Kaia picked her up, and she began to purr.

Bane scratched the cat's head, but she bared her teeth like a dog and he drew back. "I don't know why she hates me," he complained.

"She's very discerning." Kaia grinned when Bane smiled back.

"Thanks for letting me stay with you," he said, heading to the coffeepot. "You know how Mano and I get along. It would have been pure torture to spend this month off duty with him, and I'm up too late to stay with *Tûtû kâne.*"

At least he quit nagging about brushing her teeth. "Only because you can never keep your mouth shut. Mano is entitled to his own opinions."

"But he's wrong!" Bane's face reddened.

"Pele Hawai'i might not be as bad as you're making out. You haven't checked it out. Extend Mano a little aloha."

"He needs to grow up."

When Bane set his jaw like that, there was no getting through to him. Kaia sighed. "Whatever. Let's not argue about it. I'm too tired."

Bane's face softened. "Sorry. You're right. I should check out the organization before I judge them. But the Hawaiian sovereignty groups make me nervous."

"You take our Hawaiian heritage too lightly, and Mano takes it too seriously."

"Whereas you are in the middle and just right, like Goldilocks."

Kaia grinned at her brother's tone. At least he was over his snit. She hated being on the outs with him. He was her mentor, the one person in the world she most trusted with the secrets of her soul. "I'm the last person to accuse of being perfect. You've heard me sing."

He clapped his hands to his ears. "And I hope never to hear it again. You're far from perfection, all right." Bane tipped his head to one side. "Though I saw the way the handsome navy guy was giving you the once-over."

Kaia felt a volley of heat race up her neck to burn her cheeks. "Don't be ridiculous!" Hiwa yowled, and she realized she'd been squeezing the cat too tightly. She loosened her grip, and the cat jumped down and stalked away with her tail in the air.

"If you'd been a dish of *'ono* ice cream, the commander would have consumed you on the spot." Bane dodged the dish towel Kaia threw at him and went to the refrigerator. He rummaged for a minute and pulled out a mango. "Is this fresh?"

"Pffett!" She crossed her eyes and stuck out her tongue. "I thought you weren't hungry. You know how I am about fresh fruit."

He grinned and shut the refrigerator. "Looking at this house, I wasn't sure." He cut the mango and put it on a plate then carried it back to the table. "That omelet just reminded my stomach how empty it was."

She realized they were still skirting around Laban's death. Bane must still not be ready to talk about it. She stared out the window at the palm tree swaying in the breeze. "I bet that lieutenant commander is dealing with a lot of garbage today."

"I wouldn't doubt it. That was some accident. What a fluke for a missile to go astray and hit a boat." His voice grew thick. "Laban was in the wrong place." He put the dish of mango on the table.

"I'm sorry, Bane." Kaia put her hand on his shoulder and he nodded.

"Someone needs to call his mother."

"Let's go see our grandfather. He may already have done it."

"I doubt it."

"I know." Ever since she could remember, her grandfather never talked about anything unpleasant. His mission in their lives was to make up for what their mother had done. He turned a blind eye to unpleasantness.

Bane went to the sink and opened the dishwasher. "These clean?"

"Don't they look clean?"

"Just checking." He dug a fork out of the dishwasher and sat at the table then began to eat his mango. Kaia began to empty the dishwasher.

He might make fun of her housekeeping, but she'd done a great job of decorating her small home, she thought. Her collection of Hawaiian art was shown off to advantage by the pale lemon walls. Tile floors added to the beach-house feel, as did the high ceilings and the gauzy curtains at the windows. It might be a little messy today, but it wasn't as bad as what Bane made out. She liked her little home.

Too bad she never had much time to enjoy it.

"Have you heard anything about your next assignment?" Her brother loved his job as an oceanographer, and she knew his hiatus would make him restless in the coming weeks.

He shook his head. "The ship repairs should be done in a month. I hope they stay on schedule. In the meantime, I'll get to bug you and *Tûtû kâne*."

"And Mano."

"I doubt we'll see much of him."

"He was excited to hear you'd be staying at least a month. You're too hard on him, Bane." Kaia watched him rub this thick black hair and look away. Bane sometimes forgot how his intensity affected those who loved him. His black-and-white perspective allowed little room for life's gray areas.

"I'll try to watch what I say," Bane said finally.

Kaia nodded. It was best not to rely too much on Bane's comment. For one thing, she would be surprised if he followed through. Sometimes she wondered if Bane saw his teenage self in Mano. Though Mano was thirty-two, he was one of those men who looked at life as something to be conquered.

They all carried the scars of what their mother had done. Bane said Kaia threw herself into her dolphin studies to show she was worthy, he traveled to forget, and Mano laughed at danger to prove it didn't hurt.

Her brother was too perceptive sometimes.

"You're thinking too much," Bane said. "Whenever you get that look on your face, I know you're wondering where she is."

"I don't care where she is."

"You care. We all care, but we can't change what happened. If we found her, maybe we could all move on and shed the crazy things that drive us. I've been thinking about trying to locate her."

Kaia shut the dishwasher with more force than she intended. "I couldn't stand it. Another rejection would be more than I could take." Kaia scooped up Hiwa, who had wandered back to the kitchen. Cuddling the cat helped soothe the woeful feelings that always accompanied the mention of her mother.

Bane's dark eyes softened, and he got up and took his empty plate to the sink. "She might have grown up, Kaia."

"Let's drop it," she said. "*Tûtû kâne* will be wondering where we are." She put the cat on the floor and went to the door.

Bane followed her. "You need to get some sleep. Me too. I'm beat."

"You can sleep when you're dead. Besides, I want to check on Nani. Last night was stressful for her." She led the way to the steps cut into the rock outside her front door. The railing was rusty but still sturdy, which was a good thing because the stairs were steep. She used them nearly every day.

She hurried down the steps to her grandfather's cottage in the jungle just off the beach. After Hurricane 'Iniki, the family had tried to talk *Tûtû kâne* into moving, but he'd repaired the house and moved right back in. She had to admit, she loved having him just a few steps away.

The aroma of roast pig wafted on the morning breeze and reminded Kaia of the lu'au tonight. Every Friday her grandfather hosted a lu'au on the beach for a local hotel. Dressed in his Hawaiian chieftain finery, he was a sight to behold, and most visitors came to get a look at him rather than for the outstanding food.

Her grandfather, Oke Kohala, still as fit as he was in his years as a pearl diver, sat on the sand making a sandcastle. Dressed in shorts and a red and yellow Hawaiian-print shirt, he didn't look seventy-eight, in spite of his white hair.

Kaia joined him on the sand and bent down to kiss him, inhaling the aroma from the cloves he perpetually had in his mouth. "Where's Mano?"

"He called, and he's on his way." Her grandfather stood and dusted the sand from his hands. He pointed to the porch chairs. "Have a seat."

Bane moved toward the chairs, and Kaia followed. "We wanted to make sure you knew what happened." Bane dropped into a chair then sprang to his feet when a loud *whoopee* pierced the air. He went sprawling on the sand in his haste to escape.

Tûtû kâne laughed, his face as expressive as a child's. Kaia giggled, her fatigue dropping away at the expression of horror on her brother's face.

"Where'd you get that?" His smile feeble, Bane picked up the cushion.

"Mano bought it for me yesterday." Still chuckling, their grandfather took the cushion from Bane and tucked it under his arm. "He bet me a shave ice that I couldn't get Bane to sit on it."

Bane managed a weak smile then sat gingerly back in the chair, sans cushion.

Still chuckling at the pleasure in her grandfather's face, Kaia sat beside him. "I have a feeling Mano is going to pay for this."

"I'm glad to see you and know that you are both okay," their grandfather said. "Any idea what happened? The news this morning was still pretty sketchy."

Bane shook his head. "Kaia and I were talking about how it almost looked deliberate. But the navy wouldn't have tried to take out a pleasure craft."

Her grandfather put his big hand on Kaia's shoulder. "I see the self-recrimination in your face. You always think you can fix everything. This wasn't your fault."

She sighed. "I keep wishing we'd been closer, that I was there sooner. At least five people died. We're pretty sure . . ." She stopped and her gaze went to her brother. He gave a slight nod. "We can't find Laban."

Her grandfather's smile leaked away. "It was Laban's boat? Are you sure?"

"Mano saw the name. There's no mistake."

"And Laban's missing?"

She nodded, not sure what to expect from her grandfather. He seldom showed his emotions.

"Maybe he'll be found yet."

Tūtū kāne was never one to face facts. Kaia suppressed a sigh. "Someone needs to call his mother."

A look of dread crossed her grandfather's face. Bane must have seen it as well, because he stood. "I'll do it. Where's the number?"

"The address book is in the drawer by the phone," Oke said. He plucked at a string on his shirt.

Bane nodded and went to the house. Kaia glanced toward the water. "Have you seen Nani this morning?"

"She chattered her usual good morning before going off to find some fish."

"There she is!" Kaia spotted the dorsal fin coming into the small inlet. All dolphins looked a little different. She could recognize Nani out of a pod of dozens. She went down the steps to the edge of the water and waded in. The warm caress of the Pacific waves brought a comfort she never felt on land. Sometimes Kaia thought she was half fish herself.

Nani glided to her and nudged her with her nostrum. The dolphin squeaked and whistled a particular tune that Kaia recognized as Nani's greeting. She sank to her knees and rubbed Nani's skin. The dolphin rolled to her back so Kaia could rub her stomach. With her dolphin, Kaia felt accepted and whole. Once Nani found her own kind, she could have chosen never to come back, but she had never missed a day.

Snagging her research job at Seaworthy Labs had been a stroke of unbelievable luck. She'd gotten her PhD last year, and now at the ripe old age of twenty-nine, she was living the dream she'd had since she was ten and swam with her first dolphin. Every day she and Nani moved closer to understanding one another. Someday people would know her name as the woman who bridged the language barrier with sea mammals. She'd be able to hold her head high without shame. That day had been too long in coming.

Nani bore no injuries from the day before that Kaia could see. She gave the dolphin a final pat then slogged through the waves to the pier that tottered like a drunken man out into the water. Damaged in the 1992 hurricane, it needed replacing, but her grandfather had been reluctant to do it. He'd helped his father build it seventy years ago, and he couldn't let it go.

She hoisted herself onto the weathered boards and let her legs dangle in the water. The sound of the surf soothed her as she watched the dolphin frolic. After about fifteen minutes, Nani swished past Kaia's legs then rolled onto her back. When Kaia reached to touch her, the dolphin darted away as if to coax Kaia into going for a swim with her.

"Not today, Nani," she said. She began to sing a song she remembered from her childhood, one her mother had made up. It was about 'ohana, or family. Singing the words about the closeness of family, she felt her depression lift. Sometimes she felt she didn't have an 'ohana with her mother and father gone, and the song reminded her that family was more than parents. She needed to go talk to her grandfather, but not yet.

THAT GIRL NEVER COULD SING," OKE KOHALA SAID. HIS SMILE stretched across his brown face. He rose and moved toward the house.

Jesse's lips twitched. Kaia's voice had carried over the waves, and he had to admit she sounded a little like a tern—all squawk and no tone. But he'd still felt the heart in her song. He watched Kaia come toward him like Ni`ihau, the Hawaiian goddess of the sea. Fanciful stuff, but she really was lovely. Her long hair was bound in a French braid that hung over one shoulder and nearly touched her waist. High cheekbones jutted out from the sweet curves and angles of her face. Shapely black brows made an emphatic statement over her large dark eyes fringed with thick lashes. Her full lips drooped with weariness. Her naturally tanned skin looked kissed by the sun, and her eyes were as soft and melting as a black-tailed deer's.

Her eyebrows winged up when she saw him. "Good morning, Commander." Dressed in white shorts and a turquoise tank, she seemed an extension of the Pacific behind her. "Have they found any more survivors?" she asked.

He shook his head. "Not that I know of."

"I thought I'd run over to the hospital later today and see if there is anything I can do."

"You did plenty. I've never seen anything like it."

A blush touched her cheeks, and she looked away. "Anyone would have done the same."

"Not everyone has a dolphin to help them."

Her eyes brightened. "Nani is remarkable, isn't she? She's so intelligent and knew what to do without being told."

He took a deep breath. "That's the other reason I'm here. I need your help. Yours and Nani's."

She frowned. "I don't know what I could do to help the navy. Or is this personal?"

"No, this is for the navy, for your country actually."

She raised her eyebrows. "Why does it sound like I won't like it?"

At least she sounded amused. He took hope. "As a native of Kaua'i, I'm sure you're aware of how important this new defense system is?"

She nodded. "Everyone has been talking about it."

"The missile system we're testing is vital to national security. It's the best we've tested yet—until yesterday." It revved Jesse to talk about it, and he leaned forward.

"Sounds exciting. But where do I come in?" She took a step back.

He realized he was getting into her personal space and retreated. "We've had some disturbing security leaks at the base—desks riffled, hard drives destroyed, things like that. The last breach left one sailor dead." Kaia's eyes widened. Maybe he shouldn't have mentioned that part. "We think it came from the sea. You and Nani could help patrol offshore to make sure that doesn't happen again."

She was shaking her head before he finished. "I don't want Nani in danger. She's special. Nothing can be allowed to happen to her."

"Nothing will. We'd put a camera on her and let her patrol the waters. If anything showed up, we'd be right there. She would never be asked to stop an intruder, just tag them like the dolphins did in the Persian Gulf War. Apprehension would be my job."

"The whole thing is your job," Kaia said, crossing her arms over her chest. "Count us out."

"I can't. I need you."

"I'm sorry. It's just not possible."

He hadn't expected such uncompromising refusal. She had to know how valuable dolphins had been to the navy in the past. They had cleared the shipping lanes of explosives during the Iraqi war in a fraction of the time it would have taken divers to do the same. Her dolphins could save lives and man hours. But Jesse could tell from the finality in her voice that he'd get nowhere being a nice guy. Her boss at Seaworthy Labs needed to agree to this anyway. Maybe he could get him to order her to help.

THREE

Two days later, Jesse waved at Duncan Latchet, who stood outside Jo-Jo's Clubhouse in Waimea. Jo-Jo's made the best shave ice on the island, though the ramshackle wooden building that housed it was enough to scare away the tourists. Duncan already had his treat. Jesse's mouth watered just thinking of his favorite—banana shave ice with macadamia-nut ice cream in the bottom. He'd missed it during the twelve years he'd spent on the mainland. The pale imitations they'd called Hawaiian ice were nothing like the real thing.

"Thanks for meeting me," Jesse told his friend as he joined him with shave ice in hand. He scooped a bite into his mouth before sitting beside Duncan. Duncan was a year older than Jesse, but they'd played football together for the Red Raiders, the Kaua'i High School team. Duncan looked every inch his forty years and then some. His blond hair was thinning on top, and weary lines marked his mouth.

"No problem. You said it was important."

"Yeah, I hate to have to involve you, but I don't know what to do. I heard your brother just bought Seaworthy Labs, right?"

"You're sure on top of things. That just went through. He's excited about it. He's got some great contacts in the park business. Why do you ask?"

"I need a favor from one of their employees." He told Duncan about Kaia and her dolphin.

"No problem. It's the least I can do after you helped me get that navy contract. Though some days I wonder what I'm doing there." Duncan laughed, a tired sound.

"More work than you imagined, huh?" It felt good to talk to Duncan again. They had exchanged heated words when Christy died, and their relationship had never fully recovered. Jesse doubted that it ever would. Duncan tended to imagine himself a knight in shining armor, and in this instance, he'd failed to rescue the fair maiden.

"More work for less money. I shouldn't have cut my margins so low." Duncan took a bite of the ice cream in the bottom of his shave ice. "I'm not complaining though. It will pay off with more work in the long run." He wiped his fingers on a napkin and tossed it and the ice cup into the trash. "I'll call you tonight. I'm sure Curtis will see to it that you get the help you need. This is for our own security."

"Exactly," Jesse said, digging into the macadamia-nut ice cream in the bottom of his cup with as much satisfaction as he could muster. He knew he'd hear fireworks from Kaia when she found out. For some reason, he almost looked forward to it.

"You heard from Jillian lately?"

Duncan's question was almost too casual. Jesse glanced at him and suppressed a grin. Duncan and Jesse's sister had dated in high school but had broken up when Duncan went away to Honolulu for college. Jillian, several years younger, wasn't ready to settle down.

"Not in about two weeks. She was trying to get out of her latest assignment but wasn't having much luck. They want to send her to Italy, to a volcano about to blow. She needs the money, but she doesn't want to leave Heidi behind."

"Tell her I said hello." Duncan glanced at his watch and rose. "I should get back to work. It will be nine before I get home tonight as it is."

"*Mahalo*," Jesse called, thanking his friend. He wished he could do something to help Duncan. He seemed so lonely since his wife divorced him three years ago and took their two young children to the mainland. But even if Jesse could think of some way to help, Duncan's pride would never let him accept it.

Jesse's cell phone rang and he punched it on. "Matthews here."

"We've got problems." Ensign Will Master's voice came over the line.

"On my way," Jesse told his aide and ran for his Jeep Wrangler.

THE *PORPOISE II* SKIMMED THE TOPS OF THE WAVES. LABAN'S mother, Edena, held the vase containing her son's ashes between her knees as she perched in a seat beside Kaia. Her face was set and stoic. Kaia hadn't seen her cry at the funeral either.

"It was about here," Kaia said, cutting the engine. Her grandfather had been hurt that his niece hadn't wanted him along to scatter the ashes, but Edena had wanted only Kaia, and she likely would have gone alone if she hadn't needed Kaia to show her where Laban had died.

Edena nodded and stood. She began a funeral *mele*, her keening sharp as the words of the chant flowed out. Tears burned Kaia's eyes. Edena opened the vase and slowly scattered the ashes into the white crests of waves. As the *mele* mingled with the sounds of the terns overhead, Kaia prayed that she would never forget how short life could be.

Still dry-eyed, Edena put down the vase and turned to Kaia. "Was this more than an accident?" she whispered.

"The navy says the computer malfunctioned."

Edena nodded. "Do you believe it?"

"I have no reason not to," Kaia told her. Where was her aunt heading with this?

"If you learn anything that suggests it was more than an accident, would you promise to let me know—and to see what you can find out?"

"I'm not a cop or anything," Kaia pointed out. "There's not much I could do about it."

"Just keep your eyes and ears open. Something doesn't smell right to me about it. I think the navy is trying to cover up something."

Kaia shrugged. Her aunt had always been a little bit of a conspiracy theorist. She could humor her. "Okay," she said.

She took her aunt back to the dock then headed to work. She'd had the weekend to recuperate, though her muscles still ached from the ordeal in the water. Today she felt alert and ready to get back to her research. Dressed in a blue tank suit, she kicked off her Locals flip-flops, known in Kaua'i as "slippers" because they were easy to slip on and off. She dropped her bare feet over the edge of the dock into the warm water. The caress of the seawater made her eager to get to work.

The facility was already hopping with activity. The part-time students, Bobby Hannigan and Mindy Endo, were carrying buckets of fish to the large training pool for trainers Cindy Fletcher and Doug Murakami to use in the day's session.

Cindy Fletcher, a dishwater blonde with a baby face in spite of her nearly forty years, hurried past Kaia with a wave. The other trainer, Doug Murakami, about thirty, strolled behind her in his usual leisurely stride. His straight black hair fell over a smooth forehead. His family had emigrated to the islands from Japan before Doug was born then had moved back without him five years ago. His easy manner made him a favorite with the staff.

He paused to smile at Kaia. "Nice vacation? You look rested."

"Other than last weekend's crisis, it was great. I'm ready to get back to work though." Kaia turned to watch the dolphins jumping in the oversized pool. "Looks like they're impatient this morning." Seaworthy Lab had several Atlantic bottle-nosed dolphins. Though they looked similar to Nani, the Atlantic bottle-nosed thrived in shallow water, a trait dolphins like Nani didn't possess.

Dolphin research had ebbed and flowed over the years since the navy first began to investigate dolphin intelligence in the sixties. Opinion had run the gamut; some believed dolphins were like dogs, and at the other extreme, some believed they were even smarter than humans. Of course, the fact that dolphins lived in a unique environment made it hard to know for sure. It had only recently been discovered that dolphins could recognize themselves in a mirror, the only other animal besides a chimp to have such self-awareness.

"We'd both better get to work," she told him.

He grinned. "A poor man's work is never done." He patted her on the arm and continued his jaunt to the pool.

Cindy and Doug worked on regular dolphin training and put on shows for the public that brought in needed research money, while Kaia headed up the research project on dolphin intelligence. Her assistant, Jenny Saito, waved at her. Jenny, a thirty-two-year-old of Hawaiian and Japanese descent, came toward her carrying their communication device. The Dolphin Advanced Language Environment—DALE for short—was a computer gadget that utilized a touch screen and microphones to transmit clicks and whistles and was used with a hydrophone. The researchers dropped a touch screen in the water and used it to interact with the dolphins.

"Nani is raring to go." Jenny put DALE beside Kaia.

The dolphin chattered and rode the wave. She sank into the water then zipped past Kaia's legs before leaping out of the water and splashing Kaia with a huge wave. Rushing to Kaia, Nani rose and presented her nostrum for a kiss.

Kaia grinned and hugged the dolphin. "How have the other dolphins done while I've been away?"

"Liko has been bullying Mahina, and I had to scold him."

"They seem fine now." Kaia watched the three dolphins interact. It never ceased to amaze her how like a family they were. The pods all spoke the same "dialect" of whistles and clicks and taught it to the babies. They looked out for one another, and the mothers exposed themselves to danger to save their calves. If a member of the pod was too injured or sick to get to the surface for air, other dolphins bore the injured member to the surface and supported it so its blowhole was above the water.

Her own mother should have been so self-sacrificing. Kaia blinked and dragged her attention back to the dolphins. What was with all these thoughts about her mother? The woman was about as relevant to her now as the abandoned sugar plantations were to the island.

"You're supposed to go to the office," Jenny said.

"What's up?"

Jenny glanced around and lowered her voice. "We've got a new boss."

"You're kidding." She'd hoped to be further along in her research by the time a new owner came on board.

Jenny shook her head. "Nope. It must have sold last week, and no one told us. He came first thing this morning and took over the office. Not only is he the owner, but he's going to be the director."

"Who is it?"

"Curtis Latchet. Seems nice enough. Maybe he'll be more open with you than he was with me about his plans."

Kaia's earlier ebullience faded. "I guess I'd better go see what I can find out." She scrambled up and shoved her feet into her Locals and hurried to the office, a sterile box that looked out on the training area through a wall of windows.

The man behind the desk looked up and gave her a confident smile. Nearly fifty, she guessed, the wings of white at his temples gave him an air of distinction that seemed out of keeping with the casual lab. His grin was amiable though, and she smiled back cautiously. "I'm Kaia Oana," she said.

"Ah, so you're the marvelous Kaia. I've heard wonderful things about you and your work," he said. "Have a seat." He indicated the cracked vinyl chair across the desk from him. "I'm Curtis Latchet. You might have met my brother, Duncan, owner of Latchet Engineering."

She shook her head. "I've seen his buildings, but I've never met him." She sat in the chair and regarded him warily.

He steepled his fingers together. "Tell me how the research is going. I'm fascinated with dolphin communication. How close are we to a breakthrough?"

She wished she had better news to tell him. "I invented DALE, a computerized Dolphin Advanced Language Environment, and have begun to work with Nani and two other wild dolphins. I'm trying to teach them clicks and whistles that stand for certain words."

He shuffled through the papers on his desk. "Three dolphins? I thought the facility owned eight."

"Actually, we own five. The three I work with are wild. I found one of them, Nani, as an orphaned calf. After I rehabilitated her and released her back into the wild, she kept returning. Eventually the other two joined her."

His eyes did a slow blink as he stared at her. "So we're pouring our money and time into dolphins that are free to come and go? Why aren't you working with the dolphins we own? What happens if Nani and her friends choose not to come back one day?" He directed a gaze at her. "I think we need to build an enclosure and keep them in. I've paid a lot of money for this lab, and I don't want to see it escape with the dolphins. The communications research is key. Our future rests on being the first to break through the barrier."

"Captivity would be so wrong." She leaned forward. "It shortens the life expectancy of dolphins. Right now these three dolphins *choose* to interact with us. We want to be the first researchers to establish true communication between humans and dolphins, not just another place that trains sea mammals. Our approach is truly revolutionary."

"I see." He released the pen. "Coffee?" He lifted his coffee cup in the air.

"No thanks." She had to convince him. "Nani was fabulous the other day." She told him about the explosion and how the dolphin had towed people to the boat.

"That isn't all that unusual with dolphins, is it? Sometimes even wild dolphins rescue people." Curtis took a sip of coffee.

"Nani is different," Kaia insisted.

Curtis Latchet sighed heavily and sat down his cup. "Look, Kaia, I have plans for Seaworthy Labs. I'd like to see us go beyond what we're doing now. It's fine to draw in tourists to watch the dolphin show, but it's not the moneymaker it could be, and we're spending a lot of our resources on the research end. I have in mind to turn this area into an actual sea park and aquarium with water rides."

Kaia couldn't believe she was hearing this. "Then why did you purchase the lab if you didn't believe in our research?"

"It's an ideal location for a sea park. I've got designers working now on the plans for the rides and the tanks we'll need for the aquarium display."

She half rose out of her chair. "Please, Curtis, don't stop us now."

Curtis eyed Kaia thoughtfully and leaned back in his chair. "It will take several months for the plans to be ready. I can give it a trial period of two months. If you can't show me you're on to something really revolutionary, I'll move ahead with my plans."

"Two months! That's not enough time." Kaia stood and flipped her braid over her shoulder.

"All I'm saying is I'll withhold judgment for now. If you can show me the benefits of your research, I'll listen," he said mildly. "I don't want to be your adversary, Kaia. I want to be the first, but if we can't, I'll need to be practical. But I still want you to build a pen to keep the dolphins in. I can't lose them. They're too valuable."

Kaia bit back the words she wanted to say. "You can't do that!" she said.

"I can and I will. Those animals are worth a hundred thousand dollars each."

"If Nani belongs to anyone, it would be me. She doesn't belong to Seaworthy. If I have to take you to court over it, I will." As soon as the words were out of her mouth, she wondered if he would fire her on the spot.

He pressed his fingers against the bridge of his nose. "I don't want to fight with you, Kaia," he said softly. "This is not what I expected." He fell silent for a few moments. "Okay, I'll hold off on the pen for now. But if the research project fails, I'm not letting those dolphins escape."

"I won't fail." The bright promise of the day lay in ashes. There was no guarantee she would win if she went to court.

"One more thing," he said as she went toward the door.

She turned.

"I have an assignment for you."

Kaia waited, wondering why he didn't look at her.

Curtis glanced up and caught her gaze finally. "The navy needs some help, and I've agreed to assign you to them."

She couldn't have heard him correctly. "Who needs help?"

"The navy." He finally met her gaze. "Specifically, I've assigned you to work with Lieutenant Commander Jesse Matthews."

"You just gave me only two months to get results. I can't be spending my time anywhere but on my research."

"I've already promised our help."

"You want me to fail, is that it?" Her eyes burned, and she fought to keep her composure. "The offer of two months' trial was just a bone?"

"I can have Jenny take Nani and help Matthews if you'd rather. You could concentrate on the other two dolphins."

He was boxing her into a corner. "Nani is a free dolphin. She doesn't have to cooperate."

"Jenny assured me the dolphin would work with her too."

He was right. Nani loved Jenny too. She would come if either of them called. Jenny was good, but she wasn't as attached to Nani as Kaia was. The best chance Kaia had to make sure her dolphin wasn't injured was to take charge of the project herself.

The words seemed stuck in her throat. She swallowed. "Fine. I'll just have to work with Nani on my time off. I'll prove to you she can do it."

"Don't act like this is the end of the world, Kaia."

"How did Jesse get to you? Did he threaten the lab?" She wouldn't put it past him. He was probably a man who was used to getting his own way.

"Of course not. Not everything is a big conspiracy, Kaia. You probably don't know this, but my father had a hand in creating the missile defense system that's under testing right now." His pride shone through in his smile. "Though Dad is gone, I want to do everything I can to help make sure this system is implemented. My brother's business is tied to the project as well. I couldn't refuse their request for help."

"I bet he was smug." She could imagine his self-satisfied smirk.

"I imagine he will be happy when he hears."

"You didn't talk to him?"

Curtis shook his head. "My brother is a friend of his, and he asked on the commander's behalf."

"Figures." How like a military man to go through channels instead of asking right out, though she admitted to herself he had asked her. She'd just turned him down, and he couldn't take no for an answer.

"This isn't all bad, Kaia. We'll have the opportunity to observe Nani using all the skills you've worked so hard to hone. The two of you make a heck of a team. You'll be able to work with her out in the ocean."

Easy for him to say. He wasn't the one who would have to put up with being ordered around by Lieutenant Commander Jesse Matthews.

JESSE SURVEYED THE RANSACKED OFFICE. FILES LITTERED THE floor, metal drawers stood open, and chairs had been upended. It looked more like the work of vandals than that of a serious saboteur. Generally, spies tried to cover their tracks. If spies had done this, they were either insolent or incompetent.

He turned to his aide. "What's missing?"

"Some papers on the missile system," Ensign Masters said.

The shave ice he'd wolfed down sat in his stomach like a lump of cold lava. "How did this happen?"

"Someone came ashore last night, slipped through our defenses.

Security detected no breach, but I found this when I opened the door." Ensign Masters swept his hand over the room.

"Was anyone injured?"

Masters shook his head and pointed to an open window. "Whoever it was came in there and bypassed the guard outside."

Jesse had no idea how that could be accomplished. "Post a guard inside this room from now on."

"Yes sir."

Jesse's cell phone rang and he answered it.

The man on the other end identified himself as an SP on duty at the entrance. "Your sister is at the front gate, Commander."

"Jillian?" Their other sister, Livia, was in Africa the last time he heard.

"Yes sir. Jillian Sommers and her daughter are here to see you." The man's voice betrayed no emotion.

"I'll be right there." He left the ransacked office in Masters's capable hands and headed to his Jeep. He slung his long legs under the wheel and took off with the wind in his hair. He barely missed a flock of chickens crossing the road. He braked at the entrance and found his sister leaning against a rental car in the pull-off outside the security gate. Heidi was squatting in the sand watching an anthill. Her favorite bear, Boo, was clutched under her arm.

"How're my girls today?"

Heidi's head jerked around and she bounded to Jesse, throwing herself into his arms. "Uncle Jesse!"

He swung her around and kissed her soundly on the cheek then turned to his sister. Jillian had lost weight since he'd seen her last. Her high cheekbones were more pronounced, and she was pale beneath her tan, though she still looked younger than her thirty-seven years. Her ashy blond hair lay against her head in wisps without its usual curl and bounce. Jesse wanted to strangle his brother-in-law, Noah. And if he could find him, he would, but Noah had disappeared after he'd broken Jillian's heart.

"Hi, sis," he said. He threw his right arm around her and gave her a hug while holding Heidi with the other hand.

"Hi, Jesse. Sorry to drop in on you unannounced, but when you didn't answer the message I left on your answering machine, I came anyway."

"Something wrong? I haven't been to my place in two days. You could have tried my cell phone." He shuffled Heidi to his back, where she wrapped her legs around his waist like a monkey and dangled Boo in front of his nose.

"I tried but it said the number was no longer in service."

"Oh rats, I forgot to give you the new number."

Jillian nodded. "That's what I figured." Jillian looked at her shoes. "Jesse, I have to go to Italy. I tried to get out of it, but it was either go or lose my job. With Noah gone, I have to work." Her attempt at a smile fell short. "They promised no longer than a month. I'm going to have to take you up on your offer to keep Heidi. Livia is out of touch in Africa. You still cool with it?"

Jesse hated the false optimism in her voice. She used to be so sunny and genuinely cheerful. Nothing ever got her down. Pollyanna, he'd always called her. She was trying to maintain that spirit for Heidi's sake, but he could hear the desperation under the surface.

"I haven't heard from Livia in a couple of months either. The Peace Corps must have her in the wilds where she can't get to a computer. She wouldn't be much help anyway. Africa is no place for the monkey." He hitched Heidi higher on his back. "What about Aunt Irene?" He lowered his voice. "This isn't a good time for me. Base security has been compromised."

"I'm not going to Aunt Irene's." Heidi dropped her legs from his waist, and he let her down. She came around to face him with her arms folded over her chest and a mutinous thrust to her chin. "She makes me go to bed at seven like a baby. And she always nags me about being ladylike. I *hate* wearing dresses!"

Which was the final word, as far as she was concerned. She flounced away and went to sit in the car. Jesse sighed and turned back to his sister. "I'll have to find someone to watch her. I'm working long hours at the base."

Jillian looked suddenly decisive. "I'll just tell them I'm not going. Maybe I can find another job."

She turned her head, but not before he saw the tears in her eyes. "This has been your dream all your life," he said. "You can't quit. I'd love to keep the monkey. We'll figure it out. This is the opportunity of a lifetime for you. You have to go." Feeling like the most inept man alive, he patted her on the shoulder. Her tears made him feel he was twelve again and standing at the blackboard with no clue to the right answers.

He hoped having some goal would help his sister get over what Noah had done. He dropped his voice and placed his body so Heidi couldn't hear from the car. "Noah is bound to surface at some point. Maybe he'll be in Italy as well. There has to be some reason for what he did."

"What could there be, Jesse?" Jillian wiped at her face. "He took all my research and published it under his own name. What kind of man would do that to his wife? He stole from me. And to top if off, he vanished without a trace just before the journal came off the press."

"I know, I know," Jesse soothed. At least she was getting mad again. He much preferred an angry Jillian to a sad one. How could he care for Heidi though? All he knew about children was that they liked to be carted on his back and they made a lot of messes. He still remembered the way Heidi had smeared Jillian's lipstick all over his boots one night.

Of course, she'd only been a year old, he reminded himself.

Jesse let out his breath. "Don't worry about Heidi. I'll take care of her. You just go and make some brilliant new discovery." He didn't know what he was getting himself into or who he could find to help, but maybe a teenage girl out of school for the summer would want to earn some extra money.

Jillian chewed her lip. "I don't know, Jesse. Maybe I should just quit. I hate to leave Heidi."

He forced optimism into his voice. "And deprive me of her company? We'll have a great time."

A truck pulled up to the gate. He heard low voices, then a female voice began to shout to be allowed on the base. That irate tone sounded familiar, and he turned to look. Kaia's angry gaze met his.

She looked like she was about to spear a whale, and he was in the direct line of fire.

FOUR

Jesse had the audacity to smile, his teeth nearly as white as his service uniform. The air had ruffled his sun-streaked hair and left it boyishly tousled as he stood, hat in hand, talking to a woman beside a car. Kaia had a feeling he wouldn't be reprimanded easily.

She wasn't sure she could keep from crying while she yelled at him. His demands just might cost her the research project. She got out of the truck, leaving it running where it sat blocking the main gate.

The SP stepped in front of her with his hand on his gun. Jesse waved him away. "She's fine. I don't think she's dangerous." He lifted a brow. "Though I could be wrong."

A lot he knew. The way she felt right now, she could toss him from the top of Mount Kilauea as a tasty treat for Pele, the goddess of fire.

He held up his hands as she drew near. "Truce. We're going to be working together for the next few weeks. Let's not start out squabbling."

"Squabbling? I have every right to be upset. You knew I didn't want to work with you, but you went around my back to my boss. That's low, Commander Matthews."

"I was looking out for the good of the country. And call me Jesse."

From the coaxing expression in his eyes, she knew he expected her to be dazzled by the brilliance of his smile. She wasn't. "My responsibility is to look out for my dolphins. I'm warning you right now that Nani had better not be in danger." Kaia blinked rapidly. She wouldn't give him the satisfaction of seeing her cry.

A frown replaced his smile. "If I thought you or your dolphin would be hurt, I wouldn't have asked for your help. It's a simple assignment, Kaia. Patrolling offshore, that's all I ask. The navy hasn't lost a dolphin in combat yet."

"Maybe not in combat, but their callous handling has resulted in several deaths," she snapped.

He nodded. "Those dolphins weren't able to withstand the shock of transportation. We're not taking Nani anywhere."

He seemed so earnest and sincere. She wished she could believe him. "It seems I have no choice. What do I have to do?" Instead of answering, Jesse turned to the woman standing next to him. Kaia suddenly felt embarrassed by her outburst. "I'd like you to meet someone, Jillian. This is Kaia Oana. She does dolphin research."

Jillian and Jesse shared the same blond hair and blue eyes, though Jillian was slim and petite, and her eyes were rimmed in red. Something was going on here. Kaia shook Jillian's hand. "It's easy to see the two of you are related."

A small voice piped up from an invisible source. "Dolphins? You have dolphins? I'm an expert on them. What kind do you have—bottle-nosed or spinners?"

Jesse stepped aside and grinned at a little girl, a small but happier replica of Jillian, who was leaning out the car window. "I think Heidi knows more about dolphins than most trainers. This is my niece. She lives, sleeps, and breathes dolphins."

Kaia's anger began to cool. "You'll have to come meet Nani then. She's bottle-nosed."

"She's yours?" Heidi asked, her eyes round.

"Well, not exactly. She and some other dolphins are part of a research project at Seaworthy Labs where I work. We have some captive dolphins and others like Nani, who are free. We treat the wild dolphins more like friends. They can come and go as they please, and we don't train them with food deprivation. We're working on interacting with language."

"Food deprivation?" Heidi stepped out of the car and joined the threesome.

Kaia nodded. "The dolphins perform for food. They only want the food if they're hungry, so in the beginning at least, most trainers keep the dolphins slightly hungry. We don't do that."

"That's cool! How many wild dolphins do you have?" Heidi dropped her suitcase at her uncle's feet.

"Three. Nani, Liko, and Mahina. Mahina is still a calf though."

"When can I see them? I'm going to stay with Uncle Jesse while Mom chases volcanoes."

"Volcanoes?" Kaia looked at Jillian with a question in her eyes, and the other woman nodded.

"I'm a volcanologist. Vesuvius is about to blow in Italy for the first time this century."

"Sounds dangerous," Kaia said, then wondered if she should have mentioned the danger in front of Jillian's daughter. But the girl seemed too busy twirling the tie on her shirt to notice Kaia's bad choice of words.

Kaia glanced into Jillian's eyes and was surprised to find no excitement there in spite of her smile. Maybe it was the prospect of leaving her daughter. Kaia guessed her to be in her mid to late thirties. Her listless air detracted from her porcelain-doll good looks.

"Maybe Kaia will take you out with her and Nani sometime on the boat," Jesse said.

The gleam in his eye irritated Kaia. The best way to foil him would be not to let him rile her, but it was easier said than done. She managed a sweet smile. "I'm sure I could arrange that."

Heidi squealed and hopped around. "Thanks for bringing me, Mom!" She hugged her mother then ran back to the car for more of her things to add to the pile at Jesse's feet.

A smile finally lifted the corners of Jillian's lips. "I guess I can leave with a clear conscience." She looked up at her brother. "You call me if anything—and I mean anything—goes wrong. I'll quit and come home if I need to."

"We'll be fine. Don't worry. Me and the monkey will have a grand time."

"Do you have any idea who can help you?" Jillian still seemed loathe to leave.

He shook his head. "You have any idea? You've lived here just as long as I have."

Jillian glanced at her watch and chewed her lip. "My plane leaves in a few hours. I should just cancel and take another flight so I can help you find someone." She rubbed her forehead. "This was a crazy idea, Jesse. I can't go."

Jesse frowned and shook his head. "You're going. I'll figure something out."

Kaia decided to take pity on them both. "You're needing a day-care person? I had a wonderful nanny growing up. I could give you her name and number."

Relief flooded Jesse's face. "Could you get it now?"

"I have her number at home. I could call you tonight with it."

Jesse lowered his voice and glanced toward his niece, who was busy tossing out snorkel gear from the trunk of the car. "I have a friend at work, Donna, who might be happy to keep her today until I can find some day care for her," he said to Jillian.

A woman. Kaia had to wonder if it was a girlfriend, and the disquieting feeling that swept over her surprised her. She wasn't interested in the handsome commander.

"I could take her to see the dolphins today." She blurted the words without thinking.

Kaia liked kids, and Heidi's interest in dolphins intrigued her. Besides, Kaia wouldn't want to be stuck in Jesse's office all day if she were a child.

Jillian looked from her brother to Kaia uncertainly. "Are you two friends?"

"Not exactly," Jesse muttered. "But I think we can trust her.

If she's so conscientious with her dolphins, she'll take good care of Heidi."

Heidi came in on the last of the conversation. "I get to see the dolphins *today*?" She began to jump up and down.

Jillian bit her lip. "Are you sure? Have you been around kids much?"

"I love kids," Kaia assured her. "I teach hula to ten eight-year-olds every week."

"Okay," Jillian said. She dug in her purse for a scrap of paper and scribbled a number on it then handed it to Kaia. "Here's my cell phone number. Call me with any questions."

"Okay," Kaia said. She almost laughed at Jesse's expression of relief. "We'll go out in the boat with Nani."

"You're a lifesaver," Jillian said. "This job is important, but not as important as my daughter. She's all I've got now."

Kaia wanted to ask where the *keiki*'s father was, but looking into Jillian's shadowed eyes, she decided to bite her tongue. She turned to Heidi. "Want to meet Nani?"

"Can we go now?" Heidi kicked up red dust as she danced around Kaia.

"As soon as I get some instructions from your uncle." She turned to Jesse. "What exactly do you want me to do with Nani?" Kaia asked.

His relaxed, easy manner had returned. "The dolphins the navy has trained can carry a camera on their back that allows us to monitor underwater activity. They can also attach a buoy to a swimmer so guards can find and pick up the intruder. Could Nani do that?"

"I'm sure she could figure it out. What do you want to work on first?"

"Let's start with the camera. We can monitor what the lens picks up from onboard the boat. I'll meet you at the base dock and we'll put a harness with a camera on the dolphin. Then we can see whatever's down there. I'd like you to work nights, if you could. That's when we'd be most likely to have intruders. The first couple of days we can have the two of you out during the day until Nani knows what she's doing, then switch to nights. Once she figures it out, you wouldn't even have to be along. Our sailors could handle it."

This might be kind of fun. Nani would probably thrive on the challenge, and Kaia would still have plenty of opportunity to test the communication skills between her and the dolphin. Plus, if Nani successfully foiled an intruder, Kaia could use her success to help convince Curtis to keep the research going. And she'd be on hand to see if the navy was trying to cover up anything about her cousin's death. Kaia's thoughts drifted to the catamaran tragedy and the missile testing. Could this intruder problem be related?

"I'd want to be there anyway to make sure Nani isn't hurt. What exactly are we looking for?"

"In the past two weeks, we've had several intrusions that came from the sea. Probably a diver, maybe more than one. If we could apprehend whoever is doing this, we might be able to get him to tell us what he's after and why."

"Information about the missile defense system you just tested?" she suggested.

Jesse nodded. "Maybe. That's what we need to find out."

"Give me an hour. I'll meet you back here." She wanted to talk to her brother first.

He nodded then added his cell phone number to the scrap of paper Jillian's was written on before turning to talk to his sister and niece.

Kaia jogged to her truck and drove out to the lagoon to her grandfather's cottage. Bane had told her this morning he was going to help their grandfather in the garden today.

Mynas called from the trees as she got out in front of the cottage. She found Bane pulling weeds beside their grandfather. *Tûtû kâne*'s dark eyes brightened when he saw her. "Ah, *lei aloha*, you look as bright as the mynas." He held up a dirt-covered taro root. "Hungry?"

She smiled. "Um, no."

She glanced at her brother. He raised his eyebrows. "What's up, sis? You look frazzled."

"What a day I've had," she said, bending down to pull a handful of black wattle. "First I found the lab has been sold to a man who wants to enclose the lagoon and put Nani and the others in captivity for a *sea park*. Then he tells me he's giving me to the navy to help patrol the waters offshore with Nani. I'm about ready to give up the whole thing. I'll never break that communication barrier."

Her grandfather smiled. "I've got a hammer you can use."

She laughed. Her grandfather's wit always cheered her up, but she needed some advice. She glanced at Bane. He straightened up and brushed the dirt from his hands. "Need to talk?" He nodded toward a white iron garden bench surrounded by hibiscus to his left. Kaia nodded, and he headed for it. She followed and sat beside him.

Bane stretched his legs out in front of him. "Give me the scoop."

She shrugged. "I just did."

"There's more to it than you said. You hate change—admit it."

She held up her hand. "Okay, guilty as charged."

"I've always believed things happen for a reason, Kaia. God might be shutting this door and opening another opportunity for you to reach Nani. One that will work."

"I don't see how," she said. "I'll have very little time to work with my equipment. This could set me back, maybe for good."

"Give God time to work, and look for the opportunities He sends. There is a reason this has happened. Don't shortchange Him."

Kaia hadn't thought of that. "Maybe you're right. But I sure don't see how this is a good thing." She knew things didn't always work out. Even when her life went well, she waited for the other shoe to drop. And it always did. She wished she could be more like her brother. But his faith was way beyond hers. While she was a

Christian too, her own faith was as weak as a newly hatched chick—her own fault, she knew. It had been weeks since she'd even been in services. Her research had consumed her attention lately.

Bane grinned. "I see the resistance in your eyes, Kaia. I have a feeling you're in for a major lesson of some kind this summer. Relax and enjoy the ride."

Easy for him to say. He didn't have to kowtow to a certain navy commander. She sighed and went to do her duty.

She rolled her window down and let the sea air in the truck as she drove out to Barking Sands. The SPs made her wait at the gate for Jesse. He looked frazzled when he appeared fifteen minutes later.

"I really appreciate this," he said again as she climbed into his Jeep Wrangler.

He accelerated quickly and the momentum threw her back against the seat. "Where's Heidi?"

The Jeep rocketed around a corner, and Kaia grabbed the door for support. Jesse didn't answer until his SUV slid to a stop in front of a building.

Jesse killed the engine. "She's here with Donna."

Kaia got out and followed him inside. She had to admit she was curious to see this Donna. Jesse led her down a long hallway clad with institutional tan tiles and painted a sickly green. He stepped into a room filled with banks of computers. The dizzying display of electronic equipment dazzled Kaia; then she saw Heidi seated beside a woman with red hair. Donna's face brightened when she turned and caught sight of Jesse. The proprietary expression on her face deepened when her gaze wandered to Kaia.

"Donna, this is Kaia Oana. She and her dolphin are going to help patrol the waters offshore."

Donna nodded coolly. "Pleased to meet you," she said, her tone indicating anything but pleasure. Her eyes tilted upward at the ends in a way that made her appear exotic and interesting.

"We've come to take Heidi off your hands," Kaia said, glancing at the little girl who was engrossed in a computer game. "Ready to go meet the dolphins, Heidi?"

Heidi dropped the mouse and sprang out of her chair. Donna's face darkened. "Heidi and I have been having a good time, haven't we, Heidi?" She put her hand on top of Heidi's head.

"Sure, but I want to see the dolphins!" Heidi slipped her hand into Kaia's. "Can we go now?"

Kaia didn't want to be rude. "In a few minutes."

"You don't know how much I appreciate your help," Jesse said to Donna. He extended a hand to Donna.

Donna's dazzling display of teeth set Kaia on edge. If he wanted to flirt with the beautiful ensign, he could do it on his own time. She needed to get out on the water. Aware she was irritated with Jesse for no good reason, she took Heidi's hand. "We'll wait for you in the hall."

WITH THE WIND IN HER HAIR AND THE SUN SLANTING OVER THE cliffs of Na Pali, Kaia was in her element. This was the third day Heidi had gone out with her. Jesse had tried to call Kaia's old nanny but hadn't gotten an answer. Something would have to be done soon, however, since Kaia was about to start working nights. Not that she minded having Heidi along—the little girl's pleasant chatter made the day go faster.

She waved to her friend George Thompson in his Fathom Five Divers boat just outside the no-navigation area. Two other crew members, Mark Davy and Charlie Schmitt, sent piercing wolf whistles in her direction. She grinned and stuck out her tongue at them as she passed. She'd done her dive training with Fathom Five and still dove with them occasionally.

Heidi wore a life vest and sat in the bow, a smile as big as Kipu Falls on her face. Her bear, Boo, had been all but forgotten under a deck chair. Nani raced along beside the boat. Kaia had hardly seen

Jesse. From the grim expression on his face over the past couple of days, she knew things at the base weren't going well. She'd offered to keep Heidi with her tonight to attend one of her grandfather's lu'aus, and the relief on his face had spoken volumes.

Her skin felt taut and windburned. They'd been out here since seven this morning, and it was already nearly six. Nani surfaced and leaped into the air. Kaia frowned. "The camera is missing." She stood and scanned the waves for the buoyant device. "Nani keeps scraping it off." She suppressed her disappointment. She'd thought Nani would love this new challenge, and she hated to admit the dolphin was failing her assignment so far.

"There it is." Heidi pointed at the bright yellow bit of plastic housing floating about fifteen feet from the boat.

Kaia steered the boat toward the camera then cut the engine and fished it out of the waves. She whistled for Nani, and the dolphin zipped to the side of the *Porpoise II* then turned and raced away when she saw the camera in Kaia's hand.

Kaia pressed her lips together. "We might as well go in."

"I want to stay out here." Heidi crossed her arms over her chest. "Can't we work with DALE?"

Kaia glanced at her watch. "For a few minutes. Then we have to go in." She grabbed her knapsack and pulled out the communication device. When she dropped it in the water, Nani came back to the boat. Kaia began to input clicks and whistles into the machine. Nani pressed the wrong picture on the underwater screen three times.

"She's not cooperating," Kaia said. She pulled the device out of the water. "We might as well go in. We're not accomplishing anything." Sometimes she wondered if she was ever going to get through to the dolphin in a way that really mattered. Nani rolled over by the boat, and Kaia managed to get the camera back on her.

"You promised we could stay out awhile. It's only been fifteen minutes." Heidi's lip trembled, and tears clung to her lashes. "All grownups break their promises."

Kaia bit her tongue and tried not to snap back. "You sound tired. I think you need a nap."

"I'm not!" Heidi rubbed the back of her hand against her eyes. "Naps are for babies. My mom doesn't make me take a nap."

Kaia knew what the problem was. "You miss your mom, don't you? Maybe we can call her when we get to shore."

Heidi picked up an oar and threw it overboard. "Stop talking about my mother!"

Kaia wasn't sure how to handle this acting out. Heidi had to be upset by her father's abandonment and now by her mother's absence. Poor kid. Kaia cut the engine, and the boat slewed sideways. She tossed the anchor overboard. "How about a swim before we go ashore?"

Heidi looked at her uncertainly as if she had expected Kaia to be mad. "I'll get the oar. Can I snorkel?"

"We can both snorkel a little while." Kaia waved to the navy boat that was monitoring Nani. She and Heidi adjusted their masks and pulled on their swim fins. "See you in the water." Kaia rolled over the edge of the boat.

Kaia's disappointment in Nani's performance today left her as she entered the world she loved best. Schools of Raccoon Butterfly fish surrounded her then darted away. She spotted several Orange Bandit surgeonfish, a small school of Hawaiian Cleaner wrasse, and a Hawaiian puffer. Her favorite, the Moorish Idol, swam by and disappeared behind a lava rock. The scores of brilliantly colored fish dazzled her eyes in a display of bright yellow, turquoise, and green.

Heidi joined her and grabbed Nani's dorsal fin. The dolphin pulled the little girl through a school of wrasse. Kaia wished she had her camera.

A shadowy movement caught her eye, and she turned to see a scuba diver swimming toward her. Dressed in a black wet suit, the man paused when he saw them. Though she was sure he was merely out for a pleasure dive, her orders were to take pictures of any divers or anything unusual. Kaia motioned to Nani, and the dolphin swerved, dislodging Heidi's grip on her dorsal fin. Her body in torpedo mode, Nani darted past Kaia toward the diver.

Kaia pointed toward the surface, and Heidi nodded and swam to the boat. Once Kaia saw that the little girl was safely aboard the boat, she turned to help Nani. The dolphin was swimming around the man. She could see the camera would get a good look at the diver. The man spotted the camera mounted on the dolphin and swam away.

Maybe it was nothing. He might not have known he wasn't allowed here, just offshore the naval base. Still, she wanted a look at his face in case the picture in Nani's camera didn't come out. Nani raced along beside her, and Kaia grabbed hold of the dolphin's dorsal fin to let Nani drag her along faster.

Descended from a line of pearl divers, Kaia could hold her breath for four minutes, a fact she hoped would allow her to get close enough before she had to surface. The man glanced back at them then stopped by a large pile of lava rock that had fallen into the sea.

Kaia squinted through her mask. He had something in his hand. Her hold on Nani's dorsal fin slackened as she realized the man had a dart gun. A dart zipped through the water by her head, and she let out a gurgle of bubbles. Nani paused at Kaia's sound of distress, then shot forward and plowed her nostrum into the diver's arm. The dart gun loosened from his fingers and drifted toward the bottom.

He turned and swam away. Too shaken to go after him, Kaia signaled for the dolphin to come to her. Nani pulled her to the surface, and Kaia drew in a deep breath of air and looked around wildly for Heidi. Her breath eased when she saw the little girl still safely in the boat. She grasped the side and rested until her limbs stopped shaking.

"Are you okay?" Heidi peered down at her.

"I'm fine." Kaia hauled herself aboard. Her legs felt like limp seaweed. She grabbed the ship-to-shore radio the navy had given her and told the sailor on the other end what had happened. He signaled to her from the boat and spoke reassurances to her through the radio, but she glared across the water at the sailors. Where had they been when she, Heidi, and Nani were in danger?

Jesse had promised Nani would be perfectly safe. They'd both nearly been shot with the dart gun. Even worse, Heidi could have been hurt. That guy was no casual diver. She and the dolphin weren't equipped to handle terrorists.

She dangled her fingers over the side of the boat, and Nani came to her. The dolphin bumped against her hand then chattered, her bright eyes seeming to ask if Kaia was all right. Kaia smiled and patted Nani's nostrum. "I'm okay," she told the dolphin. Nani chattered again then plunged into the waves.

Kaia sat back in her seat. "We're going in," she told Heidi. "The navy has the coordinates. They don't need us to wait." And even if they did, her priority was to get Heidi to safety. Kaia had no idea where the diver had gone. If he came back with some buddies, they would all be in danger.

To be fair, she knew Jesse had thought of these daytime exercises merely as training for real detection that would go on at night. That intruder was brazen to be out here in the daylight. Kaia was sure Jesse never would have let the little girl come out here if he'd thought there was any danger.

She kept an eye out for other boats as she turned on the engine and sped toward home. All she saw was a navy cruiser heading out to where she'd been anchored. They were unlikely to find anything. The diver was long gone, but maybe they could find the dart gun.

Where had the man gone though? She'd seen no other boats around. They were only a hundred yards offshore, but he couldn't have gone ashore on base. He would have been caught by the navy.

Kaia looked up and down the stretch of Polihale Beach just north of Barking Sands. Nothing there. Na Pali stretched toward the sky just beyond the beach. The verdant green vegetation juxtaposed against the blue sky looked like a picture postcard, too beautiful to be real.

She looked the other direction. Barking Sands gave way to several contract installations. There would be no reason for any of those companies to have divers out here, though she supposed the man could have made it to a safe stretch along there.

She steered the boat toward her home dock of Echo Lagoon. It was dark by the time she and Heidi arrived, and she had to flip on her headlamps. A bonfire lit the beach outside her grandfather's house, and she could hear the thump of drums and smell the aroma of roasting pig. The familiarity eased her tension. Safe harbor. Nothing could harm them here, not with her brothers about.

Heidi bounced on the seat. "I forgot about the lu'au! Can we still go?"

"If you promise to let me teach you to hula."

"It's too girly."

Heidi was all tomboy. Kaia smiled. "You'll be hooked before the night is out."

He watched the fish in his tank. Everything he'd ever wanted was close enough to smell and taste. His imminent success should taste like the sweetest pineapple his father had ever grown, but instead it was like mashed taro—much more bland than he'd imagined. Maybe because he had no one to share the joy with. At least that's what he told himself. Believing that was better than backing out of what he had to do.

He had no choice but to make the tally of lost lives huge. The failure had to be big—big enough to change the course of the trials. He glanced at the wall to the left. Awards his father had won surrounded a large portrait of his father. He stood and walked to the picture and stood staring into his father's smiling eyes. "I'm doing this for you," he said. "You're going to be so proud of me."

He turned as his assistant came into the room. "What's the status? It's almost time."

His assistant didn't meet his gaze. "Remember the dolphin that arrived when the boat exploded? Lieutenant Commander Matthews has hired the dolphin and her trainer to patrol the waters with a camera."

"So arm our divers with spearguns." He shrugged. "One dolphin shouldn't be hard to dispose of." Nor would Jesse, for that matter. He examined the thought for a moment. Would there be a way to become wealthy beyond his wildest dreams *and* have the revenge he desired?

FIVE

Kaia had left with Heidi by the time Jesse reached the site. He peered over the side of the patrol boat into the gloom of twilight. The scent of the sea, fresh and invigorating, filled his lungs. Lights twinkled along the shore and in the canopy of stars above his head. Waves ran to the beach and lapped against the sand in a sound that soothed him. He needed soothing after the diver incident.

He had not anticipated an attack in the daylight. Could it be one of the "friendly" nations engaging in a bit of espionage, or was it the work of a terrorist group or some other rival nation? He was going to have to find out.

So far there was no evidence to indicate the disastrous missile test had been anything but a computer glitch—a glitch Lawton said he'd fixed. Jesse wasn't sure. It seemed too coincidental that there'd been a death, a test failure, and a break-in pertaining to the missile. His instincts said differently, but the navy didn't listen to intuition. If he recommended delaying the test, Lawton would be howling for proof. And Jesse didn't have a shred to offer.

He didn't care that much about the missile—the government was always working on something new—but the thought of civilians at risk bothered him. With sixty thousand residents and over a million visitors a year, there was a lot to worry about.

It was his fault his niece had been out there. Jillian would kill him when she heard about it. He'd been a poor substitute parent these past days. He needed to get his act together. Now. He hadn't even gotten hold of Kaia's old nanny. That would have to be the first thing on his list tonight. Donna was a little overeager in her willingness to help, but he needed someone who did this for a living.

"See anything?" he shouted to Ensign Masters.

His aide shook his head. "I've got divers ready to go down. The dolphin's camera only showed the diver's backside." He made a cutting motion across his throat to signal the sailor at the helm to stop the engine. The boat slowed, waves lapping against the hull. The gloom made it almost impossible to see more than a few feet down, in spite of the rising moon.

"Send down the divers," he told Masters.

Masters nodded and gave the order. Three divers dressed in wet suits fell backward into the inky water. The salty spray hit Jesse in the face, but he barely noticed. He stared into the clear water, but the shadowy forms of the divers quickly disappeared from view. One diver carried a camera mounted on his suit, and Jesse watched the monitor. The halogen floodlight illuminated the blackness about thirty feet in front of the divers. Fish darted away from them as they swam. A dolphin moved in to bump against the lead diver's hand.

One diver moved to the seabed and picked up something. Jesse couldn't tell what he'd found, but it obviously wasn't a body. It seemed hours before one of the divers surfaced, but glancing at his watch, he realized it had been only half an hour.

"No divers down here, sir," the SEAL said, saying what Jesse already knew. "Nothing but the dolphin."

"Nani?" He was surprised the man recognized Nani.

"It had a camera mounted on it."

He nodded. "She must have come back out. I wonder if Kaia knows." Though Nani was free to come and go as she pleased, Jesse was astounded by the dolphin's desire to be around people. Seaworthy Labs was doing some amazing work. He should stop over and meet the director, Duncan's brother.

A second SEAL surfaced. "Found the dart gun, sir." He swam to the boat and handed it up to Jesse.

At least they had that much. "Take me back to shore. I want at least six boats patrolling tonight," he told the men. The engine roared to life, and the boat bounced along the waves, riding the swells with ease. He stepped to the bow and put his face to the wind. He inhaled the scent of the sea in the breeze. The ocean was as much a part of him as his type O blood. He felt keenly alive and alert, eager to get to the bottom of this problem.

The boat docked, and he stepped off the deck onto the pier. Sailors milled around, and he spotted Lawton, who was headed toward him.

"A patrol just found a body floating offshore," his captain said. Lawton's tanned face bore no expression other than grim determination. "A diver."

"Identity?"

Lawton shook his head. "Nothing to tell who he is."

"Where's the body?" Jesse wanted to check this out himself. Lawton nodded toward a group of men near the beach, and Jesse went toward the huddled sailors.

The men stepped aside when Jesse arrived. He knelt beside a man about thirty-five. He was dressed in a black wet suit. The man had removed his tank and buoyancy compensator—or BC—and had unzipped his wet suit.

"Any idea what killed him?" Jesse asked the doctor standing at the edge of the group.

The physician stepped forward and crouched beside Jesse. He pulled back the edges of the man's wet suit to reveal the diver's abdomen. A dart was still in the man's flesh. "You found a dart gun. Maybe ballistics can figure out if that's the weapon that killed him."

The more Jesse stared at the man's face, the more he looked familiar. He bore Hawaiian features. It might be wise to have a lifelong native of the island look at him. Kaia's face flashed into his mind.

"Get me a camera," he told Ensign Masters. When his aide brought him a Polaroid, he snapped several photos, taking care to get only the face so it wouldn't be too graphic for Kaia.

He handed the camera back to Masters. "*Mahalo.* I'll see what

I can find out. Call me if anything else happens." He pocketed the pictures and headed for his Jeep. Once on the road, he pulled out his cell phone and called Duncan.

"Hey, buddy, you've lived here a long time. Have you ever had any day care for your kids?" Too late he realized he should have asked someone else. With Duncan's kids on the mainland, it had to be a sore subject for him.

Duncan inhaled softly, but when he spoke his voice was still full of good humor. "Not really. My wife didn't work." He paused a minute. "You know, my brother's wife is looking for work. Maybe she would have time to watch Heidi. Want me to ask her?"

"What's she like?"

"Faye? She's great. She and Curtis have only been married a year, but they're nuts about each other. I think she has some kids from a previous marriage and she's pretty congenial. I think she'd be good with kids."

"Go for it then, if you don't mind." Duncan promised to get back to him by morning, and Jesse clicked off the phone and tucked it onto his belt. If only his problems at the base could be so easily solved.

KAIA CLOSED HER EYES AND LET THE BEAT OF THE DRUMS REACH inside to the woman most people never saw. In the thrall of the drums, she wasn't the unloved and abandoned daughter of Paie Oana, but a daughter treasured by God and worthy in His sight. The fluid movements of her hands and body told the story of her life and how God had found her. The hula healed the inner place where she was still a child crying for her mother.

At least until the music ended.

The thump of the drums echoed across the waters then ebbed with the tide. She opened her eyes and let out her breath. If only the refreshment she felt in the dance could last beyond the harsh light of tomorrow's sunrise.

Heidi's eyes were round. "Could you really teach me to do that?"

Kaia smiled. "Sure. Come here." She placed the little girl in front of her and put her hands into position then began to help her mimic the simplest movements. "This means 'praise to God.'" She showed Heidi how to lift her hands into the air with the palms extending upward. "Every movement in hula has a specific meaning, and every expression of the dancer's hands has great significance. The movements of your body can even express plants and animals."

Heidi pursed her lips and tried to follow Kaia. After about fifteen minutes, she dropped her hands. "I don't think I'll ever learn it. Why bother?"

"The hula is not just a dance," Kaia said, "but our culture. Important things like Hawaiian history and legends, the Hawaiian language, prayers, poetry, daily life—it's all in the hula dance. Study the hula, and you learn a whole lot about Hawai'i besides just the dance."

Kaia touched Heidi's head. "It takes time. We'll work on it more another day." Kaia watched her join the children who had attended the lu'au with their parents. She found a large piece of driftwood near the bonfire and dropped onto it. The blaze had died to embers now, and people had begun to depart. The aroma of roast pig from the now-open pit off to her right no longer smelled appetizing with her stomach full.

Her brother Mano sat on the piece of driftwood with her. He glanced at her but didn't say anything. He seemed lost in thought, his usually smiling face pensive. Mano was the shark that his Hawaiian name meant. He carried not an ounce of extra fat, his strength stood him in good stead as a Navy SEAL, and he was the fastest swimmer Kaia had ever seen. Given the tension between her brothers, she wondered if it had been a good idea for both of them to take leave at the same time.

The festivities were almost over, and she felt every minute of the late hour. The children began to sing a song about dolphins, and

Kaia smiled. She loved this song, and she chimed in. Several people glanced at her, and the song died on her lips.

Heidi scooted over beside her. "Your voice sounds funny. Like all the notes are the same."

Their grandfather was on the other side of the bonfire. He grinned. "Kaia has a beautiful face but the voice of a frog." He directed his gaze at Kaia. "Your rendering of the hula made me wish my old limbs could move like that. I could try it, but I'd likely be too crippled to walk tomorrow." He grinned and laid his gnarled hand on her head.

Kaia dug her toes into the cool sand. "As much as I love music, you'd think God would have given me a singing voice as well." She watched Heidi get up to roast a marshmallow.

"I am proud of you just like you are, *lei aloha*."

Her grandfather's words and the way he called her "dear child" in Hawaiian filled Kaia's chest with a tight feeling. Her grandfather wasn't often so serious. Laughter was as essential to her grandfather as approval was to her. She wished she didn't have such a need to make other people happy. In her head she knew God's approval should be enough, but she craved praise the way crabs craved the hot sun. It had driven her to excel in school and to seek a career that was hard to attain. In the back of her mind, she knew reaching great heights as a marine biologist wouldn't bring her mother back.

"*Mahalo, Tûtû kâne*," she said.

Oke glanced toward Mano. Avoiding his grandfather's gaze, Mano kicked off his slippers then slid from the driftwood onto the beach. He stared into the embers the wind kicked into the sky.

"If that face gets any longer, I can use it for bait," Oke said in a jovial tone of voice.

"Don't try to cheer me up, *Tûtû kâne*."

"I wouldn't think of it," Oke said, his smile widening. "If misery makes you happy, who am I to complain?"

"Did you and Bane have a fight?" Kaia wished she could heal the breach between her brothers. Sometimes she felt like a juggler with a burning torch in each hand.

"You could call it that." Mano didn't look at either of them.

"Your fault, huh?" Kaia sympathized. Sometimes Bane took his position as older brother too seriously. They all had to make their own mistakes.

He shrugged. "I get tired of him telling me what to do. He's not the all-knowing, wise kahuna. That title goes to *Tûtû kâne.*"

Their grandfather smiled. "I think I've abdicated that position to Bane. He's wiser than I was at his age. You should listen to him."

"Easy for you to say," Mano ground out. "You don't have to deal with his constant disapproval." He glowered at his brother, who stood talking to a few lingering patrons. "I get here after working all day, and he starts in."

"What was the argument about?" Maybe she could get him to cool down.

"He keeps harping on Pele Hawai'i. I get tired of hearing his opinion. If he'd go with me one time, he'd see it isn't the radical group he thinks it is." Mano glanced up at her. "He wants me to get out."

"Bane proves his wisdom by this advice." Oke frowned and reached down to take a handful of sand, which he sifted through his fingers.

"*Tûtû kâne*, how can you say that? You of all people? The oyster beds are gone because of politicians. You can no longer find more than a handful of pearls. Our islands were annexed by the United States without a treaty, the U.S. lied to the United Nations and said we had become a state, and our heritage has been systematically stamped out. Even Clinton formally apologized for the overthrow of the Hawaiian government."

Oke smiled. "I couldn't hold my breath now long enough to grab a handful of sand twenty feet down. Change is sometimes hard, Mano, but you can never go back. You romanticize the old Hawai'i, but you forget the hardships and bloodshed our ancestors endured, the human sacrifice they committed. We are Americans now. I fought in World War II as an American. I would not go back, even if I could."

Mano gave the rock in his hand a hard toss. "Things would be better if we were self-governing."

Oke rolled his eyes. "That makes as much sense as putting a myna in control of your boat." He smiled and patted his grandson on the arm then stood and walked to the last group of tourists.

"*Tûtû kâne* doesn't understand." Mano stood and kicked sand over the last of the fire. "I wish someone in the family would listen to me." He turned and his gaze caught hers.

The last thing Kaia wanted to do was attend a political meeting that promoted Hawai'i's secession. Looking into Mano's face, though, she knew she had to do something. "I'll go with you."

"You will?" His eyes widened.

She frowned. He sounded almost disconcerted. She'd thought he would be thrilled. "As long as you don't expect me to keep quiet if they start spouting nonsense about leaving the United States."

"Just listen, okay? Don't make any judgments. And don't offer your opinion. And really, you don't need to go. I was just aggravated with Bane."

She sighed at his anxious tone. He was probably afraid she'd embarrass him. "I said I would go, so I'm going. Will there be talk of secession?"

"Yes, but try not to get riled about what they say. Just listen and don't make a scene."

"Of course I won't make a scene. But I'm an American, Mano. So are you. I love my Hawaiian heritage, but I love America too."

The sound of a motor mingled with that of the rolling surf, and Kaia turned to look. Jesse waved to her from the helm of a small white craft that glowed in the moonlight. She stood, brushing the sand from her legs. Her hair was probably a wreck from the wind, and she felt sweaty and unkempt. She wished she had time to brush her teeth. She needed all her courage to face the confident Jesse Matthews.

Heidi spotted him and raced to greet him. "Uncle Jesse!"

He lifted her in his arms and swung her around. "Having fun?"

"I'm having the best time," she proclaimed. "Did you find the bad guy who shot at us?"

"Maybe."

His gaze sought Kaia's. He stared at her as if he were trying to see inside her head. Whatever he had come to tell her, she had a feeling she wasn't going to like it.

"Heidi, why don't you go fix your uncle a plate of roast pig?" she suggested.

"Okay." Heidi slid from Jesse's arms. "I'll be right back."

Kaia waited until she was out of earshot. "Let's hear it. Did you find the man?"

"I'm not sure. A diver washed ashore. I wondered if you could look at a picture and identify him. He was dressed in black like the one who attacked you, though that doesn't tell us much since so many wear black. We recovered a dart gun from the bottom of the ocean as well." He fished in his pocket.

"He's dead? He was very much alive when I saw him last. Drowned?"

Jesse shook his head and held out a group of Polaroid pictures. "Shot with a dart in the stomach. The autopsy will show what poison was used."

She took them but couldn't bring herself to look yet. "You're saying there was more than one diver out there?"

"We don't know yet. We don't even know if this man is connected with the one you saw. Take a look."

Mano joined her. "I heard you about got my sister killed today. I don't want her doing this anymore."

"I'll make sure she's protected." Jesse's voice was steady, and he turned to face Mano.

The two men looked like two sea lions about to butt heads. Kaia put her hand on her brother's arm. "It was no big deal, Mano."

Jesse's fists uncurled at her soft tone. "Don't worry. Really, I'll make sure she's protected."

Conscious of his intent gaze, Kaia turned away and stared at the photos in her hand. She had to look at them. "Got a flashlight? It's hard to make out in the dark."

"I've got one." Jesse jogged to the boat and came back with a light. He trained it on the photograph.

Kaia studied the man. The Hawaiian face was square and swarthy with thick lips and nose. The man had a goatee, and she tried to remember if the man who'd attacked her had sported facial hair. Everything had happened so fast, it was hard to remember. "The build seems right. But I didn't get a good look at his features. He looks familiar though."

She'd seen this guy somewhere. The knowledge played hide-and-seek at the edge of her consciousness. Mano crowded her to look at the photo as well. He drew in a sharp, quickly smothered gasp.

"You know this guy?" she asked him.

He wouldn't meet her gaze. "I don't think so."

She narrowed her eyes. "I can always tell when you're lying, Mano. Who is he?"

"For a minute I thought it was a guy I knew." He shrugged and laughed, an unconvincing sound.

"Who does it look like?"

He sighed. "You're like a pit bull sometimes, you know that? I'm sure it's not him, but it almost looks like Jonah Kapolei."

The name didn't ring a bell with Kaia. "How do you know him?" Mano grimaced and she thought for a minute he wouldn't answer.

He finally shrugged. "He's the treasurer for Pele Hawai´i. But I don't think this is him."

"The sovereignty group?" Jesse asked.

Kaia nodded. She didn't like where this was heading. What was Mano involved in? Maybe it was a good thing she was going to that meeting on Saturday. She could see if maybe the group was behind everything going on at that base.

Six

Six

Faye Latchet tied her tennis shoes then stood and looked in the full-length mirror. "I'm too pale," she told her husband. She pinched her cheeks and tried a confident smile on for size. It only succeeded in deepening the lines around her mouth and eyes. She hated growing old.

She dropped the smile and stared into her own dark and haunted eyes. Those eyes had seen too much pain and disgrace. Caused it too. Maybe this was the wrong thing to do.

"You're obsessing. Just be yourself and he'll love you."

"I should have stuck with the original plan to be your secretary," Faye said. "At least I can type."

"You can still do that if you want to wait, but Kaia won't be at the lab for a couple more weeks. It seems heaven-sent that Duncan called with this need." He patted her shoulder.

"I'm frightened," Faye admitted. She turned and buried her face in her husband's chest.

"You'll be fine." He hugged her then dropped a kiss on her hair. "You can't go back now. We've talked it over, and you know this is what we have to do. It's too good an opportunity to pass over."

"I know, I know," she said, pulling away. Why couldn't he see how hard this was for her? And to watch a child at her age wouldn't be easy either. A tiny resentment flared, but she quickly squelched it. Curtis was doing this for her. She couldn't get cold feet now.

She pasted a happy look on her face. "I'm ready. It was just last-minute jitters."

"That's my girl," he said, giving her an approving hug. He glanced at his watch. "We're going to be late if we don't get moving."

She grabbed her purse from the bed and followed him to the car.

"Should I give the little girl the gift right off or wait until he hires me? *If* he hires me."

He dropped the gearshift into drive and pulled onto the street. "He'll hire you. He's desperate. But I'd still wait until things are settled."

Faye fell silent as her husband drove from Waimea to Seaworthy Labs. "You sure he said to meet here instead of at the base?"

"I'm sure." Curtis's voice was patient, and he gave her an indulgent look as he pulled into the parking lot. "There's his Jeep. He's already here."

Her heart surged to her throat, and she felt faint. She hadn't had a panic attack in years. She couldn't have one now, she thought, licking dry lips.

Curtis pulled beside the Jeep and shut off the engine. "Showtime," he murmured.

He made it sound so easy. She would be the one on display, not him. *Quit obsessing,* she told herself. After all the scams she'd pulled over the years, this would be easy. Almost as easy as turning tail and running away.

But she was through running. It was time to stay in one place and fight for what she wanted. She'd always been good at getting what she wanted. This would be no different.

JESSE LOOKED IN HIS REAR-VIEW MIRROR AND SAW CURTIS'S CAR pull in. He was curious for his first glimpse of Faye Latchet. He just hoped and prayed she would work out. Duncan seemed to like her. He wished things were different and he could take leave to spend this time with Heidi, but things at the base demanded his attention now. He felt caught between a lava flow and a tsunami.

Heidi pouted in the backseat of the Jeep. "I don't know why I can't stay with Kaia." Her lips trembled. "Or Donna," she added grudgingly.

It might have been easier if Heidi had taken to Donna as well as she had to Kaia. Jesse thought if he'd asked Donna, she might have taken leave to care for his niece. The problem was that she might expect something from him in return. Something he wasn't prepared to give.

He glanced at his niece. "Kaia has to work nights now. I already told you that." He had, in fact, told her that at least twenty times. He'd never seen such a persistent kid, but then Heidi was the only one he'd been around much. She was a good kid though, and he hated to upset her.

"I could stay at her house and sleep when she did."

"She'd never get any rest with you around. Besides, it's too dangerous now. I never would have let you go out there in the first place if I'd thought a diver might try to hurt you."

"I could protect Nani."

"Leave it, Heidi. This is the way it has to be." He was sorry for his tone when he saw big tears roll down her cheeks. He steeled his heart and clenched his teeth together. There was nothing to say. Things were what they were. He knew she was missing her mom, but he couldn't help that. He opened his door and stepped out of the Jeep.

He glanced at Curtis. It was easy to see he and Duncan were brothers, even though Curtis was much older. Jesse had never met him when they were kids. Duncan had been born to their father's second, and much younger, wife. They both had their father's pale blue eyes and soft chin.

His gaze skipped over Curtis's head and lingered on the woman. Faye. About fifty or fifty-five, she oozed a cool sophistication that startled him. He'd expected a motherly type. This woman was slim to the point of emaciation. Her glossy black hair was cut short and stylish with a youthful flip to the ends. Her skin was flawless, and her features were classical Hawaiian. Jesse could imagine her in a hula lineup in her younger days. How old was Curtis—forty, forty-five? She was a little older, though she hid it well.

Crisp linen trousers and a silk blouse completed the perfect picture. How would she be able to play with Heidi in a getup like that? She looked more like an accountant than a nanny. Misgivings furled his brow.

He saw Faye's eyes widen, and her smile faltered at his delay in greeting them. Quickly forcing a smile, he stepped forward with his hand outstretched. "You must be Curtis. You look a lot like Duncan. Thanks again for your help in getting Kaia and the dolphin assigned to me."

"My pleasure." Curtis shook his hand then pulled his wife forward. "This is Faye." He bestowed a doting look on the woman that said he thought she was perfect and everyone else had better agree.

Duncan said they had been married only a year, and Jesse wondered how they had gotten together. Curtis was a genial man but the type who might wear plaid with stripes. His hair looked like it could use a trim, and Jesse doubted he'd shaved today. Faye looked like she could spend the house payment on her clothing budget. If she even agreed to a budget.

Jesse dragged his attention back to what Curtis was saying. "I'm sorry. I was woolgathering."

"My wife has that effect on men." Curtis smiled and nodded toward a picnic table along the beach area. "Let's have a seat and talk about this."

Jesse called for Heidi, who came out of the Jeep reluctantly. He took her hand and squeezed it. They gathered around the picnic table. The heat of the weathered wood baked through his trousers, and he shifted restlessly. This wasn't a social event. He wanted to get things settled and get back to work.

"I really appreciate your interest in caring for Heidi. Have you done this type of thing before?" Was it his imagination or did her bright smile lose a watt or two?

She wet her lips. "Curtis is gone so much, and I love children. If I weren't so old, I'd think of having a child with Curtis." She sent her husband a loving look, which he returned. "Heidi is an age I enjoy, and I have some fun things planned to do this summer, but Curtis is going to be really busy working at the lab and it would be fun to see the island again through young eyes. Though I've never been a nanny, I think Heidi and I could have fun together." She leaned forward and directed her attention to Heidi. "I thought we might go to Waimea Canyon one day, go kayaking and snorkeling on other days. Do you like that idea?"

Heidi's look of reserve gave way to interest. "I love to snorkel. Did you know that a third of Hawai'i's 480 species of fish are en—endemic to Hawai'i?" She stuttered slightly over the unusual word. "And we have forty species of sharks. One almost ate me when I was a little girl."

Jesse grinned. He'd forgotten that story. Faye looked uncertainly from Heidi to him as though she didn't know what to believe. "Heidi is a fish," Jesse said. "She knows everything there is to know about the ocean around here. Or almost. She was swimming with her dad when she was four. A tiger shark nudged her leg but left her alone."

"He could tell I wasn't a fish," Heidi said.

"Of course not," Faye agreed. The corners of her mouth twitched.

Faye seemed nice enough. "It's only for a month," Jesse said. "Maybe not even that long if I can get things squared away on base so I can take leave."

Faye nodded. "Sounds perfect. We can have fun and get to be friends. Neither of us will be likely to get bored."

Though he'd found it hard to warm up to her at first, her enthusiasm for being with Heidi put him at ease. "Great!" He glanced at his watch. "When can you start?"

"Today if you need me." She smiled at Heidi. "How about a shave ice this afternoon?"

"Super!"

"Then horseback riding?" Faye's eyes gleamed.

"On the beach?"

"Yep. I'll need to change into jeans. You too. Your legs will get sore in those shorts."

"Okay!" Heidi jumped up and put her hand in Faye's.

Jesse felt like a load of taro had just rolled off his back. With Heidi so enthusiastic, he could leave the guilt behind.

THE WIND BLEW HER HAIR INTO BLACK STREAMS BEHIND HER. Kaia wished she'd brought a scarf. Mano's car was in the shop, and he reveled in the chance to drive their grandfather's car. She clung to the door handle as Mano careened around the corner and pressed the accelerator of the convertible. "Slow down!"

He ignored her plea, laughing as she hit him on the arm. The old muscle car had seen better days, but their grandfather kept it in pristine condition. Everyone on the island knew Oke in the blue 1965 Plymouth Grand Fury. He generally took up more than his half of the road, but the island people respected him enough to get out of his way.

"Live a little, sis. You need some excitement in your life," he shouted over the roar of the wind in her ears.

"I have plenty of excitement. Slow down, or you can take me home." She didn't want to go anyway. It was already five, and by the time the meeting was over, she'd barely have time to bolt down a teriyaki burger and get to the boat for her patrol duties. The thought of cruising along the inky water wasn't something she was looking forward to. She'd tried to sleep today, but the bright sunshine wasn't conducive to rest when she wanted to be at Seaworthy Labs working on her research.

Mano let up on the accelerator, and the convertible's speed eased. At least Kaia felt she could breathe again. The wind had snatched her air away before she could suck it into her lungs. "How big is this meeting anyway?"

"About sixty. It varies. We should have good attendance

tonight." Mano's broad hands handled the car with expertise, and he pulled into a tight parking spot.

"They meet at the old rice mill?" Kaia stared at the weathered structure outside Hanapepe. It sat in the middle of an open field surrounded by red dirt and scruffy shrubs. The grayed boards hadn't seen a paintbrush in decades. The dozens of cars parked around it seemed out of place.

"It's got plenty of room, and it's private." He got out of the car and headed toward the building.

Kaia hurried to catch up with him. "Where's the fire?" she panted.

"The meeting has probably already started. I don't want to miss anything."

She followed him through the door and into the old mill. This was not her idea of a good time. Cane spiders tended to overtake abandoned buildings, and she hated the huge, aggressive spiders. She'd once had one nearly the size of her hula skirt chase her across the room even though she had a broom in her hand, and she wasn't eager to repeat the experience, even though they weren't poisonous.

Men and women milled around the rough wooden floors. The musty odor of grain and dust made her sneeze. No one seemed to notice them slip to the back of the crowd, which was intent on the man speaking from atop an old piece of machinery.

He waved his arms as he spoke. "The *haoles* brought their diseases to our islands, used our women, took our land, brought religious ideas and ethics that eradicated the Hawaiian culture. But we can take it back, my friends. The United States has apologized for their atrocities; now we must insist they prove their sincerity with action. They must return the lands they stole and allow us to govern ourselves. As we make inroads with Congress, we need to work to repair our culture, to revitalize the old ways."

Kaia listened to him expound on the virtues of a sovereign Hawai'i. She could see why Mano was enthralled. Even she felt a tugging in her heart. Hawaiians like the Oana family would stand to benefit if the old monarchy was resurrected. She and her siblings descended from royalty, all the way back to the last reigning queen, Liliuokalani. They could be part of the new government. Maybe that was the allure for Mano.

The man continued. "We could make our own trade agreements, keep what we make here, use the taxes we pay to the U.S. for our own islands. We can turn back the clock and return to the old ways, to our rich culture of aloha."

She glanced around the mill and saw groups of men and women listening intently. There was a mixture of races as well, full-blooded Hawaiian, part Hawaiian, and even some *haole* and Japanese. The man's appeal was apparently broad based.

"Who is he?" she whispered to Mano.

"Nahele Aki. He's brilliant."

Kaia had to admit he had a special charisma. He spoke with such passion and authority. She listened as he extolled the way of life they'd had before the white man came. He made it sound like a paradise. Though admittedly inspired, she wondered how many of these people would like to go back to mashing taro and living in huts.

When the meeting was over, Mano left her to talk to a group of men. She grabbed a cup of coffee from a folding table set up by the door. Sipping it, she tried to look inconspicuous.

"What did you think?"

She realized with a start that the speaker, Nahele Aki, had stepped down from his perch and was talking to her. "It was interesting," she stammered.

"Interesting? You and your family would be in line for the monarchy."

"How do you know who I am?" she asked. His dark eyes crinkled, and she had a feeling he was laughing at her.

"I make it my business to find out about important people. Ready to join us and be a queen in the new kingdom?"

She knew he expected her to feel flattered. She wasn't. "No thanks. I wouldn't want that kind of responsibility. I'm perfectly happy with my life the way it is."

"Mano says you keep the old traditions with the hula and our language. Why would you not want to bring back the old Hawai'i— the way we were before the United States stole our land and our wealth from us?"

She sighed. "There were many reasons why we lost our sovereignty. By the time we were annexed, the damage had been done to our culture anyway. I'm an American now as well as a Hawaiian. Both are my heritage. I wouldn't mind seeing us awarded nation-within-a-nation status, like the Sioux or other Native American nations. But I don't plan to vote to pull away from the United States. My father died defending his country in Vietnam. I couldn't spit on the memory of his sacrifice like that."

The amusement in Nahele's eyes faded. Kaia shivered at the bleak depths in them.

"I'm going to pay America back for all they've taken from us. Most Hawaiians are content to sit back and wait for the government's goodwill. I'm not that stupid."

She wet her lips. "It's a lost cause."

The man's fingers curled into the palms of his hands. "Mano believes in our cause. You would do well to follow your brother's example."

"He is hot-blooded." She decided to turn Nahele's attention away from her family. "I heard you lost a member recently. Jonah Kapolei."

He raised his eyebrows. "Did you know Jonah?"

Bingo. The dead man was Jonah. "No, but Mano did. I suppose Jonah wanted to see the naval base leave Kaua'i. Did you send him to sabotage something?"

Amusement touched Nahele's face. "Why do I feel you're fishing, Miss Oana? I'm not hungry for the tasty worm you're dangling.

I have no idea what Jonah was doing on a dive alone. He knew better."

"Maybe he wasn't alone. He was shot with a poisoned dart."

"I wouldn't know anything about that. I hope you'll attend again with your brother and give us a chance to change your mind." He nodded and walked away without waiting for an answer.

Kaia watched him go. If Jonah's death had nothing to do with the murders and break-ins at the base, why was Nahele so defensive? She needed to tell Jesse about this conversation, but what if it got Mano in trouble? She chewed on her lip and wished she knew what to do.

SEVEN

Faye walked along the beach with Heidi running ahead of her. The little girl stopped and tossed lava rock into the turquoise waves before skipping ahead again. Faye didn't know where the child got so much energy. In the three days she'd been watching her, they'd gone horseback riding, been to Fern Grotto, and gone on a picnic to Waimea Canyon.

She was already exhausted. How she would keep this up for another month, she had no idea. Faye found herself remembering how it was when her own children were young. She hadn't enjoyed this age then, but maybe she'd been too much of a kid herself. Once Heidi got used to her, maybe things would be less tiring.

She caught up with Heidi only after the girl plopped down to the sand and began heaping it into a pail. "Want some help?" Faye asked her. The little girl shook her head and didn't look at her. She'd been sullen and uncooperative all day, and Faye was fed up with it. She was only doing this because Curtis thought it was a good idea, and at least the kid could cooperate.

"I'm going to swim, Auntie Faye." Heidi got up and went to the edge of the water.

Faye watched the little girl's pink bathing suit blur into the brilliant blue of the ocean. In a few minutes Heidi rode a rolling wave onto the beach. Faye looked down at her own modest black suit. She could join the child in the water, but it would mess up her hair, and she and Curtis had an engagement with business associates later. She didn't want to have to wash it again.

She pulled a beach towel out of her bag and spread it on the pale golden sand. She'd just lie in the sun and watch Heidi play. A few other women and children were playing along this section of Queen's Pond at Polihale Beach, but not many. She settled her sunglasses on her nose and lay on her stomach with her face turned toward the water where she could watch Heidi.

The sun baking into her skin felt good, and the tightness in her muscles began to relax. She still hadn't met Kaia. Every day when she got home, Curtis asked her if she'd met Kaia or her brothers. His face clouded every time she said no. She was going to have to disappoint him again today. They'd both been sure the women's paths would cross, considering Kaia's connection to Jesse and Heidi.

Her eyes closed against the glare of the sun that penetrated the edges of her sunglasses. A shout startled her. She sat up and looked toward the water. She relaxed when she saw Heidi dumping sand from her pail.

Someone shrieked again. "Where's Michael? Where's my son?" The hysterical mother ran toward the water.

The cry was something no woman could ignore. It touched the deepest fears in every female. Faye stood and ran to the water's edge with the woman. "Are you sure he's in the water?"

"He was right here a minute ago," the woman said, her tone frantic.

The other mothers began to call for the little boy. While they checked the water, Faye hurried toward the restrooms. Children were never where you expected them to be. She rapped on the men's door. "Michael, are you in there?"

The door opened, and she looked down on a small boy of about four. "Are you Michael?" He nodded. "Your mommy is looking for you." She took his hand and led him toward the beach.

She looked across the sand to the water. The waves were bigger now, tipped with foam. She handed Michael off to his mother then looked around for Heidi. There was no sign of the little girl. "Have you seen Heidi? She's blond, about eight."

The women shook their heads. "We were looking for Michael," one woman said.

Faye cupped her hands around her mouth. "Heidi, time to come in."

Only the terns' harsh calls answered her. She scanned the waves again and told herself not to panic. Just as Michael had been found, Heidi would be too. Maybe she was in the restroom as well. But she would have passed her on the way back, she reminded herself. Faye ran down the beach toward another group of children but Heidi wasn't with them.

She ran the other direction. Clouds had gathered in the west, and the wind began to freshen. Her knees felt weak and wobbly, and she was lightheaded. Heidi had to be here. But there was no sign of a blond head in the water anywhere.

Tears sprang to her eyes, and she turned and looked up and down the sand. She saw small footprints leading toward an area where palm trees marched along the water's edge. Terror squeezed her lungs, and she followed the prints. "Please, Lord, please let her be all right," she muttered.

The footprints ended near a battered pier where the beach petered out into jagged black rock. Straining her eyes, Faye stared out at the waves and saw a distant sea kayak with a blond head poking up in the middle. Heidi. Faye looked around for another kayak or dingy—anything. But there was no other craft at the crumbling dock. She needed help. The child was no match for the growing waves.

She sprinted back to her bag and rummaged for her cell phone. She couldn't find it. Biting back a groan, she upended the bag onto the sand. Her cell phone went skittering across the beach. She grabbed for it and fell as it slipped past her. The sand scraped the skin from her knees, but she hardly noticed the sting.

She picked up the phone and dialed Curtis at the office. When she told him what had happened, he promised to call Jesse and have him come right away. Faye dropped her phone onto the sand and ran back to the pier. She couldn't see the boat any longer. Sobbing, she sank to her knees and prayed like she'd never prayed before.

KAIA RUBBED HER EYES. SHE WAS NEVER GOING TO GET USED TO this night work. Her body clock needed sunshine glinting off the surf and the sound of terns cawing overhead. She got dressed, brushed her teeth, then looked around for her keys. They weren't on her bedside table where she thought she'd left them.

Hiwa meowed as she scooped her up and carried her through the house. She went through the pockets of the clothes she'd left on the kitchen floor by the washer last night but didn't find them. She glanced on the counter. No keys. It was already nearly five, and she wanted to stop to see her grandfather before she had to report for work.

She set Hiwa on the floor and threw last night's pizza into the trash. This kitchen was a pit. She'd punched the snooze button on her alarm too many times. Her goal for the afternoon had been to clean house, but it wasn't going to happen today. Three days' worth of dirty glasses sat on the counter as well as the dirty pots from making a week's worth of granola. She was a health nut about her food, and she wished that care extended to housekeeping.

She took ten minutes to set the kitchen to rights, but she still couldn't find her keys. What a scatterbrain she was. Where had she left them? This morning she'd gotten home at six, gulped down a bowl of granola with flaxseed, and headed for bed. No, wait, she'd thrown a load of clothes in the washer first. Maybe they were in the laundry room.

The phone rang and she grabbed it.

"Kaia, can you meet me at the pier below you? I'm about to pass it right now. Heidi took a kayak out by herself." Jesse's voice held a touch of panic.

Kaia didn't ask questions. "I'll be right there." She clicked off the phone, grabbed her jacket, and ran out the door.

Hadn't that woman he hired been watching Heidi? Kaia's anger and fear grew as she reached the top of the cliff and saw the size of the swells from the storm blowing in. Easily twenty feet, they could swamp an inexperienced kayaker in minutes. Heidi was resourceful, but she was just a child, and Kaia doubted she had the expertise to manage these waves.

The navy boat was just pulling up to the dock when she arrived. Jesse's face was grim and strained. Kaia wondered how much sleep he'd had over the past few days. She'd half expected him to accompany her on the patrol at night, but another sailor had joined her.

She hopped aboard the boat without waiting for it to dock and dropped the backpack containing her diving gear onto the deck. Jesse grabbed her hand to steady her against the rolling of the vessel, and she dropped into a seat beside him. "Any sign of her yet?"

He shook his head. "Can Nani help us?"

"I'll call her." She opened her backpack and pulled out the equipment she'd been carrying with her on the patrols. Leaning over the side of the boat, she put DALE into the water and turned it on. The clicks and whistles it emitted couldn't be heard above the sound of the surf. White spray struck her in the face as the boat headed out to sea, and she licked the salt from her lips. It was hard to hang on to DALE with the bounce of the vessel.

She was beginning to think Nani wouldn't respond when she finally recognized the dolphin's dorsal fin running along the side of the boat. "There she is!"

Nani leaped into the air and splashed down then raced alongside the boat. Jesse told the pilot to head along Polihale Beach just north of Barking Sands. Kaia spotted a figure waving from a dilapidated pier along a piece of land that jutted into the sea. "Who is that?" she asked, pointing.

Jesse squinted. "I think it's Faye, Heidi's nanny." He directed the boat to veer over to pick her up.

The woman's eyes were red, and her mascara had left tracks of black under her eyes. She clambered aboard. "Oh, Jesse, I'm so sorry. I don't know how she managed to slip away from me like that. A mother had lost her child, and I was trying to help find him. I was only distracted for a few minutes."

Jesse pressed his lips together. "How long has she been gone?"

Faye glanced at her watch. "Maybe an hour?"

Kaia checked the other woman out. She recognized Faye's bathing suit as one that had cost the earth, and she smelled like she'd bathed in expensive French perfume. The Kate Spade sandals she wore would have cost Kaia's wages for the week. She looked Hawaiian, but Kaia had never seen her before.

She frowned. Why would a woman of such wealth be baby-sitting? Kaia hadn't had a chance to ask Jesse much about the new nanny. But the woman was obviously distraught, and Kaia knew how quickly a child could slip away. She'd had a hula student wander off once, and it was something she never forgot.

"She could be far out to sea by now." Jesse turned and looked out over the water. He ordered the pilot to head back out.

Kaia leaned over the side of the boat. She'd tried to teach Nani the series of clicks and whistles that she'd assigned to Heidi's name the first week they'd been out together. She could only pray the dolphin remembered and had figured it out. The device emitted the sound of Heidi's name, and Nani leaped in the water then zipped ahead of the boat.

"Follow the dolphin!" Jesse shouted over the noisy surf.

Nani had made the connection. Kaia could hardly believe it. Now if only the dolphin could find the little girl. The skipper revved up the engine, and the boat's bow slammed against every wave. The repeated jarring would have knocked Kaia to the deck, but she held on to the railing and strained to see through the spray. As Nani swam toward the Na Pali mountain chain, Kaia looked ahead then turned to look behind her. She saw something bobbing in the water.

"Is that a kayak?" Kaia pointed toward the shore. The upended kayak dipped and rolled with the waves tumbling it toward shore.

"It is!" Jesse leaned into the wind, his gaze on the boat.

Faye started to sob. Kaia jumped to the railing and cupped her hands to her mouth. "Heidi!" she shouted. *Please, Lord, let her be alive.* Her eyes burned. She knew Jesse was just as aware as she was that the little girl was unlikely to survive for long in seas like these.

Nani paused then turned back. Kaia felt a stab of disappointment in the dolphin. She hadn't been leading them to Heidi. The clicks and whistles hadn't represented anything meaningful to her. So much for their breakthrough.

Kaia squinted in the sunshine and continued to scan the waves and shout Heidi's name. Nani sped by the boat and veered toward shore. In that moment, Kaia spotted Heidi in the water. "There she is!" She shucked her jacket, kicked off her slippers, and dove overboard.

The swells hampered her vision, but she struck out with adrenaline-driven strength in the direction she'd seen Heidi. She glimpsed Jesse off to her right in the water as well. She rode a swell to the top and saw the little girl clinging to Nani's dorsal fin. The dolphin was pulling Heidi toward the boat.

Kaia shouted and pointed. Jesse heard her and shook the water out of his eyes. He waved that he'd seen them too, and they turned around and swam to intercept Nani and Heidi. They reached the boat the same time as the dolphin with her precious cargo.

Heidi let go of Nani and grabbed for her uncle's hand. Kaia came alongside and together they hoisted Heidi to the waiting men, who lifted her to safety. A wave grabbed Kaia and flung her away from the boat.

She went under, gulping water. An undertow caught her, and she instinctively fought it for a moment. Heidi needed her, and she wanted to get to the boat, but the current was too strong. She let herself go limp and went with the riptide until it released its grip.

Her head broke the surface. The boat was even farther away. Then Nani came to her, and she grabbed for the dolphin. Nani towed her back to the boat.

Jesse was at the ladder, spitting water. "I thought you were a goner," he sputtered.

Kaia grabbed the ladder and hauled herself up. Jesse followed, and they both collapsed onto the deck.

Kaia lay gasping then rolled to all fours and looked for the child. "How's Heidi?" She felt strung as tightly as a ukulele until she saw the *keiki*. Heidi lay in Faye's arms. They were both crying. Faye was smoothing the child's wet hair out of her face.

Too tired to stand, Kaia collapsed back onto the deck. Jesse grabbed her arm and helped her to a seat then went to his niece. Heidi turned and buried her face against her uncle.

"I'm sorry," she gulped. "Are you mad at me?"

He embraced her with one arm and held on to the rail with the other. Then he sat down and pulled her onto his lap. "You could have been killed, Heidi. You almost were."

She burst into fresh sobs. "The waves were so big. I kept swallowing water. Every time I got to the top of a wave, it sucked me under again. I asked God to send Nani, and he did. I was drowning when she came. She saved me."

"Don't ever scare me like that again." Jesse tucked her against his chest and propped his chin on her wet hair. "I don't know what I'd do if something happened to you."

"What were you thinking to go off by yourself?" Kaia asked. "We're lucky to have spotted you in the waves. Nani was just wandering aimlessly until I saw your kayak."

"We couldn't find the little boy, and I saw the kayak. I thought I could save him."

"That's a job for grownups," Jesse said.

"The waves got really big, and I got scared. I yelled, but no one could hear me." Heidi's tears began to taper off.

"How long were you in the water?" A real understanding of the close call was beginning to set in, and Kaia's limbs trembled.

"A long time. I tried to swim to shore, but the undertow wouldn't let me." She looked up at Jesse. "At first I forgot what Daddy told me about how to swim if I got caught in one. I kept getting farther and farther from the shore. Then I remembered how Daddy said I was supposed to swim with the current. I tried, but it kept pulling me under. I thought I was going to drown." Fresh tears sparkled in her eyes.

"It was strong." Kaia wasn't sure she could have overcome the undertow, and she was a strong swimmer. Thank the Lord Nani had been there, even if the dolphin had reacted to instinct rather than communication.

Heidi leaned over and vomited seawater on her uncle's feet. He didn't react much, just grabbed a towel Ensign Masters handed him and wiped his niece's face. The ensign upended a bucket of water onto Jesse's feet and the surrounding deck.

"Your mother is going to have to know about this escapade," he said sternly.

Heidi nodded. "She's going to be mad."

"We're just glad you're okay," Faye said. She seemed to be recovering some of her color. "Here, let me clean that up." She knelt and began to swab ineffectually at the mess. She finally gave up and let the ensign use his mop.

The wind blew Faye's black hair around her head and whipped it into her face. She brushed it out of her eyes. "Jesse, I hope you won't hold this against me. I don't want to give up my friendship with Heidi."

Heidi's eyes grew wide. "Does this mean I get to go back with Kaia?"

Faye flinched and covered her mouth with her hands. "She's not been very happy," she admitted. "I think she misses her mother."

"I realize that," Jesse said. He patted her shoulder. "If you're still willing to keep Heidi, I think we'll keep to our arrangement."

Faye's shoulders sagged. "*Mahalo*, Jesse. It won't happen again." Her dark eyes blinked rapidly, then she turned and gazed at Kaia. "I've been wanting to meet you, Kaia. Curtis has said such great things about you."

Kaia frowned. "Curtis has?" She couldn't imagine what her boss could have said. They'd butted heads right from the start.

"Curtis says you're brilliant." The boat lurched in the waves, and Faye almost tumbled to the deck. She caught herself against the back of Jesse's seat.

Kaia hadn't put the two together. In fact, she found it hard to imagine the pragmatic Curtis with Faye. But maybe she was judging the woman unfairly. Just because she wore nice clothes and shoes didn't mean she was shallow. Kaia had to admit her twinge of envy might have affected her first impression of the woman.

In fact, maybe Faye could be her ally to help Curtis understand the importance of her dolphin research. "Make sure you tell him about how Nani saved Heidi today," she said. If only Nani had found Heidi because she'd understood the language. Still, Heidi was safe, thanks to Nani.

"Oh, I will," Faye assured her. She hesitated for a second. "Why don't you meet me and Heidi for breakfast when you get off work tomorrow?"

Faye could be the help Kaia had been looking for. She had to convince Curtis that the real future of Seaworthy Labs lay with research into dolphin communication, even though Nani had failed her again.

"I just might do that."

EIGHT

Jesse parked in front of Kaia's charming cottage. "Cute place," he said. He grabbed Kaia's knapsack. "I'll carry this for you. Heidi's sleeping anyway."

Kaia yawned and nodded. She stepped over a hose and pushed open the door.

"Holy cow," Jesse muttered. He realized he'd said it out loud when he saw Kaia's cheeks go red. "Sorry, but—wow." He dropped the knapsack and picked up a discarded T-shirt.

Kaia grabbed it from his hand. "It's not like I haven't been busy," she snapped.

"Yeah, sorry." He'd never pegged her for the messy sort. It was a good thing they weren't in a relationship. A mess like this would drive him crazy.

He stepped over a catnip mouse and looked around then realized he hadn't thanked Kaia properly when they'd docked. "I really appreciate all you did today. You saved Heidi's life, you and Nani."

She didn't meet his gaze. "That's okay. I'm glad we were there. I was surprised you decided to let Heidi stay with Faye when she obviously wasn't watching her closely enough."

"I almost didn't. But I looked at Heidi and realized she was hoping to get Faye in trouble. It could have happened to anyone. I wandered off from my mother often enough. Especially when another child was in trouble. Faye has a good heart."

Maybe he was right. Kaia was beginning to realize Jesse had good judgment about people. She glanced out the window. "Here comes Bane."

"I'd better go. Heidi needs to get to bed." He exited the house, waving at Bane as he got in the Jeep. At his place, he parked and carried Heidi inside before wandering into the living room. The room felt even more sterile than usual. Beige paint, carpet, and furniture. No pictures on the walls. He'd been back on the island for three months and hadn't bothered to unpack so much as a picture of his family. But when had there been time?

Even though Kaia's place had been messy, it was homey and cheerful. It had character, whereas this place could have been anyone's home. Christy had never been much for decorating either. He sighed and went to the phone. Jillian's hotel number was right on top of the stand. The ringing went on for what seemed like forever on the other end of the line before she finally answered.

"Hello?" Jillian's voice echoed across the line.

He glanced at his watch. The time difference was twelve hours. "Hey, Jillian, I was about to give up."

"Is something wrong? Is Heidi okay?" Her voice rose and held a tinge of panic.

"She's fine. But we had a scare." He told her what had happened.

"She's always been one for getting into scrapes. She forgets she's only eight." Jillian sounded worried. "I should be there."

"You can't; you'd lose your job," he reminded her. "I've got everything under control here. I just wanted to keep you up-to-date on things."

"I want to be with Heidi." Her gulp echoed over the phone. "I miss her. Are you sure she's okay?"

"She's fine. I think she'll listen to Faye now."

Jillian began to cry softly. "I should just quit, find another job. This separation is too hard. How is Heidi doing?"

"She's fine."

"Does she ask about me?" Jillian's voice sounded wistful.

"She talks about you." Jesse didn't dare tell her Heidi had been acting out some. "Don't do anything foolish, Jillian. You worked your whole life for this job. What kind of position could you get if you quit? This time will pass sooner than you think. You can't afford to let emotion overrule your common sense."

"I know you're right, but it's so hard." Her voice broke again.

He hated to hear either of his sisters cry. His father had always expected him to take care of them. Sometimes, though, he couldn't. And this was one of those times. Jillian needed to do this project.

Jillian gulped again. "Who is this woman you've got watching her? Why isn't Kaia keeping her?"

"That was only temporary. Kaia is helping with base security at night. She sleeps during the day. This is an older woman—in her fifties I'd guess. She's Duncan's sister-in-law. She's been taking Heidi to see all the sights."

Jillian was silent. "How is Duncan?"

Jesse propped his feet up. "Same old Duncan."

"That sounds a little cynical."

"You know how he is—always looking to blame someone else for his own troubles."

Jillian was silent a minute. "I think maybe I was too hard on him. He wanted so badly to do well in college."

"He was smart enough to do it without cheating. He said to tell you hello, by the way. You could always look him up when you get back to the islands."

"We'll see." Her voice hardened. "I'm still not impressed with this Faye."

"That's not fair, Jillian. Something like this could happen to anyone."

"Even you, Jesse." His sister's voice was soft. "Maybe you should listen to your own words. What happened to Christy wasn't your fault either."

He knew that. They all thought he blamed himself, and he had for a while. But now all he felt was sadness and regret that Christy's family had turned their backs on him. But there was no way was he going there with Jillian. "Let me know when you'll be winding up things there."

"I'll get out of this as soon as I can," she promised.

Clicking off the phone, Jesse knew Jillian wouldn't go back to sleep. She would probably get up and reorganize the hotel room dresser. Cleaning and organizing was generally her way of coping with worry. If he were a betting man, he'd bet she wouldn't last the month out before she'd be back for her daughter. She was a good mother. Until then, looking out for Heidi was his responsibility.

ARE YOU EVER COMING TO BED?"

Curtis sounded petulant, but Faye couldn't bring herself to leave the bathroom and mollify him. Staring at herself in the mirror, she told herself she deserved nothing less than what had almost happened today. Maybe it would have been better to have been exposed for the fraud she was. Better for Heidi at least.

She rinsed the expensive cleansing cream from her face, taking care not to stretch the fragile skin around her eyes. Slathering on a special nighttime mixture with a light floral scent, she tipped her chin to the right and the left. Not bad for a woman of fifty-five. People told her she looked forty, but she had watched the lines around her eyes and mouth advance and knew they were being kind.

One of these days it would be easy to see she was ten years older than Curtis.

"You're not talking." Curtis stood in the bathroom doorway.

The pale green silk pajamas she'd bought him had been a mistake, she thought, turning to look at him. They were the wrong color for his florid face, and they were too tight across his stomach.

Curtis sighed and reached out to draw her against his chest. "I see that look in your eyes. You're not running away from this, Faye. We've come too far to back out now. And I've plowed too much money into Seaworthy Labs to just walk away. You wanted this, and now you're going to stay here and face it."

"I know, I know," she murmured against the silk pajama top. "You're so good to me, Curtis. So much better than I deserve."

He leaned her away from his chest and gave her a gentle shake. "Quit that kind of talk. You're deserving of so much more than I can give you, Faye. This is going to work out—you'll see."

She nodded and laid her head back against his chest. The beat of his heart thudded against her ear in a steady, rhythmic beat that calmed her like a baby laid against its mother's breast. "I met Kaia today too. I wasn't sure it was ever going to happen. So something good came out of the day."

The hand he'd been petting her hair with grew still. "What did you think of her?"

"She's beautiful, more lovely than I could have imagined. Smart and strong too. You should have seen the way she dove into the water and went after Heidi. She seemed almost as much fish as human."

"She's really remarkable. Her affinity with the dolphins is going to make her famous someday. And Seaworthy Labs too, she says."

"She's meeting me and Heidi for breakfast in the morning."

"Here?" Curtis drew back. "Do you think that's wise?"

"Wise or not, she's coming here when she gets off work in the morning. Don't worry. I'll be good. She'll never suspect a thing."

KAIA SHIFTED RESTLESSLY IN HER SEAT ABOARD THE NAVY cruiser. A misty rain had fallen earlier, a remnant of the system that had blown in during the afternoon with the large swells. The clouds had dissipated, and the stars had come out around one o'clock in the morning. The two SPs Jesse had assigned to accompany her spent their time at the helm and largely ignored her—a state of affairs she welcomed. They were both older and married, which helped put her at ease.

Tonight they were anchored just off Nohili Point, south of Barking Sands. The waves had died down to gentle swells. She sat under the overhang and looked out over the water. There were hardly any lights along the shore here, and she felt alone.

She hadn't wanted to have Nani in danger again, but she had to try to figure out what was going on so she could protect Mano from himself. She was certain Pele Hawai'i was involved, and if they were behind the break-ins, Mano might be too.

Nani chattered from just off the bow, and Kaia got up to speak to her. "What's the matter, girl? Are you lonely?"

The dolphin flung herself into the air and splashed Kaia. Nani chattered again as she danced along the waves. If Kaia weren't so tired, she'd join Nani for a swim. Heidi's rescue had taken a lot out of her. She could curl up on the deck and take a nap.

Now was as good a time as any to do what she had to do. After Nani's failure to realize she needed to find Heidi, Kaia had come to the conclusion she had to do what Curtis suggested: train Nani and the other dolphins to jump through hoops and perform the tricks that brought in more people. If enough money came in that way, maybe they could continue the research long enough to make the communication connection.

She turned to get the equipment she'd brought when she became aware of the sound of a boat engine in the distance. The lights were out as though they didn't want to be seen. She doubted they could see the navy boat sitting quietly in its anchorage. The other boat hugged the coastline as close to shore as possible without running aground. In a few minutes, the hum of the engine fell silent.

She should check it out. She poked her head into the engine room and told the sailors what she was doing.

"One of us should go with you." Mick Wilson, the burly petty officer who'd been assigned to her, stood.

"I've got Nani. She and I can slip in without being seen. If I get in trouble, I'll signal you with my flashlight and wave into Nani's camera."

He hesitated then nodded. Kaia stepped out of her slippers and went down the ladder. Nani met her at the bottom. Kaia began swimming toward the boat, and when Nani caught on, Kaia grabbed the dolphin's dorsal fin. Together they sped through the water.

The boat was anchored just offshore in an inlet cove. No lights shone, and if she hadn't heard the motor before it was cut, she never would have noticed it. The waves streamed past her body in a silken flow. She released Nani's fin and treaded water while she assessed the situation.

There was no sound from the boat, no sign of movement. Maybe the passengers had gone ashore. She glanced toward the beach. The moon came out from behind a cloud and illuminated a small dingy pulled up on the sand.

Bingo. Someone was here. She swam closer to shore. Her feet touched bottom, and she moved to the left where coconut palm trees leaned over the water. She came ashore under the thick leafy shelter. Pausing to catch her breath, she stepped against the smooth trunk of the tree and peered around into the open area to her right.

Three men stood talking in a soft hush. The wind blew their words away from her. She was going to have to get closer. She sidled along the edge of the trees as they changed from palms to monkeypod. She was careful to stay in the shadows. The sharp lava rock scraped her bare feet, and she winced when she stubbed her toe on an unseen boulder.

Still hidden in the shelter of the trees, she finally stood about six feet from the men. She recognized one of them as Nahele Aki, the head of Pele Hawai'i. The other two looked familiar, and she assumed she'd seen them at the meeting she'd attended with Mano.

"Are we all set on our jobs?" Nahele asked.

"Yep," the taller of the two men said.

All three were dressed in black wet suits. Kaia suspected they were about to make an unannounced visit to the base, though why they'd come ashore here, off base property, she had no idea.

Nahele motioned toward where Kaia crouched. "Get the gear."

She looked around for someplace to hide. The monkeypod tree

branches grew low and heavy, so she grabbed one and hoisted herself into the tree. She settled on the branch and strained to hear. A movement along the branch above her head flickered at the edge of her vision. She turned her head to look and found herself eyeball to eyeball with a cane spider. She froze.

The thing was huge, nearly eight inches in diameter. It lifted one leg delicately as if to reach out to touch her. Her heart tried to get to the ground before the rest of her could move. Then her taut muscles loosened and she lunged back along the branch as far as she could go. It wasn't far. She was wedged into the crook of the tree.

Her horrified gaze stayed fixed on the spider. It moved closer. She couldn't breathe, couldn't think beyond a certainty that she couldn't let that thing touch her. The spider was going to be on her any minute. She was afraid to look at it and afraid to let it out of her sight for fear it would scurry up her arm. When the spider made a sudden movement and raced toward her, she lost it. Screeching, she flung herself away and fell from the tree. Her ankle twisted under her as she hit the ground.

She lay on the sand as the men surrounded her. Nahele yanked her to her feet, and she moaned as her foot slammed against a boulder.

"Miss Oana, what are you doing here?"

Trying to ignore the throbbing in her ankle, she lifted her chin and met his gaze. "Nothing. I'd been out for a moonlight swim."

"A little late for a swim, isn't it? And tree swimming is something I've never heard of."

"I couldn't sleep." She wondered how long it would be before the sailors came looking for her.

"What did you hear?"

Though the words were mild, the dislike and suspicion in his eyes made her freeze. She tried to smile. "Hey, I just got here. I didn't hear anything other than when you told the men to get the gear." It might be a good thing she hadn't heard anything.

His gaze probed her face, and she forced herself to tilt her head up and meet his suspicious stare.

"I'm inclined to believe you," he said.

"Nahele!" The younger man scowled and took a step closer. "We can't risk it."

"I know that, Kim. Take her." He stepped aside.

The younger man grabbed her by the arm and dragged her away from the grove. A hot burst of pain jolted up her leg, and she sagged to the ground. She wasn't sure if she wanted to moan or vomit.

Kim jerked her back onto her feet. She swayed on her good leg. She regarded him through a haze of pain. How was she going to get out of this? She glanced toward the dark water and saw the dolphin's dorsal fin at the top of a wave. If she could just make it to the water, Nani would be there to get her back to the navy boat.

"Carry her, Kim," Nehele said.

Kaia couldn't let that happen. He'd have too tight a grip on her. "I can walk," she said. "I just twisted my ankle." She eased part of her weight onto her foot and took a tiny step. Kim slackened his grip on her arm, and she wrenched herself free and stumbled toward the waves.

He shouted and grabbed her, missing her arm but snagging her by the hair. She tore loose. Her scalp stung where she'd left strands of hair in his grip. Just a few more feet. She waded into the water, the cool touch of the waves soothing the pain in her ankle.

The men came splashing after her. She dove into the next wave. The water engulfed her and hid her from her pursuers. She kicked out and surfaced then took another gulp of air and plunged under the water again. Something brushed her ankle, a hand fumbled to snag her foot, but she shot forward in the waves.

The next time she surfaced, her pursuers were farther behind. Nani's dorsal fin sliced the water toward her. Kaia reached out and took hold. She looked back and saw them scrambling for their boat. She had to get to her own, or they'd nab her again.

NINE

*J*esse *tried to move, but his arms were tied to his sides with long
strands of black hair, dark as midnight and just as thick. He
could smell the scent of orchids, sweet and cloying. Christy called
his name, and he tried again to move, to go to her. The horn on the car
blared an evil sound that made him want to scream. He turned to look
at Christy again, but instead of her lovely face, he saw her father. His
lips were twisted in a snarl that made him look like one of Kaua'i's wild
boars, all crooked teeth and wild eyes. Jesse tried to pull his hand free,
but he was pulled toward those jagged teeth.*

Jesse thrashed to free himself and woke up in his bed with the
sound of his own voice crashing like tropical surf. Covered in a thin
sheen of perspiration, his limbs felt weak and shaky. He untangled
his legs from the damp sheet and took several deep breaths. It was
just a dream.

"You yelled, Uncle Jesse." Heidi stood in the doorway clutching
her tattered teddy. Rubbing her eyes, her hair was rumpled around
her red pajamas.

"I was having a bad dream." He'd thought they were over, but
this one was as bad as in the early days. He passed a hand over his
damp forehead then rubbed his hair. The memories wouldn't stay
locked away.

Heidi scampered to the bed and clambered onto the covers. She
patted his face and tucked Boo under his arm. "Want me to sing to
you? Kaia taught me a new song in Hawaiian. Mom always likes me
to sing to her when she can't sleep at night."

"It would be better than hearing me sing. Or Kaia," he said,
grinning at the memory of Kaia's froglike voice. Jesse knew nothing
could induce him to go back to sleep now, but Heidi would feel use-
ful. And it might distract him.

She sat back with her legs tucked under her. Raising her hands above her head, she began to sing a hula *mele*. *"E hô mai i ka `ike, mai luna mai e."* She closed her eyes and swayed with the beat. *"I nâ mea huna no`eau o nâ `ôlelo e, E hô mai, e hô mai, e hô mai e."* She bowed her head when she was done.

"That's beautiful. What's it mean?"

"It asks God for wisdom from above," Heidi said.

"I sure need that now." Jesse could still hear the echo of the chant in his head. What was wisdom anyway? He'd read in Proverbs that the fear of the Lord was the beginning of wisdom. God could take things he treasured most away in a heartbeat—Jesse had learned well the lesson on fearing God. But he still didn't know much about being wise.

Aware of Heidi's expectant face, he hugged her and kissed the top of her head. "You need to go back to sleep, princess."

"Okay." She returned his hug with a fierceness that warmed him then climbed down from the bed and went to the door. "Call me if you have another bad dream."

"Okay." You'd think she was the grownup and he was the child. He grinned and settled back against the pillow.

He prayed for peace to settle over him and Heidi for the rest of the night, though he still felt uneasy. But his eyelids grew heavy, and he settled down into the bed.

The phone rang just as he was beginning to drift off. The bright numbers on the clock radio said it was four. He grabbed the phone before Heidi awakened again. "Matthews."

"Kaia's been attacked," Ensign Masters said.

"On my way." He dropped the phone back into the cradle and sprang out of bed. There was no way around it. He'd have to take Heidi with him.

KAIA SAT IN THE CONTROL ROOM WITH HER FOOT PROPPED ON a stool. The doctor probed her swollen ankle with impersonal hands, and she winced when he moved it around.

"I take it that hurts," he said, standing up.

"Is it broken?" That was her biggest fear. The thought of being laid up when the future of her research was at stake frightened her.

"I don't think so. We'll get some pictures and see for sure, but I think it's just a sprain. I'll wrap it, and you can stay off it a few days."

"I don't have a few days. Can I get back on the boat and just keep it propped up?"

"If you have to." He took off his bifocals and rubbed his eyes.

She noticed the bags under his eyes. "Sorry to get you out of bed at this hour."

"I was on duty, but it's about time to go off." He patted her toes. "Come see me at the base hospital when you're done being debriefed. I'll get X-rays and wrap it."

She nodded, her gaze on the tall figure coming through the door. Jesse's gaze swept the room and came to rest on her face. Heidi clung to his hand, her eyes droopy with sleep. She saw Kaia, and her mouth made an O.

She dropped her uncle's hand and ran to Kaia. "Is Nani okay?"

"She's fine." Kaia shifted in her seat and stifled a grin. The *keiki* knew where her priorities were.

Jesse approached. "What happened?"

"I ran into some men just off base. I'm not sure what they were up to, but whatever it was, they weren't happy at my appearance." She told him about her ordeal.

"Did you recognize them?"

She hesitated. If she told him about Pele Hawai´i, Mano might fall under suspicion. As well as implicating her brother, it could lead to even more demands by the navy for her help. She couldn't afford any more distractions from her research. She decided to ignore his question. "I wasn't sure I'd make it back to the boat before they got to me, but Mike was just starting to look for me. When the men saw the navy boat, they headed off in the opposite direction."

Jesse's composed face never altered as she went through her

story. He nodded at a few points then asked his men some questions. They hadn't seen anything other than the boat speeding away.

"You should report this to the police," Jesse said.

Kaia splayed her fingers palms up. "Why? I injured myself falling out of the tree. My only bruises are self-inflicted."

Jesse frowned. "Maybe they could help identify the men. They've got artists to help you recreate the faces."

"I just want to go home." Kaia reached forward and rubbed her ankle. She needed to keep him from asking her again if she recognized the men.

"That looks bad," he said. He touched the purple bruises with gentle fingers.

She tensed at the way her nerve endings sprang to life. His hair was only inches away, and she had an urge to put her fingers in that short blond cap. Her hand crept toward his head, and she snatched it back. What was she thinking? He was ten years older and not her type at all.

Jesse seemed oblivious, but Kaia couldn't look him in the eye. "What's next?" she asked, careful to keep her tone impersonal.

Before he could answer, an older man stepped into the room. Kaia recognized the insignia on his uniform as that of a navy captain.

Jesse stood at attention and saluted.

"At ease." The man didn't smile.

Jesse went to an at-ease stance with his hands clasped behind his back. He introduced the man to Kaia as Captain Stanley Lawton. Lawton's gaze raked over her, making Kaia feel she was a beached starfish on display. And what was that noise? She realized the captain was grinding his teeth.

The captain's probing eyes zeroed in on Jesse. "Matthews, I've been patient with you and your family problems. But this missile defense system is *critical.* I don't want any more attempted break-ins. You're going to have to prove to me you can handle this job, or I'll ask the base commander to replace you."

A muscle twitched in Jesse's jaw. Kaia wished she could come to his defense, but she knew it would humiliate him further. Heidi scowled at Lawton and took Kaia's hand. Kaia studied her ankle and tried to disappear.

"I can handle it, sir. I'm going to need more men."

"Then request the men you need, but I want results—not excuses. If there are any further security breaches, I'll take steps." Lawton's scowl deepened, and he spun on his heel and stalked out of the room.

Kaia was glad the man hadn't addressed her. She was in no shape to withstand his withering tongue.

Jesse gave orders to his aide then turned back to Kaia. "We're going to make some changes. I'm going to see if Faye can let Heidi sleep at her house. I'll pick her up after work and feed her dinner before I take her back at bedtime so I can join you on the boat."

"But, Uncle Jesse!"

Jesse shot Heidi a look that said the topic wasn't open for discussion. Even so, Kaia thought she saw regret there too.

"You won't get any sleep." And she wasn't sure she wanted him looking over her shoulder every minute. His confident strength disturbed her and made her wonder what it would be like to kiss him, to share her past hurts with him.

"I'll survive it. The tests will be over in two weeks. I can crash for a few minutes at a time on deck." His stance tense, he stood with his arms folded across his chest.

This wasn't up to her, so she nodded. "I'd better go get this ankle wrapped." She stood and swayed from the pain that shot up her leg.

"Let me help you." Jesse caught her hand then swung her up into his arms.

Taken off guard, she stiffened.

"Relax," he said in her ear.

She could hear amusement in his voice but didn't dare look at his face. She could have fried an egg on her cheeks.

"Follow me, Heidi." He carried Kaia outside and across the parade ground to the naval hospital emergency room. A nurse tried to stop him at the desk with a wheelchair for Kaia, but he ignored her and carried Kaia back to a room.

In short order, he had a doctor taking her to X-ray. Kaia felt bewildered at how fast he got things moving. An hour later she'd been X-rayed and bandaged and was back outside on the sidewalk. Dawn was pushing back the edges of the darkness as she stood there with Heidi's hand in hers.

"Where's your car?" Jesse asked.

"Back at the dock where I reported for work last night."

"Wait here. I'll get my Jeep and drive you there."

"I'll stay with Kaia," Heidi said.

Jesse nodded and jogged off toward his office. Kaia's ankle throbbed, and she was discovering muscles she never knew she had. Maybe she'd stop for coffee on her way home. The thought of an iced Americano sounded tempting.

"Are you going to marry Uncle Jesse?" Heidi asked.

Kaia froze. "Of course not. Why would you ask such a question?"

"Your face was all red. I think he likes you. He needs a wife."

"Why does he need a wife?" Kaia knew she shouldn't pursue this line of questioning, but she had been wondering why Jesse was unattached. A man that attractive didn't often escape matrimony into his late thirties.

"He's been sad a long time. Mom worries about him."

"Sad?" Kaia wouldn't have called Jesse sad. Intense, focused . . . those were the words that came to mind. She took Heidi's hand and went to a bench to await Jesse's return.

Heidi nodded. "From the accident. Aunt Christy died. They were going to have a baby too. Poor Uncle Jesse."

"Was Aunt Christy his wife?"

"Uh-huh. She was nice, but I don't remember her real well. I was four when she died. Aunt Christy's family is mad at him."

Heidi was eight now, so it had been about four years ago. "I'm sure it wasn't your uncle's fault. Sometimes we have to blame someone when a bad thing happens."

"Well, it was kind of his fault." Heidi swung her legs to and fro on the bench. "Do you have some gum?"

"My purse is in the car. Sorry." She wanted to ask what Jesse had done that made it his fault, but the presence of a group of sailors standing behind them stopped her. She'd be mortified if they noticed the way she was taking advantage of Heidi's tendency to chatter. Jesse wouldn't be pleased to find she'd been prying.

The red Jeep Wrangler pulled up in front of them. Kaia stood and managed to use her crutches well enough to get to the vehicle. She felt as awkward as a monk seal on land. Jesse hopped out and opened the door for her and Heidi.

"I'd better get in the back so I can prop my leg on the seat," she told him. He nodded and helped her in.

"I'm taking you home. You're in no shape to drive. I'll pick you up when it's time to go out tonight."

She knew better than to object. Besides, he was right. The pain medicine the doctor had given her had made her woozy. She settled back against the door and lifted her leg to the seat. She found herself watching Jesse and wondering how she could have been so blind. Lines of suffering edged his mouth, and a furrow in his brow that she'd taken for arrogance was likely the expression of a man waiting for life to hand him another blow. His wife's death was none of her business, but she was curious.

She couldn't imagine how he could have been to blame for it. He seemed the type to handle anything life threw his way, but sometimes looks were deceiving. Her gaze lingered on him. What had his wife been like? Shame touched her at the thought of how she'd treated him, and she resolved to be more amiable. It wouldn't kill her to be pleasant.

"You okay?" he asked. He flipped the radio to an oldies station.

"Fine. Can we stop for coffee though?"

"You've got it." He released the parking brake and drove off the base. A stiff wind was blowing in from the sea and rocked the SUV as Jesse navigated it along the curving road toward Waimea.

"I told Kaia about Aunt Christy," Heidi said.

Kaia saw his hands grip the steering wheel tighter. His jaw hardened but he didn't say anything. She wasn't sure what to say either.

"That's not a topic for discussion, Heidi. You know that," he said finally. He turned into the espresso bar and turned to face Kaia. "What do you want, Kaia? I'll get it and you can rest your foot."

His expression warned her not to probe. As she listened to the Fab Four sing "Yesterday," she wondered if Jesse was ready to move on from the past. Watching his set face as he got out of the Jeep and went inside the espresso bar, she doubted it.

TEN

Faye could hardly sleep. Finally, things were moving in the right direction. In the morning, she felt vibrant in spite of her lack of sleep, and she hummed as she measured flour into a bowl and added macadamia nuts to the waffle mixture. She cleaned and diced papaya, strawberries, and pineapple for fruit smoothies.

In her perfect kitchen she felt in control. The smooth granite counters and floor, the European-style cabinets with their sleek lines, and the stainless appliances made her feel like a veritable Rachel Ray from TV. If Kaia and Jesse saw her here, they'd know she could handle any problem.

The clock on the mantel chimed eight times. Kaia and Heidi should be here any minute. Curtis would be so proud of her. She knew exactly how to handle this and just what she was going to say. Curtis said to be subtle. She'd show him just how good she was at that.

The doorbell rang and she jumped. She glanced at herself in the hall mirror as she rushed to the door. Her face was flushed, and there was a smudge of flour on her nose. She brushed it away and flung open the door. Her smile faded as she saw only Jesse and Heidi.

"Kaia isn't with you?" She stepped aside for them to enter.

Jesse guided Heidi inside. Her expression was mutinous. "She twisted her ankle last night, and I made her go home to bed. She said to tell you she'd come for breakfast in a couple of days. She'll call you."

Faye's lips trembled, and she pressed them together. She couldn't let Jesse see how disappointed she was. He'd wonder why it mattered so much. "I have breakfast ready. Macadamia-nut waffles with strawberry syrup."

"Sounds great. I need to get back to the base, but I think I can force down a waffle or two." He smiled and followed her to the kitchen. Heidi trailed behind them.

Faye brought him a plate of food. "We can eat in the dining room."

"Oh, this is fine," he said. He took the plate and sat at the bar stool at the counter.

Oh dear, none of this was going the way she'd planned. She bit her lip and gave Heidi her breakfast. "I'd thought to take Heidi snorkeling today, but she looks like she could use a nap." The little girl propped her head on one hand and picked at her food.

Jesse mouthed, "She misses her mom." He began to wolf down his food. "Wow, this is good. It's been forever since I had a breakfast like this."

Faye smiled and sat beside him. She picked daintily at her own breakfast, her appetite gone as quickly as her plans.

They ate in silence for a few minutes, then Jesse shoved his plate away. "Let me tuck her into bed; then I need to talk to you for a minute."

He sounded serious. Faye caught her breath and prayed he hadn't discovered her secret. She showed Jesse to the guest bedroom. He kissed Heidi then slipped her sandals off. Her eyes closed before Jesse and Faye had exited the room.

Faye ushered Jesse to the living room. She wasn't sure she wanted to hear what he had to say. Her gaze swept the room. It was in perfect order, unlike her life.

He perched on the edge of the sofa. Folding his big hands in front of him, he cleared his throat. "I need a favor."

Relief as sweet as pineapple swept through her. "Is that all? I thought the fate of the world hung in the balance from the way you looked. You know I'll do whatever I can to help you."

He nodded. "You've been great. I don't know what Heidi and I would have done without you. I'm not sure why you're being so good to us, but I appreciate it."

Faye couldn't look him in the eye. If he only knew. She resolved to try to get to know Heidi for her own sake. It was wrong to be using the child. And caring for a rambunctious eight-year-old hadn't been easy.

She pleated her skirt and looked at the carpet. "What can I do to help?"

"I'm going to need to start going out on the boat with Kaia. She was injured last night on duty, and I want to make sure that doesn't happen again."

Faye put her hand to her throat. "What happened?"

Jesse told her about Kaia's sprained ankle. Faye wished she could go check on the younger woman, but they were merely casual acquaintances. It would look odd.

"I see. And how do I come in?"

"Could you let Heidi sleep here? I'll come get her after work so you can have the evening with your husband. Then I'll bring her back and put her down to bed."

For a moment, Faye was taken aback at his temerity in asking such a consuming "favor." This would disrupt her whole life, not just the day. She was tempted to say no. But Kaia would hear of it and think her selfish. She bit her lip.

Jesse's coaxing smile faded. "I know it's a lot to ask. I'll see if I can find someone to stay at my place with her at night. It's too much for you."

"No, no, I was just surprised." Faye swallowed her irritation. "For how long?"

"Two weeks. Just until the missile tests are over. Less than that if we can nail who's breaching security."

She resisted the inclination to sigh. "I'll do it."

Jesse's blue eyes clouded. "On second thought, this isn't a good idea. If you could do this for a few days, I'll find someone to stay at the house. Let me see what I can do."

"No, no, it's fine. I like Heidi." She managed a smile. Why on earth was she trying to talk him out of it now? It was going to put a major crimp in her life. She'd basically have the *keiki* 24-7 with the exception of a few hours in the evening. Curtis might have a fit. On second thought, he probably wouldn't mind.

This could work to their advantage.

BANE HAD CLEANED THE HOUSE BEFORE KAIA GOT UP THIS morning, and she wished Jesse could see it now. From her view, she could see clear to Ni'ihau. The breeze had died down, and the sea rolled smoothly in to shore in mesmerizing waves of blue. The crutches had been more a hindrance than a help, and she'd left them in her house. Kaia hopped down the stone steps to her grandfather's. Clinging to the iron rail, she made her way to the bottom. The pain in her ankle was much less than she'd expected. Though the joint was still purple, it was more stiff than painful.

A curl of smoke rose from her grandfather's front yard. The aroma of another roasting pig floated to her nose, and her mouth watered. When was the last time she'd eaten? She thought back. Probably about this time yesterday. No wonder she was famished. *Tûtû kâne* would be more than happy to feed her.

Bane and Mano were raking the yard and putting out chairs for tonight's lu'au. "Hi, guys. What are you doing off work this morning?" she asked Mano.

"I'm not. I just don't have to report for duty until noon." Propping the rake against the house, Mano put his hands on his hips. "What did you do this time?"

"Fell out of a tree." Kaia's gaze lingered on Mano's face. She wondered if Nahele had called her brother and warned him what to expect. But no, she couldn't believe her brother would have anything to do with something that might put her in danger.

"Figures. When will you learn to be more careful?" Bane scolded. He grabbed a chair and pushed it toward her. "Sit down."

"I'm fine. It's just stiff." She wished she could confide in her older brother, but she didn't dare. Not this time. Bane would go marching off to see Nahele in high indignation, and he might blame Mano as well. And anything she said to Mano might get back to Pele Hawai'i. If she wanted information from Mano, she needed to shut up and wait until they were alone.

Was there a flicker of guilt in Mano's face? Maybe not, she decided. It could be fatigue. Dirt smeared one cheek and the side of his neck. *Tûtû kâne* had worked the guys hard today.

"How's the training going?" Bane asked.

"Slow."

"It would be a lot easier if you just used a food reward."

Kaia shook her head. "Then it would be just training, not really her learning on her own volition. I don't want there to be any doubt about her intelligence when the study is done. It's harder and it takes longer, but it will be something worth working for." If Curtis would only give her the chance to prove it.

"You think you're going to get shut down?" Bane's gaze lingered on her face.

She sighed. "Curtis is more interested in amusement parks than scientific research. So it's a possibility. But he hasn't cut me out yet."

"You'll get there." He patted her shoulder.

She laid her hand over his then looked toward the cottage. "Where's *Tûtû kâne?*"

"I'm right here." Her grandfather stepped through the front door and came toward her with a welcoming smile on his face. His gaze went to her bandaged foot. "Klutzy as usual, I see." He handed each of his grandsons a glass of soda.

"It was either fall or get eaten by a cane spider." She shuddered at the thought. She'd had nightmares about that one.

Bane whistled. "No wonder you let go of the tree limb. But you never said what you were doing in the tree in the first place."

"Climbing it, what else?" She poked Bane in the ribs.

"But why?" he persisted.

He was like Nani with her ball. The only way she'd get him to leave it alone would be to find him something else. "You have to report back to work in two weeks, don't you?"

Bane grimaced. "Don't remind me. I've been enjoying my leave."

"Will you still be on the Big island?"

He nodded. "No sign of new orders."

"How's it going with your navy work?" her grandfather asked her.

"Okay. But I haven't quite caught on to sleeping during the day yet."

"How much longer do you have to do this?" Mano asked. "I hate that you're helping them." He took a swig of his soda.

"Get over it," Bane said sharply. "I don't know what's happened to you, Mano. You didn't use to be so militant. And you're navy yourself."

"Just until I can get out." Mano took another swig.

Kaia watched the muscles move in his broad back. How could she get him alone to question him about Nahele?

Bane turned his gaze to her. "Did you see the paper this morning?"

"No. Something interesting in there for a change?"

He nodded and went to fetch it for her from the porch. "Look here," he said, pointing to a front-page article.

She scanned it, and her heart fell. "Oh great. Another lab says they're close to having a breakthrough in dolphin communication." She tossed the paper aside. "And here I'm stuck with this navy detail when I could be working more with Nani and the others."

"You think the paper is right?"

"There are a lot of groups working on the same thing." She tried to treat it lightly, but in truth, it looked like all her dreams might come crashing down. She glanced at Mano. "Would you mind running me over to the base to get my truck?"

"Sure. No problem." Mano drained his glass. His eyes grew wide, and he threw the glass across the yard.

"What is it?"

"A scorpion in the glass."

Kaia shuddered. Scorpions were even worse than spiders, if that were possible.

"Was it still alive?" Bane walked to the glass and scooped it up. He began to grin. "This your big, bad scorpion?" He dug into the glass and came out holding a hideous-looking specimen.

"Don't touch it!" Kaia said.

When her grandfather began to chuckle, she knew they'd all been had. "*Tûtû kâne*, is that rubber?" she scolded.

He laughed, a delighted sound that made him sound sixty years younger.

Mano flushed, then he began to laugh too. "You'd think I'd learn after all this time."

"Life is meant for laughter," *Tûtû kâne* said. "Not for dwelling on gloomy things."

"What enjoyment do you get out of making us look like fools?" Bane asked. The amusement on his face softened his question.

Their grandfather shrugged. "A cheerful heart is good medicine," he said, quoting Proverbs 17.

"If that's the case, you're never going to die," Mano quipped.

They all laughed, and Kaia felt her spirits lifting. Her grandfather had always been able to do that to her. In the dark days after her mother left, he'd kept a cheerful banter going that soon made her forget her abandonment. Or at least she'd tried to.

Oke smiled at her. "How about I fix us all lunch tomorrow after you get off work and have a rest."

"Sounds great."

"There is something I want to talk to you about," her grandfather said. "But it can wait until tomorrow."

"What is it?"

He waved his hand. "No matter. We can discuss it tomorrow. I want all three of you to be here."

She frowned. *Tûtû kâne* didn't often call a family meeting. "I guess I have to wait then."

"You are always so impatient, *lei aloha*. It will keep."

She wasn't going to get anything out of him today. He was still smiling inanely over the rubber scorpion.

She ducked inside and brushed her teeth with a spare brush she kept at her grandfather's. She checked in the mirror for any spots she'd missed then put her toothbrush away and hobbled outside.

Mano's truck was back from the garage, and he brought it around from the back. Shiny black, the big Dodge Ram truck was his pride and joy. She settled onto the plush seat and rolled down the window. The trade winds lifted the hair on the nape of her neck, and she breathed in the scent of plumeria. Her stomach rumbled.

"I heard that," Mano said. "Let's stop and get something to eat. I'll run through Pacific Pizza and we can share. I'm hungry too."

"Perfect." She rubbed her ankle while she considered how to bring up the subject of Nahele.

"You've got something on your mind. I can see the wheels turning." Mano pulled onto Highway 50.

"I was wondering if you'd seen Nahele lately."

Mano's eyebrows winged up, and he swerved across the center line. Mano gave a shamefaced grin. "Sorry. That would be more like something you'd do."

"Hey, I'm not that bad a driver." Was he trying to avoid her question? Her spirits sank.

He gave her a sidelong glance. "Nahele had me come by yesterday. Why?"

Rats. She had hoped Mano was completely out of it. "Do you mind telling me what he wanted?"

"It had to do with business stuff." He shifted in his seat.

"This is important, Mano. I wouldn't ask otherwise."

"It's nothing to do with you, Kaia," he said.

"He was just outside naval property yesterday. And one of his goons manhandled me last night."

Mano's fingers tightened on the wheel. "Manhandled you?" He stopped at Pacific Pizza and killed the engine. "I think it's about time you told me what really happened to your ankle."

Kaia hadn't seen him look so grim in a long time. Maybe never. Mano had always been her easy-going brother. The intensity he'd shown over this Pele Hawai'i thing had surprised her.

She sighed. "I think Nahele is trying to sabotage the missile tests." Mano rolled his eyes. "Mano, if Pele Hawai'i had *anything* to do with Laban's death—"

Mano shook his head. "You're wrong."

She told him what had happened the night before. His eyes grew flinty when she showed him the bruises on her arm where Kim had grabbed her and dragged her toward the boat.

"I'll take care of it, Kaia. You stay out of it. I think you should quit working with the navy on this."

"I wish I could. I just want to get back to my research. But my boss has ordered me to do this project. I need to finish it out and get back to Seaworthy Labs. This piecemeal research isn't getting me the answers I need."

"I don't want you hurt."

There was more he wasn't saying. She squeezed her eyes shut so she wouldn't have to see the determination in her brother's face. He was involved in this somehow.

ELEVEN

Jesse was waiting at the boat when he saw the headlights of Kaia's truck. She'd left a message on his voice mail saying that her brother had taken her to get her vehicle and she would meet him at the boat at ten. It was fifteen after. Nani was waiting for them when he arrived. She splashed around in the waves and flipped water all over his uniform. She seemed to laugh at him when he scolded her. That dolphin was really something. No wonder Kaia was hooked on her research.

Kaia parked and got out of her truck. Carrying her backpack, she half jogged, half limped toward the boat. "Sorry I'm late." She hopped on the boat and smiled when she saw his damp clothing. "Looks like Nani was getting rambunctious."

"You could say that." He took her backpack from her and laid it on the deck.

She felt through her pockets then frowned. "I bet I left my cell phone at home."

"I've got mine."

"I'd forget my head if it wasn't attached." She clicked her tongue at Nani.

Jesse watched her. "You look a little tired."

She didn't answer, but he saw her lips tighten. She untied the rope from the dock and tossed it on the deck. "Let's get out there."

She must not want to talk about whatever had shadowed her dark eyes. He guessed it was worry. "You got it." He slung his legs under the wheel and started the engine while Kaia coaxed Nani into allowing her to attach the underwater camera. Then the boat puttered out to sea, and darkness swallowed up the security lights at the dock. Nani followed.

"Where we headed today?" she asked.

"I thought we might hug the shoreline tonight."

As Jesse turned the boat northward, Nani sprang out of the water then crashed back, throwing water over them. The dolphin surfaced again, chattering in agitation.

"What's wrong with her?" he asked, cutting the engine.

Kaia looked at the camera monitor but couldn't detect anything unusual. "I think she sees something. I'm going in." Kaia started pulling on her wet suit.

"Not without me." He grabbed his own suit and thrust his legs into it. She had her fins and mask on before he could get his arms into the neoprene fabric. She shrugged her shoulders into the BC, then he heard a splash as she went overboard.

Fuming, he fumbled with his suit before he succeeded in getting it zipped. He grabbed his BC and got the tank on his back.

Kaia surfaced just off the starboard bow. "I forgot my flashlight," she said. "It's in my backpack. Would you throw it to me? Turn it on first."

He ought to make her come after it. She was disobeying orders already. Rummaging in the backpack, he found the halogen light. It should have been clipped to her BC. He turned it on and tossed it to her. It landed about a foot from her right hand and floated in the waves until she grabbed it.

Nani was circling, still agitated. Jesse rubbed anti-fog on the inside of his mask, then rinsed it out and adjusted it on his face. He looked around for Kaia but found only a dim glow from her light under the waves. He took a deep breath and joined her.

Under water, it was impossible to see more than the area illuminated by the light—about thirty feet in a straight line. Beyond that, it was like staring into space—a blackness so impenetrable it brought an atavistic fear at the gut level. Anything could lie in that inky well: man o' war colonies, sharks, giant squid. Jesse always required a moment to adjust to the differences of nighttime diving.

His fear safely stowed away, he swam after Kaia. He joined her where she floated with Nani. She was peering at a sea cave, aiming her light toward it. His light was bigger and more powerful, so he did the same.

The cave's shadows fled and revealed the cause of Nani's agitation. A diver was caught. Her airlines had been snagged by a rockfall. She was gesturing wildly and trying to tug herself free. A flashlight lay at her feet, but the lens was shattered and dark.

Jesse and Kaia shot forward. Kaia grabbed her octopus regulator and offered it to the young woman. She shook her head and pointed to the bubbles still escaping from her tank. She had enough air.

Jesse pulled out his knife and pried on the rocks that held the woman's lines. He could feel the blood pounding in his ears as he worked. A million things could go wrong before he got her free.

Nani hovered over them all, seemingly at peace now that Kaia and Jesse were helping the diver. The lava rock was soft and porous, crumbling under his sharp knife, though it still took five minutes to release her hoses. As soon as the rock released her, they all headed to the surface as fast as they dared. Jesse rose on relief alone. The moon was bright as their heads broke the surface.

The woman spit out her regulator and pulled her mask down around her neck. "I thought I was a goner!"

Jesse glanced around to make sure Kaia's head was above the waves. She was floating with her hand on Nani's dorsal fin. He dropped his mask and took out his regulator. "What were you doing diving alone? It's bad enough to do it in the daytime, but never at night. You're lucky Nani found you." Fear made him shout.

"You're right," the woman said gravely. She swam toward the boat and climbed the ladder.

Kaia and Jesse followed her. Jesse insisted Kaia go up the ladder first, then he followed. He was eager to get a look at the reckless young woman and find out what she was doing out here. The fact that she was just barely outside navy waters was suspect.

He grabbed a towel and rubbed the salt out of his eyes then turned to stare at her. Under the boat's lights and with her mask down, she was older than Jesse had thought. Probably thirty-five, with straight dark hair and hazel eyes.

"Jenny Saito! What were you thinking?" Kaia scolded. "You know better than to do something like this."

"You know each other?" he asked. Kaia looked mad enough to shake the other woman.

Jenny nodded. "I'm Kaia's research assistant." She took the towel he handed her and began to dry off.

"Then you're a professional. You know how insane it was to go out there alone," he said.

Jenny shrugged. "I was bored tonight and thought I'd do a little shore diving. I've done it before. I saw Liko and Mahina playing off the point and thought I'd join them. Liko took my light and dropped it in the sea cave. I went to retrieve it, and you saw the results."

Kaia shuddered. "Don't ever do that again, Jenny. That was stupid."

Jenny dropped her gaze, but not before Jesse saw the flare of rebellion in her eyes. He began to wonder if the woman was telling them the whole story. A little investigation into her background might be in order.

When she left Jesse at the dock, Kaia was still charged from the night's excitement. Working at the lab for an hour or two before heading home to get some rest wouldn't kill her. She changed into the clean shorts and top she'd brought in her backpack then took DALE down to the lagoon. The rising sun made her blink, but it kept her awake.

She worked with Nani for an hour; then her lids began to grow heavy, and she knew she had to get some rest. On her way to the truck, she heard the phone ringing in the office over the loudspeaker. They had it set up that way so no one felt they had to stay inside when they could be working with the dolphins. No one was here but her. Maybe it was Jenny. Kaia hoped her coworker didn't have any ill effects from the night's escapade.

She entered the office and grabbed the phone. "Seaworthy Labs."

An unfamiliar man's voice came over the line. "I was about to hang up."

The guy sounded irritated, and Kaia's back stiffened. "We're actually closed," she informed him. "It's Saturday."

"Is Mr. Latchet around?"

"No, like I said, the lab is closed."

"You can take a message. Tell him Aloha Sea Park called, and I need to reschedule my tour of the facility. I don't want to cancel it though. I'm very interested in partnering with Mr. Latchet in building a sea park."

Kaia promised to relay the message and hung up. Anger drove away her exhaustion, and she considered heading straight for the Latchet house to plead with Curtis to stop all plans to capture her dolphins. But she knew she'd get nowhere when she was this mad. She glanced at her watch. She could go see Mano. Worry about what he was getting into with Pele Hawai'i wouldn't leave her alone. She still hadn't decided whether to confide her fears to Bane and ask him to try to extricate their brother from his involvement.

She drove out to her brother's house. A block one-story house, it was basic and plain, but Mano had spent a lot of time and money on the yard, and flowers bloomed along the lava-chip path to the door. As she approached, she saw Mano talking with another man. The man wore a navy uniform, and she saw the captain's bars on his shirt. Mano stood at attention, but even from here she could see the tension in his jaw matched the rigidity in his back. His hands clenched and unclenched as he stared the other officer in the face.

Maybe she should stay in her truck. She didn't want to interrupt something important. The officer shook his finger in Mano's face, and it was all Kaia could do to stay in her vehicle and not fly to her brother's defense. Mano wouldn't thank her for humiliating him by interfering. She'd tried that once when he was in high school. He'd been in a schoolyard fight, and she'd launched herself onto the pad to pummel the back of a boy who had pinned him.

It had been months before Mano deigned to look at her or speak. Guys were weird about girls defending them. Kaia rolled her window down, but the wind was blowing the wrong direction for her to be able to hear. It rustled the leaves in the monkeypod tree along the driveway. She was going to have to wait it out.

Her nerves were already strung as tightly as vines through the jungle. She wondered if Mano's obsession with Pele Hawai'i had gotten back to the navy. They wouldn't be happy about one of their own putting himself in a potentially traitorous position.

Chewing on her thumbnail, she wondered what she could do to prove to Mano that his so-called friends were behind the problems at the base. Kaia was sure Nahele and his cohorts had been planning something the night she ran into them at the lagoon. If only she had some kind of proof. Mano was too firmly entrenched in their camp to listen.

Leaning her head back against the headrest, she closed her eyes. Her anger toward Curtis had waned, and the night's hard work was beginning to take its toll. The buzz of insects outside and the rustle of the wind in the leaves soothed her, and she felt her muscles relax. She sank down into the welcome arms of sleep.

Kaia awoke and sat up. She glanced at her watch. It was nearly eleven. She'd been sleeping here for an hour and a half. She heard the roosters crowing, something that occurred any time of the day. Groaning as her muscles complained of their cramped position in the truck, she got out and headed to the house.

"Mano?" She opened the screen door and went inside, but her brother wasn't in the small three-room house. He had a hobby shop in the shed out back. Maybe he was there. She went through the kitchen and out the back door. The shed's door stood open, and she could hear the murmur of voices as she approached.

She recognized the deep tenor of her brother's voice. The shop door opened outward, and she paused behind it where she couldn't be seen. She shouldn't be eavesdropping on Mano, but she had to know what was going on.

Peeking through the crack by the hinges, she could see the two men with her brother. One was a big Hawaiian. When he turned slightly, she could see a birthmark on the side of his nose. She thought she might have seen him at the Pele meeting she'd attended.

Nudging nearer the crack, she listened.

Mano was raising his voice. "I don't know how you can question my loyalty. The navy just told me I have to quit the organization. I told them no. Because my boss likes me, he's giving me the option to resign my commission or I'll be court-martialed."

The big man spoke. "We heard. But you've got to prove it to us one more time. The navy has taken our land long enough. They're going to find out they have no right to be here."

"What did you have in mind?" Mano's voice was low and intense.

Kaia tensed. Surely her brother wouldn't strike at the military. He'd been proud of his military service until Pele Hawai'i had twisted his values.

The other man laughed, but it wasn't a nice sound. "I was thinking a nice, big bomb. Something that will put us on the front page of every paper."

"What will that accomplish?"

At least Mano was questioning the insane suggestion. Kaia wondered if she should enter the shop and break up this little meeting. Mano would be furious though.

"They'll know we're about more than just talk. Our numbers will grow as Hawaiians see we are serious enough to put action behind our words."

Mano seemed to weigh this. "Okay," he finally said. "I've got an idea. Where do I get the explosives?"

Was that eagerness in his voice? Kaia wanted to slam the door and lock Mano in until she could get Bane and her grandfather here to talk sense into him. On second thought, he'd never listen to Bane. She was going to have to figure out a way to save Mano from himself.

The big man took a paper out of his pocket. "We have the fire-power stashed here." They all bent over the paper.

AFTER ONLY FOUR HOURS OF SLEEP, KAIA STILL FELT SLUGGISH. Traipsing down the stone steps, she felt beaten down by what she'd overheard at Mano's. This was too big for her. Could Mano's involvement with Nahele have caused their cousin's death? She didn't have the strength or the resources to help her brother. She'd have to ask Jesse for help and pray he wouldn't turn her brother in.

When Kaia stepped into her grandfather's cottage, she was enveloped by the aroma of sweet potatoes and roast turkey. She followed the fragrance to the kitchen and found her grandfather at the oven. "What can I do to help, *Tûtû kâne?*"

"Everything is almost ready, *lei aloha*. You can set the table."

Kaia nodded and went to the old pie safe her great-grandfather had made. She pulled out the Banana Patch Studio pottery she'd bought him for Christmas last year. The Plumeria Collection of dinnerware in blue and yellow lifted her spirits. Though she'd spent two weeks' wages on it, it was worth every penny, she thought, running her hands over the bottom of a hand-painted plate.

Glancing at the table, she saw her grandfather had *opihi* as an appetizer. Whatever he wanted to discuss with them must be important if he'd plunked down the money for the highly prized limpet.

Her brothers came in as their grandfather set the last of the food on the table. *Tûtû kâne* sat at the head. He gave thanks then began to pass the food around. Bane talked about his day out fishing, but Mano didn't have much to say. Kaia wished she could tell him she'd overheard him, but she bit her tongue.

When their grandfather had finished serving the dessert—haupia, a custard made with coconut—he placed his hands on the table and glanced around at his grandchildren. "I have something I wish to discuss with you. This affects all of you, so I didn't want to do it unless I had unanimous approval."

All three grandchildren put down their spoons and looked at him. Kaia could feel the curiosity zip between them. Their grandfather was seldom so serious. Dark circles rimmed his eyes, and she wondered if he'd slept last night. Could he be sick? She tried to remember if he'd been to the doctor lately.

"Are you okay, *Tûtû kâne*?" she asked timidly.

"I'm fine. Physically at least." Her grandfather's smile was kind. "But I'm seventy-eight. Who knows how many more years the good Lord will grant me? There is one thing I want before I die—to know what has become of your mother."

Of all the things Kaia had been expecting, she'd never imagined this. Her gut clenched, and the taste of coconut rose from her stomach. "Is this another of your jokes?" she asked, her suspicions rising.

"No joke this time."

He was still smiling, but not with mirth.

"Do you have any idea how we might accomplish that?" Bane asked.

Her brother's calm tone upset Kaia more than her grandfather's request. How could Bane act like it was perfectly all right? Was she the only sane person left in this family? No one in their right mind would willingly seek out someone who had left so much pain in her wake. Paie Oana had been like an octopus who sucked the life out of her family and left the shell of the remains behind.

"I don't want to find her. She's better left in the past." Kaia folded her arms over her chest. "Why do you want to find her after all this time? If she wanted to see us, she knows where we are."

"I've told myself that for years," her grandfather agreed. "I've been thinking about it for a year. It was the one regret your grandmother had when she passed on—that she never knew what had become of Paie. I woke up in the night last week and realized I didn't want to die with that same regret. And I want the three of you to have closure as well."

"It's closed as far as I'm concerned," Kaia said. More than closed. Dead and buried.

"I'm for it," Bane said. "How do we do it?"

"We hire a private investigator," their grandfather said.

"No!" Kaia cast a *help me!* look at Mano and began to gather the dirty dishes. Mano looked away.

"And you need to think about extending aloha to our mother." Bane's voice was grim. "*Tûtû kâne* is right. It's time we know. Pray about it."

Kaia carried the dirty dishes to the sink. Her mother deserved no aloha. There was nothing to pray about as far as she was concerned. She stormed into the bathroom, grabbed her toothbrush and began to brush.

TWELVE

The man paced across the room. The woman and her dolphin were beginning to be a problem. If they found his underwater transmission site, he was in trouble. He pressed the phone against his ear.

The voice on the other end of the phone raised a notch. "She has no idea what we were doing. She's not really a problem."

"So you say. The big day is in less than two weeks. I've got everything riding on this." No one knew just how much. If he succeeded, he stood to regain all he'd lost. Money, prestige, a purpose. If he failed . . . but he couldn't let himself think that way. It would be sinking back into the old patterns that had brought his first defeat so many years ago.

His father's name was rarely spoken now, but that would change in a few short weeks. His name would be on lips across the world. He shook off the fear that clouded his mind. Fear was his only real enemy. If he could defeat the fear of failure, he could beat anything.

KAIA WENT HOME AND TRIED NOT TO WORRY ABOUT MANO'S betrayal or her grandfather's plans. She tried to focus on what she'd try next with Nani but found it impossible to concentrate. Her thoughts kept drifting back to Mano. She had left *Tûtû kâne's* without talking to him. Now was as good a time as any. She had a couple of hours before it was time to meet Jesse.

Grabbing her keys, she hurried to her truck and drove back to her brother's. A yellow glow of lamplight shone from his front window when she pulled into the driveway. She wasn't sure how to bring up the subject. He'd take one look at her face and know something was wrong.

She didn't even have time to knock on the door when Mano threw it open. "I heard your truck." His gaze lingered on her face. "Have you been crying?"

She thought she'd washed all traces away. Her lips tightened, and she shut the door behind her. "I need to talk to you." He was going to get mad and defensive, but she couldn't help that.

"So talk." Mano pointed at the brown couch, a hand-me-down from Aunt Edena. He sat down and began to twirl a pencil in his fingers.

Kaia sank onto the worn fabric. "I might as well tell you—I overheard you today."

His fingers stilled. "When—what do you mean?"

She could hear the caution in his voice, and it broke her heart. There had never been this distance between them. "When you were talking to the Pele Hawai'i men," she said softly. "Don't do this, Mano. Don't commit treason. That's what this is. I couldn't bear it if you were sent to prison. It would kill *Tûtû kâne*."

"You don't understand, Kaia," Mano began. "Stay out of it."

"I can't. You're my brother. I love you." She leaned forward. "Walk away. Now."

"I can't. It's gone too far." His jaw was hard as he stood and turned his back to her.

She touched his shoulder. "I'm here for you, Mano. I'll do anything I can to help."

"I don't need your help." He turned toward the kitchen. "I'll get you some coffee and we can talk about something else."

JESSE WAS NAPPING ON THE COUCH IN HIS OFFICE WHEN HIS cell phone chirped. He raised his eyebrows at the name on the caller

ID. Kaia rarely ever called him, and even before he answered it, he had the feeling it was bad news. "Matthews."

"Jesse, we need to talk. Where can I meet you?" Kaia's voice sounded strained.

He glanced at his watch. "What are you doing up already? It's only twelve."

"Can you meet me at the front gate in fifteen minutes?"

"Sure." He clicked off his phone and went to tell his aide he'd be off base for a while. He hopped in his Jeep and headed toward the gate. The two-hour nap had refreshed him. Kaia wasn't there yet, so he parked and waited.

His cell phone chirped again. The caller ID revealed a name he hadn't seen in a long time, and he stared at it, wondering if he was seeing it right. It chirped again, and he reluctantly pressed the button. "Matthews."

"Hi, Jesse. It's Steve."

The familiar voice made Jesse's stomach clench. "Steve. I saw your name on the caller ID." He didn't know what to say.

"I bet it gave you a start. Got your new number from Jillian. Surprised to hear from me?"

"You might say that." Surprise was an understatement. Christy's family had cut off all contact with him after Christy's death. Three years had passed since any of them had spoken to him. He gritted his teeth and wondered what Christy's brother wanted from him.

Steve gave a nervous chuckle. "You're not making this easy, Jesse. You haven't so much as sent a Christmas card."

"Was I supposed to? You told me you never wanted to talk to me again. As I recall, you called me a 'baby killer.' I'm sure your parents still hate me. They'd be furious if they knew you'd contacted me."

"Dad's gone now. You didn't know?"

"I hadn't heard. I'm sorry."

His father-in-law hadn't had much use for Jesse. Resignation filled Jesse, and he pinched the bridge of his nose hard.

"We used to be good friends, Jesse. Do you know what today is?"

Like he could ever forget. "Of course. The baby would have been three today if he'd been born on his due date."

"I wasn't sure you ever thought about it."

He didn't bother to hide the anger he felt rising. "Do you think I'm some kind of monster? My life changed that day, Steve. There's not a day goes by that I don't think about it." What did he really want? Jesse couldn't read his voice. Steve had always been a little strange—one minute friendly and the next as aloof as if Jesse had been a playground bully who had taken his toys. He was Christy's twin, and the two had been close.

"I'm sorry. I probably shouldn't have called." Steve's voice grew husky.

Jesse sighed. "Well, you did, so you might as well tell me what you want."

There was a long pause, then Steve cleared his throat. "It wasn't your fault, Jesse. I know that now."

"Come on, Steve, don't throw me any bones. You and I both know the truth. It's something I live with every day." He didn't even try to keep the regret from his voice. Part of it *had* been his fault. He'd come to grips with it, but it didn't change the truth.

"No. No, it wasn't. Christy was to blame, and that's the truth."

"I shouldn't have argued with her that day. I knew she wasn't thinking clearly, but I'd thought once the baby was born . . ." His voice broke. Jesse didn't want to relive that day, but the memories crowded in like a school of piranha fighting over a wounded animal. He closed his eyes. Christy's agitated voice rang in his ears.

"You never let me do anything! I'm stifling in this house. I wasn't meant to be only a mother, Jesse. I want to have a career. We can hire a sitter. This kind of job offer only comes along once in a lifetime."

"The doctor said you need to rest, Christy. You're not able to do it now." He glanced at her then turned his attention back to the road.

"If I don't, I'll lose the opportunity. I'll be sitting at a desk all day.

I can take a stool and put my feet up. Just think of it, Jesse. 'Chat with Christy.' My own radio spot. It's my dream come true. I'm not giving it up just because you want me barefoot and pregnant."

"Our baby is more important than a job, Christy. You can't endanger the baby and your own health like that."

Her voice rose. "I'm doing it, Jesse. And you can't stop me. If I have to, I'll abort this baby."

Shocked at her words, he jerked his head to look at her. "You wouldn't!"

"I will." She thrust her jaw out.

While he stared at her in shock, her eyes widened. "Jesse, look out!"

His gaze whipped back to the front but too late to react to the curve coming up fast. Too fast. He slammed on the brake and fought the wheel. The tires screamed in tune with Christy's shriek of terror.

Jesse blinked and realized Steve had said something. "I'm sorry?"

"I just said I wanted to put the past behind us. I've been attending a church lately." He paused and cleared his throat again. "I treated you badly, Jesse. Can you forgive me for the harsh words I said at Christy's funeral?"

"You didn't say anything I haven't said a thousand times over to myself. I should have been paying attention to the road. I deserved every word."

"No, you didn't. And I'm sorry."

Jesse found it difficult to swallow.

Steve's breath sounded erratic and shaky. "We should have been comforting one another. Instead we acted like wounded animals snapping at a helping hand. It made the grief worse not to have you there too. You'd been part of the family since we were kids."

"Christy was eight the first time I saw her." He could still remember the gap-toothed smile she'd given him that day. He'd fallen for her right then. They'd fought and made up and fallen in love over the fifteen years they'd lived next door to one another.

"Mom and Dad loved you like a son."

"They turned on me fast enough." He rubbed his knuckles into his burning eyes.

"They had to blame someone for the pain they felt. So did I. You were handy."

Jesse's vision blurred. He didn't want to talk about it anymore. "I have to go, Steve. It's been good talking to you."

"Don't shut me out, Jesse," he pleaded. "I'll be—"

Jesse cut him off. He couldn't take any more. "Good-bye, Steve," he said. He clicked off the phone and leaned against the headrest.

Kaia didn't want to do this. She'd tried to think of a way to get to the bottom of things alone, but she had to be honest. She didn't have the skills to figure it out without help. She needed Jesse's help, much as she didn't want to involve the navy. And Mano's current situation demanded immediate action.

Besides, she needed to get her mind wrapped around something other than her grandfather's crazy plan. She didn't want to think about seeing her mother again. What if she left again? Kaia knew she could never bear that kind of rejection more than once.

Jesse was standing beside his Jeep when she got to the front gate. She pulled behind his vehicle and got out, conscious of the way the SPs watched her. Her heart felt as heavy as a boat anchor. Even now, she cast about for some way out of revealing everything to him.

She thought he looked a little pale today. His eyes were cloaked with some dark emotion she found hard to name—fear, or sorrow maybe. His uniform was a little rumpled too. Maybe there had been a problem with Heidi. This was probably a bad idea. He had enough on his plate without her problems too.

He didn't waste time on pleasantries. "You sounded upset. What's wrong?"

The concern in his voice released the valve on her emotions, and she wanted to cry. "I need your help, Jesse. I think my brother is in trouble."

His blue eyes softened, and he touched her arm. "Bane or Mano?"

She was surprised he remembered her brothers' names. "Mano." Jesse wasn't going to be happy with her when she told him why. She dropped her gaze to the ground. "You know those men who tried to grab me the other night when I sprained my ankle?"

"Yeah." His voice was deepened with wariness.

"I recognized them. I just didn't want to tell you."

His face didn't change. He just nodded as though he already knew. "Okay, tell me now."

He was being too nice to her. It made her want to throw herself against his chest and wail out her fear, let him carry it all. She took a step back and told herself she needed to look at him like a father figure. "You remember I mentioned Pele Hawai'i once before?"

He nodded. "Yeah. I haven't been back on the island long, but it's been long enough to hear about them and their violent tactics. They want to force the U.S. government into giving Hawai'i sovereignty. They sound more like a terrorist group than a bona fide political group."

"I guess that's exactly what they are." It hurt to admit her brother could be involved in something like that. "The leader, Nahele Aki, was there with two of his men."

"Why didn't you want me to know? Is he a friend of yours?"

His voice had risen, and she wondered if he could be jealous. She shook her head. What a stupid thought. He was justifiably angry with her for not doing what she should have done sooner. "No. I didn't want you to suspect Mano of being involved with those three. He joined the group in the past month." She rushed on before she lost her nerve. "I've seen such a change in him. He's turned into a zealot." It felt wrong to be talking about her brother like this. She should have gone to her grandfather first. Maybe he could have reined in her brother. She bit her lip and reminded herself this affected national security.

"He's navy, isn't he? How does he reconcile the two?"

"That's what I'm afraid of. I think they're using him to gain information about the base. And that he's involved in the security breaches." She closed her eyes as she whispered the last sentence. She never would have thought that Mano would do something like this. Or that she would ever cast suspicion on him. Her eyes moistened, and she opened them to stare into Jesse's face.

He raised his eyebrows. "Do you have any proof?"

Kaia told him what she'd overheard.

"Do you have any idea when they plan to do this?"

"No, but I think I know how to find out."

"Tell me."

At least he wasn't brushing her off. "I want to follow Mano, see what he's up to, and try to get him away from the organization before he does anything irreversible. You're a security professional. You have surveillance equipment that could help, right?"

"Have you tried talking with him?"

She nodded. "He's not listening. But something is wrong. The brother I know wouldn't willingly participate in this kind of sabotage. I think he's being manipulated. But if he knows *you* know what's going on, maybe we could persuade him to help us bring Nahele down."

Jesse's gaze never left her face. She could see him considering what she said. "If Mano is as involved as you say, my duty is to turn him in, Kaia. If I hesitate, I could compromise the entire base."

"You can't! Not yet!" She never should have asked him for help. "If you won't help me help my brother, I'll take Nani and pull out and you can track down your intruders yourself." She folded her arms across her chest. "Besides, you have no proof without me. I won't testify against him. *And,* if you take out Mano without getting Nahele, you've still got a huge problem on your hands: they'll just get someone else to do their dirty work!"

He pressed his fingers against the bridge of his nose. "You drive a hard bargain, Kaia." He sighed. "Okay, we can poke around first and see what we can find out. But this might turn out wrong. He might be more involved than you'd like to believe. What if you end up proving he's in this up to his neck? He could be charged with terrorism or espionage. He could go to prison."

Kaia gulped. "All the more reason to save him before he does something truly stupid. He's already getting kicked out of the navy. When he's thinking clearly, he'll be heartbroken. He was always so proud of being a SEAL."

"You'd better face the possibility. Sometimes we think we know someone and find out we didn't know them at all."

His blue eyes looked bleak, and fatigue deepened the lines around his mouth. Kaia wanted to touch his hand, to reassure him, but she dropped her gaze instead. They needed to keep their relationship strictly business. He obviously carried baggage she wasn't sure she wanted to deal with.

He glanced at his watch. "I can get my equipment and meet you at quitting time. We could have a couple of hours before we hit the patrol duty."

"What about Heidi?"

"She's with Faye. I'll call and let them know I can't come by tonight."

"How about if I go get her for a while? I feel bad that I didn't make breakfast the other day."

"Have you slept at all today?" His gaze traveled over her face.

"About four hours."

"I imagine Faye would like a visit. She seems lonely."

"Maybe I could take them both out for a shave ice to make it up to her. *Tûtû kâne* would enjoy having them come to the lu'au on Friday too."

"I'm sure Heidi would love it, the way she talks about the last one." His gaze softened. "I appreciate all you've done for Heidi, Kaia. She's crazy about you."

She wished he wouldn't look at her like that. It made it hard to concentrate on remembering she wanted to keep her distance. "I'm glad she likes me."

"What's not to like?"

The warm smile extended to his blue eyes. She turned to get into her car and pretended not to hear.

THIRTEEN

Faye wished she could go to her room and shut the door. She'd forgotten how tiring it was to listen to a child's prattle all day long. And her nails were a mess. They'd made sand castles, and her red polish was worn and chipped. The last thing she had time for right now was to sit for another manicure.

She glanced at her watch. Jesse wouldn't be here for three hours. Faye didn't know if she'd make it that long, though she would have some relief for a few blessed minutes. The girl had fallen asleep on the living room floor just a little while ago.

Why had she ever agreed to this job? So far, every attempt to get close to Kaia had failed. It was just one more failure to add to Faye's collection.

The phone rang, and she saw Curtis's cell number pop up on the caller ID. He was out running errands. "Can you come rescue me?" she asked, making her voice as pitiful as she could.

Curtis's booming voice lifted her spirits. "Not going well, huh?" he asked, worry giving his voice a rough edge that she liked.

She hurried to soothe his concern. "It's nothing. I'm just not used to dealing with a child all day. I'm not sure this was the best approach to take. And I don't think Kaia likes me." Admitting her biggest fear brought her near tears.

"I'm sure that's not true," Curtis said. "Give it time, Faye. Things will work out."

"I don't think so. Do I have to even try? Let's just pack up and move back to the mainland." She knew Curtis would never agree to that. Not until he'd reached the goal he'd set for both of them.

"You know better. Try again."

She sighed. "I will." The doorbell rang. "I've got to go. Someone is at the door."

"Okay. I'll see you after work."

Faye clicked off the phone and hurried to the door. She nearly stumbled when she saw Kaia through the glass panes. She wished she'd had time to clean up a little. Flecks of sand still clung to her shorts and legs.

"Sorry to drop in unannounced," Kaia said when Faye opened the door. "I'm so sorry about missing breakfast the other day."

"Oh no, you can come by any time. And Jesse explained about your ankle. Is it better? How are you? Come in and sit down." Aware she was babbling but unable to stop, Faye stepped aside and closed the door after Kaia.

"My ankle is fine now, thanks." Kaia looked around. "Where's Heidi?"

Faye gestured toward the living room. "She's asleep. We made sand castles. That's why I'm such a mess." Faye hid her hands in the pockets of her shorts.

"You don't look a mess. I've never seen someone so perfectly put together all the time."

The way Kaia said it, it didn't seem like a compliment. Faye's smile felt false. "Have a seat and I'll get you something to drink. How about a fruit smoothie?"

"Actually, I came to take you out for a shave ice."

The way Kaia smiled made Faye's spirits rise. Her gaze lingered on the younger woman. Kaia's large, dark eyes dominated her face. Intense and intelligent, they were a window to the inner woman Faye wanted to get to know better.

"A shave ice sounds wonderful! But Heidi is asleep."

"There's no hurry. We can sit and get to know one another for awhile." Kaia sat on the sofa and curled one leg under her in a relaxed position. "I'm pooped anyway. A rest sounds nice."

Faye watched Kaia lean back against the cushions. She looked quite at home. Maybe it was a good omen. Faye would like to see Kaia in this room all the time. "Tell me about your research."

"I would think you would be tired of hearing about it."

"Oh, Curtis doesn't bring his work home. Getting him to talk about it is harder than prying open a clam." Kaia's dark eyes lit with enthusiasm as Faye listened. Kaia's animation was mesmerizing, and Faye couldn't take her eyes off her.

"We're working on interacting with the dolphins with language," Kaia said. "They talk to one another in clicks and whistles. We're trying to establish a defined set of clicks and whistles that mean something to both of us so we can actually communicate with each other."

"How exciting!" Faye didn't care what Kaia said; she just wanted to keep her talking, keep her in the house. All her earlier plans to get Kaia to open up about important things went out of her head.

"Yes, it is. Although so far I've had more setbacks than anything. But I'm optimistic."

"Curtis says if the dolphins don't figure things out soon, he's going to have to train them for the sea park." Kaia's eyes narrowed, and Faye knew she'd said the wrong thing.

"He can't capture them. They're wild dolphins who choose to come in to interact with us. I won't let him betray their trust." Kaia clenched her hands into fists.

"I'm sorry, I shouldn't have said anything."

"No, I'm glad you did. I'm going to have to talk to Curtis about this again." Kaia began shifting in her seat, agitated now.

"Oh dear." Faye wanted to wring her hands. Now Curtis would be mad that she'd gotten the whole staff up in arms.

"Don't worry; I'm not going to blab that we've talked. But I am going to stop him," Kaia said fiercely.

Faye chewed on her lip, tasting the lipstick she thought had worn off long ago. She'd have to confess to Curtis herself. If she let him be blindsided by Kaia's plans, he'd never forgive her.

Kaia made an obvious effort to control her anger. "Tell me about yourself. Where are you from? You look Hawaiian."

Treacherous territory. But maybe this would be the opportunity Faye had been looking for. "I am Hawaiian. I left Kaua'i a long time ago though and went to the mainland. I've been gone from the islands for twenty-two years."

"I can't imagine leaving here for so long! Didn't you miss the sound of the sea and the scent of the orchids?"

If Kaia only knew. "Once upon a time I thought I wanted excitement and fulfillment I couldn't find here." She folded her hands in her lap. "After tasting everything the world had to offer, I found it wasn't as thrilling as I thought it would be. I was empty when I met Curtis. He changed things for me, and I realized all I'd missed here. When he suggested moving back, I jumped at the chance. Things have changed though. I can't believe how busy Honolulu has gotten."

Kaia nodded. "Kaua'i has stayed much the same though."

"Yes, it has." Faye needed to tread carefully. "What about you and your family?"

"It's just me and my two brothers. Our grandfather raised us. Our father died when I was two."

Faye's eyes stung. "What about your mother?"

Kaia's mouth grew pinched. "I'd rather not talk about her. She left me with strangers when I was four and never looked back. I've never gotten so much as a card or a phone call from her."

"You poor child." Faye just barely managed to get the words out. "She must have been a terrible person."

Kaia shrugged. "I don't remember much about her, except that she sang when she combed her hair. She took me with her when she left, at least for a little while. Until she dumped me with a friend who called my grandfather to come get me a year later. Bane remembers her better than I do."

"What does he say?"

"He's been thinking about trying to find her. I told him not to bother. She wouldn't thank us for interrupting the perfect life she's

found without us." She sighed. "But our grandfather agrees with
Bane." She gave a slight smile. "I don't know why I'm telling you all
this. It must be boring."

"Not at all. You still sound so hurt." Faye wanted to embrace
Kaia and tell her it would be all right.

Kaia's smile was sad. "*Tûtû kâne* says I was in rags when he found
me and brought me home. I imagine the abandonment affected me
in ways I can't remember. And I've lived with the whispers all my life.
My mother's departure was big news on the island."

"Why did people talk about it so much? It happens every day,
sad to say."

"My mother was someone special. Paie Oana grew up the darling of the island. A Hawaiian princess that everyone recognized.
She was the best hula performer in the islands, I'm told. I'm surprised she was able to vanish without a trace, to tell you the truth."

Faye hesitated. She didn't want to upset Kaia even more. "Could
she be dead?"

"I doubt it. I think she just got fed up with raising three kids on
her own. She was used to acclaim and honor and the drudgery got
her down. When a rich man appeared, she was more than ready to
be spoiled again."

"I see. Maybe she's changed."

Kaia must have heard the note of disapproval in her voice,
because she looked up. "The guy she ran off with owned a bunch of
companies. He had a private jet and a house in Paris as well as two
on the mainland."

"Where did you hear all this?" Faye shook her head. "Sounds
like a lot of gossip to me. If you were left with a friend, maybe your
mother was abandoned too and didn't have the money to feed you
or something."

Kaia's cheeks reddened, though from anger or embarrassment
Faye couldn't say. "I shouldn't be talking like this. I'm sorry. You're
right; it's gossip. I didn't come here to air my past anyway, but

you're a good listener." She glanced at Heidi. "Maybe we should wake her."

Kaia's words warmed Faye. The walls between them were starting to come down. She glanced at the sleeping child. "She's so tired I hate to do that."

Kaia rolled her wrist to look at her watch. "I've only got another hour before I have to meet Jesse."

"Oh? Jesse is supposed to come get Heidi at five."

Kaia gasped. "Oh, didn't he call you? He wanted to ask you to keep Heidi this evening. I wanted to give you a break from her for a few hours and instead I've yakked my head off. I'm sorry."

Faye's initial dismay faded. After talking with Kaia, she realized she'd been going about this the wrong way. It was time she put her own selfishness behind her and focus on Heidi's needs. She'd fallen too quickly into the old patterns of pursuing her own ends no matter what the cost to others. She wouldn't hurt Heidi the way Kaia had been hurt.

THE RED DIRT ROAD HELD MORE DIPS THAN WAIMEA CANYON. The wind whipped her hair in the exposed Jeep. Kaia was beginning to think the shave ice she'd gulped down with Heidi and Faye had been a bad idea. She'd enjoyed the time with Faye. Though the older woman had seemed cold and polished on the outside, the genuine caring in her manner had cut through Kaia's usual defenses. Strange that Faye had done it so easily.

Jesse turned into a pull-off to a canyon and killed the engine. "This seems pretty remote."

Taro fields spread *mauka*, and the flooded fields glistening in the sunshine. "The place where they meet is just down that hill," Kaia said, pointing to the sloping hillside opposite the taro fields. "They use the old rice mill." She started off in the general direction of the mill.

"This is probably a bad idea," Jesse grumbled. "Your ankle is still too weak to be climbing rough ground."

Her ankle throbbed at the reminder, but Kaia wasn't about to say so. "I'll rest it up on the boat later. And a swim will fix everything." He helped her down the steep incline. Thin soil slid from under her hiking boots. Stones rattled down the hill. "We're sure not sneaking up on anyone," she told him.

He grinned, and she found herself smiling back. Suddenly the fading afternoon sun seemed brighter. His quiet strength made her feel secure. It was such a direct contrast to the way she'd felt when she first met him. They'd sure gotten off on the wrong foot.

They reached the bottom of the slope. The mill crouched over a dry spring about a hundred yards away. A slight breeze shifted a dangling piece of metal sheeting on the roof, and it gave an eerie creak that startled them both. Kaia clutched Jesse's hand.

"I don't think anyone is here," Jesse whispered.

"Oh yes there is." Kaia pointed at a black sedan sitting under a palm tree. Red dust dulled the shine, but she didn't think it had been out of the showroom more than a few weeks.

He nodded and held his finger to his lips. Crouching low, they stepped to a window along the back of the building. It was too high to see in, but Jesse stepped onto a large boulder. A gecko scurried away at their approach.

"See anything?" she whispered.

"I think I hear voices." He hopped down beside her. "We need to get closer."

"We used to play out here when we were kids. There's a side door, if it's unlocked. It opens into a small room." She led him to the west side. He peered around the corner then motioned for her to join him in the enclosure that jutted from the side of the building.

Out of reach of the trade winds, the air here seemed still and oppressive. Jesse tried the door. "It's unlocked," he mouthed.

He turned the knob in small increments, and Kaia waited for

the door to creak as it opened, but it made no sound. He opened it just far enough to get his head in. "No one's in there." He stepped through first and held it open for her.

She joined him in the ten-foot-square room. The door into the milling room was partially ajar. One loud noise, and they'd be discovered. Jesse tiptoed to the door and peered out. Kaia looked around his shoulder.

Two women stood near some machinery. Kaia leaned forward to hear, and her weak ankle gave way. She tumbled into a group of boxes.

The women looked around at the clatter. They rushed toward the door, and Kaia scrambled to her feet and moved to intercept them. "Stay hidden," she mouthed urgently to Jesse.

The women paused when they saw her. "We're just looking around," the oldest woman said. About fifty, she wore alohawear shorts and a matching top. Her short black hair held a trace of gray at the temples. She was Hawaiian. The other woman hung behind. She looked like a younger version of the older woman.

Kaia thought they'd be more inclined to talk to her than a navy officer. "Aloha," she said, smiling. "I was just looking around myself. Are you members of Pele Hawai'i?"

"I know you," the woman said. "You're Kaia Oana. I'm Lei Kanahele. I was a friend of your mother's once upon a time. You look just like her."

Kaia had heard that before, and though it was intended as a compliment, it never failed to irritate her. "Thanks," she said shortly. "What are you doing here?"

"I forgot my picnic basket the other day. What are *you* doing here?" The woman's sharp look of suspicion increased.

"I came to a meeting here with my brother recently. I was hoping to ask someone a few more questions. It was very interesting."

Lei's frown eased a bit. "Isn't Nahele amazing?"

"He's a riveting speaker," Kaia agreed. She decided to take a wild stab in the dark. "I was wondering how quickly Nahele thinks we'll be able to get rid of the navy. They've been interrupting my research."

Lei's expression softened. "You won't have long to wait. Hasn't Mano told you about the plan?"

"What plan? We haven't had a chance to talk lately."

"I probably shouldn't say anything then," Lei said. "I'm sure Mano will tell you what he wants you to do." She tugged on her daughter's arm. "We'd better go."

"Does it have anything to do with my dolphins?" Kaia asked.

"I've said too much already. Talk to your brother." Lei edged past Kaia, and the women rushed for the door.

FOURTEEN

J esse knew better than to try to comfort Kaia. He kept glancing at her as he drove down to the dock. Any words he might offer would be hollow now that they'd confirmed the extent of Mano's treachery. He obviously intended to drag her into the situation, or at the very least, pump her for information.

Jesse helped Kaia aboard the boat. Nani chattered in the waves just off the bow, and Kaia leaned over the side and talked to the dolphin. At least Kaia was beginning to lose that sick green color she'd taken on when she realized Mano planned to use her.

"Well look who's here." He nodded toward Kaia's brother, who approached the dock.

Kaia frowned and kept her voice low. "What does he think he's doing?"

"Picking the right time to unveil his plan? We should make the most of it. Tell him he's welcome to join us."

She turned to look. "I don't know if I can." Her mouth trembled, and she bit down on her lower lip. "He knows me too well."

"You've got to." He gripped her shoulders and turned her to face him. "I'm praying for you to be strong." The sweet scent of her hair drifted to his nose, and he had to suppress the urge to pull her close. She was too young for him. He'd seen too much of life, and she'd seen too little.

She shut her eyes for a moment. A shudder passed through her, then she raised her head. "I'll try."

"Good girl." He squeezed her shoulders gently and released her, though he really wanted to pull her into his arms and kiss her. The thought shocked him. He hadn't had an impulse like that since Christy died.

"Hey, wait up!" Mano jogged toward the boat. His broad face

wore a smile. "I thought I'd go out with you guys tonight." His glance cut to his sister. "You cool with that?"

"Sure." Kaia didn't look him in the face.

He hesitated. "You still mad at me?"

A smile tugged at Kaia's lips, and she finally raised her eyes. "I can never stay mad at you for long."

Mano's smile burst forth. "Great. I'll come along for the ride."

"We can always use some extra help," Jesse said. "You're off duty for the weekend?"

"Yeah. I was bored and didn't want to hang out with Bane and let him hammer me."

"He doesn't hammer you," Kaia said.

"You're not the one getting ragged on." Mano wore khaki shorts and a T-shirt that advertised Lappert's Ice Cream. He slung his backpack to the deck. "Where are we going tonight?"

Jesse exchanged a glance with Kaia. "Just trolling back and forth in front of the base."

"Sounds fun." Mano settled into a seat and propped his feet on the railing. "Maybe we'll go for a swim with the dolphins later."

The other two dolphins had joined Nani, and the three raced along beside the boat. The trade winds' silky touch blew along Jesse's body, and he lifted his face into the wind and breathed deeply of the scent of the sea. Very little kelp washed onto beaches here, and the fresh scent was unique to Hawaiian waters.

He dropped onto a seat beside Mano. "How are your duties going?"

"Okay. I'm getting a little tired of training and ready to get out and do something."

Jesse and Kaia exchanged a quick look. Mano was a good liar. Too good. What else was he hiding?

They dropped anchor just off where the Na Pali coastline began. Black, green, and red converged into a breathtaking collage of sheer rock cliffs that rose vertically to touch a blue sky with a special glow that came just before twilight.

Jesse glanced at the sun beginning to sink into the ocean. "Have you ever seen the green flash?" he asked Kaia.

"A couple of times. You?" Jesse shook his head. "Let's watch for it tonight," she said. "You have to look away until only the very top of the sun's disk is about to disappear below the horizon. Then it's just for an instant you see a brief splash of green color, kind of like a prism."

They stood quietly as the sun sank lower and lower into the sea. Kaia frowned. "I think there were too many clouds to see it tonight."

"Maybe tomorrow."

"I think I'll go for a swim," Kaia said. She kicked off her slippers and dove into the water, her sleek body slicing into the waves with precision.

In the water, she became the mermaid Jesse had seen the first day they met. Her black hair streamed out behind her, and the tinkling sound of her laughter blended with the rush of the waves in a mesmerizing sound that made him want to jump into the water with her.

Mano joined her, but Jesse stayed aboard the boat. Kaia took DALE into the water and worked with the dolphins for about an hour. Jesse admired her patience as she went over and over the words she was trying to teach. At one point, he could have sworn Nani was repeating the sounds back to her.

"Sounds like she's got it," he called.

Treading water, Kaia flung her long hair over her shoulder then shook her head. "She's just trying to repeat it so far, and it's not exact either. We're not there yet."

"You'll figure it out," Jesse told her. The genuine enjoyment on her face was a welcome change from the pinched expression she'd worn earlier.

"At least she's quit knocking the camera off her back."

She finally got out of the water and stood dripping seawater onto the deck. Wrapping a huge beach towel around herself, she went to stand by the rail to watch the dolphins. Mano got out too, then grabbed a towel and rubbed his hair. He dropped back into his chair and leaned his head back.

Jesse joined Kaia at the railing. "I love watching you with the dolphins. They're really something. They're all so different. How did you find Nani?"

"Her mother was caught in a tuna net and died. Nani was caught too, but my *tûtû kâne* was aboard a nearby boat and saved her. He brought her to me just as I was beginning my doctorate. Perfect timing. That was three years ago. I bottle-fed her, and I've been with her every day since then."

"Amazing." A light snore startled him and he glanced back at Mano. "He's not prying much," he whispered.

"I noticed. Maybe he's waiting for the right time."

A light rain had fallen earlier in the evening then stopped, but a mist still lingered in the air over the ocean.

She squeezed water from her hair and began to braid it. "The mist over moana is lovely tonight," Kaia said, referring to the sea by its Hawaiian name.

"Yes, it is," Jesse said, his gaze lingering on her face. *Kaia* meant sea as well, and she looked as beautiful as the sunset touching the coast-line with gold. He wished he had the nerve to touch her hair, but she exuded an almost other-worldly appearance. She could be a Hawaiian princess from an earlier time, standing there surveying her domain.

She raised her hands toward Na Pali and began to chant a Hawaiian *mele*. The words lifted on the wind.

"Pretty," he said.

She stopped and smiled. "At least a *mele* doesn't require singing." She lifted her hands to the sky and began again. The chant was so beautiful it made the hair stand up on the back of his neck.

She was as far above him as the stars.

THE CLOUDS PARTED, ALLOWING THE MOON TO PEEK THROUGH. Its rays glimmered on the Polihale sands and deepened the night's shadows in the crooks and valleys of Na Pali. Kaia rubbed her gritty eyes. She was paying for the day's lack of sleep. The green glow on her watch revealed the time as four o'clock. Another two hours and she could go home and get some rest.

Mano was snoring in his chair, and even Jesse was asleep, his head tipped to one side and deep breaths issuing from his slightly parted lips. Kaia knew the crew running the boat was still awake, but she felt the comfort of solitude on the deck as she looked out over the water.

A movement in the water caught her eye, and she squinted. A gray fin cut through the waves and approached the boat. A shark, probably a reef blacktip. Nothing to be really alarmed about. The dolphins, which had been swimming beside the boat, vanished at the big fish's appearance. Kaia leaned her arms on the railing and listened to the wind whistle along the sand dunes on Polihale Beach. The roar of the night surf filled her head. She loved times like this when it was just her and the ocean.

She saw a blinking light ashore on her left. Watching it, she realized it was a message in Morse code, something she had learned from *Tûtû kâne* as a child. She held her breath until it came again. She counted the longs and shorts and mouthed silently the meaning, but when the light vanished she was no wiser than she'd been before.

Hammer fall. What did that mean? It sounded ominous. She glanced at Jesse's sleeping face. Maybe he would know. It would be best if Mano didn't awaken and ask any questions. Her bare feet whispered along the smooth deck as she approached Jesse.

The moonlight illuminated his square face. Her gaze traced a tiny bump on his nose she'd never noticed before, and she wondered if he'd broken it playing ball when he was growing up. There was so much she didn't know about him, and she realized she wanted to plumb the depths under his calm surface.

She touched his shoulder and he opened his eyes, immediately alert, as though he had been waiting for her to awaken him. She smiled and held a finger to her lips then motioned for him to follow her. He rose, and they went to the stern of the boat.

"What's up?"

He was standing closer than was comfortable for her growing awareness of her attraction. She stepped back a few inches. "I saw a light offshore. Morse code. It said 'hammer fall.' Does that mean anything to you?"

He seemed not to notice her discomfort. A frown crouched between his eyes as his gaze went to the shore. "'Hammer fall.' You sure?"

"Positive."

Jesse shook his head. "Doesn't ring a bell. I don't like the sound of it though. Let's go investigate. You up for a swim?"

"There are sharks out there tonight."

He froze. "What kind? I hate sharks."

"Reef probably, though it was too dark to tell for sure."

"We'll take the lifeboat then. I'm not swimming with sharks." He hesitated and glanced back at her brother. "I'd rather not take Mano. No offense."

"I tried not to wake him. The last thing we need is for him to sabotage our efforts." It hurt to admit her brother might do that. She'd hoped this day would end with Mano cleared of any suspicion.

The approval in his face warmed her cheeks, and she looked quickly away before he noticed. When she was close to Jesse, she felt she was suffocating. That should have been an unpleasant sensation, but somehow it wasn't. She slipped on her Locals and followed him.

Jesse lowered the lifeboat into the waves then helped her step down into it. The boat rocked in the water as he joined her. Nani chattered off to their starboard side.

"Shh," she told the dolphin.

Jesse hopped to the middle seat and grabbed the oars. "Sit down," he advised.

She nodded and moved to the bow. The spray hit her in the face, and she licked the salt from her lips. Glancing back to the boat, she saw Mano still inert in his chair.

The oars slipped silently through the water, and the waves pushed them toward the shore. When the sand scraped the lifeboat's bottom, she started to get up.

"I'll get it." Jesse stepped over the side and dragged the boat ashore. He held out his hand and steadied her as she got out.

This stretch of beach was one of the most deserted on the island. Monkeypod trees loomed over sharp lava rock. Kaia shivered at their sinister look in the moonlight. Her last interaction with a tree still gave her nightmares when she remembered the size of the cane spider.

They stumbled over the rocks. Jesse took her hand, his fingers warm and reassuring. It felt almost romantic. Kaia knew she should pull away, but she left her hand clasped tightly in his.

They stopped at the edge of the jungle where they could go no farther. Jesse's other hand went to her back to guide her in turning around. She stumbled and lurched against his chest. He caught her and held her there. His sharp exhale ruffled the hair at her temple. His breath smelled of cinnamon.

"You smell good," he said. "Like flowers."

His voice sounded a little hoarse. Kaia looked up and found his gaze fastened on her. He reached out and touched her cheek.

She was so caught by the look in his eyes, it took a moment for the sound above their heads to register. The *whup-whup* of a helicopter overhead finally penetrated, and she gasped.

Jesse released her and craned his head to look. "Kind of early for a pleasure copter to be out, isn't it?" he observed. "It's not even dawn yet."

Helicopters flew tourists out to see the fantastic Kaua'i sites. Most wanted to make sure they saw where *Jurassic Park* had been filmed, and some of the scenery was best viewed from the air. She nodded. "It sounds close." Kaia took off toward the helicopter noise.

Jesse caught her by the arm. "Wait here."

"No way." She pulled her arm free and ran across the damp sand to the edge of the jungle. It was lush and covered with thick vegetation that rimmed the sand.

The helicopter was almost directly overhead. The loud throb of its engines reverberated in her head, and she clapped her hands over her ears. A light shone from the copter onto the sand right over them, and she instinctively crouched behind a boulder though she knew they had to have been seen.

"Is it navy?" she shouted above the noise.

Jesse shook his head. The craft swung around over their heads, then the rapid-fire sound of artillery zinged over them.

They dove to the ground as bullets kicked up sand that stung Kaia's legs and arms. The breath left her lungs as Jesse's heavy weight came down on her. His arms circled her. "Lay still," he shouted as she instinctively struggled to get free.

She stopped her thrashing and lay sheltered in his arms. *Please, God, don't let him take a bullet for me.* She wanted to shriek with the whining sound of the bullets as they plowed all around them. Then the attack stopped as quickly as it had started.

She was trembling so hard she could barely lift her head. Jesse got up as the sound of the helicopter's engine rose. He pulled Kaia to her feet then put his arm around her shoulders, and they watched the "bird" hover then veer off toward Na Pali. The sound faded into the distance. Jesse was talking softly on his phone with the navy base. He clicked it off. "Help's on the way."

"Are you hurt?" She wanted to run her hands over his torso to make sure he was unharmed.

"I'm fine. Did they hit you?"

"No, no, not a scratch." She became aware that he had his hand wrapped in her hair. The look on his face as he stared into her eyes made her cheeks hot. She should step away, but the strength seemed to have left her legs. She saw a muscle work in his jaw, then he released her and stepped back. She wasn't sure if she was relieved or disappointed.

"Could the Morse code have been coming from the copter?" Jesse asked her.

So he was going to ignore the emotion that had zipped between them as briefly and brilliantly as Hawai'i's green flash. She collected herself. "It was in this area, so yeah. I wonder what they were doing out here?"

Jesse flipped on his flashlight. The powerful halogen beam threw the rocks and plants in the area into sharp relief.

"I think we're going to have to start digging deeper ourselves," Kaia said. "How about talking to Jonah Kapolei's family? Has the navy done that yet?"

"The dead diver? Probably. But maybe you could get more out of them. Do you know anything about the family?"

"No, but Mano might." She told herself if her brother could pump her for information, she could do the same. She squinted in the moonlight and could make out a dark figure moving around on the deck of Jesse's craft. "Looks like he's awake."

Neither said much as Jesse rowed them back to the navy boat.

Mano was scowling when they stepped back onto the deck. "You should have woken me up. What was up with the helicopter?"

"Nothing. We decided to go for a walk along the beach and

happened to see it," Jesse said. "We didn't know it was there until it lifted off over our heads."

"Sounded like gunfire."

"It was."

Kaia watched her brother. She saw concern and a trace of guilt arc over his face. She was going to have to press him, and she feared it might cost them their relationship.

FIFTEEN

Jesse stood on the white sand of Polihale. The bullets from early this morning had dug ridges in the soft lava rocks. He'd retrieved several samples, but he didn't expect them to prove much. He glanced down the beach and saw Kaia coming toward him. The lack of rest was beginning to show on both of them. He glanced at his watch. He needed to get Heidi at ten.

"I don't get why the helicopter cared that we showed up unless whatever they were doing was illegal," Kaia said as she approached him. "There's nothing out here but sand."

Jesse nodded toward the mountains. "Waianae Range has the munitions storage in the caves up there. I sent some men up to check it out. I'm wondering if the helicopter planted the explosives to carry out their plan."

Kaia winced. "They're not wasting any time. Maybe they were just scouting it out."

"I hadn't thought of that. It's possible. Maybe I should go take a look myself."

She clutched his arm. "I wish you wouldn't. What if they managed to plant explosives and they went off while you were up there?"

Did she care if he got hurt? The thought left him smiling. There was something developing between them, and neither of them wanted to talk about it. Jesse was afraid to look at it too closely. He didn't want to care about another woman. What if he failed again?

He pulled his arm free of her grip and turned away. "I'll be fine. I'd better check it out."

"I'll go with you then."

He stopped. "No, I don't want you up there. You'll be safer here."

"So would you." She stuck out her jaw.

He nearly laughed at the pugnacious expression on her face but knew it would make her madder. "You're not military anyway. This is my job, Kaia."

"We were nearly shot last night. This is getting scary." She clasped her arms around herself as if the warm wind were thirty degrees cooler than the balmy eighty degrees.

"I know. And I need to make sure the next missile test is secure."

"When is that?"

"Next week. Thursday." He didn't want to tell her how uneasy he was about that test. He'd been thinking about the Morse code from last night. *Hammer fall.* What if it had something to do with the missile test? Lawton still believed the problem with the first test had been a malfunction of the computer and that everything was fixed now.

But what if it wasn't?

Faye cracked eggs for omelets into a bowl and got out the juice. Curtis entered the kitchen, kissed her, then sat at the kitchen table. She whipped the eggs with vigor and didn't look at him.

"Am I in trouble?" he asked. "You're beating those eggs like they have personally offended you."

Tears flooded her eyes. "I'm going to make a hopeless grandmother. I'm tired and cranky and want to go back to bed. I'm feeling my age."

He stood and put his arms around her. "You're jumping the gun a little. The kids aren't even married yet. Besides, it's different when the children are your own. Heidi is sweet, but she's not your own flesh and blood."

Faye leaned against his chest. "I'm just tired. It's been a long week."

"What time is Jesse coming?"

"He called a little while ago and said he'd be here around ten when he finishes an errand. I'm so tired, Curtis." She sighed and laid her cheek over his heart. Its steady beat calmed her nerves.

"You could tell him to find someone else."

She pulled away and hurried to flip the omelet. "No, I can't do that, and you know it. Besides, Heidi needs me too."

"We could figure out another way to keep you and Kaia connected. If nothing else, I could pull her back to the office. Maybe that would be best anyway."

Faye shook her head. "No, I'm just overreacting. I had a nice talk with her yesterday."

"Did you ask any questions?"

"No. The time didn't seem right. I'm not sure it ever will be. Maybe you'll have to do it."

"I think you can handle it better than I could." Curtis sat back down at the table, and she put his breakfast in front of him.

"I don't know if I can talk to her or not. Maybe I should talk to one of the boys."

"I thought you wanted to start with Kaia."

"I did. Now I just don't know." Faye pulled out her chair and sat at the table. The omelet looked unappetizing, and she picked at it. She wished she could go to her bedroom, shut the door, get out her novel, and forget what was happening in her world.

"I don't know what to tell you, Faye. We agreed this was the best way to handle it. You can't give up before we've even started."

"I want to give up," she said. "I want to get on the plane and fly away from here. This is too hard."

Curtis put down his fork. "You have to stop running someday. It's time to face up to what you've done."

"I'm not sure I can." The old, familiar panic clawed at her chest. She couldn't handle this. It was too much. Though Curtis didn't know it, she had a voucher for an airline ticket to Chicago in her dresser. The safety net it gave her had calmed her more than once. Maybe it was time to use it.

But no. She couldn't leave Curtis. She loved him. He would be so hurt and disappointed in her. Even if the future brought pain, she needed to see this through. She was too old to keep running. Faye had thought she'd grown up, but she was beginning to see the old habits were harder to kill than she'd realized.

She must have some kind of defect that made her hate confrontation and trouble. Maybe she would never overcome it. And if she didn't, what would she do with her life? Where would she go? She wouldn't be able to stay here and face all her failures. Was there ever a woman with more regrets than she carried?

JESSE PARKED AT AN OVERLOOK WITH THE PANORAMA OF WAIMEA Canyon spread out before them. "You sure this is the place?" he asked Kaia.

From here Kaia could see the reds and greens of the canyon that nearly took her breath away. Dubbed "the Grand Canyon of the Pacific" by Mark Twain, the smaller canyon was no less spectacular than its larger namesake. The colors were deep and rich and spoke to her soul.

Kaia nodded. "Mano gave me directions."

"How'd you weasel them out of him?"

"I told him the truth that I wanted to talk to Jonah Kapolei's family. He tried to talk me out of it, but he knew I could find out in town if I asked."

"Did he ask to come with you?"

She nodded. "I told him you'd be along to protect me." She turned in her seat and smiled at him. It felt good to be here with him. When had she begun to drop her defenses? She needed to be careful. He was not the type of man she'd always thought of marrying. He was older and not Hawaiian.

"We'd better get moving. I need to pick up Heidi at ten. And you look beat."

"I am," she admitted. "I'm hitting the bed as soon as I get home."

"Want to go on a picnic with me and Heidi after church tomorrow?"

"Sure," she said before she thought. What was she thinking? She'd just decided she needed to be more careful. She got out of the Jeep and wished she could find a way to bow out gracefully.

"I thought we'd go to Po'ipu and watch for monk seals. Heidi loves them."

"Sounds fun. Where have you been going to church?"

"Nowhere yet. I haven't had a chance to look for one, but I thought I'd figure out where to go."

"I haven't been in ages," she said. "I've been feeling pretty guilty about it. You could come with me and my grandfather," she offered. She was getting herself in deeper and deeper. Maybe he'd refuse.

"I'd love to. Want me to pick you up?"

"Okay." She slammed her door and headed toward the path that led down the hillside.

The house they approached looked as though it had been perched on the ledge since King Kamehameha had ruled the island. Wood weathered to silvery gray covered the small home, and a stone porch added substance to the structure. Wild orchids, plumeria, and ginger grew in profusion along the brick path to the front door. The trade winds brought the sweet scent to Kaia's nose.

"Let me start us off," Kaia whispered as they got to the door. With Jesse in a uniform, he was liable to choke off any information the woman might give.

He nodded and let her go in front. From inside she could hear the strains of a ukulele. Kaia rapped on the door. There was no answer at first, then the sound of footsteps echoed on hardwood floors.

The woman who opened the door was about Kaia's height. Her Hawaiian features were framed by black hair cut into a short bob.

She wore khaki shorts and an orange top. Maybe the outfit would have been attractive on a twenty-year-old, but it made her forty-something skin look sallow. Kaia guessed she was at least five years older than her husband had been.

"Mrs. Kapolei?" Kaia held out her hand. "I'm Kaia Oana and this is Lieutenant Commander Jesse Matthews. We'd like to ask you a few questions about Jonah, but first I'd like to say I'm so sorry for your loss."

The woman blinked rapidly and bit her lip. "*Mahalo*. Who are you? I already told the other military guys and the police everything I know."

"We're also investigating for the base," Jesse said. "Do you have any idea why he was diving by himself? Did he usually dive with a partner?"

"I'd begged him not to go out alone, but he always laughed at me. He thought he was invincible." Mrs. Kapolei rubbed her forehead.

"Did he always dive with a dart gun?" Jesse put in.

Kaia shot him a look. He wasn't paying any attention to what she'd told him, and Kaia could see the woman bristling.

The woman took a step back. "I know the military is trying to pin that dart gun on Jonah, but I've never seen him with anything like that. I doubt he would have known how to use one."

"So you think he was murdered and didn't shoot himself by accident?" Kaia asked, her voice gentle.

"Of course he was murdered! And I can tell you who the culprit is, though no one will listen." Mrs. Kapolei stepped onto the porch and shook her finger in Kaia's face. "It's that no-good Nahele Aki. He hated Jonah."

"I thought your husband was a member of Pele Hawai'i," Kaia said.

"He was. But he's been trying to get Nahele out of power for months. Aki is taking the organization in a radical direction." Her eyes flooded with tears. "And Nahele couldn't stand the competition, so he got rid of my husband and made it look like he was involved in something suspicious."

"Did you tell the military this?" Kaia asked.

Mrs. Kapolei nodded. "But I could tell they didn't believe a word of it." She rubbed the back of her hand over her eyes. "As far as they were concerned, he'd been tried and found guilty."

Kaia opened her purse and pulled out a tissue. She pressed it into the other woman's hand.

Mrs. Kapolei blew her nose. "*Mahalo.* Are you going to do something about Nahele?"

The hope in her eyes rattled Kaia. This was beyond her reach. "We'll do what we can," she promised.

The light in Mrs. Kapolei's eyes dimmed. "In other words, no."

"We'll follow what leads we can find," Kaia told her. "Is there anything else you can tell us? Did Jonah have a best friend who might be able to help us?"

The woman's jaw hardened, and her dark eyes closed to mere slits. "You might ask his girlfriend. I doubt she'll talk to you, but you can try." Mrs. Kapolei opened the screen door and stepped back into the house. "She works at the Waimea Brewing Company."

Kaia knew the pub. She exchanged a quick glance with Jesse. "What's her name?"

"Lindy Martin. She lives in a gray house next to the school."

The door shut, and Jesse took Kaia's elbow and guided her back to the path. "That was informative. You think she knows what she's talking about?"

"I don't know. She knew about the girlfriend though, so she's no dummy."

Jesse looked at his watch. "I've got forty-five minutes before I need to pick up Heidi. You game to see what this Lindy Martin has to say?"

"Sure."

They reached the road, and Kaia followed him to the Jeep. She was quiet as they drove back down the winding road to town.

"You doing okay?" he asked.

"I'm fine. Just tired. I've fallen from a tree, twisted my ankle, been grabbed, shot at, and endured practically no sleep for the past few days." She shifted in the seat and turned to face him. "To tell you the truth, I'm beginning to wonder if this is something I need to back away from. If I get killed, Nani will be at the mercy of Seaworthy Labs and likely be made to perform in a sea park. I can't let that happen. My research doesn't have a chance to move forward with problems like these."

"Can you just hang in there with me until the missile test is complete?"

She was silent then leaned her head back against the rest. She didn't know when she'd been so tired. Her life was racing from one crisis to the next, and she wanted the stress to end. "Okay, but if anything happens to me, you're to take care of Nani. Agreed?"

Jesse chuckled. "Agreed. But I won't let anything happen to you." He slowed as they entered the town.

"That must be the house." Kaia pointed to a gray house next to the school.

The small structure had peeling paint and a broken window-pane in the door. A flock of chickens ran from under the Jeep's tires when Jesse pulled into the rutted driveway. They got out and went to the door. Splinters had been gouged from the wood, and the red paint had faded to pink.

Jesse pounded on the metal screen door that didn't fit securely into the frame. Almost immediately, a young woman in her twenties answered. She had red hair of a shade Kaia had never seen in nature. A cigarette hung from her crimson mouth.

She looked blearily at them through the door. "If you're selling something, I'm not interested."

"We'd like to ask you some questions about Jonah Kapolei,"

Kaia said. She smiled, but the young woman wasn't moved by the warmth. "We won't take more than a few minutes."

Lindy's manner thawed only slightly, and she stepped out onto the porch. "I'm about to go to bed."

"We wondered if you knew of any problems Jonah might have had with Pele Hawai'i." Jesse took off his hat and rubbed his forehead.

"The military has already been around asking their questions. Why do you care?" Her gaze lingered on Jesse's ribbons. "You're a little higher rank. The big boys are getting involved, huh?" She blew a ring of smoke in his face.

"You have a chance to help your country out by just telling us what you know."

She gave a bitter laugh. "What's my country done for me lately?"

Kaia had a feeling she was enjoying putting them off. "What was Jonah's relationship with Nahele Aki?"

"I suppose you won't leave until I answer your stupid questions." She dropped the cigarette to the porch and ground it under a foot clad in a pink fuzzy slipper. "He hated that Aki guy. They had a big fight a couple of days before Jonah died. But why the questions? Didn't he shoot himself with a dart gun accidentally?"

Jesse shrugged. "That's what we're trying to find out. Did he have a diving buddy?"

"Sometimes. Some guy from the group. I can't remember his name. Big Hawaiian guy with scary eyes." She shuddered.

"Did he have a birthmark on his nose?" Kaia asked.

Lindy nodded. "That's him."

"I don't know his name either, but I've seen him," Kaia said.

Lindy glanced at her watch. "Look, I'm bushed. I don't know anything about Jonah's death, and I'm going to bed."

"*Mahalo*," Jesse called through the door as she slammed it in their faces.

Sixteen

The man glanced at his watch. The others were late. A grove of monkeypod trees surrounded this clearing in a sheltering fence of tangled roots and overgrown vegetation. Mynas chattered from the trees above his head, and his nose caught the faint scent of orchids blooming along the wild path that led to this remote spot.

The mynas squawked and flew off just as he heard the sound of careless feet crashing through the vegetation. He rose from his seat on a tree stump and brushed the debris from his pants then turned to face the two who stepped into the clearing. "You took your time about getting here."

His blond assistant gave him an apologetic smile. "Sorry. We got lost." He approached and held out a file.

The man took it and opened it. He flipped through the pictures. One photograph showed Jesse Matthews aboard a boat, another at his quarters, still more at Seaworthy Labs. "This is all you got?" He closed the folder and stuffed it in his briefcase.

"Yeah. He's pretty wily. We had to make sure he didn't see." The third man stomped on a line of ants heading for the safety of the jungle.

"Why did you want them anyway?"

"I have my reasons." While revenge on Jesse Matthews hadn't been part of his original plan, he couldn't deny the thrill the opportunity brought him. One of life's serendipities. He pulled out his cell phone and an electronic voice synthesizer.

"What are you doing?"

Ignoring his assistant, he dialed the phone and asked to speak to the base commander. "Hello, I have some information about the recent break-in where missile schematics were stolen. I think if you look in Lieutenant Commander Jesse Matthews's quarters, you'll find what you're looking for." He shut the phone quickly and wished he could see Jesse's face when he found the military riffling through his belongings.

A RUSH OF EXCITEMENT PROPELLED KAIA OUT OF BED. JESSE HAD arranged for navy personnel to patrol the waters so they could both have a day off and get caught up on their rest. She needed the break.

She showered then blow-dried her hair, leaving it down in a curtain of black that fell to her waist. The red print dress she chose showed off her tanned arms and legs. She wondered at her desire for Jesse to notice her. Never before had she really cared whether a man found her attractive.

She took special care brushing her teeth then flossed as well and put on red lipstick. It was all she could do to keep herself from pacing. Jesse was different from any man she'd come in contact with though. He was more—well, *manly*. Everything about him exuded confidence and strength. She felt safe with him. It had been a long time since she'd felt safe. Not since her dim memories of being held in her father's strong arms, of looking up into his laughing face. Not that she equated Jesse with being a father figure. He was much too attractive to be thought of that way.

She tucked her hair behind her ears and put on silver hoop earrings, then touched a drop of perfume behind each ear. *Tûtû kâne* had been delighted she was attending church this morning. He'd been after her to get back to church, and she'd intended to. Jesse's leadership in that direction was another quality that appealed to her. Not very many men had the kind of spiritual strength she sensed in Jesse.

She slipped white leather sandals on her feet and admired the red polish that twinkled on the ends of her toes. She couldn't even remember the last time she'd painted her nails. It didn't stay on long with all her exposure to seawater. Glancing in the full-length mirror, she decided she would pass. She just needed the bracelet that matched her earrings as the final touch.

It wasn't on her dresser. She sighed. If there was one thing she would change about herself, it was her propensity for misplacing things. She didn't think she could blame the cat today. She generally kept her bedroom door shut to keep him from taking things. This one was her own fault.

She dug in her jewelry box. Not there. Maybe she'd left it in the bathroom. She checked there but didn't find it. It was past ten before she found it in the pocket of a pair of jeans in her closet. Kaia fastened the clasp around her wrist and went into the living room to wait for Jesse.

She found Hiwa curled on the couch with Kaia's cell phone. "I would have been looking for that in a little while," she scolded. She tucked the cell phone into her purse.

The driveway gravel crunched, and she looked up to see Jesse's red Jeep outside. He'd been thoughtful enough to put the soft top up on it. That man thought of everything. She hurried to the door.

"Good morning," he said.

Dressed in off-white chinos, a light blue shirt that made his eyes look like the sky, and deck shoes with no socks, he looked too good for Kaia's peace of mind. He was going to make all the unmarried girls at church take a second look.

His gaze seemed glued to her face. Her cheeks flamed. "Do I have a smudge on my nose?" She glanced in the mirror by the door.

"No, you look beautiful," he said. "You ready?"

"Yep." She grabbed the Bible on the hall table. Her grand-mother had given it to her when she was seven. The white cover was tattered and barely clung to the rest of the book, but it was dear and familiar with many marked pages.

He escorted her to the Jeep and opened the door for her. "Whoa, you cleaned out your Jeep," she exclaimed. The inside sparkled, even the windows. Not a speck of sand marred the floor.

"I thought you deserved it." He went around to his side.

Heidi was scowling in the backseat. "What's wrong?" Kaia asked.

"Uncle Jesse made me wear a dress." Heidi folded her arms across her chest and cast a scornful look down at the blue dress she wore.

"You look very pretty," Kaia told her. "Sometimes it's fun to wear a dress."

"Not for me." Heidi's mutinous scowl deepened.

A change of topic might be good. Kaia smiled. "Did you bring your bathing suit and shorts for after church?"

Heidi nodded. "And my pail and shovel. I'm going to bury Uncle Jesse in the sand." She glared at her uncle as he got in the car.

He grinned. "Just punishment for the dress wearing, huh?" He glanced toward Kaia. "You both look beautiful."

His comment warmed Kaia. She fastened her seat belt and glanced at the Bible on the console between them. The leather cover was worn. That was a good sign. The deeper she delved into the real man under the surface, the more intrigued she grew.

Her grandfather was already at church when they arrived. Kaia took Heidi to junior church then joined Jesse in the pew with her grandfather. The scent of flowers that blew through the open windows put her in the right frame of mind for worship.

Jesse laid his arm along the back of the pew. Kaia settled in to pay attention to the service. The music and message were like water and breath to her soul, and she wondered how she'd been able to stay away so long.

She saw a man and woman pause at their pew on the way out. Kaia heard Jesse gasp, and she glanced at him. His gaze was riveted on the man.

He stood. "Steve, what are you doing here?"

Kaia had never seen the couple before. The man was about thirty-five with light brown hair and pale blue eyes. The woman was a few years younger and heavier, built almost like a man. They didn't seem to go together, but Steve clasped her hand with tobacco-stained fingers like he was afraid to let go.

The man smiled uncertainly. "Hello, Jesse. I hoped you would be here."

Jesse's shoulders were rigid, but he returned the man's smile. "Were you looking for me?"

"Not really. This is Becky, my wife. You got off the phone the other day before I could tell you we were moving here. I just bought a new security business."

Jesse seemed frozen in place. Kaia held out her hand. "I'm Kaia Oana, a friend of Jesse's."

Her words seemed to shock Jesse into action. "This is my brother-in-law, Steve Prickett."

Kaia's first instinct was to stare, but she quickly recovered her manners. "Hello." She shook Steve's hand and noticed he was doing his own share of staring at her. Jesse seemed uncomfortable, and she had to wonder if he felt guilty to be with her.

"Pleased to meet you," Steve said. "I'm glad to see Jesse is moving on with his life." He stared into Jesse's face. "I just wanted to see you face-to-face and see if we can still be friends. I could use a friend here on the island."

Jesse rubbed his forehead. "I'm pretty busy, Steve."

Kaia wondered what Steve had done to Jesse. The awkwardness between the two men was as obvious as the fragrance of the flowers.

Steve smiled uncertainly. "I'm going to work on Mom. The breach needs to be healed between all of us. Maybe when she comes for Christmas, we can all get together."

"Good luck with that. I doubt you'll have much success with it."

Steve reached out and gripped Jesse's hand with sudden strength. "It's good to see you again, Jesse. I'll keep in touch." He and his wife moved on toward the door.

"I wish I knew what he was up to," Jesse muttered as he guided Kaia down the aisle to exit the church.

"What makes you think he's up to anything? He seemed very nice."

"He hasn't wanted anything to do with me for three years, then he calls to apologize and shows up here. It just seems weird to me."

"Maybe he's sincere."

Jesse shrugged. "Maybe."

As they were leaving, Kaia noticed Jenny Saito go by in the passenger seat of an unfamiliar black SUV. She stopped and stared at the man driving the Durango. It looked like the big Hawaiian who had grabbed her on the beach. The man with the birthmark. But what would Jenny be doing with him?

"What's wrong?" Jesse asked.

"Remember my assistant, the woman we found trapped in the sea cave? Jenny Saito?"

Jesse nodded. "What about her?"

"She just went by with that big Hawaiian guy. The one with the birthmark that Lindy said was Jonah's diving partner. Nahele called him Kim."

His brow furrowed, and he was silent a moment. "You think Jenny's involved in this somehow?"

"It looks suspicious. I think I'd better talk to her."

"The Durango looked like it was heading toward the beach. Maybe she'll be there."

Kaia nodded and got in the Jeep with Heidi. The *keiki* chattered all the way to Po'ipu Beach Park. Heidi had enjoyed junior church and had made several new friends. Kaia listened with half an ear. Her thoughts whirled. Maybe Jenny didn't realize what the big Hawaiian was up to. Though she and her coworker weren't close, they'd been friendly, and Kaia couldn't imagine Jenny being part of such a sinister organization.

There were only a few people on the beach when Jesse parked, and they got out. By the time they'd changed in the bathhouse, the beachgoers had gathered in a circle to the right of the tombola, on a narrow strip of sand that ran out to Nukumoi Point.

"Looks like we're just in time to see the monk seals," Jesse said. He'd changed into blue shorts. His snorkel and mask hung around his neck, and he carried a pair of fins in his hand.

"I want to see!" Heidi ran forward, her red suit a bright splash of color against the golden beach.

Kaia followed her and watched a monk seal flounder up onto the beach. A lifeguard had already strung up a yellow rope to keep gawkers from getting too close to the seal. The endangered mammal was found only in Hawaiian waters, and the fine for disturbing one could run as high as twenty-five thousand dollars. They were interesting to watch from a distance though.

Her gaze wandered around the circle of people watching the seal's antics. A flash of bright blue caught her eye, and she saw Jenny standing almost directly across from her. She had an animated smile on her face. She talked with her hands as she chattered to the man beside her.

Jenny's companion turned and saw Kaia watching them. His gaze narrowed and darkened as he looked at her. Kaia knew he'd recognized her. Her heart pounding, she shrank back into the crowd. She didn't know why the guy scared her so much. There was so much menace in his face. He couldn't do anything to her here though, not with all these people around.

"Are you all right? You look a little pale." Jesse studied her face.

"Jenny and the Hawaiian guy. They're here." She tried to find them again in the crowd, but she'd lost them.

"I don't see them," Jesse said.

"Me neither." She turned and looked toward the parking lot. "There they are!" She pointed at the two of them getting into the black Durango.

Jesse started to go after them, but Kaia grabbed his arm. "They'll be gone by the time you can get there." The SUV spit gravel as it pulled away and disappeared among the condos around the beach.

KAIA COULDN'T REMEMBER WHEN SHE'D ENJOYED A DAY MORE than she'd enjoyed yesterday with Jesse and Heidi. After a full night's sleep, she was ready to take on the world. She glanced at her watch. She hadn't had a chance to talk to Mano since she and Jesse had spoken to Lindy, and there would be no time today. She wanted to work with Nani for a few hours before heading to the base.

Curtis was puttering around the equipment shed when she arrived at Seaworthy Labs. Watching him, she tried to decide how to tackle the subject of the dolphins. Maybe Faye had talked to him already and he would be receptive to what she had to say. She squared her shoulders and stepped toward him.

He must have heard the sound of her slippers slapping the pavement, because he turned and shaded his eyes with his hand. "How's the research coming?"

"It's coming."

He frowned. "I suspected you weren't making progress. Kaia, I want to be straight with you. We're not getting the grants I'd expected. When that article came out last week saying another lab was close to a breakthrough, we lost funding I was counting on. Face it: we're about done with research here. I'm going to move ahead with the sea park."

No other lab was doing *exactly* the work they were. "We'll beat the other lab—all I need is a little more time. Besides, you just bought the lab. You've got to expect to lose a little money at first."

"And I was prepared to do that in the beginning. But things are going downhill fast. I had to pay last week's salaries out of my own pocket."

She hadn't realized the lab was in such dire straits. "Then why did you loan me out to the navy?"

He sighed. "I didn't have much choice. When the navy asks, a patriotic citizen helps out."

"The missile test will be over in a few days. I'm sure I can get that breakthrough in just a few more weeks of work."

"We don't have a few more weeks." He nodded toward the lagoon. "I've arranged to begin construction next week. I'll need to bring in the younger two dolphins and start their training right away. Maybe I can leave Nani in the research project for now."

"I need all three dolphins," she said. "They interact and follow one another's lead in learning the clicks and whistles. It will set the project back if you take them from the pod. I raised Nani. She followed me here to learn, and the other two dolphins followed her. You have no legal right to do this. Besides, they are Pacific dolphins. They need deep water."

"You're saying you own Nani?"

Why was this so hard for him to understand? "Nani isn't owned by anyone. And neither are the other two. They are free, wild dolphins."

"And all I'd have to do would be to put a net fence over the lagoon to keep them here."

Over her dead body. She curled her fingers into her palms and felt her nails bite into her flesh. The only way to save the dolphins was to prove they were capable of language. She needed time for the research, but Jesse needed her for several more days. The only way to do both was to get along on five or six hours of sleep a night.

"You look as though you'd like to punch something," Curtis said. "Kaia, Seaworthy Labs won't cease to be humane just because we're dropping our research function. They'll be happy in the sea park."

"I'm going to get you the proof. You're not capturing the dolphins." The pressure was almost unbearable. Everyone was depending on her, and the thought of failing was unacceptable.

Curtis sighed and his stance relaxed. "It's nothing personal, Kaia. I'm in business, not just research."

Kaia didn't answer him. If she had to, she'd make sure the dolphins never came into the lagoon again. They wouldn't survive being cooped up. "I've got work to do." She left him standing by the shed door and walked to the water.

Nani greeted her with an excited chatter. Kaia kicked off her slippers, sat on the pier, and dropped her feet into the water. "What are you trying to tell me, Nani?" Tears blurred her vision. She'd been trying so hard and still no breakthrough. What would it take to bridge the gap between her and Nani? The missing link was there somewhere. She just had to find it.

She pulled her fins and snorkel from her backpack and slipped into the water, adjusting her equipment into place. Nani brushed against her, and Kaia grabbed the dolphin's dorsal fin and swam through the clear water with her friend. A school of bright yellow tangs scattered as they approached, and Kaia paused and floated as she watched them.

If only she and Nani could really communicate. Nani bumped her with her nostrum, her signal she wanted affection from Kaia. Kaia could feel Nani's love and devotion to her, and she was sure the dolphin could feel how Kaia loved her as well, but the sense of connection wasn't enough.

Kaia floated in the buoyant water and watched Nani try to imitate her. Why was this so important to her anyway? Other people, even her own family, sometimes acted as if they thought she was a little obsessed. But until she could share *words* with Nani, there would always be a wall between them. She wondered if Nani ever felt the distance the way Kaia did. Maybe the dolphin sometimes tried to communicate with her like God tried to communicate with man. Each group had such a different frame of reference.

Jenny was standing on the pier when she surfaced. "How's it going?"

Kaia pulled her mask and snorkel down around her neck and squinted through the glare of the sun. "Okay. Any successes this week?" Kaia watched Jenny carefully for any sign of guilt. The other woman's smile never wavered.

Jenny shook her head. "They don't work as well without you here. And Nani hasn't been showing up as much with you gone either."

"I saw you at the beach yesterday," Kaia blurted out. "Who was the guy you were with?"

Jenny's eyes flickered. "Just a friend of my brother's. No one important."

"I've seen him before. I just wondered what his last name was." Kaia pressed a bit more, but Jenny turned and looked out to sea with a closed expression.

"Hey, have you gotten in any work while you're on patrol?" Jenny asked.

She could tell Jenny wasn't about to reveal anything to her. "Some. We've both been tired." She told Jenny what Curtis said about the sea park.

"Yeah. He's been pretty open about his plans. We may not be able to stop him," Jenny said. She sat on the edge of the pier and dangled her feet over the edge. Liko swam nearer and rubbed against her feet.

"Well, I've got a plan of my own." Kaia swam to the dock and grabbed hold of the pilaster to steady herself. "What if we teach the dolphins *not* to come in here anymore? We've got a couple of weeks before the construction on the new lagoon is done."

"But won't that slow our progress on the communication?"

"Maybe not. We have to try. Unless you have a better idea?" Kaia didn't see that they had a choice. She would do anything in her power to save the dolphins.

Jenny shook her head.

"Let's get started on it today." Kaia nodded toward the car kicking up red dirt under its wheels as it left the parking lot. "Curtis is gone. He won't see what we're doing."

Jenny got to her feet. "I'm game. Tell me what to do."

That was what Kaia wanted to hear. She heaved herself out of the water and blew the whistle around her neck to call the dolphins.

JESSE JOGGED DOWN THE PATH THROUGH THE PARK JUST OFF base. He was smiling as he remembered the day he'd spent with Kaia yesterday. Their conversation had been so free and easy, almost like two old friends. Or even a married couple. He cut that thought short. Best not go there. He glanced at his watch. Three o'clock. Almost time to get Heidi for a few hours before meeting Kaia for tonight's patrol.

He wiped his forehead and turned to head back to base when he saw Duncan's car stop by the curb. He walked over to talk to him. "I figured you'd be hard at work today."

Duncan was smiling. "I was, but my daughter's birthday is next week and I needed to pick up something for her and get it sent."

"How long has it been since you've seen them?"

Duncan's broad smile faltered. "Nearly six months," he admitted. "I could kill Mary for taking them so far away."

"I'm sorry. It must be hard."

"You have no idea." Sadness settled on his features. "I always thought marriage would be forever. So much for faithfulness." His lips twisted. "Matthew was only too glad to step in for me."

Jesse couldn't imagine how it must have felt to be so utterly rejected by one's wife. He reminded himself, however, that there were always at least two sides to a problem. Maybe Duncan had worked too many hours. After the college cheating fiasco, he'd changed—become driven. "Maybe she'll let them come for a visit now that summer is here," Jesse suggested.

"Not a chance. I already asked. Evan is in T-ball and Beth is in swim competition. I've lost them."

Jesse pointed to a framed photo on the passenger seat. "Is that a picture of your dad?" Duncan's dad had been a surrogate father to Jesse.

Duncan picked up the picture. "I'm actually taking it to the office. It seems appropriate with the new missile being tested."

"I'd forgotten your dad came up with the original plans for the missile, didn't he? You must be very proud. I hope you're planning on watching the test from the base."

"Wouldn't miss it. The captain invited me to watch with him." He glanced at his watch. "I've got to run. Duty awaits."

As Duncan drove away, Jesse wondered if his sister Jillian ever regretted breaking it off with Duncan. He might have treated her better than her AWOL husband, Noah.

He jogged to the street and entered the base. Perspiration trickled down his back from his run, and his tank top clung to him. Fingers of steam from the sun's rays rose from the flowers growing along the path. He crested the hill and paused to catch his breath, bending over at the waist and drawing in oxygen.

A movement caught his eye, and he straightened to stare at his quarters. Other soldiers milled around his yard and more men streamed from his front door. What was going on? He swiped at the sweat beading his brow and jogged down the hill to find out.

Captain Lawton met him at the front door. "I'm sorry, Jesse, you can't go in right now."

"What's wrong?" Jesse glanced from Lawton's stern face to the window. Inside his quarters he could see security personnel going through the drawers in the kitchen.

Lawton put his hand on Jesse's shoulder. "We've had a tip that you're the one behind the break-ins on base, Jesse." He removed his hand after a final squeeze.

His blood heating, Jesse stared at the captain. "That's ludicrous!" He started past Lawton, who put out a warning hand. Jesse stopped and resisted an urge to bat down his arm. That would get him thrown into the brig.

"The accusations were serious enough to warrant an investigation. I'm sorry, Jesse."

Was that disappointment in the captain's voice? Jesse examined Lawton's expression. Surely the captain didn't believe any of this. "I see," he said slowly. "I thought you knew me well enough to trust me, Captain."

"I've learned there is always more to a man than meets the eye." Captain Lawton turned at a shout from inside the house. "Watch him," he barked to an SP standing nearby.

Watch him? Jesse was no criminal. He started to follow the captain.

"I'm sorry, Commander, but you heard the captain." The SP put his hand on his gun.

Jesse unclenched his fists and shoved his hands in the pockets of his shorts. He was too angry to be worried about anything they might find. His supervisor's suspicion cut like sharp coral.

He stared down the SP until the man dropped his gaze and shuffled. Jesse strained his ears to try to figure out what was going on inside his house. Who could have called in a prank like this? His mind raced through the list of friends who might have thought this would make a good joke. He rejected them all. All his sailor friends would know how seriously an accusation like this would be taken, and none of his civilian friends would even know how to go about calling the captain.

Could it have been Mano? The thought refused to be dislodged from his head. Mano would have the know-how and contacts, and if Jesse was busy defending himself, he wouldn't be investigating Mano.

The captain reappeared in the doorway holding a booklet. It

looked suspiciously familiar. A sick feeling settled in the pit of Jesse's stomach.

"Can you explain how this happened to be under your mattress, Jesse?" The general opened the booklet to reveal several pages of the schematics of the new missile system. It looked to be the same set that had gone missing after the first break-in.

Jesse forced his gaze up to meet his commander's. "No sir, I can't. I haven't seen them since they were stolen from the safe."

"I know you, Jesse. I don't want to believe you could be guilty of espionage. But you must admit the evidence looks bad."

"Yes sir, it does. But I didn't put those drawings there. And *under my mattress?* C'mon, Captain. The fact that you received an anonymous call has to be suspect. The real spy must be trying to discredit me so I can't continue my investigation."

Lawton's teeth ground together as he thought. He glanced at the booklet then frowned. Turning it over, he rubbed at the ink. "This isn't the original."

"See? It's a practical joke."

Lawton scowled. "Maybe. Because I know your character, I'm going to give you the benefit of the doubt and not confine you to the stockade for now, but I can't allow you to have access to sensitive material either, not with the testing of this new system coming up in three days."

"But, Captain, this proves——"

Captain Lawton held up his hand. "You'd normally be in the brig, Jesse. Count your blessings, and be glad you're on an island where it would be difficult for you to bolt. I want to believe you're innocent, but I can't take any chances."

Jesse clamped his teeth together. "Yes sir," he ground out. He spun on his heel and stomped into the house. An SP followed him and watched as Jesse grabbed a duffel bag and began to stuff clothing and toiletries inside.

Jesse felt like a mouse caught by the tail and held up by the taunting cat for ridicule. He'd never had his integrity questioned before, and this experience was not one he ever wanted to repeat. His military record was spotless.

He grabbed his wallet and keys and stalked back outside. The captain showed no emotion as Jesse went past him to his Jeep. Jesse couldn't bear to look at him. He slung himself under the wheel and cranked over the engine, then stomped on the accelerator. An SP jumped out of the way as Jesse peeled out. He'd dedicated his life to serving his country, and this was the thanks he got? The desolate sensation of betrayal chased him off the base.

SEVENTEEN

"You beat me, you little twerp." Faye threw her Uno cards onto the table and gave Heidi a mock glare.

The little girl giggled. "Let's play again." She picked up the cards and began to shuffle them awkwardly.

"I wish we could, sweetheart, but it's almost time for your uncle to get here." Faye had enjoyed the day. She was finally getting into this nanny thing. The break yesterday had helped too.

"He's usually late," Heidi said in a matter-of-fact voice. "He's been really busy at work."

"I know. What did your mom have to say when she called today?" Faye always tried not to pry too much, but Heidi had seemed more content and happy after the phone visit with her mother. Faye didn't know the full story of why Heidi's parents were split up, and she wasn't sure she wanted to know.

"She thinks she should be done in a few more weeks. She'll come get me, and we'll go see Grandma Sommers."

Faye nodded, but said nothing else. Mention of Heidi's father was treacherous territory and would likely lead to tears. Faye knew the *keiki* missed her daddy badly.

The doorbell rang, and Faye got to her feet. "I bet that's your Uncle Jesse." A smile lifting her lips, she went to the door and threw it open.

Jesse's face was white, and his blue eyes seemed almost wild. "Is Heidi ready?" He pushed past Faye without a word of greeting.

"Jesse, what's wrong?" Faye whispered.

He took off his hat and rubbed his short blond hair then put his hat back on. "Everything. I don't want to talk about it." He strode into the living room. "Ready to go, monkey?"

"Uncle Jesse!" Heidi scrambled out of the chair and threw herself into her uncle's arms. He lifted her against his chest, tucking his head into the crook between her head and neck. "You're squeezing me too hard," Heidi protested, wiggling.

Jesse released her and set her back on the floor. "Sorry." He turned to Faye. "Thanks for keeping her today."

"Can't you tell me what's wrong?" Faye laid her hand on his arm.

He put his hand over hers. "Maybe tomorrow. I can't talk about it right now. Work stuff." He swallowed hard and dropped his hand then moved away.

Heidi returned with her backpack. "I'm ready to go."

Jesse put his hand on the little girl's head and guided her out the door. "See you after while."

"After while, crocodile," Heidi chimed in.

Faye shut the door behind them. She had several hours before Curtis was due home, and the house seemed claustrophobic. She grabbed her car keys and went out through the kitchen to the garage. The Volvo convertible rarely got used, but today she felt like letting the wind blow through her hair. Punching the garage-door opener, she got in the car, lowered the top, and backed out.

Her tires kicked up red dirt as she headed down Highway 50. She passed three men talking along the roadside. The Acura parked on the shoulder must belong to them. They turned so their backs were to the road. She stared at them as she passed. With all the problems going on for Jesse, she wondered if they were up to no good. The base was just over the hill. One turned to look at her, and she shivered and looked away. It was none of her business.

The car seemed to know where it was going even if Faye didn't, and fifteen minutes later she stopped by a driveway. Did she dare drive in? Her lungs constricted, and she felt faint. Dragging in oxygen, she told herself she could do this. Curtis would be so proud when she told him.

She dropped the Volvo into gear and turned into the driveway. The koa tree that stood guard over the property was nearly sixty feet tall, its long, straight trunk at least eight feet in diameter. Plumeria, orchids, and hibiscus bloomed along the drive, and their sweet fragrance wafted to her nose and settled her nerves. Talk about aromatherapy. She smiled at the thought.

When she was a little girl, she often hid under the koa tree and pretended to talk with the Menehune and the Mu, tiny aborigines who were said to have lived on Kaua'i in the early days. Whenever she played jokes on her parents, she told them it was the Mu, because the little people were supposed to be tricksters. It never worked with her parents.

The memories washed over her, and she stopped in the middle of the driveway, unexpected sobs heaving from her throat. She couldn't do this. The memories were too strong and painful. She'd give herself away.

Gripping the steering wheel, she took several deep breaths until she could feel a sense of calmness begin to settle over her. She took her foot off the brake and put it back on the accelerator. Rounding the last curve, she shut off the engine in front of a small Hawaiian cottage. The red shutters looked freshly painted, and the front porch was just as she remembered it, such a dark wood it was almost black.

Her knees shook as she got out of the car and went to the front door. There was no sound from the other side of the screen. A gecko looked at her then raced along the siding. She lifted her hand then dropped it and rubbed slick palms against the sides of her slacks. Biting her lip, she raised her hand again and rapped on the door. The soft knock startled the myna on the porch railing. It squawked and flew off. Faye rapped a little harder, but only silence greeted her.

"He's not home."

She turned, and her heart tried to escape her chest when she saw the man approaching the porch. He could have been Palani in his younger years. She wasn't sure she could talk. She swallowed past the constriction in her throat. "Hello. I hope I didn't take you away from your work."

"I was just doing a little fishing. I'm not working this month."

The young man's wide shoulders and open, generous expression filled her with delight. He'd grown up strong and handsome in spite of her desertion.

"Catching anything?" she asked, stepping off the porch. She approached him. If only she had the courage to tell him who she was. In his firm jaw and full lips, she could still see the pudgy cheeks from his childhood.

He shrugged. "A few small 'ono." He tipped his head and stared at her. "Do I know you? You look familiar."

The words lodged in her throat. "Not really," she finally managed. "But I'm hoping you will want to. I'm your mother."

KAIA SAT ON THE PIER WITH HER LEGS DANGLING IN THE WATER, disheartened. DALE lay discarded on the pier beside her. Nani could repeat sounds back to her, but the dolphin had no idea what they meant. Maybe she never would.

Kaia heard a noise and turned to see Jesse and Heidi coming toward her. Jesse's mouth was grim. She stood and moved toward them.

"Can I swim with Nani?" Heidi demanded when Kaia reached them.

"For a few minutes. We're going to have to go to the base in a while." She smiled as she watched Heidi shuck off her shorts and top to reveal her bathing suit underneath. The little girl shouted then ran pell-mell into the waves. Nani leaped in the air then moved to meet Heidi.

Kaia turned back to face Jesse. "What's happened?"

He picked up her hand and squeezed it. "I've been relieved of my duties."

"What? Wait, what duties?"

"My duties as security officer. Some anonymous caller accused me of being a spy."

"You've got to be kidding. And the captain believed it?"

His words were clipped, and she found it hard to read his expression. "They're investigating." He rubbed his forehead. "Until they get to the bottom of it, I'm no longer head of security."

"*Auē*! Why would someone do that to you?"

He shrugged. "To halt my investigation? Someone planted a copy of the schematics that had been stolen from the base in my quarters."

"Wait—what schematics?"

"Of the new missile system. They think I'm a spy."

She covered her hand with her mouth. A spy. Could it be true? She stared into his face, her eyes noting the firm chin, the direct way he met her gaze. She couldn't imagine he could be a spy, but wasn't that the reason most spies went undetected? They were the last person you'd suspect.

She didn't want him to know her doubts, so she tried for humor. "Does that mean someone else is going to order me around?"

"Was I ordering you around?" His tight mouth relaxed, and he smiled.

"You do it without even thinking."

"Come on, you must be talking about someone else. I've treated you with kid gloves."

"With nails embedded," she said, punching him lightly in the stomach.

He caught her hand, and she unfurled her fingers in his. He squeezed them. She tried to squelch her doubts, but they kept rising. Maybe he'd asked for her help to allay suspicions at the base. She didn't want to be a pawn—she had too much on her own plate to figure out.

She stepped away. "So what's next? I don't have time to tiptoe around someone else. I found out today that Curtis is going ahead with the sea park plans and will take Nani and the others in as soon as the lagoon is ready."

Jesse frowned. "Can he do that?"

"They're free but trusting. They would have no idea what he was up to until he penned them in. I've got to bridge the gap between us. So you see, I don't have the time to give to the navy right now."

"What about getting Mano out of the fix he's in? We only have three days to figure out what's going on."

She bit her lip. Mano. She had to make sure he was out of this. "How?"

He nodded toward the boat floating in the lagoon. "Would Curtis let you take that out?"

"Sure."

"What if I take leave and we don't have to answer to the navy? We could patrol on our own at night. That would give us time to work with Nani during the day and run down some leads too. We can catch catnaps when we need to. It would only be for three days."

"Won't you get in trouble?"

He pressed his lips together. "I can't get in much more trouble. I need your help to find who's behind all this. That's the only thing that will clear my name."

She wanted so badly to believe him, to trust him. "Okay."

"What about Heidi?" Kaia nodded toward the little girl frolicking with the dolphin.

"How many bedrooms does the boat have?"

"One master with sleeping room for four more in the galley."

"Could she share your bed? And some backup would be good. Would Bane have time to join us?"

"I think so. He's been wanting something to do."

"It's settled then. I'll head over to the base and get some gear." He glanced at his watch. "I'll meet you back here in an hour."

"Who's going to tell the navy I'm pulling out of the project?"

"I will," he said. "I'm going to take great pleasure in it."

EIGHTEEN

Faye let her gaze trace the contours of her son's face. The strong jaw, the curling lashes that were just like hers, the slightly pointed ears he inherited from his grandfather. He was staring at her as if he expected her to disappear any minute. She averted her eyes. No wonder he thought she'd leave. She had done it before.

It did no good to dwell on her past failures, she reminded herself. "Aren't you going to say anything?" she whispered.

Bane blinked slowly as if awakening from a long sleep. *"Makuahine?"*

She hadn't heard the Hawaiian word for "mother" in so long. The melodious sound of it brought tears to her eyes. She blinked her eyes rapidly. "Yes, Bane. I've come home," she said simply. It would be up to him to accept or reject her. She had no power to sway his feelings, no excuses for what she'd done.

A light crept into his eyes, and he took her in his arms, wrapping himself around her as if she were the child. Her oldest *keiki*. She remembered when he was born, the way the coppery odor of blood and the salty smell of the amniotic fluid had clung to him and overlaid the sweet scent of his own newness. She held him now and thought she could never let him go again.

When his strong arms finally released her, she clung to him for a long moment then reluctantly let go and stepped away. Searching his eyes, she found questions she wasn't sure she could answer. "I'm so sorry, *Keikikâne*," she whispered. "I was selfish and willful. I can only ask your forgiveness. I have no excuses for what I did."

The light in his eyes faded. "Why did you leave? And why didn't you take me with you? You took Kaia."

She lifted her shoulders helplessly. "It would be impossible to explain how trapped I felt, Bane. And I knew taking you and Mano would kill your grandfather. You *keikis* were the light of his life. Besides, the man I left with was only willing to take Kaia."

"You picked a man over your own children?" A frown wrinkled Bane's brow.

"Yes." The bald truth was all she could offer. "I was young and stupid. I've since learned just how stupid. I never got over hearing your voice call for me the night I left."

Bane's Adam's apple bobbed in his neck, and he ducked his head, but not before she caught the sheen of moisture in his eyes. "I'm sorry, Bane. So sorry. You have no idea how I wish I could go back and change everything."

He backed away, then turned and raced down the beach. Faye started to go after him, then she stopped and sank to the sand. She fell face forward and sobbed out her grief and remorse. Her children couldn't blame her any more than she blamed herself.

KAIA TRIED TO SQUELCH THE EXCITEMENT SHE FELT AS SHE stood on deck and waited for Jesse to join her. Bane had been quick to agree to accompany them, though his voice had sounded strained when she called. From her perch on the railing of Seaworthy Lab's boat, she could see Bane's pickup pulling into the parking lot. He got out with a duffel bag slung over his shoulder.

Kaia waved to him. He lifted his hand in greeting then jogged to the pier. He tossed her his bag then hopped aboard.

"Mahalo," she told him.

"Hey, no problem." His strong, brown legs were clad in shorts.

His eyes seemed dark. Kaia frowned and wondered if he'd had another run-in with Mano. He looked great though. Some girl was going to get a wonderful husband in Bane one of these days. Not that she'd seen him noticing all the lovely women casting glances his way.

"What are we doing tonight?" he asked, settling into a deck chair. "I brought my GameBoy for later. I'm going to trounce you."

"You'll have to wait awhile," she told him with a smile. "Until dark, I'm going to work with Nani on learning words, then we're going to cruise back and forth in the waters off base. Jesse thinks we might see more a little farther out."

"Sounds fun." Bane rubbed his hands together. "I'm surprised you didn't invite Mano."

Kaia hesitated. She wasn't sure how much to tell Bane, but if he was going to help them, he needed to know the truth. "We think Pele Hawai'i might be involved."

Bane stared at her. "You mean Mano might be mixed up in espionage and sabotage?"

"I hope not. But it doesn't look good." She told him what Lei had said at the rice mill.

"Why are you just now telling me this? I need to have a talk with baby brother." He sounded grim. "And he hasn't said a word about being in trouble with the navy."

"We can't tip him off that Pele Hawai'i is under suspicion. He might tell them."

"I knew that group was trouble," Bane muttered. "No good ever comes from that kind of anger."

"There's a guy I saw at the meeting and at the beach. First or last name is Kim. Big Hawaiian with a birthmark on his nose. Ring any bells?"

Bane frowned as he thought about it then shook his head. "I can't say it does. What's he done?"

She wasn't about to tell him about the guy manhandling her. "Nothing that we can prove. But he was a diving buddy to the man who washed ashore on the base, Jonah Kapolei. We'd like to talk to him."

"And you saw this guy at the meeting? So Kapolei was a member of Pele Hawai'i too?"

"He was the treasurer."

"Did you ask Mano about him?"

Kaia nodded. "He wouldn't tell me much."

"Then how are we going to track this guy down?"

"There's a meeting of Pele Hawai'i tomorrow night. I'm hoping you'll go."

Bane grimaced. "It would tax my soul to sit there and listen to them spout their treason." He sighed. "I don't have much choice though. What if Mano sees me?"

"Tell him you're curious about the group. It's the truth."

"Yes, I could do that. Maybe I'll just ask to go with him. You went once. He probably wouldn't think much about it other than how he could use the opportunity to convert me." He sighed. "I don't know what's gotten into our brother lately."

Bane's eyes had turned brooding, but for some reason Kaia didn't think it had anything to do with Mano. "Anything wrong, Bane?"

"Nope." Bane shaded his eyes with his hand. "Jesse's here." He grinned when Kaia turned to look. "I see you're very interested in the handsome navy man."

"We're working together," she reminded him. The burning in her cheeks told her she wasn't fooling her brother.

"'e, 'ê, 'ê," her brother said, indicating he heard her but didn't believe it.

She ignored him and turned to smile at Jesse and Heidi. "Aloha." She held out her hand to help them aboard.

Jesse took it and stepped aboard. "Mahalo," he said.

Heidi looked around with a bewildered expression on her face. Kaia realized Jesse hadn't told his niece much about what was happening. "Let me show you to our quarters." She took Heidi's hand and led her to the ladder into the galley. They stepped down into the boat's hold, and Kaia had the little girl stash her belongings in the cabinet in the master quarters.

"Can I go swimming with Nani?"

"Not right now. I need to work with her for a little while. She gets too excited when you're in the water with her to pay attention to me." Kaia rubbed Heidi's soft blond curls. "Bane brought some video games. You want to play with the GameBoy?"

"Okay! Where is it?"

"I'll get it." Kaia went on deck and grabbed the backpack with Bane's game then went back below. They pulled it out and she got Heidi started on the game. "It's best to use it below deck just in case a big wave would happen along."

Heidi just grunted in answer as she became engrossed in the game. Kaia smiled and went topside. She grabbed her laptop and went to the railing. She attached it to the hydrophone and dropped DALE over the side into the water. She showed Jesse how to use the computer program that translated the words into clicks and whistles that emanated from the hydrophone.

She shucked down to her modest one-piece swimsuit and put on her snorkel and fins. Jumping overboard, she kicked alongside Nani. The hydrophone was connected to an underwater computer screen that showed four figures. The clicks and whistles coming from the device meant "ball." Nani poised next to the screen then punched the picture of the ball with her nostrum. A little figure came onto the screen and began to dance. Nani swished her tail then jumped out of the water with obvious delight.

Kaia smiled at the dolphin's joy in choosing the right figure, but though Nani could recognize the picture and replicate the noises for the picture of a ball, she had yet to recognize a real ball and call it by its name. Kaia felt like Anne Sullivan trying to help Helen Keller make sense of language. If she could make the connection with just one thing, the rest would follow, but that missing link still eluded them.

Kaia surfaced and waved for Bane to throw her a beach ball. "Keep having the hydrophone repeat the word for ball," she shouted to Jesse.

He nodded and bent back over the computer. Kaia tossed the

beach ball to Nani, who balanced it on her nostrum and threw it back to Kaia. They played for a few minutes, then Kaia gave the ball back to Bane for hiding, hoping Nani, in her playful mood, might ask for it back with the right clicks and whistles. Instead, Nani just bumped Kaia's leg with her nostrum. Kaia tried again.

She repeated the process for over an hour until she was exhausted, both from the exertion and from the lack of progress. Desperation gripped her. Nani was so trusting, she could easily be captured if Curtis was determined.

Kaia climbed back into the boat, and Jesse handed her a towel and a bottle of water. *"Mahalo,"* she said. She took a swig of water then toweled off and wrapped the large beach towel around herself. She sat in the chair beside the captain's seat then propped her feet on the dash, crossing them at the ankles.

Jesse drank from his water bottle. "I've been thinking while you were working with Nani. We've got to find that guy with the birthmark on his nose."

"I've got it covered. Bane is going to attend a meeting tomorrow night and try to figure out the man's name. Once we have that, we can talk to him and see what he knows about Jonah's death."

"What did you tell Bane?" He sounded cautious.

Was he worried she'd told Bane about Jesse's suspension? All her earlier doubts surged again. Could Jesse be involved more than she thought? She sipped her water and stared out over the blue ocean. The sun was beginning to set behind them, its rays gilding the craggy heights of Na Pali with glitter.

Jesse leaned forward and started the engine. He steered the boat out to sea a bit then began to troll back and forth in front of the base, just outside navy waters.

"You never told me what the base commander said."

"He thought my taking leave was a good idea."

Jesse didn't look at her, but she could sense the pain in his words. *"Aloha nô,"* she said, expressing her sympathy the best way she knew how. She wanted to touch him but wondered if it would be too forward. Her brothers hated being pitied.

"Mahalo," he said.

She sensed he'd like to be alone. "I think I'll fix some dinner," she said. She went below to the galley. Kaia prepared a quick meal of fish and fruit salad, tossing in papaya, coconut, banana, mango, and strawberries. They polished off the food, then Jesse tucked Heidi into bed while Kaia and Bane cleaned up the galley.

"I like your Jesse more and more," Bane remarked as he put the plates away.

"He's not *my* Jesse," she said.

"He'd like to be. I think you'd like it too."

Bane's voice was amused, but Kaia wasn't. She could only hope and pray Jesse couldn't hear from in the bedroom. She quickly changed the subject. "You've been quiet all evening. What's that all about?"

"I've had a lot to think about lately."

"Like what? You're not questioning your profession, are you?"

"Oh no, not at all. I love oceanography. I can't wait to get back to it." He hesitated and glanced at her from the corner of his eye.

She hung up her dish towel and frowned. "Then spill it. What's up?"

"Nothing much. I've been thinking about what our grandfather said last week. We've been too busy to get back together and discuss it, but I think we should find our mother."

"He aha ke àno? I don't want to talk about it." She grabbed two containers of yogurt and flounced up the ladder. If he was going to talk nonsense, she'd go talk to Nani. She wondered if she'd brought her toothbrush. Had she left it on the sink at home?

Bane followed her. "We're going to have to deal with this sooner or later, Kaia."

"Then make it later," she retorted. "I told you I have no interest in finding her. Let her come looking for us."

"If she did, how would you feel?"

"I still wouldn't want to see her."

"Then you're the one with the problem. You need to forgive her and put it behind you. Maybe you can't do that until you see her face-to-face."

"I can't do that *ever*. I don't see why you keep bringing her up. She doesn't love us, Bane. She left three kids without a backward glance. For all she knows, *Tûtû kâne* died and left us to the welfare system. She never cared about us, so why should we care about her?"

"We don't really know anything about it. Maybe she watched us from a distance all these years."

"You're dreaming, Bane. And you know better. If she cared, we would have at least gotten a postcard, a birthday card, something. But there has been nothing for almost twenty-five *years*. Years, not months or days. What kind of woman would do that? Not one I want to know." Or could ever trust. Her throat ached.

"Well, I want to know her."

He set his jaw, and she recognized the stubbornness in it. "Fine, go find her. But don't bring her around me when you do." She wanted to burst into tears. She still remembered crying for her mother in a strange house with people who yelled at her all the time. By the time her grandfather had found her, she'd been a timid child who barely spoke.

Mano and Bane had escaped that part. And while she was glad they hadn't had to go through it, a part of her wished they had so they could understand how she felt. But they would never fully comprehend what their mother's desertion had done to her.

"You think you had it so bad," Bane said in a low voice. "Have you ever stopped to think how it felt to me and Mano to know that she loved you more? She took you."

Kaia's eyes widened. The thought had never crossed her mind. "That's not true, Bane. She left me with strangers. At least she made sure you were with our grandfather."

His dark eyes bored into hers. "That's the trouble with being a human on this earth. We can never fully enter into how another person feels."

She wished there was someplace she could go to escape this conversation. She was too cold and tired to go back in the water. It was going to be a long night.

Bane's hands touched her shoulders. "Just as you don't know what Mano and I went through, we don't know what she went through either," he said gently. "But you have an unforgiving spirit, Kaia."

"I don't." She batted his hands away.

Jesse's head poked up from the galley below. "Sounds like you two are having an argument."

"My sister has a hard head."

"I have the hard head? It's the other way around." She handed Jesse a container of yogurt.

He accepted it and pulled off the foil top then sat beside her. "What are you fighting about?"

"Bane is on a quest to find our mother." She inwardly winced at her shrill tone.

"You're impossible. I'm going below." Bane stood and disappeared below deck.

Kaia knew she should go after him and apologize, but she stayed put. He was the one who had brought it up.

"I take it you don't want him to look for your mother?"

"I have no interest in dredging up the past." She took the foil top from him and tossed it in the trash bag hanging from a hook beside her. "What about your family? Did you have a good relationship with your parents?"

Jesse shrugged. "Yeah, I still do."

"You grew up here, didn't you?" Kaia asked.

"Yep. My parents were church-plant missionaries. Me and my sisters always felt part of something big. My parents are in Indonesia now."

"Sounds wonderful." She heard the harsh tone in her voice.

"Your grandparents must have been kind."

"They were. But it's hard to live in a place that prizes family and know your own mother hated you so much that she left you at the mercy of strangers." A lump formed in her throat. She should be able to put the past behind her. Why couldn't she? It's not like her mother had the power to hurt her anymore.

Maybe Bane was right and she had an unforgiving spirit. She found it hard to overlook slights, and staring into Jesse's face, she realized she still blamed him for dragging her away from her research when she should be grateful for his help extricating Mano from his trouble.

Jesse squeezed her hand. "I'm sure your mom didn't hate you, Kaia. That would be impossible for anyone."

The air suddenly seemed more fragrant and silky. Kaia couldn't look at him. The earnest tenderness in his voice made her feel like a dolphin on land. "Tell me about your wife," she said.

The feel of the air changed. She could sense Jesse's withdrawal.

"What do you want to know?"

"How did you meet?"

He sighed and rubbed his head. "You sure you want to hear this?"

She nodded. "Go ahead. Maybe it will help to talk about it."

"It was a typical girl-next-door thing. She lived right here on Kaua'i. She was best friends with my sister Jillian. I fell for her the first day I saw her and we were married fifteen years later. I thought I knew her. I didn't."

"You sound a little bitter."

"Maybe I am. Killing your wife will do that to a man." His gaze never left her face as he said the words.

"If you're trying to shock me, you'll have to do a better job than that. Heidi already told me she died, and you think it's your fault." His rueful grimace stopped the rest of her words.

"It was my fault. We were arguing and I looked away from the road. I missed a curve. I lived. She died carrying my son. I killed two people that day."

"It was an accident."

"It didn't make them less dead."

"You need to forgive yourself."

"Actually, I have, but it doesn't make what I did any less wrong."

Kaia had had all she could take. She rose. "I think I'll let you take the first watch and try to catch a little nap."

NINETEEN

I t didn't work. Jesse Matthews just took leave and is patrolling the water on his own time with the dolphin lady. If anything, they'll be more of a nuisance."

The man looked up from the papers on his desk. "He can't be allowed to stop our strike. Not now. We're too close." He tapped his teeth with the pencil he held in his hand. He needed leverage. His thoughts lingered on the kid. He couldn't do that, could he? He sifted through the emotions clouding his thoughts: regret, pity, hatred. His hate was strongest. Just like a butterfly had to fight to emerge from its cocoon, so he had to struggle through emotions that would paralyze a weaker man.

He glanced up and grabbed his can of Red Bull. "We might need a hostage to keep him in line. I hadn't thought to do this yet, but maybe it's time. Get his niece."

His assistant nodded and left. Best not to think about it. Just do it.

JESSE'S EYELIDS WERE HEAVY. HE FOUGHT TO STAY AWAKE. Glancing at the luminous dial on his watch, he realized he should awaken Bane or Kaia and let one of them take over. It was nearly 2 a.m. and they'd both been sleeping over four hours.

He knew Kaia needed her sleep. If he could just stay awake, he'd let her sleep the whole night through. Maybe Bane could take over for an hour or so.

But it was so pleasant to sit here and watch the moon on the water. The sound of the surf was soothing as it ran toward shore like a playful sea lion. He'd get one of them to relieve him soon. But not yet. His eyes did a slow blink. He'd close his eyes for just a minute.

The boat would troll along at this slow speed for a long time before it ran aground on the rocky shore. Jesse closed his eyes.

He awoke with a start and sat up. He dug his nails into his hand, and the pain sharpened his senses. He glanced around to get his bearings and realized he couldn't have slept more than fifteen minutes. What had awakened him?

He listened, but all he heard was the throb of the engines and sound of waves against rock and sand. Then the noise that had been out of kilter came again. A soft thump. It came from below. Maybe one of the others had awakened.

But it didn't feel right. The sound was stealthy, but he told himself it was because whoever it was didn't want to wake up the rest of the sleeping passengers. He listened, but the noise didn't come again. His gaze swept the horizon, then he frowned and squinted. Was that a small boat moored about twenty-five feet away?

He grabbed the night goggles beside him and adjusted them to his eyes. The boat sprang into focus. A man sat hunched in the bow of the boat. He seemed to be looking right back at Jesse. That couldn't be good.

He put down the goggles and started to rise when something came crashing down on the back of his head. Falling heavily forward, his face smashed into the steering wheel. Warm blood gushed from his nose, and the coppery taste filled his mouth. Splatters of blood sprayed the dash in front of him. He reached out and grabbed the goggles again, using them as a shield against his bigger, heavier attacker.

He grappled with the man in the darkness before being struck again. Heidi and Kaia were sleeping below deck, he thought. He had to save them. He vainly tried to force back the darkness that rolled over him like a crashing breaker.

KAIA AWAKENED IN THE DARKNESS. SHE ROLLED OVER AND glanced at the dim glow of the alarm clock. Jesse should have come to get her by now. He was going to get a piece of her mind. Reaching out her hand, she felt for Heidi's warm presence but felt nothing but empty bed. She raised her head and saw a dark shadow pass by the door. The moonlight illuminated the room enough to see that it was a man. Not Bane or Jesse though. The guy was too bulky.

He was carrying Heidi up the galley ladder.

Galvanized into action, Kaia sprang from the bed. "You there. Put her down!" She ran forward, tripping over her slippers lying on the floor. "Bane, Jesse, stop him!" The cry was hard to force out of her tight throat.

Heidi murmured, and Kaia felt a sense of rising horror at the scent of chloroform that drifted toward her. The man had drugged the little girl.

The boat tilted in the waves, and Kaia staggered, nearly falling. She righted herself and barreled through the doorway. She threw herself onto the intruder's back. He thrust an elbow into her stomach and tossed her aside like an empty clam shell. She went down hard.

"Bane, help me!" she screamed. She could see her brother's sleeping form on the bed. He rolled over, his mouth open. He'd been drugged too.

She had no idea why the man had left her alert. Maybe he'd thought she would be no match for his strength even if she awakened. Was Jesse unconscious as well? It might be up to her to save Heidi.

Kaia sprang to her feet and looked around for a weapon. The man's bare feet were about to disappear onto the deck above her head. Nani chattered in obvious agitation. Kaia grabbed an iron skillet hanging from a hook and charged up the ladder. Shrieking like a myna, she jumped up the last rung and onto the deck.

The man was at the railing. She raised the skillet over her head and charged again, bringing the skillet down with a loud clang onto the man's head.

He uttered a small sigh then toppled overboard with Heidi.

"Heidi!" Kaia dove over the side. She came up, flinging water from her eyes. Where was Heidi? Then she saw the little girl floating face-down in the water.

The dolphin surfaced beside her and got to Heidi before Kaia could. She came up under the little girl and bore her on her back to Kaia. Kaia reached out and pulled Heidi to her, flipping her over as she did. Was she breathing?

She couldn't tell, and she couldn't tend to her in the water. Pulling the little girl behind her in a lifesaver's hold, she got to the ladder. Holding Heidi against her, she tried to climb the ladder, but the weight was too much for her.

"Help me, God!" she cried out. Panting and sobbing, she tried again, this time balancing Heidi on one shoulder. She got her foot in the first rung of the ladder and heaved straight up.

Heidi began to slip, but Kaia grabbed her with her right hand while using her left to continue pulling them up the ladder. She finally lay gasping next to Heidi on the deck.

She glanced toward the radio. There was no time to call for help. She rolled Heidi to her stomach and grabbed a coil of rope to put under her stomach for pressure. Pressing on the little girl's back, she forced water out of her mouth then laid her on her back. What was the protocol for CPR for a child? For a moment she couldn't think. Then her training came flooding back. One full breath, five compressions. She leaned over Heidi and breathed into her mouth then began the compressions. She prayed while she went through the routine. *Please, Lord, let her live.*

It seemed an eternity before the little girl sputtered and coughed. She vomited seawater onto the deck, but she was breathing.

Kaia ran her hand over the water beading Heidi's forehead. "Heidi, can you open your eyes?"

Moonlight and dim decking light illuminated Heidi's face. Her lashes fluttered, then she opened her eyes. "Kaia?" she asked in a weak voice. "What happened?"

"I'm not quite sure," she said. "You fell overboard." Heidi didn't need to know the whole story unless Jesse okayed it. The little girl might suffer nightmares from the ordeal. Kaia prayed Heidi wouldn't remember it.

"Oh."

She managed a smile and pressed her palms against Heidi's cheeks. "Nani brought you to me on her back. It was something to see." She helped Heidi sit up.

Heidi coughed. "I don't feel so good."

"I'm not surprised. Why don't you just lie down here for a minute?" Kaia snatched a dry towel from the chair and snugged it around Heidi. "Better?"

Heidi nodded, her small face pinched and white. "I'll be warm in a minute." Her eyes closed.

Kaia left her there and went to check on Jesse. Along the way, she glanced overboard but didn't see the man she'd hit with the skillet. In the distance, she heard a motor and saw a small craft speeding away from her boat. The guy must have survived the incident.

She hurried to the helm and found Jesse on the floor in the dim light in the room. She choked back a shriek when she saw the blood pooled around his head. Sinking to her knees, she rolled him over. His eyes were closed, and blood matted his hair.

She touched his face. "Jesse, can you hear me?" There was a first-aid kit in the compartment to the right of where she crouched, but she didn't want to leave him to get it.

He didn't respond. Panic flared in her chest. She had to leave him for a minute. She crawled to the compartment and pulled out the first-aid kit. Opening it, she found an ampule of smelling salts. With the kit in her hand, she went back to Jesse, broke the ampule, and waved it under his nose. The acrid smell stung her nose and made her eyes water.

Jesse gasped and his head lolled from side to side trying to escape the odor. "Smells like your cat," he muttered weakly. His eyes opened more fully then watered from the stinging fumes of the smelling salts. He struggled to sit up.

"Lie still; you're hurt," she ordered. She dug in the kit again and pulled out a pad and alcohol.

"Ouch!" He pushed her hand away. "That hurts."

"Don't be such a baby," she told him. She dabbed at the cut. It wasn't as nasty as she'd feared. Head wounds bled so badly. She put a butterfly bandage on the cut. That would have to do until she could get him below deck and get the blood washed out of his hair.

His eyes snapped open in a more alert way. "Heidi!" He pulled out of Kaia's arms and sat up.

"She's okay. Some guy was hauling her off though." She told him about the chloroform and how she'd beaned the man with the frying pan.

"This is all my fault. I fell asleep." His shoulders slumped. "I failed her too."

She stood and helped him up. "We didn't fail. Heidi is sleeping on the deck." She led him to where his niece lay under the towel.

They watched the rise and fall of her chest. "You're sure she's okay?" he asked.

Kaia nodded. "I need to try to get Bane awake. He was drugged too." She knelt and scooped Heidi into her arms.

"I'll take her," Jesse said. He staggered as he lurched forward with his arms outstretched.

"You're too weak. Go first down the ladder, and I'll hand her to you."

She could see the protest in his eyes, but he shrugged then did as she suggested. Kaia dropped Heidi into his waiting arms then went down the ladder into the galley. "I'll be down to put dry pajamas on her," she called after him.

He nodded, and she went to try to rouse her brother. He didn't move when she shook him, though she could see his chest move up and down. He might have to sleep it off. She tried again, but Bane was like a dead weight in the bed. She could try the smelling salts, but maybe it would be better to let him sleep.

Jesse came back into the galley. He looked terrible with the blood black and caked in his blond hair. Like a Frankenstein monster. "She woke up enough to say she could change into dry pajamas."

Kaia nodded. "Let me wash that out of your hair," she said. "I want to see your wounds in the light."

"My head is throbbing like this engine at full bore," he admitted. He went to the nearest chair and sank into it. Dark circles cupped his eyes, and he was pasty under his tan.

Kaia got out some Tylenol and gave it to him with water. He downed it and closed his eyes while she probed his hair.

"You've got another cut back here," she said.

"He clocked me with something from behind," he murmured, his eyes still closed.

"I wonder why he didn't drug you?"

"I think he was going to, but I woke up before he had the chance."

Kaia cleaned the cuts she could see. She got a cloth and washed as much of the blood from his hair as she could without dunking him in the sink.

"That will have to do for now." She stepped back and regarded him critically. "You're getting a little more color to your face."

"Your torture would make anyone red-faced," he said. He opened his eyes and grinned.

Kaia found herself smiling back. Before she could react, he had pulled her down onto his lap. The shock held her still.

He put his arms around her waist and leaned his head against her neck. "Um, you smell better than chloroform any day, my little mermaid."

She smiled and smoothed his stiff hair. He must be concussed. "You'd better not go to sleep until we get you checked out by the doctor."

"I'm fine, Kaia. Even my headache is getting better."

He sounded better. Stronger and more like himself. But he was still holding her, and she was still liking it. She moved to free herself, and he immediately released her. She wasn't sure what to say.

"I'm not a shark," he said, his grin forming like a wave. "I won't bite. Well, except for maybe a nibble."

"Maybe a killer whale?" she suggested.

"Nope. Not even a beluga. I'm your plain, ordinary, garden-variety tang. Yellow and all." He rubbed his blond head. "I'm totally harmless."

"I'm not so sure about that." Not if her racing pulse was any indication. She felt like she'd just swum across the ocean to Ni`ihau.

"You're way more dangerous than me," he said. His gaze lingered on her face then sank to her lips.

If he kept looking at her like that, she'd be back in his lap in no time. She backed away. "I should go clean up the blood on deck. You need to call someone to tell them about this kidnapping attempt."

His smile faded. "You're right. I get way too distracted by you." His smile surged back. "But it's a welcome distraction."

Even more flustered, she grabbed some paper towels and went to the ladder.

"Don't clean that up yet," he called after her. "We might need some evidence."

She rushed up the steps to get away from him. In school and later in college, she'd never had much time for guys. Her work was too important to risk messing up her plans for a man. Now she found herself questioning that decision.

Jesse was hard-headed and opinionated, but gentle with his niece and his family and a rock in times of trouble. She found herself leaning on him and didn't like that dependency.

He followed her up the ladder and examined the pool of red on the deck. "I bled enough to have been the lu'au pig," he said.

He grabbed the ship-to-shore radio and called in the attack to the Coast Guard.

"I thought you might call it in to the captain," she said.

"I thought about it. But I think our patrol out here is going to yield more results than trolling navy waters. Better to leave things alone with the navy for now."

"Captain Lawton may hear of the attack anyway."

"He might," Jesse agreed. "If he does, I'll explain it to him then. In the meantime, we have to figure out what's going on with Heidi."

"Could her father be trying to get her?"

"All he'd have to do is show up at the door and ask to see her. I wouldn't deny him visitation rights. He wouldn't drug everyone and try to open my skull. Me and Noah have always gotten along pretty well."

"Maybe he wants her all to himself. You hear about fathers stealing kids."

"I don't think Noah would do that. He loves her too much."

"So much he left her and hasn't called." Kaia couldn't keep the asperity from her voice. Maybe their similar histories were what made her feel such a connection to the *keiki*.

Jesse shook his head. "I just don't think it's Noah."

"Then who would want her?" Kaia was almost afraid to ask.

"The fact that I have no idea scares me spitless."

TWENTY

A misty curtain of rain hung over the ocean, giving it a soft, dreamy look. But the man was in no mood to appreciate the beauty. "You nitwits! I give you a perfectly simple assignment and you blow it. How hard can it be to snatch an eight-year-old?"

"We had her. But that dolphin woman was too quick. She woke up before I had time to drug her. When she saw me with the kid, she came after me with a frying pan." The younger man rubbed his head where a massive swelling had parted his hair.

"And it didn't occur to you to *both* go aboard?"

"We wanted the boat ready to get out of there in a hurry."

"There would have been no need for hurry if you'd drugged them all!" There was no use in talking to them. They were as dumb as a piece of coral. He took a deep breath. There was still time. The test would be in two days. Even if they snatched the kid hours before the test, it would work out.

Maybe there was some other way. He still hated to involve the kid. He looked down at his hands. No, it had to be this way. And he'd enjoy watching Matthews squirm on a hook he couldn't get off of. The man gave a grim smile then looked back at his men. "You'd better not screw up again," he barked. "I've got too much riding on this now."

FAYE PACED THE FLOOR IN THE LIVING ROOM. SHE'D MADE THE first step in healing the breach with her family. Her son hadn't thrown her off the property. She'd expected hostility, but he had been open enough to talk to her. Until he'd run away. But she still had hopes Bane would come around. She knew meeting him had been the first and easiest step in an uphill climb as steep as Na Pali.

Her euphoria faded, and she felt tired. A dull headache began to gather at the base of her skull, and she pressed on it. Curtis was reading the morning paper, and Heidi should be here any minute so Jesse could get a little rest. It was going to be hard to keep her attention on the little girl when she wanted to go back to the cottage by the sea.

Curtis put down his paper. "Why so glum, sweetheart? I would have thought you'd be floating on air this morning." He patted his lap.

Faye tried to smile as she went to perch on her husband's knees. "I don't think it's going to be so easy with the rest. Especially my father. He's going to be so angry with me." She blinked rapidly to keep the tears from rolling.

"I think you're going to be pleasantly surprised how well it goes. The prodigal daughter's return is probably something that he's dreamed of and prayed about for years. Remember what Kaia told you about him wanting to find you?"

"You're more optimistic than me. My father was never that way. I couldn't do anything right while I was growing up. I don't expect that to change now." Faye leaned over and kissed him. "You'd better get going. You'll be late."

"I'm not too eager to get in today." He frowned and picked up his coffee cup.

"What's wrong?"

"Two more investors bailed on me yesterday. Our funds have dwindled to practically nothing. I never would have gone into this if I'd realized it would be such a drain on our resources."

"Are we going to be okay?" Her muscles stiffened. Faye had worried about money all her life until she married Curtis a year ago. She wasn't eager to be living on a shoestring again.

"Don't worry; we'll be fine. But I'm not going to continue to let Seaworthy lose money. If I can't come up with a way to make it a viable business, I'll sell off the assets."

"The equipment?"

"And the animals."

Faye frowned. "The dolphins are wild, aren't they?"

"Now you sound like Kaia. I bought those animals. All eight of them are listed as assets." He was sounding more annoyed by the minute.

"You can't sell Kaia's dolphins! You'll alienate her from me for good." The thought of it made Faye jump to her feet. Her movement spilled coffee down the front of Curtis's shirt.

"Ouch!" He held his shirt out from his skin.

"Oh, Curtis, I'm so sorry." Faye rushed to the kitchen and grabbed a towel. She soaked it in water and hurried back to her husband. He was already peeling off his shirt. "Let me take it. I'll get you a clean one."

"I'll get it. I need to get out of here." He hesitated then kissed her. "Don't worry about this, Faye. You keep your mind on meeting your family, and I'll take care of the business stuff. We might turn things around yet. I don't want to sell the dolphins, but I may have no choice."

"We could just take a loss," she pleaded. "I could get a job if I need to."

His gaze softened. "That won't be necessary, sweetheart. We'll be fine. It's the principle of the thing for me, I guess. I don't like to lose. I'll try to figure out something." He kissed her again then went down the hall to the bedroom.

Faye wrung her hands. Kaia would hate her if Curtis sold the dolphins. She took the empty coffee cups to the kitchen. The phone rang as she put the last dish in the dishwasher and turned it on.

She glanced at her watch. Heidi was late. "Latchet residence."

"Faye, it's Jesse. I'm not bringing Heidi today. I hope you don't mind."

"Oh no, that's fine. Is everything all right?" She thought his voice sounded strained.

"Someone tried to take Heidi last night." Faye gasped and put her hand to her mouth. "I'd better keep her close until we figure out what's going on."

"Oh, Jesse, that's terrifying! Is she all right?"

"She was fine once the chloroform wore off. I hope we're not messing up your day too badly."

"Not at all. I've got some errands to run. But how will you get any rest?"

"We'll all take turns guarding her. We'll be fine."

"Okay, well, give Heidi my love. Let me know if there's anything I can do."

"I will."

The phone clicked in her ear, and she put it down slowly. She wished she'd told Jesse she could come there to be with Heidi. Jesse was competent though, she reminded herself. No harm would come to Heidi while he was around.

She heard the garage door go up then saw Curtis drive his car onto the street. The day stretched ahead of her. She could spend it cleaning house or shopping, but she knew what she needed to do.

WHERE ARE WE GOING?" THE WIND TUGGED TENDRILS OF HAIR loose from Kaia's braid, and she pushed them out of her eyes as she turned in the seat of the Jeep to face Jesse.

Jesse tried not to watch her. He imagined that glorious hair flying in the wind. "My brother-in-law bought a security business. Remember when he mentioned it at church? He might be able to help us. I thought we'd get some motion detectors for the boat and maybe some security lights." Jesse turned the SUV into the parking lot of Prickett Security. He pulled into a spot near the door. "You'd both better come with me. I don't dare leave you alone."

"I think I did pretty well by myself last night," she reminded him. "I'm not some insipid female who faints at danger."

He grinned. "Sorry if that sounded chauvinistic. You were

amazing." He got out of the Jeep and flipped his seat forward to let out Heidi. He noticed Kaia's cheeks turn pink and hid a grin. Maybe she wasn't immune to him. He'd tried to ignore his attraction to her, but after last night, he realized there was something more between them, something he couldn't blame on the goose egg on his head.

Slamming her door behind her, she followed him into the first building. The complex consisted of four slump-block buildings painted an institutional gray and trimmed in navy.

A receptionist greeted them and went to tell Steve they would like to see him. Steve stepped out of his office. His shirt was rumpled and his eyes shaded with fatigue. His face brightened when he saw them though.

"Jesse, it's good to see you." Steve grabbed Jesse's hand and pumped it.

"Looks like you haven't been home all night," Jesse remarked after making small talk for a few minutes.

"I haven't," Steve said. "You know how a new business is. Let's go back to my office."

"Things that busy?" Jesse pointed out a chair to Kaia then dropped into the one closest to Steve's desk.

"It's crazy here. We're behind schedule, and my foreman quit, so I stayed to keep things on track." He went to a coffeepot on a caddy by the door. "Coffee? I've got Red Bull in the fridge too."

"Coffee's fine." Kaia and Jesse spoke together.

He poured them all coffee and asked the receptionist to bring Heidi some juice. "Now what can I do for you?"

Jesse told him what had happened. Steve's abstracted air turned to sharp focus as he listened.

"I've got just the system for you. I'll have it delivered this afternoon. Will you be at the boat?"

"We'll be there by six or so." Jesse sipped his coffee. He glanced at Kaia. She needed to get some rest. She looked ready to fall asleep in the chair. They were going to need someone to keep guard while they slept a few hours.

Walking back to the parking lot, he tried to think of who he could call.

"I see that look," Kaia said. "You're worrying."

"We need help. I'm all in and so are you. We won't be much good without some shut-eye."

"I've been thinking about that too. We could stay at *Tûtû kâne*'s cottage. No one will look for us there. I can call some cousins to hang around while we get some rest. Bane is there too."

"You think your grandfather wouldn't mind?'

Kaia laughed. "He'd relish the chance to smother me."

"Should we call him first?"

"No, we can just go over. But I need to call some of my cousins." She dug her cell phone out of her purse and made a couple of calls. "You mind if we stop for some cat food for Hiwa?"

"No problem." As he drove along Highway 50, Jesse's mind raced. They couldn't keep reacting to things. He needed to take charge and dig out the truth. Once they got some sleep, he would pay a visit to Nahele Aki and see if he could rattle him enough to make him admit he'd tried to take Heidi.

He didn't know what Pele Hawai'i would want with his niece though, especially since Jesse was no longer in charge of base security. They couldn't threaten her as a way to make him do anything. Nothing made any sense.

They stopped to get cat food for Hiwa then went on to Kaia's. As he stopped in front of Kaia's house, his cell phone rang. "Heidi and I will wait here," he told Kaia. He answered his phone. "Matthews."

"Jesse, what is going on?" Jillian's voice was agitated. "I called Faye and she told me someone tried to kidnap Heidi last night."

"I was going to call you."

"You should have called me last night! It was probably Noah."

"Jillian, you don't believe that."

"I don't know what I believe anymore." She took a ragged breath.

"Noah might be a lot of things, but he wouldn't put Heidi through an ordeal like last night. The thugs used chloroform. You know how Noah hates drugs."

His sister sounded near tears. "Is Heidi suffering any effects from it? Faye didn't say anything about chloroform."

"She's right as rain this morning." He glanced in the rearview mirror and watched the concentration on his niece's face as she played Mario. The beeps and noises from the GameBoy assured him she was back to her old self.

"I'd better get there," Jillian said. "I should have brought her with me. I wasn't thinking."

"I can't let you take her until we get to the bottom of this."

"You can't let me take her? She's my daughter, Jesse." Jillian's voice rose. "I'm coming home. I couldn't bear it if anything happened to Heidi."

"I know she's your daughter. Just calm down. You would have been no match for those men last night. Heidi needs to be protected. If you want to come here, fine, but don't expect to take Heidi until I'm sure she'll be safe. The men could follow you to whereever you are and just take her. We don't know why they wanted her. Until we do, we have to keep her safe."

"They wouldn't follow us to Italy," his sister insisted.

"They had obviously laid their plans well last night, sis. I think whoever is behind this is capable of anything." He told her about being relieved of his duties and the investigation.

"That's nuts, Jesse! The captain has to know your character."

"It was a shock," he admitted. "But it's for the best now. I can go about things my own way."

"I'm scared." Jillian's voice fell to a whisper. "What can I do?"

"I've got it under control, little sister. Try not to worry. Nothing will happen to her. We'll get the culprit soon."

"You've always been there for me, Jesse. For both me and Livia. School would have been impossible if you hadn't protected us."

"What doesn't kill you makes you stronger."

Jillian laughed. "You and your motto. I don't feel very strong right now."

"You're stronger than you realize. Some women would have gone into hiding after what Noah did." He could tell his sister was getting her spunk back.

"The wheels of justice grind exceedingly fine," Jillian said. "He'll get what's coming to him, and I wouldn't want to be in his shoes when he does."

"Have you heard from him?"

"There was a message from him on my answering machine. He just said to call him and left a number. I looked it up. He's in India."

"What's he doing there?"

"I don't know. I didn't call him."

"Are you going to?"

"And say what? If I have to listen to any of his excuses, I'll puke. What he did was unforgivable."

"I've always liked Noah. Maybe you should listen."

"You listen then," Jillian retorted. "I never want to hear his voice again." Her voice changed. "I'll book a flight tomorrow. I'll call and let you know when to come get me."

Jesse wished he could make everything right for Jillian. Once he figured out what was happening here, maybe he'd go looking for Noah.

TWENTY-ONE

Faye wiped sweaty palms on her shorts. All she had to do was lift her hand and knock on the door, but her limbs felt frozen. The safety of her car was right behind her. She could rush back there or go forward. The way her heart was throbbing out of her chest, she wasn't sure she could even say anything to her dad.

God has not given us a spirit of fear but of love and a sound mind. She reminded herself of the verse that had gotten her this far. Though the preacher who'd prayed with her had assured her God had answered her prayers and was waiting to listen to her, she still felt inadequate and undeserving when she tried to pray. She didn't see how God could want to hear from anyone like her.

Steeling herself, she raised her hand and knocked on the door. Maybe he would be gone. Then she heard the sound of movement from inside.

"Coming," a man's voice said.

The familiarity of those gruff tones sapped the strength from her knees, and she nearly crumpled on the porch. Her smile felt frozen in place.

The door swung open, and the familiar scent of cloves greeted her. Otherwise, she almost didn't recognize the man standing there. His thick black hair was now as white as the oyster shells he used to dive for, and his muscles had thinned. He looked almost gaunt compared to her mind's picture of the vibrant man of fifty-three she'd last seen. Twenty-five years had passed since then. He was seventy-eight now, though he still held himself erect.

"May I help you?" her father asked. His sharp eyes settled on her face. He gave a start, and a tiny frown crouched between his eyes. His gaze swept her figure, then he blinked rapidly as though to clear his vision. He leaned against the doorjamb. "Paie?" His voice trembled as he called her by her Hawaiian name.

"Yes, *Makuakane*, I have come home." The screen door still separated them. Faye wanted to fling it open and throw herself into her father's arms.

As if he felt the longing in her heart, he pushed open the screen door and stepped onto the porch. "You've come home." He lifted his hand then dropped it as if he didn't know if she'd welcome his touch.

Faye was sobbing in earnest now. "I'm so sorry, *Makuakane*. I hurt you so much. You and the children." She burrowed into his arms, pressing her face to his cotton shirt and inhaling his spicy scent.

His hand finally came up, and he smoothed her hair. His touch felt alien to her. He'd never been one for hugs and kisses like her mother. She could feel his chest heaving and thought he might be crying as well. Peeking up into his face, she saw tears trickling down the furrows in his cheeks. His hands gripped her shoulders, and he ended their embrace. "Come inside, Paie. I want to hear everything."

She followed him inside and glanced around the living room. The sights and scents of her home swept over her like a rogue wave and nearly threw her onto the rocky shores of unendurable remorse. She closed her eyes and swayed on unsteady legs.

"Sit."

Her father pointed to her favorite chair, a wooden rocker he had made when Faye was a child. Her mother had always used that chair, and Faye had often sat on the floor and leaned her head against her mother's knees. "I didn't know about *Makuahine* until I came back to the island. I wish I could have asked her to forgive me."

Her father was silent. "She always longed for you."

Faye's throat closed. "I brought you both so much pain."

"Perhaps. But I've learned from it. Where there is great joy there is always great pain as well. They are two sides of the same shell."

"I'm afraid you experienced more tears than laughter with me," she said.

His head bowed. "You are here now."

"Do you forgive me, *Makuakane*?" she whispered.

He looked up, and his dark eyes pierced her soul. "I worked through that long ago. I forgive you, Paie, but you have amends to make with the children."

"I know." She hesitated. "I saw Bane yesterday."

"Ah. And Mano and Kaia?"

"Kaia knows me but not who I am. I've been watching Heidi, her friend's niece."

His eyes widened. "You are the Faye I've heard so much about?"

"When she learns I am her mother, I don't know how she will react."

Her father's gaze went to the window. "Perhaps you are about to find out." He nodded toward the vehicle pulling in front of the house. "Unless I'm mistaken, there is Kaia with Jesse."

KAIA FELT CLUMSY AND AWKWARD AS SHE LET HEIDI OUT OF THE backseat. "I forgot to take the cat food in," she said when she saw the cans still in the back of the Jeep. It was no wonder. She was so tired it was hard to make her hand obey her brain. She knew Jesse felt the same way. The thought of the soft bed she'd slept in every night of her young life was as tempting as a rainbow shave ice.

"Looks like your grandfather has company." Jesse nodded toward the Volvo convertible.

"Faye's here! Yay!" Heidi shouted.

Faye? Kaia was almost too tired to wonder what the older woman was doing here. Maybe Jesse had told her to meet them. Kaia was in no mood to socialize, though they'd bonded. That afternoon seemed very far away now, however, and the thought of smiling and making small talk was overwhelming when all she wanted to do was creep under the quilt her grandmother had made.

Heidi rushed inside the house without knocking. Kaia smiled at how the little girl had become part of the family.

"I'll get your bag," Jesse said. His steps were slow as he reached in the back and grabbed Kaia's suitcase.

"Mahalo." She waited for him then led the way up the flagstone path to the cottage. How many times had she walked this yard? Thousands. Being here was like entering a cocoon where nothing could hurt her.

She poked her head in the door. *"Tûtû kâne?* We've come to throw ourselves on your mercy. We need a place to crash." She forced a smile when she looked at Faye. "Couldn't stay away, huh? I'll admit Heidi is a *keiki* who is hard to resist."

Faye had risen from her chair and was clasping her hands together as though they might keep her from toppling over. Her mouth trembled in her white face. Red rimmed her eyes.

Heidi went to her and took her hand. "Are you sad, Faye?"

"I'm fine," Faye said. "Would you like to fix us both a cup of tea?"

"By myself?"

"You can use the microwave like a big girl, can't you?"

"Sure." Heidi gave her a puzzled look then disappeared down the hall.

The pleading expression on Faye's face puzzled Kaia. Kaia's gaze traveled to her grandfather. His face was wet, and he looked strange—almost *exalted,* though that made no sense. "What's wrong?" she asked. She felt pummeled by the problems of these past weeks and wasn't sure if she could handle anything more.

No one answered her for a long moment. Faye glanced at Kaia's grandfather, and he nodded his head.

Faye wet her lips. The expression on her face could only be described as beseeching, Kaia thought. Unease stirred in her gut. She glanced at Jesse, and he raised his eyebrows and shrugged.

Kaia looked back at Faye. "Isn't anyone going to speak?"

"I—I have something to tell you," Faye said. Her face grew red, and she looked as though she might burst into tears again.

Kaia froze. "Did Curtis sell the dolphins?" Her voice rose. She hadn't seen Nani all morning.

Faye raised her hand. "No, no, nothing like that. The dolphins are fine." She bit her bottom lip and looked down at the wood floor then back up at Kaia again. "Sit down. Please."

Kaia advanced into the room, and Jesse followed. She perched on the edge of the sofa and folded her hands in her lap. "I'm sitting. Now tell me what's wrong. You're scaring me."

"I'm sorry." Faye wrung her hands. "I think I told you I lived here when I was younger?"

Kaia nodded.

"I want to tell you a story," Faye said. She drew in a deep breath then sank back into the chair and leaned forward. "I had an idyllic life here. I grew up along the edge of the sea with loving parents who spoiled me rotten. I thought the world was mine for the asking." She wet her lips. "When I met a handsome man who adored me like my parents had done, I was sure nothing could ever bring me pain or heartache." She looked down at the floor. "I was wrong."

"You're divorced now?" Kaia had seen the pain divorce had brought to her friends. At least she'd never been torn between two parents.

"Several times. But I was widowed before any of that. I couldn't cope, couldn't face life without him. Everywhere I looked was a painful reminder of all I'd lost. When I met a wealthy businessman who promised me the moon, I took it. The fact that he was a slack key guitarist was just icing on the cake. He'd had an offer to make a record in Nashville, so I left with him. I always thought I'd only be gone a little while. I took my daughter with me."

Unease stirred. This story sounded a little like her own.

"One wrong step and we can go down a path that takes us far-

ther and farther from what's right, from where we intended to go."
Tears rolled down Faye's cheeks. "I was lonesome and found solace
in the drugs Richard brought home. Within a couple of months, I
knew I couldn't come home. I was too ashamed. Everything went
downhill from there. Richard left me. I had no money and a drug
habit that was eating me alive. I left my daughter with friends and
went to a clinic to dry out. It didn't work. I was back on the streets
within two months of getting out."

A tightness began to squeeze Kaia's chest. "What about your
daughter?" she whispered.

"She was raised by loving grandparents. I knew she was fine,
but I wasn't. My next marriage lasted ten years, but neither of us
was ever really happy. I was searching for the paradise I'd lost, but I
never found it."

Kaia couldn't speak.

Faye sent Kaia a beseeching look. "What really made the change
was finding Jesus. I felt clean and new again. Happy for the first time
in years." She took a deep breath. "Except for one thing. I knew I
had to try to make right the wrong I'd done here."

Kaia couldn't move, couldn't breathe. She didn't want to hear
this. She shut her eyes, but the other woman's voice continued
inexorably.

"It's you I wronged, Kaia. You and Bane and Mano."

Kaia opened her eyes again and stared at the woman she knew
and yet didn't know.

Faye glanced at Kaia's grandfather. "And *Makuakane*. I wronged
him terribly, as well as *Makuahine*."

Father and Mother. Kaia felt frozen in time with each minute
moving by like a sea turtle on land. Her gaze went to her grandfather. She didn't want to believe it.

He nodded. "Faye is your mother. Paie."

Faye in the Hawaiian language was *Paie*. Why had she never
thought about that? Kaia knew Faye had grown up here yet had

never questioned her name. She couldn't breathe, couldn't think. Her brain felt like poi.

Jesse reached over and took her hand. His strong fingers gripping hers gave her the comfort she needed. She clung to his hand with all the desperation she felt. Her gaze went back to Faye. In the pictures she'd seen of her mother, Paie was wearing Hawaiian attire, and she looked very different in her perfectly tailored linen shorts and beige top, so unlike the colorful clothing in the pictures. But focusing on Paie's face, she saw some of her own features staring back at her.

"Why have none of your friends recognized you?" she asked. She almost didn't know her own voice. It was hoarse and strained.

"I've pretty much kept to the house except on outings with Heidi. I tried not to go places where I might run into old friends."

Faye held out her arms. Kaia knew she should be feeling something—anger, joy, something. But she felt only cold and empty. Mechanically, she rose and went into Faye's arms. But the touch of her arms made her feel even colder.

She pulled away quickly. "Why are you here?"

"I want you to forgive me, Kaia. I'm so sorry for leaving you and your brothers. I can't make any excuses because there are none. I was blind and willful."

"Forgive you?" Kaia turned the words over in her mind.

"Yes, I want to make it up to you. Can we be friends first and maybe feel our way to a deeper relationship?"

Friends. Her *mother* wanted to be friends with her. The pain was more than she could bear. She wanted a mother to love her, not a friend. "You walk out and leave us orphaned and then expect to just pick up twenty-five years later like you'd just taken a little walk?" She stood and clenched her hands together. "My real mother was my *tûtû*. She was there to teach me to braid my hair. She was there the day I learned to swim, when my first tooth fell out, when I had my first date. How dare you come back now and want to be my *friend!*"

The betrayal gathered and built until she felt she would burst from the pressure. She whirled and faced her grandfather. "How long have you known about this?" she demanded.

"She came to me just minutes before you arrived," her grandfather said, his tone slow and measured. "Sit down, *keiki*. Think; reason this out. Your mother is asking for nothing more than for you to put the past away and make a new future."

"It's more than I can do." Kaia stared at her mother. Faye—Paie—or whatever she wanted to be called—looked pale. Kaia hardened her heart.

"Please, Kaia. I'm so sorry," her mother whispered. She rose and came toward Kaia.

Kaia took a step back as her mother reached out to touch her again. She put her hands up to her face. "Leave me alone. I can't think." She looked down at Jesse. "Can we get out of here?"

"Sure." He stood, and his eyes were filled with sympathy.

Kaia looked back to her mother. "You've talked to Bane, haven't you? That's why he was trying to tell me it was time to look for you."

"Yes," Faye admitted.

"I suppose he welcomed you with open arms." Kaia's lips twisted. She could imagine Bane's response.

If her mother thought she was going to be welcomed with a fatted calf like the prodigal son, she was mistaken. The most Kaia could summon right now was a mess of pottage.

TWENTY-TWO

Kaia ran toward the ocean. She heard Jesse shout her name, but the waves beckoned her, and she could see Nani zipping through the water to greet her. As she ran, she shucked her shorts, tank top, and slippers off until she wore only her swimsuit. The warm sand grated against the soles of her feet.

She reached the edge of the water and waded in. When the water was to her knees, she dove into the next white-crested wave. The warm water welcomed her in a loving, unconditional embrace. Nani bumped against her, and Kaia reached out and grabbed the dolphin's nostrum. She closed her eyes and listened to the song of the sea whisper to her aching heart.

She'd always imagined what it would be like if her mother came back. In her dreams, she was able to coldly tell her mother she had no desire to see her. There was no pain in her dream, no wrenching agony of being torn between love and hate, betrayal and loyalty.

She put her feet down on the bedrock of lava and sand and stood. "God, be my foundation right now. I can't stand this by myself," she whispered. Nani nudged her knee, and she leaned down and ran her hand over the warm inner tube of dolphin skin. Nani rolled to one side and one eye stared up at Kaia as if to ask if she could help.

Kaia sank into the water and let the waves lap around her neck. Her knees scraped bottom, and she steadied herself then put both arms around Nani. The tears she'd managed to hold back began to mingle with the salt water on her cheeks. The little girl in her wanted to run back into the house and feel her mother's arms around her. She'd lacked that all her life. Why would she want it when she'd always had the love of her grandparents though? That should have been enough.

She had dim memories of her mother. A faint fragrance of blossoms, a tinkling laugh, soft hands. Maybe that's where these longings came from. Faye was very different from the image Kaia had of her mother. She remembered a ready smile and loving arms before her mother left. Faye was nervous and uncertain, not at all the confident, laughing mother.

But people change. Was her mother really as sorry as she claimed, or was it all a ploy? *Tûtû kâne* was getting older. Could Faye have come back to make sure she inherited the family property? Kaia wouldn't put it past her. She had proven herself capable of anything.

She stayed in the water until her fingers turned to prunes. She could see Jesse sitting patiently on a piece of driftwood on the beach. Her cat, Hiwa, was at his feet. Giving Nani a final pat, she rose from the water and walked toward him. He stood as she came out of the water and handed her the shorts and top she'd discarded.

"*Mahalo.*" She pulled on her clothing and picked up her slippers. "Sorry I ran out like that."

"I understand."

His tone surprised her. "How would you know? You grew up with both parents. They're still alive."

"I understand that forgiving myself was harder than forgiving someone else. I had to face what I'd done to Christy and my son and let go of it."

"I can't."

"I know. You're afraid."

Her eyes widened. He'd put his finger on it exactly. "I didn't realize it until you said it, but I *am* scared. Scared I'll let my guard down and learn to love her and she'll betray me all over again."

He nodded. "She's going to have to earn your trust."

"I don't think she can." Kaia started toward the house. "It will take more than a pretty smile and a casual 'I'm sorry' to make me believe her."

"Try," he suggested.

"I'll think about it," was all she could say.

Jesse didn't bring up Faye to Kaia again. He figured if she wanted to talk about it, he'd listen, but there was nothing he hated worse than someone badgering him. Kaia surely felt the same. Faye was gone when they went back to the house, and Oke said nothing as Kaia stalked through the living room and down the hall toward the bedroom wing.

Oke shook his head sadly and went to the kitchen. Jesse crashed on the couch. After four hours of sleep, his cell phone awakened him. It was Jillian, who told him her flight was getting in tomorrow. Yawning, he promised to pick her up then stood and went to find Kaia. They needed to get moving. The danger facing them hadn't diminished just because Kaia had personal problems.

Bane was in the living room talking in soft tones to his grandfather. Jesse glanced around but didn't see Kaia or Heidi.

Oke saw him. "If you're looking for your niece and my granddaughter, they are out working with Nani."

"Alone?"

"Mano is with them," Bane said.

That wasn't much comfort. Mano was still under suspicion, and while Jesse didn't think he'd harm his own sister, he wouldn't put it past the man to allow Heidi to be taken.

He strode past the other men and looked out the window. He could see three heads in the waves, and the sound of Heidi's laughter floated to him on the wind.

"They are fine," Oke said. "No need to worry. Mano will guard them with his life."

Jesse turned back to the other men. Maybe it was time for a heart-to-heart talk.

"How much do you know of what your grandson has been up to lately?" he asked Oke.

"I believe in my grandson," Oke said. "I doubt there is anything you could say to shake that faith."

Jesse winced. He wished he'd had someone who trusted him like that. It was a shame he was going to have to shatter that confidence.

"Mano has been attending meetings at Pele Hawai´i. He seems to have become a zealot for their cause."

Oke's white head bowed. "He's young and impetuous. He'll soon see past their rhetoric."

"I'm afraid it's gone beyond rhetoric. I believe the agency is behind the deaths and security breaches at the base, and I'm positive the men who tried to kidnap Heidi last night were Pele Hawai'i flunkies."

"You're saying you believe Mano is part of this conspiracy?" A slight smile touched Oke's lips. "You don't know my grandson. He has a strong streak of justice and compassion for those in need. He would never harm a child."

"He might not have known about this particular ploy," Jesse admitted. "But he's deeper into this conspiracy than I think you know."

"Let's ask him," Oke said. "My grandson has never lied to me." He rose and went toward the door.

Jesse sighed and stood. His gaze met Bane's. The other man shrugged. "I have to agree with my grandfather. I've been upset with Mano for getting involved with them, but he's no murderer."

Jesse hoped they were right. Confronted with his family's concern, maybe Mano would help them.

He trailed behind Oke and Bane down the path to the sea. The salty air brushed his face and lifted the fatigue that still dogged him.

Kaia was laughing as they played keep-away with a beach ball. Heidi and Nani were in the middle while Mano tossed the ball back and forth with Kaia. The dolphin jumped in the air and nosed the ball over to Heidi.

Jesse's gaze lingered on Kaia. Her face glistened with water, and her sleek black hair lay plastered to her back with the line of her face fully exposed to the golden sunshine. The curve of her cheeks and lips enhanced her dark eyes. He'd never seen anything more beautiful in his life. An ache he'd never felt tugged at him.

What he was beginning to feel for Kaia was different from the love he'd felt for Christy. Christy's love had been gentle and comfortable. This was as wild and unpredictable as a Kona wind.

There was no time to analyze it though, because Oke called to his grandson. "Mano, can you come here for a minute?"

The young man tossed the ball Heidi had just thrown him to Kaia. "Be right there." Striding from the water, he looked like a young King Kamehameha. Stocky with thick muscles, Mano looked confident and in control.

Dripping with water, he stood in front of them and looked at Jesse then back to his grandfather. His eyes were filled with trepidation. "Is something wrong?"

His back erect, Oke advanced toward his grandson. "Mano, you have never lied to me. I want to know about Pele Hawai'i. Are they involved in the break-ins at the base?" Oke's voice was stern.

Mano looked down at the sand. His lips tightened and he glanced at Jesse. "Is this your doing, Matthews? Have you come here with your lies to turn my family against me?"

"That was not my intention," Jesse said. "But I need to protect my niece. And your sister."

Mano frowned. "I'll protect my sister. No harm will come to her."

Jesse noticed Mano said nothing about Heidi. "What about my niece?"

Oke interrupted. "Did you have anything to do with the kidnapping attempt on Heidi?"

Mano tossed his head in a proud gesture. "You would believe this *haole?*"

"Watch how you say that. I was born on Kaua'i." Jesse said. He tried to keep his voice mild. Mano was cornered, and it would be easy to provoke him to a fight.

"Do not evade my question, Mano." Oke reached out and gripped his grandson's arm. "Tell me the truth."

Mano gave Jesse an angry look then gently pried his grandfather's fingers from his arm. "I can't talk about it now, *Tûtû kâne.* I have an appointment." He strode off toward the house.

Jesse saw disillusionment in Oke's face. He wished he could reassure the old man, but Mano's behavior spoke for itself.

"I'm going to the meeting tonight, *Tûtû kâne*," Bane said. "If Mano is involved, I'll find out."

Oke straightened. "Until then, I choose to believe in my grandson."

Jesse tried not to look at the way love and fear vied for control of Oke's face. He hoped the old man wouldn't be too crushed when the truth came out.

Jesse glanced at his watch. Two o'clock. They had several hours before they needed to be back at the boat. He waved to Kaia, and she spoke to Heidi and they both came in on the next wave.

"Let's go get some lunch," he told her.

"I'll change. What about Heidi?"

Jesse hesitated. He didn't dare leave his niece. "We'll take her with us."

She took Heidi's hand, and they went to the house to change. Jesse stood outside and watched Bane digging the pit for Friday night's lu'au. He saw a glint from the basalt rock cliff behind Kaia's brother. Squinting, Jesse tried to make out what it was but couldn't. He had some binoculars in the Jeep. He rummaged in the glove box and found them. The hillside leaped into focus as he brought them to his eyes, and he saw a man with a rifle. The gun was pointed toward Bane as the man sighted down the scope.

"Get down!" Jesse dropped the binoculars and tackled Bane. A bullet plowed in the sand. It would have struck Bane if not for Jesse's quick actions. Another bullet struck the piece of driftwood to Jesse's left. Crouching to make themselves as small a target as possible, Jesse and Bane ran for the Jeep and knelt behind it.

Jesse flung open the car door and reached under the seat for his gun. Bane grabbed up the binoculars lying on the ground. He squinted as he stared through them. Jesse waited to see where the shots were coming from.

"He's leaving," Bane said. "In a blue car. I can't tell what kind from here."

"Let me see." Jesse took the binoculars, but the car was kicking up too much dust to make out a license number.

He put down the binoculars and looked at Bane. "I'm not sure it's safe for you to go to the meeting after all."

Bane shrugged. "I'm not afraid."

"I'll go." Kaia stood on the porch. Dressed in white shorts and a red top, she looked too fragile to take on a sniper, but her dark eyes were cool and determined as she stared at Jesse. "I heard the shots. I've been to one meeting already. A woman can blend in better anyway. There are more women there than you might imagine."

"Not someone who looks like you," Jesse said. "You'd stand out in any crowd. I'll go."

"Oh sure. A *haole* like you will blend right in," she scoffed.

She didn't say the word *haole* like a slur, so Jesse knew she meant only that he was fair skinned and blond. "And a woman will blend? Not likely."

"There were other women there. No one will notice me," she insisted.

"Nahele will recognize you."

"I'll stay to the back of the crowd. There are lots of shadows in the mill."

Jesse didn't see how that was possible, but he could tell by the look on her face that she wasn't going to listen to reason. "I want you to be wired if you go," he said. "I'll get the equipment from Steve."

"I'm not wearing a wire. Where would I hide it?" She shook her head. "I won't stay long. If I'm not back to the boat by eight, you can come looking for me."

"I don't like it," Jesse said.

"Me neither." Bane scowled and shook his head.

"Neither of you will change my mind. Nahele won't see me."

"What if Mano sees you?"

"Mano would die before he let anyone harm me."

Jesse could only hope and pray she was right.

Twenty-three

Kaia pleated her mu'umu'u with nervous fingers. The soft flowers had seemed a good choice when she first put it on, as everyone else would likely be dressed in alohawear as well, but driving toward the meeting place, she wished she'd chosen something black. The dress seemed to scream, "Look at me," and she didn't want to call attention to herself.

The old rice mill parking lot was packed with cars. That was a good sign. The crowd should be large enough to hide in. She parked beside her brother's truck. If she had to run from someone, she wanted him close enough to help her. In spite of all they suspected, she knew Mano would never let someone harm her.

She fell into step behind a group of five people heading to the mill. The two women in the group had clothing similar to Kaia's, so she hoped to blend in and be thought to be part of them.

"They're predicting a storm tonight," a man in the group said.

"All I'd heard was the usual passing windward and *mauka* showers," one of the women said.

Kaia hadn't checked the weather, but she turned to look over the water. Truly inclement weather could come from Kona winds. A faint dusting of clouds darkened the horizon, but that was no comfort. A storm could blow in quickly.

She realized the group had left her behind while she was woolgathering, so she hurried to rejoin them as they stepped into the mill. There were about seventy-five people inside, she guessed. The group she was trying to be part of stopped by a massive support beam, and she stood behind it. There wasn't much lighting in this corner, which would help conceal her.

Nahele looked like he was about to begin to speak, but tonight she wasn't interested in his inflammatory words. Her one goal was to find the man with the birthmark on his nose and discover his name. Then she was out of here.

Something about the tension in the room was getting to her. A strange vibration of danger put her nerves on edge.

Nahele climbed the machinery that served as a platform and began his harangue, but Kaia's attention was riveted on the man who was revealed when Nahele moved. The big Hawaiian, nearly as huge as the machinery, was impossible to miss. The dim lighting revealed the birthmark on the side of his nose.

She spoke to the woman in front of her. "Excuse me," she whispered. "Who is the big guy behind Nahele?"

"Shh," the woman said in an annoyed whisper.

No help there. Kaia moved through the crowd, closer to where the man stood. She saw Mano in a group of four other men. He hadn't seen her yet, and she wanted to make sure it stayed that way. She retreated into the shadows. Glancing around, her gaze connected with that of her coworker Jenny. Jenny's eyes widened when she saw Kaia, and she gave an uncertain smile.

So Jenny was involved in this organization just as Kaia had suspected. Maybe she could get some information out of her. Kaia moved quickly to her side before she said anything. "Hi, Jenny," she whispered.

"What are you doing here?" Jenny too withdrew to the shadows when several people gave them an annoyed look.

"I was about to ask you the same thing. I didn't know you were interested in Pele Hawai'i. Mano never mentioned it."

The tension between them seemed to lessen. Jenny smiled. "Oh, I suppose Mano talked you into coming. I'd forgotten he was a member."

There were several shushes from people standing around.

"Let's go outside," Kaia whispered.

Jenny nodded reluctantly then followed her out the door. "I

really wanted to listen to Nahele. I heard the organization is going in a new direction."

"Oh?"

"I don't know the details," Jenny said.

Maybe she would know the guy's name. "That big guy who hangs around Nahele, the one with the birthmark on his nose. Who is he?"

Jenny pressed her lips together. "Kim Aki. He's Nahele's son," she said with obvious reluctance.

He was an Aki? Kaia hadn't been expecting that. He looked like some kind of henchman. "He doesn't look much like his dad."

Jenny shrugged. "I think he's adopted."

"Are you involved with him?"

Jenny sighed. "We're friends," she admitted. "I've seen him a few times."

"Why didn't you tell me the first time I asked?"

Jenny shrugged. "That was our first date. I wasn't sure if it would lead anywhere."

"He looks scary," Kaia said.

"He's a sweet guy. He makes sure things run smoothly," Jenny said. "Listen, I really want to hear this. Let's go back inside."

"You go ahead. I need to go to the bathroom." Kaia nodded toward the porta-potty parked in the lot.

"Okay. I'll be back where you first saw me if you want to join me."

"Great." Kaia waited until Jenny disappeared inside the rice mill then jogged back to her car. She nearly screamed when a dark figure moved out from behind her brother's truck. She relaxed when she recognized Mano.

"You just robbed me of a year of my life," she scolded.

"What are you doing here, Kaia?" His face was stern in spite of her teasing tone.

"I was about to leave."

"You're poking around in things that don't concern you. I don't want you to come back here."

"I don't want you to come here at all," she retorted.

"I have to. It will be over soon."

She stared into his face. "What's going on, Mano? Can't you tell me?"

"Not yet." He took her arm and opened her car door then thrust her inside. "Get out of here, Kaia. I don't want Nahele to see you here."

She sat in the car and pulled her door shut then looked up at him through the window. "What about Kim Aki?"

Mano's face changed. If she didn't know her brother feared nothing, she would have sworn she saw fear.

"You stay away from Kim," he said, leaning down to whisper. "He's a dangerous man."

"Then why are you hanging around him?" She wanted to shake her brother. Why wouldn't he stop talking in riddles?

A hulking shadow moved behind Mano, and Kaia gasped when she recognized Kim Aki.

Mano whirled, his fists clenched.

"What are you doing out here, Oana? You should be inside listening." Kim's voice was a low growl that brought the hair on the back of Kaia's neck to attention.

"Just escorting my sister home."

"So early?" Kim moved closer. "I want to have a little talk with your sister. Get her and bring her inside."

"She's leaving," Mano insisted. He blocked Kim's access to Kaia's door. "Get out of here, Kaia."

Kaia had her car key in her hand, and she jabbed it into the ignition. The pickup roared to life as Kim leaped toward it. Mano tackled him.

The men wrestled on the gravel. Kaia swung open her door to go to her brother's aid.

"Get out of here!" Mano screamed at her.

Kim was nearly out of her brother's grasp. Kaia slammed her door and gunned the engine. The tires spit gravel as she raced away. She glanced in her rearview mirror and saw that Kim had managed to evade Mano and was getting in a blue car. She floored the accelerator and sped toward town and safety. She could only pray her truck was faster than his car.

On the curve where the mill access road met Highway 50, she saw a third road that shot off into a grove of trees. Without thinking, she took it and turned the car into a clearing surrounded by trees. By the time Kim reached the curve, the dust had settled and he sped by, merging onto the highway and heading into town.

Kaia sagged onto the steering wheel. She shuddered to think what would have happened if he'd caught up with her.

JESSE CHECKED HIS WATCH AND PACED THE DECK OF THE *Porpoise II*. Kaia should be here any minute. He'd been praying the whole time she was gone. It felt wrong to let her go into danger that way, but she was one female with a mind of her own. At least Steve had brought the promised security equipment.

The boat swayed with the waves, and he saw storm clouds building to the southwest. A Kona could be bad news. When Kaia arrived, they would have to make a decision about the patrol.

He turned and saw a truck speeding toward the dock. Squinting, he recognized Mano's truck. The truck stopped, and Mano got out and jogged to the boat.

"Is Kaia back yet?" he asked.

"Not yet."

Mano frowned. "She left the meeting before I did. Kim Aki was following her. We've got to find her."

Jesse didn't like the sound of that. "Who's Kim Aki? Is he related to Nahele?"

"His son. Big guy."

"Birthmark?"

Mano nodded. "I think she's in trouble." He chewed his lip.

"Let's go." He'd have to take Heidi. He called her, and the three of them piled into Jesse's Jeep.

"Any ideas where we can look?" Jesse asked.

"Let's backtrack along the way she would have come," Mano suggested.

Jesse followed Mano's directions and drove down Highway 50 through town and out to the mill road. They didn't see any sign of Kaia's car.

"Is the meeting over?"

"Yeah. There's no one left back at the mill."

Jesse turned down the mill road.

"Hey, what about that turnout?" Mano pointed out a tiny lane into a grove of trees.

"I'll check it out." Jesse turned into the lane and drove slowly over the bumps. He parked before he got to the trees. "Wait here. I'll look around." He got out of the SUV and jogged into the grove. The trunks parted to reveal a small clearing. Kaia's Mazda pickup was parked behind a big monkeypod tree, but she wasn't in it.

This couldn't be good. Jesse looked around the clearing. "Kaia? Where are you?"

There was no answer but the whine of insects. He opened her truck door and looked inside. Her purse was still on the seat. His stomach clenched. Had Aki found her?

He went back to the Jeep and told Mano what he'd found. Heidi was sleeping in the backseat.

"Do you have any idea where Kim would have taken her if he'd found her?"

Mano hesitated, and Jesse thought he might not answer. Then he sighed. "Yeah, I think I know where that would be, but we're going to need help. It's like a fortress in there."

"I've got my gun."

"They've got batteries of guns." Mano sounded resigned.

"I don't think we have time to gather more help."

"I'll at least call Bane." Mano dug out his cell phone and called his brother. "He'll meet us at the turnoff to Waimea Canyon."

Jesse glanced to his niece. "We can't take Heidi there."

"My grandfather will watch her. He'll make sure no harm comes to her."

Jesse didn't like it. Oke was a good man, but he was nearly eighty. All the good intentions in the world couldn't defeat strong young men. He hesitated. "What about Faye and Curtis?"

Mano frowned then nodded. "At least there would be two, and their house is more secure than *Tûtû kâne's*."

"Let's go." They got in the Jeep and headed to town.

He pulled into the Latchet driveway. Heidi was still sleeping soundly when he opened the back door and lifted her out. She murmured and snuggled against his chest. He carried her to the front door and rang the bell.

Faye answered. Her tear-stained eyes widened when she saw Jesse with Heidi in his arms.

"I think Kaia is in trouble. Can you keep Heidi until I find her?"

"Of course." She trailed after him as he carried his niece to the spare room. "Where's my daughter?"

"We're not sure, but we think Aki's thugs have her."

Her hand went to her mouth. "Oh no," she whispered.

Curtis came to the doorway. "What's wrong?"

His wife told him. "I'd better go with you," he said.

"We need you here," Jesse said. "I don't want to leave Faye and Heidi unprotected. Do you have a gun?"

Curtis nodded. "It's just a small pistol, but I'm a good shot."

"Have it ready. I'll be back as soon as I can." He dropped a kiss on Heidi's sleeping forehead and ran for his Jeep.

Driving out to Waimea Canyon, he asked God to keep Kaia safe.

They picked up Bane in Hanapepe and left his car parked at a gas station. The storm Jesse feared had blown in, and the wind lashed rain against the vehicle as Mano directed him up the winding road toward the top of the canyon. With the heavy downpour, the night was even blacker than usual with the lights of Waimea below obscured. There was no other traffic on the road this late.

It seemed they drove forever. The storm finally began to abate.

"There," Mano said, pointing to a nearly overgrown lane.

Jesse slowed the Jeep. "How far is it?"

"A quarter of a mile or so."

"Maybe we should hide the Jeep and walk back. We don't want to announce our presence," Bane said.

Mano nodded. "I know just the spot."

Once the Jeep was stashed behind an outcropping of rocks, Mano led the way through the mud to an imposing two-story house on top of a hill.

"It's not as easily approached as it looks," Mano said. "There are usually at least two guards walking the property."

"Can you get in by just walking to the door?"

"Probably not now. I challenged Kim." Mano's voice was low. "You might as well know, I was investigating them undercover. My cover is blown, so it doesn't matter now."

Jesse didn't know what to say. He'd been sure Mano was involved up to his neck.

"Sorry, *kaikunâne*. I misjudged you," Bane said.

"I'll take that as a compliment," Mano said with a cockeyed smile. "I figured if I could fool my own family, Aki's group would believe me too. Unfortunately, they found out before the meeting anyway. They shot at you to warn me not to betray them. I was told to follow through on my orders or next time they wouldn't miss."

"What are they planning?"

"They intend to blow up the munitions caves."

"That's why the helicopter was out there," Jesse said.

Mano nodded. "I think they might be canceling that plan now though. They know they'll never pull it off."

"Then why take your sister?" Jesse asked.

"Probably to keep me quiet until they can get away."

Jesse knew all the suspicion had to have hurt. He pressed Mano's arm. "You're a good man," he said. "Now how are we going to get in there?"

TWENTY-FOUR

The car stank of garlic. Kim Aki must have had the mother of all Italian meals, Kaia thought. He oozed the sharp stench. Pipe ashes littered the leather seat, and a cigarette burn marred the armrest near her left arm. Kaia had to figure out a way to escape. She sat tensed in the passenger seat as her mind whirled.

The night was black up here on top of the mountain. The stars hid behind clouds that had rolled in after sunset. Kim braked at the crest of a hill. With the motor still idling, he twisted in the seat and looked at Kaia. "Get out."

Kaia caught her breath at the man's growl. Her skin prickled at the intent in his voice. He was going to kill her, she just knew it. Kim Aki was too big for her to overpower, but maybe she could outrun him.

Her hand crept to the door handle. His gaze veered toward the dash as he turned the engine off. In that moment, she flung open her door and hit the pavement running. She heard Kim shout, but she didn't look back. She turned off the road and plunged into the black gravel. A grove of koa trees beckoned her up ahead. She dared a glance back and realized Kim wasn't in pursuit. The glare of the headlamps revealed his bulky figure by his car talking on a cell phone and smoking a pipe. His stance as he leaned against the car fender suggested he didn't care that she'd escaped.

Kaia reached the coolness of the grove and stopped. Panting, she glanced back toward the car again. Had he just intended to release her here anyway? If so, then why had he taken her? She'd stepped out of her car for a minute to get a closer view of the road. When she returned, he'd rushed out from behind a tree and marched her down the lane to his vehicle.

He'd said nothing the last three hours. Kaia had to find out what was going on. She circled a large black boulder and crossed the road behind Kim. Once on the other side, she crouched behind a thicket.

The wind was coming from the west and carried Kim's words to her.

"Yeah, she's gone." He listened a bit then swore viciously. "What do you mean, find her? It's as black as lava out here tonight. You said to scare her and I did. What do you want her for anyway?" His stance changed as he listened. "Then take someone else. The kid would be an easier target. That will keep Mano in line just as well. He's a soft touch. I don't know why we ever trusted him."

Kaia froze. Heidi! Jesse was undoubtedly looking for Kaia by now. Where would he have left Heidi? *Tûtû kâne's* maybe? She wished she had her cell phone, but it was in her purse back at her car. She had to get to a phone and contact Jesse before it was too late.

She backed away from Kim's car. He had taken her high onto Waimea Mountain, and the road down would be long. There were no houses along the way.

Please, Lord, send help. *Her only hope was if a passerby saw her.* She knew it wasn't likely at this hour. Few people drove up the dark canyon at night. She recognized the growl of an engine behind her and ducked behind a boulder until Kim drove past. His meaty arm hung out the window, and he crooned a Hawaiian tune with the radio.

When the sound of his car died in the distance, she stepped back onto the road and continued to walk. The moon came and went behind clouds, and the night grew darker. It was hard to keep from wandering off the road, but she knew she had to stay alert or she was liable to go over the edge.

She began to shiver as the air cooled. Her mu´umu´u offered little warmth. She shook her hair free from the French braid and spread it over her shoulders and down her back. It offered a welcome bit of coverage.

Her watch said it was after eleven. Jesse would be frantic, but

he'd have no idea where to look for her. Jesse. Bane had said she had
an unforgiving spirit. She didn't want to be like that. She would
start by releasing her anger against Jesse for taking her away from
her research.

"I forgive Jesse, Lord." She waited. Maybe she felt a little different—lighter. She wanted to say she forgave her mother, but the
words still stuck in her throat.

She rounded a curve and caught a glimpse of a flicker of light
down a narrow, nearly hidden lane. Was that a house down there?

She stopped on the road and considered her options. The light
was possibly only a security light for a park service building. She
couldn't remember ever going down this lane so she had no idea
what lay at the end. Going that way could delay her at least a half
an hour, time that would increase Heidi's risk. On the other hand, if
there was access to a phone this way, she could call for help at least
an hour sooner than if she walked down the road.

Kaia dithered. She wanted to sit in the middle of the road and
cry. *What should I do, Lord?* Almost without considering it, she
turned into the lane at an inner urging. All she could do was step out
on faith and trust that God was the one leading her down this path.

The moon came out again and illuminated her way. She saw
a dark shadow hidden in a pull-off. Squinting, she realized it was
a vehicle. Someone had to be back here. The Jeep looked familiar,
and she glanced inside. It was Jesse's Jeep. She closed her eyes.
Mahalo, Jesus.

But where was he? A rising sense of urgency propelled her back
to the road. She began to run down the cinder driveway. "Jesse!" she
called. The rising wind snatched her cry and threw it behind her.

She paused to catch her breath. Had Jesse run into Kim and
the rest of the Pele Hawai'i thugs? Maybe he was hurt or in danger
somewhere in the wilderness out here. She wouldn't know where
to look for him. All she could do was to keep trudging down this
narrow track.

She veered back to the ditch and kept walking. The light grew larger, and she realized it was a house. No, not just a house, but a mansion. The thing towered high in the moonlight, but only a single light blazed from a downstairs window.

Kaia stopped and listened. She thought she'd heard something. Her straining ears caught nothing but her own ragged breath. Though she wanted to call out for Jesse again, some sense warned her to keep quiet. Something about the house deterred her from marching to the front door and knocking. She'd never realized a place this grand was here, and she had to wonder who would have had the money or inclination to build something this fabulous so far off the beaten path.

Nahele Aki's face flashed through her mind, and she wondered if this could be his place. It looked secure enough to be a compound of some sort. A small structure stood guard at the driveway up to the house, and a heavy iron gate barred the way. She went back toward the Jeep. Maybe Jesse had left his keys in there. If not, she could honk the horn and alert them.

THE HOUSE WAS DARK AND SILENT. "I'LL GO FIRST." JESSE CRAWLED under the fence. Bane and Mano followed him. They approached the back of the house where no light shone from the windows.

"I'm not sure anyone is here," Bane whispered.

"Where else would they have taken her?" Jesse asked.

"It could be a trap," Mano said. "Pele Hawai'i never does what you expect."

"I'm going to look in the window." Jesse stepped into the yard, and instantly a flood of light illuminated the backyard from a motion-sensor security light.

He ducked to the ground. Kaia's brothers lunged for the shadows. No alarm seemed to be raised, so after a few minutes Jesse raised his head and got to his hands and knees.

"We're wasting time. I don't think anyone is here. Let's look for Kaia and get out of here." He couldn't let himself think about what she might be going through or fear would paralyze him.

He led the way toward the house. The soft grass underfoot was soft and springy. A twig snapped, and he froze. "Did you hear that?"

"It was me," Bane said.

Jesse nodded and went forward again. He peered in the window but saw no one. The house had that empty feel. He was sure Kaia wasn't there. "Let's go," he said.

He was nearly halfway to the front yard when he heard a low growl. He stopped. "Was that you too, Bane?"

Before the men could react, three dobermans came running toward them.

"Run!" Jesse turned and shoved Bane ahead of him. They raced back the way they'd come, toward the house. Bane leaped for the low overhang of the porch and heaved himself up. Mano did the same, swinging easily onto the roof. Jesse wasn't sure he was going to make it. One dog was snapping at his heels as he reached up and caught Bane's hand.

The dog's teeth fastened on the cuff of Jesse's jeans, and he nearly fell, but Bane and Mano jerked him to safety. He scrabbled back from the ledge and looked down on the three dogs. They were barking and practically foaming at the mouth.

"Now what?" Mano asked.

"We've got to get out of here."

"How? Those dogs will stand guard all night if necessary."

"Why did they just now come out?" Jesse asked. It seemed suspicious to him. He stared into the darkness in the direction the dogs had come. "I have to wonder if someone is out there laughing at us."

"The door is open on the shed," Bane said. "It was closed earlier."

Jesse balanced on the steep roof and walked to the side of the house. He thought about shouting at whoever was out there but decided not to give the man any more thrills. If only he could get to his Jeep. The cat food Kaia had purchased for Hiwa was in the back. Maybe they could distract the dogs with the food long enough to get out of here.

"I'm going to go over the roof to the front yard," he told the other men. "Keep these guys occupied."

Moving carefully, he climbed the tall house to the peak then half slid, half walked down the other side. He could hear Bane and Mano jeering and talking to the dogs, but one had followed him around the house in spite of the men's attempts. It stood near the front porch with teeth bared and growling as if it would like to eat him.

As he reached the porch, he heard his Jeep horn begin to blare. It gave three short blasts then a long one. A slight figure came from behind the rocks where the Jeep was hidden. He recognized Kaia when he saw the flowing black hair. Relief swept through him. She was all right.

He stood and waved. "Kaia!"

She heard him and her head came up. She started toward him.

"Get the cat food from the Jeep," he shouted.

She hesitated then went back to the SUV. She rummaged in the Jeep then came toward him carrying some cans.

"You need to distract the dog," he called. "But be careful, he's mean." He heard the sound of the top popping on the can.

"Oh, there's my sweet boy," she crooned to the dog. She began to chant a soothing Hawaiian *mele*. It must have been pleasant to the dog, because it quit growling and went to stand by the fence.

Kaia walked along the outside of the fence to the far corner. The dog followed, whining now. "What a good boy you are," she said softly, a placating tone to her voice.

When the dog was as far away as possible, he dropped from the porch and ran for the fence. The dog didn't seem to notice as it wolfed down food from the tin Kaia held in her hand. Brave woman. He wouldn't have gotten that close to the animal.

Jesse reached the fence and opened the gate. He stepped through then shut it behind him. How would they get her brothers out? He hurried to Kaia. "Can you go around back and do the same with the two dogs back there? Your brothers are trapped on the back porch."

"I'll need more food." The dog lifted its head and growled at Jesse. Kaia snatched her hand back as the dog lunged. "He doesn't like you. You'd better get out of here."

He left her there and hurried to the SUV for more cat food. He grabbed four cans and ran along the fence row to the far back corner. "Get to the front," he called to Bane and Mano. "Kaia is there with the other dog. I'll distract these two." He raised his voice louder and called to the dogs. "Hey, pooches, look what I have for you." He began to bang on the iron fence, and the dogs raced toward him. He pulled off the tops of two cans and dug out the insides with nervous fingers. Tossing it to the dogs, he watched Kaia's brothers hurry over the rooftop.

He fed the dogs the food as slowly as he could until he heard Mano call to him from the front yard. Wiping his messy fingers on his jeans, he tossed the cans over the fence and raced back to join the rest.

Kaia was running to meet him. "We've got to get to town! They're after Heidi!"

TWENTY-FIVE

Faye woke with a start, drenched in perspiration and shaking with regret. In her dream, her children were swimming. Their laughter changed to shrieks of fear as sharks' dorsal fins sliced through the blue water from every direction. Kaia began to scream her mother's name, but Faye had turned and walked away, left her, just like she'd done in real life.

She pressed her fingers into her eye sockets. Her head felt heavy and lethargic. She reached out to touch Curtis but found only cold, empty sheets. The green glow of the clock said it was nearly eleven thirty. Where could he be?

She slipped out of the bed and padded to the door. Stepping into the hallway, she peered downstairs, but there were no lights on. She moved into the hall and nearly fell over a figure lying at her feet.

"Curtis?" She dropped to the floor and touched him. He groaned as she rolled him to his back, and his eyes fluttered. A trickle of blood ran from a cut on his forehead. Just then, she heard a child's voice from downstairs.

"Let go of me! I want my mommy. Mommy!" Heidi's wail ended with a sob as a man's voice answered her roughly. It didn't sound like Jesse.

The *keiki's* wail had been in her dream. Faye shot to her feet. She glanced down at Curtis, her hand to her mouth. He needed her, but so did Heidi. Fear held her immobile. She'd never in her life been able to face down danger.

She shrank back against the wall then sank to the soft carpet. Crawling toward her bedroom, she thought she could hide in the closet. *For God has not given us a spirit of fear but of power and a sound mind.* The words thundered in her head. She stopped and looked down the stairway. Tears leaked from her eyes. She was such a coward. Heidi could be in real danger.

She tried to tell herself it was Jesse who'd come for his niece, but she knew the truth. Someone bad had taken the *keiki*, and only Faye could stop him. She rose on trembling legs and prayed for God to help her. Then she turned and hurtled down the stairs.

At the bottom of the steps, she stopped and listened. Heidi's sobs seemed to be coming from the kitchen. Faye heard the back door open. On bare feet, she ran toward the sound. When she entered the kitchen, she saw a tall, blond man carrying Heidi. The little girl was pummeling him with her small fists.

"Let me go. I want my mommy!" Heidi howled again.

Faye acted on instinct. She grabbed up the bowl of fruit on the table and brought it down on the man's head. It bounced off his skull and rained apples, bananas, and mangoes onto the floor. The man paused and turned his head to look at her. She quailed at the fierce glare and hesitated. Then Heidi screamed again, and Faye was galvanized into action. She snatched at Heidi and must have caught the man off guard, because she managed to pull the *keiki* from his hands.

Heidi burrowed into Faye's arms. Her wet face soaked the neck of Faye's nightgown. "I've got you," Faye crooned.

The man grabbed Faye's arm. "Fine, you can come along too," he growled. He propelled her out the door.

She backpedaled, trying to shake loose his grip. Opening her mouth, she gathered her breath to scream, but he clamped a hand that smelled of—was it cabbage? She bit him.

He swore and clamped his hand around her throat. "Do that again and you and the kid are dead. Got it?"

Her eyes wide, she nodded. She couldn't breathe, couldn't swallow. The pressure on her throat eased, and she gulped in the sweet night air. He thrust her toward a dark-colored sedan. Reaching the car, he opened the back door and pushed her and Heidi inside.

A grate separated them from the front seat. The door shut then locked. Faye couldn't find a way to release the lock. She tugged on the handle but the door refused to open. There was no way to roll the window down either. This was all her fault. She should have put Heidi down and told her to run.

And her husband was bleeding in the upstairs hallway. She could only pray he would be all right. He must have surprised the man taking Heidi. They never should have gone to bed, but Curtis had been sure things would be fine. He'd activated the security system and taken his pistol into the bedroom with them. All those precautions hadn't been enough.

Faye's mouth was dry, and she cuddled Heidi close. She had to protect her somehow, even though she'd failed at all those things with her own children. All her life she'd run from problems. Tonight that would stop. She was going to have to reach deep inside and find what small, tattered courage she possessed to stand up to whoever was behind this.

Heidi stirred and lifted her damp face. "I want to go home," she whispered. "Where's Uncle Jesse? And the man hit Mr. Curtis. You need to help him."

"I know. I saw." Faye smoothed the hair back from Heidi's face. "Mr. Curtis was moving around when I saw him. He'll be all right." She said the words as much to reassure herself as the *keiki*.

The car shifted as the man got in. Faye stared at the back of his head where a small swirl of hair crested the top of his skull. "What do you want with us?" she asked.

The man didn't answer as he rolled the window down a crack to let in some air. His dark eyes met Faye's in the rearview mirror, and she shuddered at the implacable expression in them. She began to shake deep inside, though she tried to hide her fear from Heidi.

Heidi crawled into her lap, and Faye rocked and crooned to her as if she were only three instead of eight. Heidi buried her face against Faye. Faye strained to see through the darkness, hoping for someone walking a dog or jogging along the street so she could pound on the window and scream for help, but there was no one around. Though nightlife wasn't totally unknown on this side of the island, it wasn't common either. The golden glow from streetlights revealed a sleeping town, then the car left the city limits and headed into the dark night.

JESSE WRENCHED THE STEERING WHEEL, AND THE TIRES screamed around a tight curve. He knew he was driving too fast, but he kept his foot glued to the accelerator.

"No answer at the house," Kaia said, clicking off the cell phone.

"They've had plenty of time to snatch the *keiki*," Bane said.

"Do you think they hurt Curtis and—and Faye?" It would have been typical of Faye to fail to protect Heidi. He should have known better than to take his niece to a woman who would desert her own children.

"What did the police say?" Mano asked.

"They're sending over a patrol car." Kaia's voice was strained. "They should get there about the same time as we do."

The Jeep careened around another curve then went airborne when it hit a bump. The tires slammed onto the pavement, and Jesse fought to keep the SUV on the road. The lights of town were just ahead. He jammed his foot into the floorboard and sped to the out-skirts of town where he slammed on the brakes and barreled around the corner.

The Latchet house was at the end of the lane. A police car, its motor running, sat at the curb, and two uniformed officers stood at the front door. Jesse parked behind the squad car and jumped out of his Jeep. The officers turned as Jesse got to the porch. Kaia was right behind him.

"We called you," Kaia said. "Jesse's niece was threatened by a man who forced me into his car."

"There's no answer from inside," the youngest officer said.

"Did you try the door?" Jesse twisted the doorknob, but it was locked.

"Let me call in and get permission to force the door." The older, portly policeman started toward the patrol car.

"I'll go around back," Jesse said. He jogged around the side of the house with Kaia on his heels.

The back door stood open. Kaia took hold of his arm, and her nails bit into his arm. "Oh no," she whispered.

"Go get the officers," he said softly.

Kaia nodded. "Wait until they get here." She ran to the corner of the house and disappeared around the side.

Jesse approached the back steps and examined the frame. The door didn't look like it had been broken, but it stood wide open. Jesse stepped into the kitchen. Fruit lay scattered on the floor, and his sneakers crunched broken pieces of pottery underfoot; he nearly slipped on mashed chunks of fruit. The aroma of mango filled the air.

He wiped his feet on the rug by the door and flipped on the light. "Faye? Curtis?" He went through the door to the living room and down the hall to the front door. He unlocked the door and swung it open as the officer with Kaia started around the end of the house.

They turned and ran to join Jesse. "You should have waited for me, sir," the officer said.

Jesse pointed to the stairs. "The bedrooms are up there."

With his hand on the rail, the older policeman started up the stairs. "I'll check out the downstairs," the younger patrolman said.

Jesse went up the stairs. He knew his niece wasn't down here. At the top of the stairs, he found the policeman bending over a figure on the carpet in the hall.

Curtis was moving about, and his eyes were fluttering as he struggled to gain consciousness. A pool of blood stained the tan carpet by his head. Jesse looked past him into the bedroom. The soft green comforter had been carefully folded and lay across a stand.

Every accessory had been coordinated and placed just so. It seemed an attempt to create a perfect haven. This had to be the master bedroom.

Unfortunately, it was empty.

He let the officer take care of Curtis and stepped past them to race down the hall to the guest room. Heidi's stuffed bear, Boo, lay in the doorway. Jesse caught his breath as his lungs constricted with an awful knowledge. "Heidi?" he croaked. He flipped on the light and looked frantically around the bedroom.

The covers had been thrown back, but the bed was empty, though there was still an indentation in the pillow where Heidi's head had been. Jesse picked up Boo and clutched the bear to his chest. He sagged against the doorjamb.

He felt a touch and turned. Kaia's dark eyes were soft and troubled. "She and Faye are both gone?"

He couldn't have spoken if he tried. Nodding, he gestured toward the bed.

Kaia's gaze swept the room. "Her suitcase is still here."

Jesse hadn't noticed. He'd failed Heidi and Jillian. Failed to protect his precious niece from harm. Some guardian he was. Kaia touched his arm, and he opened his eyes. He knew he needed to do something, find them somehow, but his muscles felt frozen in place. Where did he even start to look?

She put her palms on his cheeks. "We'll find them, Jesse."

"How?" he croaked, his tight throat finally allowing a word through.

"God will help us."

Jesse knew God as an exacting Father. Maybe this was Jesse's punishment for all the failures in his life. He'd failed to protect his wife and child, and now Faye and Heidi were in danger because of him. He never should have left them.

Kaia leaned up and brushed his lips with hers. The action warmed his cold limbs as nothing else could. He clutched her to his chest and buried his face in her fragrant hair. "You smell like plumeria," he murmured.

A soft laugh escaped her, and she pulled away. He let her go slowly, wishing he could hold this moment a little longer. Maybe the police would know where to look next. He didn't have a clue. He followed Kaia down the hall to where the officers crouched over Curtis.

Curtis was sitting up now with his head leaning against the wall. His eyes were closed, and an ugly bruise darkened his forehead. The cut was crusted with dried blood, and Curtis touched it then winced.

"How is he?" Jesse asked the older officer.

"He'll be all right. The paramedics are on their way."

Jesse tucked Boo inside his shirt then knelt by Curtis. "What happened?"

Curtis opened his eyes. "I'm not sure. I heard a noise and got up. My gun was on the nightstand, so I took it with me. When I opened the door and stepped into the hall, someone hit me on the head. That's all I remember."

Not much help there. "Did you see the attacker at all?" Jesse asked.

"No, not a glimpse." Curtis looked up, his face contorting with pain at the movement. "I'm sorry, Jesse." He looked around. "Where's Faye?"

"Where did you see her last?" an officer asked.

"She was still in bed when I got up. I don't think she heard whatever it was that I did." Curtis groaned and leaned forward, holding his head.

"She's nowhere in the house, sir," the other patrolman said.

Curtis looked up. "What's that mean? What about Heidi?"

"Gone as well," Jesse said. "The back door was standing open when we got here."

"I shouldn't have gone to bed," Curtis said. "Faye wanted me to stay up and stand guard, but I told her we'd be fine. I have state-of-the-art security here. I have no idea how the guy got in."

"You think there was only one man?" Jesse asked.

"I don't know. I don't know anything." Curtis's head fell back against the wall.

TWENTY-SIX

As Jesse drove along the coastal road, Kaia rolled the Jeep window down and inhaled the scent of the sea, hoping it would soothe the razor-sharp edge of her fear. Her brothers had gone to retrieve her truck and drop it at the dock for her. They wanted to tell their grandfather about his daughter's abduction, and Kaia had promised to keep them informed of the investigation.

She was still reeling from Jesse's revelation that Mano had been working undercover. She shouldn't have doubted him. What kind of sister was she?

She glanced at Jesse. "You're quiet," she said. "Are you doing okay? We'll find her."

"I'm scared," he admitted. "I couldn't live with myself if anything happened to Heidi."

"This isn't your fault." She laid her hand on his arm.

"She was my responsibility." His jaw flexed, and his gaze stayed on the road.

"The missile test is in the morning too, isn't it?" From his sudden intake of breath, she realized he'd forgotten about it.

"Yeah." He pulled to the side of the road. "I wonder if there's any correlation."

"Wait, I'm not following you. How could Heidi's kidnapping be related to the missile test?"

He ran his hand through his hair. "I don't know; maybe I'm grasping at straws. Maybe they want to use Faye and Heidi as hostages."

"For what purpose?" Kaia hated to discourage him, but she didn't see how he was coming to this conclusion. "We already know they were planning on blowing up the storage caves in the mountain.

Mano thinks they're buying time for Aki and his thugs to get away. He never said anything about the missile test."

"I don't know," he admitted. "You're right, it's probably completely unrelated." He dropped the Jeep back into drive and started driving again.

His cell phone rang, and he grabbed it. "Matthews here."

He listened then said, "Yes sir. I've got problems here too. My niece has been kidnapped." He listened a bit longer then said, "Yes sir," again and clicked off the phone. "I'm being called back to duty. The officer in charge of security was just killed in a helicopter crash."

"Right before the missile test? What about the espionage charge?"

He shrugged. "My prints weren't on the papers they found. Lawton is giving me the benefit of the doubt."

"What about Heidi and my—I mean Faye?" She'd almost said "my mother." The realization shook her.

"The captain is giving me until seven to report for duty. Everything at the base seems under control. I've got six hours to find them." He sounded grim. "And we're going to find them. This island isn't big. They have to be here somewhere."

Kaia nodded. "Could Heidi and Faye have been taken somewhere by helicopter?"

Jesse's eyes widened. "We can only pray that's not the case."

"Let's try the Aki house again. Maybe he's gone back."

Jesse shook his head. "He wouldn't be that obvious. No way would he take them there. The police are checking there and the helicopter pads on the island." He frowned. "And he wouldn't take them to the mill. Do you know of any remote buildings around?"

"There are some old sugar mills." Kaia directed him where to go, and they drove out to the closest sugar mill. The track back to the mill was overgrown, and there had obviously been no cars along this way in years.

Jesse sat staring at the road then slapped his thigh. "I'm so stupid!

My cousin Kade is here on his vacation with his family. His wife, Bree, has a search-and-rescue dog who is just phenomenal. Maybe they can help us."

"A search dog?" Kaia hadn't heard much about them, other than a brief mention or two on television after national disasters.

Jesse dialed Kade's cell phone. He explained the problem then gave them directions and clicked off his phone. "They'll meet us at Faye's house in half an hour." He wheeled the Jeep around and drove back toward town.

The police were still on the scene when Jesse parked on the street. The yard was illuminated with halogen lights, and the yard had been roped off with crime-scene tape. Kaia saw the police dusting for fingerprints at the back door.

"I'll get a personal item," Jesse said. "You wait here and watch for them." He loped to the front door and said something to the policeman then disappeared inside. When he came out a few minutes later, he was carrying a paper bag.

"Kade told me what to do." He showed the bag to Kaia. "I've got Heidi's socks in here and Faye's hairbrush."

A few minutes later, a tan SUV pulled up behind them. "There they are," Jesse said. He jumped out of the Jeep, and Kaia followed him. A stocky, dark-haired man got out of the SUV and opened the rear door to let out a big dog. The dog seemed to be a mix of German shepherd and maybe chow, Kaia thought. A petite woman with red-gold hair hopped out of the passenger side.

"Kade, thanks for interrupting your vacation." Jesse gripped his cousin's hand then introduced them. "Did you leave Davy with Lauri?" The man nodded. Jesse turned to Kaia. "I hope you'll get a chance to meet the rest of the family—my cousin Lauri and Bree's son, Davy."

Bree held out her hand to Kaia. "Jesse has told us so much about you. I'd love to meet Nani some time while we're here."

"I'll make sure to do that." Kaia looked down at the dog. "This is Samson?" The dog woofed and nosed her hand that she'd placed on his head. "What a beautiful dog."

"He's my boy," Bree said, her smile widening. "Let's get started. Jesse, what do you have for us?"

"Some socks and a brush." Jesse handed the bag to her.

She held the bag open, and Samson sniffed it. "Search, Samson," she told him.

The dog woofed then raced around to the back door. They followed him. He nosed the entry then went to the driveway and started toward the street. Bree ran to intercept him and clipped the leash onto his collar.

"Follow us in the Jeep," she called. The dog dragged her down the street, dimly lit with streetlights.

"I'll take our SUV too," Kade said. He ran to his vehicle and followed his wife while Jesse and Kaia got in the Jeep.

Once the dog determined which direction to travel in, Bree and Samson got in the Jeep and rode to the next crossroad, where Bree and the dog got out and figured out which way to go again. Within fifteen minutes they were at a dock looking out toward the dark waves. Kaia noticed her brothers had been here and gone, leaving her truck parked along the water for her.

"They're on the water somewhere," Bree said. "It will take some time to find them out there, even with Samson."

"I'll call Nani." Kaia pulled a whistle out of her pocket and blew the call signal for the dolphin. She repeated it several times over the next few minutes, but Nani didn't come. "She must be out a ways," Kaia said. "I'll try the hydrophone." She got her backpack out of her truck and took the hydrophone to the dock and dropped it in the water.

Fifteen minutes later, Nani still had not arrived. Kaia tried not to worry, but Nani always came when she called. What if the men who took Heidi and Faye had harmed the dolphin? She needed to find Nani now too.

"Thanks for your help," Jesse told Kade and Bree. He rubbed Samson's head. "And especially you, big guy." The dog woofed and licked his hand. "We'll get in the boat and see what we can find, and I'll get some birds in the air. I don't want to interrupt your honeymoon anymore than we have already."

"Glad to do it," Kade said. "Call if you need us again."

Kaia paced the dock while the good-byes were going on. She wanted to get out on the water now that she knew Heidi and Faye were out there somewhere. The breakers rolled onto the shore. Their tops foamed and formed eddies in the sand. She stared out on the horizon but couldn't see anything in the dark. No boat lights or ships were in sight.

"The *Porpoise II* is the closest boat. Let's stop by our dock and get it," she told Jesse when he joined her.

"I'll call in some helicopter searches as well."

"There are bound to be a lot of boats out there even though we can't see them right now. It's prime tourist time," Kaia reminded him.

"Yeah, I know." His voice sounded depressed. He glanced at his watch. "It's almost two thirty. Sunup won't be for a while yet."

"If only I could find Nani." Kaia looked out over the whitecaps as they glimmered in the moonlight. The bloated moon gave the ocean an eerie glitter like some gaudy painting that was meant to be viewed under black lights. She shivered. What if the kidnappers tossed Heidi and Faye overboard?

"Let's get out there. Maybe she'll come when you call again." Jesse put his hand at her waist and guided her back to the Jeep.

His touch comforted her, and she realized she craved this connection she felt with him, even though he didn't share her cultural background. She'd always intended to marry another Hawaiian someday, someone whose roots ran deep in taro like her own. Though Jesse didn't fit into the plans she'd made, she found she didn't mind much.

They drove to the dock and boarded the *Porpoise II*. Jesse fired up the engines, and they headed out to sea. Once they were about a mile from shore, he cut the engines. "Try to call Nani again."

Kaia nodded and dropped DALE into the water. She called the dolphin four times before she gave up again. "I'm worried, Jesse. She's never ignored my call before."

"I wonder if she followed Heidi. She loves that kid."

FAYE HELD HEIDI CLOSE AS THE SEA SPRAY STRUCK THEM. THE boat's bow rose high in the air as the craft slammed into the waves. She couldn't see shore from here, so they had to be far from land. Far enough to drown if that's what their kidnappers intended.

She prayed it wasn't, but she didn't know why the man would have taken them. The target had been the *keiki*, which made no sense. Faye's eyes filled with tears at the thought of Curtis. If only she knew he was all right.

The boat slewed sideways in the water then settled into a buoyant motion on the water as the man at the helm cut the motor. The moon went behind some clouds and a light mist began to fall. Faye scooted back under the canopy out of the moisture.

Heidi woke at her movement and lifted her head. "Where are we?"

"Somewhere out to sea," Faye told her.

The man who had carried Heidi from the house walked toward them. He wore a scowl. "I don't want no trouble from either of you," he said. "Do what you're told, and you won't get fed to the sharks."

Heidi cringed back against Faye's chest, and Faye patted her back, feeling the chicken skin along the child's arms. "It's okay," she whispered. She looked up at the man and attempted a smile. Sometimes charm worked where nothing else did. "Why are you holding us?"

He returned her smile, but it wasn't pleasant, and chicken skin prickled along her back. "As insurance for now. This will all be over by this time tomorrow." He turned and ducked into the helm.

There was no sound but the lapping of the waves against the hull of the boat. Faye strained to catch a glimpse of light along the dark horizon but saw nothing. She was a strong swimmer, but she knew her limitations now that she was getting older. She might have been able to manage a mile or so with Heidi in tow, but not this distance.

They were going to have to wait for help.

She heard a sound, a squeak and whistle.

"It's Nani!" Heidi slipped from her lap and went to the rail. She leaned over and dangled her fingers at the dolphin.

"Quiet," Faye cautioned. "We don't want the bad man to shoot Nani."

Heidi's smile dimmed, and she stepped back from the railing.

Faye joined her and looked down at the dolphin. "Go get Kaia, Nani," she said softly. "Kaia." She wished she knew how to make the sounds that meant "Kaia."

Nani rode the waves then plunged into the ocean. Faye saw her dorsal fin slice through the water as she headed away from the boat. She could only pray the dolphin knew enough to find her daughter.

TWENTY-SEVEN

J esse guided the boat along the cresting waves. The craft bottomed out then rose on the next wave. He glanced at his watch. "It's nearly four."

"This night has been the longest in my life," Kaia said. She must look as haggard as she felt. They'd been wandering aimlessly out here for over an hour. Jesse had received an update from the police, who hadn't found a sign of Heidi or Faye.

Her cell phone rang. "This is Kaia."

Her brother's voice sounded weary and ragged. "It's Mano. We found Aki about to leave the island with his son. He claims to have no knowledge of Heidi or our mother."

"Can't they force him to tell where he's got them?" She heard the sharp edge of panic in her voice and tried to tighten her control, but time was running out. Every moment that ticked by brought disaster closer.

"They're trying. You having any luck?"

"Not yet. I can't find Nani either. If she would come, she might be able to help us."

"You've called her?"

"Many times. I've never known her to be so unresponsive. I'm worried."

"She's fine," Mano assured her.

Kaia wasn't so sure. Something felt very wrong. "Keep me posted," she told him. She clicked off her phone and told Jesse what Mano had said.

"We know Pele Hawai'i is behind this. Are there any other officers in the organization who could be hiding them?"

"I don't know. We just have to pray the police can get Aki to talk." Kaia rubbed her eyes. She wished she could talk to Nahele Aki herself. She could look into his eyes and find the truth behind his lies.

Jesse's cell phone rang, and he answered it. His eyes widened. "Listen," he mouthed to Kaia. He held the phone tipped so she could put her head next to his and listen with him.

The distorted voice raised the hair on the back of her neck.

"Jesse, you've got a problem," the voice said.

"Who is this?"

"I'm the person you want to keep happy if you also want to see your niece again." Kaia locked eyes with Jesse. This could not be one of the Akis.

"Where is my niece?"

"She's safe. For now. But whether she remains safe will be up to you."

"What do you want?" Jesse said.

"Nothing. That is, I want you to do nothing. When it's all over tonight, we'll talk again."

"When what is all over?"

The phone went dead.

Jesse hung up and stared at Kaia. "I don't get it at all," he said.

Kaia didn't like what she was thinking. "The missile test will be over by tonight. What if the problem with the last test wasn't an accident? What if this one is going to veer off as well?"

Jesse went still. "But why take Heidi and Faye?"

"I don't know." Kaia rubbed her head. "What do we do?"

He whirled the steering wheel and turned the boat toward shore. "The first thing I want to do is talk to Duncan. His father was part of the design team who came up with this new system. Duncan would know if it's even possible for someone to tamper with it like that. His house is near here."

The boat sped toward the shore. Jesse docked it at Duncan's pier and tied the boat to the piling. "This shouldn't take long. You want to wait here or come with me?"

"I'll wait here." Kaia wanted to try calling Nani again.

Jesse nodded then headed toward the steps that led from the pier up the hill to the house on top of the cliff. "He's not going to like me waking him at this hour."

Kaia watched him disappear at the top of the hill then called Nani on DALE again. Still no sign of her dolphin. She stepped from the boat to the dock. Her muscles were stiff and sore. A walk might help. She kept her reef shoes on and stepped into the soft sand. She walked toward a small lagoon where she often swam with Nani.

A low stone wall separated her from the lagoon's beach. She stepped over it then pushed through a thicket. Maybe Nani had come here. It was a favorite spot. She half expected to see her dolphin floating dead or injured in the water. The mental image dogged her. She couldn't imagine why Nani would refuse to answer . . . unless the dolphin couldn't.

In the middle of the thicket, Kaia came up short at the sound of men's voices. At the edge of the lagoon, she saw two men talking. Duncan Latchet and someone she did not recognize. She started forward to tell Duncan their problem.

Duncan clapped his hand to the man's shoulder. "We're all set. In this game, all we need are two strikes, and they're out. And it looks like we'll be in."

Kaia paused and ducked down behind a shrub. Two strikes. What kind of strike? The sight of the missile veering off course crossed her mind. If this morning's missile test went awry . . . She told herself not to be ridiculous. Duncan's father had helped develop this missile system. He would have no reason to want to see it fail.

"Meet me at the satellite. We should have a bird's-eye view of the fireworks." Duncan's voice was filled with excitement.

He was talking about the missile test. He had to be. Kaia backed away as quickly as she could. She and Jesse had to get out of here before Duncan saw them. She escaped the thicket and ran along the sand back to the boat. She saw Jesse standing on the dock.

She raced to the end. Grabbing Jesse's arm, she pushed him toward the boat. "Go, go, let's get out of here."

"What—" he began.

"I'll explain later. Just get us out of here."

Jesse jumped to the deck of the boat and helped her aboard. "As quietly as possible," she whispered.

He nodded and started the engine. Though it purred quietly, Kaia hoped the white noise of the surf would muffle their departure as well as it had their arrival.

At a safe distance out, Jesse accelerated, and the boat sped out to sea. Then he cut the engine and turned to stare at her. "What was that all about?"

"I saw Duncan talking to another guy. He said something about two strikes. I couldn't hear everything he said, but I think he means to sabotage this morning's test." Her voice rose as fear began to vibrate through her.

A smile touched Jesse's mouth. "Not Duncan, Kaia. He wouldn't do something like that."

"What else could he be talking about?" Kaia knew he didn't want to believe it, and neither did she. She'd always liked Duncan. "We should call the police."

"I can't go charging him with something like that without proof," Jesse said. "And there's no time for them to investigate." He frowned. "His office is over by the base. Let's go see if we can find anything there."

"How do we get in?"

"I'll think of something when we get there," he said.

Kaia sat in the bow of the boat as he directed the boat toward Barking Sands Naval Base. Events were spiraling out of control, and she felt as helpless as the time she took the dingy out to sea without a compass.

The Latchet building bordered the naval base. Jesse cut the motor at the nearest civilian dock, grabbed a flashlight, and helped Kaia ashore. They jogged toward the buildings.

"Is there a guard?" Kaia whispered.

Jesse nodded. "I think so. They deal with some top-secret stuff."

Security lights illuminated the parking lot, and their hum seemed loud when Kaia and Jesse were trying to be quiet. A row of windows looked out to sea, but only a few dim lights shone in the halls.

"Do you see the guard?" Kaia stopped and peered in.

"Yeah, he's at the desk." He pointed, and she saw a man slumped back in a chair with his eyes closed.

"Maybe we can talk our way past him." Jesse took her hand as they went across the road to the parking lot. He pressed the buzzer at the front door.

The guard, a sleepy-eyed Hawaiian of about forty-five, came to the door and opened it. "Hey, *brah*, you got any kine idea of the time?"

He looked familiar to Kaia, then she placed him. She'd gone to school with his son, Simon. In fact, she'd dated Simon a few times.

"Hi, Mr. Kalakaua. I don't know if you remember me."

His face changed. "Kaia Oana. Howzit?"

He'd always sprinkled his speech with Hawaiian pidgin. "I'm fine. How's Simon? I haven't seen him in a while."

"Getting married in August." He frowned. "Whatcha doing out here at this hour?"

"It's a matter of national security," Jesse said, stepping forward. "I really need to get into the building." He dug out his military ID.

"No can." Kalakaua handed him back the ID. "Latchet be giving me stink eye when he gets wind of it. Waddascoops?"

He'd just asked them what was at stake, so at least he was willing to listen. "Please, Mr. Kalakaua. A little girl's life is at stake. And me—my mother's as well." To her shock, Kaia felt tears well in her eyes as she said the word *mother*. She blinked rapidly to dispel them.

His face softened. "I dated her once, da kine?" He frowned again. "But no can." Then he smiled. "Lesgo, it's about time for my break. Mo'bettah, I'll take a little shut-eye for fifteen minutes." He winked and stepped away from the door without locking it behind him.

Kaia and Jesse looked at one another, and Kaia felt a grin stretching her lips. "You're amazing," he whispered. He held the door open for her, and they walked past Mr. Kalakaua with his feet propped on his desk and his eyes closed.

Kaia's smile felt as wide as the Kilauea caldera. Did he really think that? He touched her hand and squeezed her fingers. Her hand closed around his, and they went to the elevator.

Stopping on the third floor, they stepped out into a dark lobby. Jesse flipped on the flashlight, and its beam illuminated the cavernous lobby. "Duncan's office is the first door on the right."

Kaia followed him down the hall and into the first office. She glanced around at the office furniture. "I'll check the filing cabinet."

"I'll check the computer." Jesse went to the desk and pushed aside a can of Red Bull.

Fifteen minutes later, they were still empty-handed. "Maybe I'm wrong," Kaia admitted. She didn't feel wrong though.

"Or we're missing it," Jesse said.

"Let me look at the computer," Kaia said. "I'm a bit of a computer nerd." Jesse moved aside, and she sat in the chair and began to poke around. "Aha," she said a few minutes later. "There's a hidden file." She tried to open it. "Rats, it has a password."

Jesse sat on the edge of the desk. "I know Duncan pretty well. Let's try a few things." He suggested word after word, but the file refused to open.

Kaia sat back in the chair. "Any other ideas?"

"I'm fresh out," he said. His gaze wandered around the room. "Hey, he's got a picture here of Christy."

"Your wife?" Kaia wasn't sure she wanted to see it. At least she'd know whose shoes she had to fill. She nearly gulped at the thought. Where had that come from? She didn't want to be Jesse's wife—did she?

Jesse leaned forward and plucked a picture frame from the desk. "Yeah, see here. She's standing with Jillian. Duncan used to date Jillian when we were in high school. He still asks about her."

Kaia took the picture and studied the lovely blond woman. In the picture, her head was tipped to one side, and she was laughing. Her green eyes were mischievous. "She's lovely."

"Yes, she was." Jesse took the photo back and stared at it. "Duncan was hung up on her once too, before she and I started dating. In fact, I always thought of her as the girl next door until Duncan took her out."

Kaia wondered what he was thinking. Was he comparing his wife's fair locks with her own dark ones? She would certainly be found wanting when compared with Christy.

"I kind of broke them up," Jesse said.

"Duncan and Christy?"

"Well, yeah, but that was no big deal. They'd only gone out a few times. But I meant Jillian and Duncan. In college he stole the answers to a test and told me about it. It ticked me off, and I told Jillian what he did. She broke it off with him."

Kaia took the photo back and looked at it again. "Do you think Duncan is still angry over that?"

Jesse frowned. "That sounds pretty extreme, though he was pretty broken up over it. He didn't speak to me for a few weeks. When he lightened up, he threw himself into his schoolwork and said he was going to beat me out for valedictorian. I beat him anyway, and he was majorly ticked for about a month. But he got over it."

"Why would he be so competitive with you? I thought you two were friends."

"We were. He'd always been a bit of a geek though. We went through that kind of thing occasionally. He was always sorry afterward, and we stayed friends."

Kaia stared at Jillian's face. "When is Jillian's birthday?"

"June fifth."

She typed in JILLIAN65. "Rats, still wrong. Think, Jesse."

Jesse thought for a few moments then squatted by the desk. "Duncan was always into secret hiding places. Move aside and let me look." He began to feel around the bottom of the desk. "Aha. He's got something taped under the drawer." He struggled briefly then brought up a small notebook. Flipping through it, he pointed at a series of numbers and letters. "Try that."

Kaia typed it in, and the file opened. Jesse leaned over her shoulder and began to read the file with her. She heard his intake of breath. "He intends to direct the missile into Honolulu." She couldn't believe it.

"Nearly four hundred thousand people live there. The death toll would be staggering."

"He can't be serious. Thousands would die."

"Tens of thousands," Kaia said. "Look at this." She pointed to the screen. "He's got another missile system in the works that he plans to sell to the government once this one is discredited. But why would he be willing to kill so many people for money?" She noticed Jesse wasn't listening. His attention was focused on a display of pictures on the wall.

He went to it. "This almost looks like a shrine to his dad."

Kaia joined him. In one picture, Duncan was looking at his father with an adoring expression on his face.

"It makes no sense he'd want to discredit his father's missile system."

"His father designed it? Why isn't it named after him or something?"

"His dad's company split apart and his partner took the credit. It killed Duncan's dad. He drove his car into a monkeypod tree, and we always thought it was deliberate."

"Maybe that's what this is really about," Kaia said. "The new system would have the Latchet name on it."

"Maybe." He glanced at his watch. "We'll have to figure that out later. Right now we have to stop that missile launch."

The phone jangled, and they both jumped. Kaia's eyes widened. "Why would it ring in the middle of the night? Maybe it's Mr. Kalakaua. Answer it."

Jesse raised his eyebrows, but he picked up the phone. "Hello," he said cautiously. "It's Duncan," he mouthed to Kaia. He motioned for Kaia to come close enough to listen in."

She pressed her ear against the phone and heard Duncan's voice. "Did you enjoy rifling through my office, Jesse? Look, I was serious when I told you to do *nothing*. If that missile test doesn't go on as planned, I'm going to kill your niece. So don't even think about calling the commander."

The phone went dead.

Jesse dropped the receiver back into its cradle. "I don't know what to do." He stared uncertainly at Kaia.

"We've still got a few hours. Maybe we can find him and rescue Heidi and Faye first."

He pulled her from the chair. "We have to try."

They left the computer on and the filing cabinet standing ajar and ran for the elevator. The guard kept his face turned away as they exited the building and headed for the boat.

As they approached the *Porpoise II*, Kaia saw a familiar dorsal fin. "It's Nani!" She was dizzy with relief.

She ran to the water and ran her hands over the dolphin. The warmth of her friend reassured her. Nani seemed fine physically, but she was agitated. She kept chattering and whistling. She dove under the water then surfaced again and made more noises.

Nani's pattern of clicks and whistles suddenly formed a pattern in Kaia's mind. She gasped. "She's saying, 'Heidi'!"

"What?" Jesse frowned.

"She's communicating, Jesse! She's telling me she knows where Heidi is." Kaia jumped to the deck of the boat.

Nani chattered again, the same word. *Heidi*. Then a different word. *Shark*.

TWENTY-EIGHT

Faye's stomach rumbled. The man hadn't fed them or given them anything to drink, though it was nearly dawn. Light began to touch the edges of the sky, but only barely.

Heidi slept on a blanket on deck, but Faye hadn't closed her eyes all night. They felt gritty and painful, and she wished she could rest. She wanted to cling to every minute because she thought this night might be her last. The men weren't going to let her walk away. She could identify them.

A light appeared on the horizon. It seemed to be a small motorcraft headed in their direction. Faye had thought she wanted something to happen, but watching the dot grow larger, she found herself praying it would pass them by.

As the boat grew nearer, she squinted in the darkness. Was that her brother-in-law, Duncan? She shot to her feet and waved her hands. "Duncan, we're here!"

The engine died on the small boat, and moments later Duncan climbed aboard. Faye rushed to hug him then stopped when she realized he wasn't smiling. And why had the other man not tried to thwart the rescue? She stared at him.

"I wish you hadn't interfered, Faye." Duncan's lips twisted and he shook his head. "I really liked you."

Liked as in past tense. She took a step away from his cynical smile. "You—you're behind this?" she whispered. "You're going to kill me?"

"I wish I didn't have to." He sounded regretful. "I hate to hurt Curtis. He looked so long for someone to make him happy. You did a good job, I'll give you that."

"Don't hurt the *keiki*," she pleaded, glancing toward the sleeping Heidi.

"If you'd let my man take her, things would have been just fine," Duncan growled.

He is going to kill us both. The knowledge sapped the strength from Faye's limbs. She shrank back to stand over Heidi. "I won't let you hurt her." Her voice was a whimper.

Duncan looked away. "Sorry, Faye. But the kid has a role to play first."

He wasn't going to kill them yet. There was still time to figure a way out of this.

"Something's wrong with the radio," the other man told Duncan. The two went to the helm.

Faye glanced at the boat Duncan had arrived in. Maybe she and Heidi could get away in it. She held her fingers to her lips and started toward the ladder. She'd just reached it when Duncan came back on deck.

He reached her before she could react and grabbed her arm. He woke Heidi then thrust them both into the salon. "Stay there. If you move, you won't like the consequences."

KAIA STRAINED TO SEE THROUGH THE DARKNESS AS NANI LED them on a chase over the sea. The waves were smaller now that morning drew near, and the sea seemed glassy smooth. Nani had said "shark." What did she mean? Could Nani have been talking about something other than an actual shark? Something else that represented danger?

Jesse cut the engine, and the boat bobbed in the water. "Why are we stopping?" she demanded. Nani's dorsal fin was still cutting through the water ahead at a torpedo's pace.

"I see a boat in the distance. We can't get too close or they'll see us." He opened the locker on the boat and pulled out snorkel gear. "If we stand any chance of rescuing them, we have to surprise them."

He tossed her a wet suit and she pulled it on, eager to get into the water with Nani. She saw Nani circling back to get her. She zipped up her wet suit then put her snorkel and mask around her neck. She squinted at the boat in the distance. "Looks like a Viking. Maybe fifty-foot or so. Nani can get us there quicker." She glanced around for the dolphin and saw two more dorsal fins out there. "Liko and Mahina are here too."

Jesse went to the radio and called in their coordinates, but told them to wait until he knew for sure if this was Duncan's boat.

"Let's go." Jesse tucked Heidi's stuffed bear inside his wet suit. "Boo will be soaked, but he might bring some comfort to Heidi if she's there." He tucked his gun into a waterproof bag.

How like him to care about his niece's emotional state as well as her safety. Kaia followed him into the water. The water closed over her head, but she couldn't see a foot in front of her face, although dawn was beginning to brighten the sky. They didn't dare use their lights if they wanted to surprise the people on the boat. She just prayed Nani hadn't led them astray. Nani brushed by her, and Kaia reached out and grabbed the dolphin's dorsal fin. Breathing steadily through her snorkel, she tucked her body close to Nani and let her pull her along the top of the water. She could only hope Jesse would do the same with one of the other dolphins.

When she surfaced, she was six feet from the boat. Glancing around, she saw Liko's dorsal fin approaching, then Jesse's head bobbed up. She pulled her mask and snorkel down around her neck. Kaia swam toward the boat's ladder. Jesse moved past her.

"Let me go first." He began to climb the ladder.

"Be careful," she whispered. She waited until he was at the top then followed. He paused and pulled out his gun.

On the aft deck, she shadowed Jesse as they listened. Nothing moved aboard the boat, and Kaia shivered. It was too quiet. She looked and saw Faye sitting in the salon. Heidi was on her lap. Kaia pointed to them, and Jesse nodded. She could hear his soft exhalation of relief.

Putting his finger to his lips, Jesse moved toward the helm. Before he'd gone more than two steps, a figure appeared in the doorway.

Duncan. He was holding a gun. Another man stepped into view behind him. Kaia didn't recognize the other man, but the impassive expression on his face made her shiver. She stepped closer to Jesse. With two guns trained on them, they were outnumbered. "Drop your gun, Jesse," Duncan ordered. Jesse hesitated, then complied and the gun clattered to the deck.

Heidi's head came up at the sound of Duncan's voice. "Uncle Jesse!" She scrambled down from Faye's lap and rushed out the door of the salon. She launched herself at her uncle, and he caught her to his chest.

"Are you all right?" He ran his hands over her face and arms.

Heidi nodded. "Did Nani bring you?"

"Yep." His voice sounded choked. He reached into his wet suit and pulled out Boo. Heidi gave a smothered sob and clutched the dripping stuffed bear to her chest.

Kaia's gaze connected with her mother's through the window into the salon. Faye rose and came slowly to the doorway. A myriad of emotions raged through Kaia. At least her mother was all right. Part of her wanted to rush into Faye's arms and part of her hung back, still too afraid to let herself feel anything. She tore her gaze away from Faye's face.

"Such a touching reunion scene," Duncan said. His hand shook.

Kaia thought she detected real regret in the man's voice. She stared into his face. He seemed pale but set on his course.

"What's wrong with you?" Jesse took a step toward Duncan but stopped when the gun came up. "What could possibly be worth this?"

Duncan's smile seemed weak. "The family honor, old friend. Honor and revenge. Two of the strongest motives in the world."

"Revenge? What have we ever done to you?"

Pain, regret, then rage flashed over Duncan's face. "Did you deliberately set out to hurt me, Jesse? You took everything from me, one by one."

"Are you talking about Jillian? You were the one who cheated."

Duncan's face reddened. "I lost Jillian because of you. And Christy before that."

"You only went on two dates with Christy!"

"Because of you. Every time I was close to happiness, you stepped in and took it from me." He sneered. "Perfect surfer guy, the jock. All the girls looked at you and didn't know I existed."

"You lost Jillian because you cheated on a test."

"I just wanted to take you down a notch or two, beat you at something. That was the only reason I bought the test answers. You made sure it backfired." His gaze hardened. "Jillian would never even talk to me after that. But don't kid yourself. This is about more than you."

"You'd kill thousands of people because you're *jealous?* And hurt Jillian in the process by taking Heidi?"

Duncan smiled. "That's the beauty of my plan. Jillian will need comforting. She'll be alone again. She'll be totally alone with Heidi gone. And you." His smile faded. "I wish she didn't have to be hurt by it all though."

"The missile system," Kaia said. "It was your father's."

Duncan's eyes narrowed. "He never got credit for it. You never see his name on it. It's always his partner who is said to be the genius, even though ninety percent of the work was Dad's. When the system is discredited, I've got the perfect one to take its place. And this time the name Latchet will be on it. And make a boatload of money in the process." He blinked rapidly. "I'll be someone, the person I was meant to be."

"Nothing that you think you want is worth this," Faye said softly. "Believe me, young man, hurting others for the sake of your own happiness is never worth it. I tried and it doesn't work. God will never let you build your life on another's misery. Better to extend aloha to those who hurt you. Forgive and love them anyway."

Duncan hesitated, and a flash of fear darkened his face. He stuck his gun in his pocket. "Cover them, Brad," he said to the other man. The man nodded and leveled his gun at Jesse.

"If any of them move, shoot the *keiki*," Duncan said. "I've got some details to take care of." He went to the helm, and Kaia saw him speaking into the ship-to-shore radio. Then he shook it and threw it down and began to tinker with the contents. He didn't seem in any hurry. Brad finally let them sit down. Kaia kept stealing glances at her watch. The minutes were ticking by. It was already a quarter to eight. An hour and fifteen minutes until the launch. They had to stop it somehow.

Duncan finally joined them. His face was tight as he went to the side of the boat. Reaching into a locker, he withdrew a piece of plastic. He pulled a tab and the plastic inflated to a lifeboat. Tossing it overboard, he got in a small motorboat that was floating beside the bigger boat.

"Let's have a picnic," he said. "You get in first, Jesse."

Jesse looked at Kaia. She could see the plea in his eyes but didn't know what he wanted her to do. He put Heidi down, and she clung to his hand. "Don't leave me, Uncle Jesse," she pleaded.

"You can take her with you," Duncan called. He was scowling, and Kaia wondered if whatever he planned was going to be more difficult for him to do than he'd imagined.

Brad motioned with his gun. "You heard him. Get moving."

Jesse helped Heidi onto the ladder. Once she was in the inflated lifeboat, he climbed down himself. Faye went next, then Kaia.

"All of you sit on your hands," Duncan said. His vessel floated about ten feet away.

Kaia looked at Jesse, and he shrugged.

"I don't want any funny stuff," he warned. Sweat beaded his forehead and upper lip. He swallowed hard then lifted the lid of the cooler beside him. He began tossing handfuls of bloody meat into the water. He wiped his hands on his jeans then pulled out his gun and aimed it toward the lifeboat.

He paused then wiped his forearm over his damp forehead. "I

hate to do this, Jesse, I really do. It's not as easy as I thought it would be. We were friends once. But I've come too far to back out. I'm not ready to go to prison."

Kaia felt sick as she realized what he intended. She looked at Jesse. They might as well try to stop him even if it meant getting shot. It was better than being shark bait.

"Don't worry; the sharks will kill you quickly." Duncan leaned over the railing to aim the gun into the bottom of the lifeboat. He fired a bullet into the raft, and air began to hiss from the hole it made.

Before either Kaia or Jesse could make a move, Nani launched herself from the water. As she passed Duncan, she gave a powerful flip, and her tail collided with Duncan's body. Off balance from leaning over, he pinwheeled then pitched into the water. His head bobbed to the surface, and he swam toward the yacht's ladder. Nani blocked his move and nudged him away from safety and farther out to sea.

Kaia saw several fins appear. "Sharks!" The raft was quickly deflating. She lurched toward the ladder, pushing Heidi ahead of her.

"Get him in," Brad shouted from the deck of the yacht. He pointed the gun at Jesse.

"Throw your gun in the water and I'll bring him in." Jesse folded his arms over his chest.

"Shoot the dolphin!" Duncan screamed, still trying to evade Nani's nudges.

Brad swung the gun toward Duncan and Nani. His hand wavered. "I might hit you," he shouted. He aimed it back at the lifeboat. "Haul him in or I'll shoot all of you."

Jesse shrugged. "We're about to die anyway. If you want to save him, you'll throw your gun in the water."

Kaia held her breath as the man hesitated. There was no time to waste. They had to get off this raft before it sank.

Duncan began to swear and scream. "Help me!" He batted at Nani, but she kept pushing him toward the approaching sharks.

Brad swore viciously then tossed his gun over the side. "Get him in the boat!"

Kaia grabbed the whistle around her neck and gave the command that told Nani to come. The dolphin left Duncan.

Taking advantage of the opportunity, Duncan swam quickly toward the smaller motorboat. "Help me," he cried.

Jesse grabbed an oar and started to reach it out to help, but Duncan reached the motorboat and managed to haul himself aboard. He lay panting and shivering.

"I need to get a weapon," Jesse whispered to Kaia. He grabbed the ladder and climbed to the deck of the yacht.

Faye hurried to the ladder, and Kaia helped her aboard. Waves were beginning to swamp the raft, and one slapped her in the leg, drenching her with water. A shark was swimming nearby, so close Kaia could have reached out and grabbed its fin. She jumped to the ladder and clambered to the deck as the raft sank beneath the waves.

As she reached the deck, she saw Jesse grab Brad by the arm and spin him around. The other man brought up a speargun. Jesse grappled with him. Kaia held her breath, sure the man she loved would be killed.

The man she loved. She squeezed her eyes shut. What a time to figure that out. She looked around for a weapon, but even as she snatched up a rope, Jesse batted the speargun out of Brad's hand and bore him to the deck. He put his knee in Brad's back and pulled his arms behind him.

"Hand me that rope," Jesse panted. Kaia rushed forward and helped him tie up Brad.

The sound of a motor firing startled Kaia. She ran to the railing and glanced over the side of the yacht. Duncan was steering the boat toward the island. "He's getting away!"

"I'll call the Coast Guard. They'll pick him up. At least there's no danger with the launch. All his equipment is here." Jesse went to the helm to call on the ship-to-shore phone. He came back to the door with part of it in his hand. "It's broken. I need to get to the radio on the *Porpoise II*."

"How? All the boats are gone," Kaia reminded him.

He rubbed his forehead. "Oh yeah." He disappeared back into the helm.

Faye stood off to one side, holding Heidi's hand. She was looking at Kaia with love shining out of her dark eyes. At least Kaia thought it looked like love. A lump formed in her throat, but she couldn't look away.

"I am so proud of you," Faye said softly.

Kaia swallowed hard. She turned away and went to join Jesse.

He threw the mic down. "I can't fix it. I don't know what we're going to do." He stood, and his gaze met hers. "I thought we were dead. If I had died without telling you how I felt . . ."

He held out his arms, and Kaia went into them without hesitation. He was soaked and shivering, but so was she. She rubbed her face against his wet suit. He tipped her chin up and kissed her. She closed her eyes when his lips touched hers. Wrapping her arms around him, she put the love she'd just discovered into the kiss.

She was trembling when they broke apart. "I love you," Jesse whispered. "I didn't want to. I'm too old for you—old and jaded. But it happened anyway." He cupped her face with his big hands.

"I love you too." Kaia felt tongue-tied. "This wasn't supposed to happen."

"We're entering uncharted territory," he said. "And I want to explore it with you as soon as we get a chance." He kissed her on the tip of her nose. "Let's finish saving the day first. We'll have to take the boat to rendezvous with the *Porpoise II*."

TWENTY-NINE

Jesse put his hand to the engine ignition. "Duncan took the key. Great."

"Can you hot-wire the boat?" Kaia asked. "It's nearly eight thirty. You said the missile test is at nine."

Jesse glanced at Brad, who was trussed up and lying in a corner. "You have a key to this thing?"

"Nope." The man smiled. "You think you've won, but time has run out. You're stuck out here in the ocean."

"Duncan's equipment is here, and you're in custody," Jesse pointed out.

"What makes you think he was going to take control of the missile from here?" Brad's smirk deepened.

Kaia heard the smugness in his voice. "What's he talking about?"

"Hide and watch," Brad said.

"Where's Duncan going?" Jesse demanded.

Brad laughed. "I'd love to tell you and watch you stew since you can't do anything about it, but on the slim chance you manage to get to shore before nine, I'd better keep my mouth shut."

Jesse went to where Brad lay. He checked the man's pockets for a key but came up empty-handed. Brad's grin grew wider. Jesse turned to Kaia. "Something's about to happen. We've got to get some help. Let's swim for it."

"I don't think so." She pointed at the sharks still circling the boat as they searched for more of the raw meat Duncan had thrown out.

Jesse paled, and Kaia remembered his fear of sharks. "I hate sharks," he muttered. He hesitated. "I'm going to have to risk it. Can you call Nani?"

She didn't want Nani in danger. "Sharks eat dolphins, you know."

"We can't stand by and let thousands of people die! Look, we have no time to stand here and argue."

She rushed past him to the aft side of the boat. "The sharks are mainly on the other side. They don't usually attack divers. I wish we had our tanks."

"Maybe there are tanks aboard." He began to rummage in the storage compartments, but they found nothing. "I have to try. I'll get the boat and come back for you."

"I'm coming too." These were tiger sharks, one of the most dangerous species. She swallowed and pressed her lips together. "Let me call Nani." She grabbed her whistle and blew it. A few moments later, she pointed. "There she is! But she's not coming close."

"If she sees me in the water, maybe she will." Jesse sat on the railing and slung his legs over.

"Uncle Jesse, you can't go! There are sharks in the water." Heidi ran to grab his hand.

He squeezed it. "You pray for me, okay? I have to go. It's really important." His gaze met Faye's. "Take care of her. I'll be back in a few minutes."

"We'll pray," Faye promised.

"Try to ease into the water with as little splash as possible," Kaia said. "And dive as deep as you dare. We don't want them to mistake us for seals on the surface." She grabbed the railing and let herself down toward the water. She was halfway submerged before she let go, and she entered the waves with hardly a ripple.

Jesse saw her and motioned her back, but she shook her head. "You may need my help. Make sure you come up for air as little as possible," she told him.

He nodded and pulled his mask into place. "See you aboard the boat." His head disappeared into the water.

Kaia took a deep breath and dove. She saw a large shadow off to her right and paused to look. A large tiger shark loomed in the murky water. She dove deeper, trying to emit as many bubbles as she could to let it know she wasn't a seal. That's what she'd always been taught, but this particular shark didn't seem to get it. It followed her down.

Her lungs burned. She was going to have to surface for air soon. She glanced up and saw Jesse moving toward the boat. The tiger swam past, nearly brushing her with its tail. It was checking her out. She was going to die in its jaws.

The shark turned and started back. Its hungry mouth displayed rows of razor-like teeth. She didn't have a chance. Then Kaia saw another form come toward her. Nani. Six other dolphins followed. To Kaia's amazement, they circled the shark. Then Nani rushed in, ramming her nostrum into the belly of the shark. The attacks from the other dolphins came thick and fast. *Wham, wham.* In moments the shark was bleeding and beginning to turn belly up.

Nani brushed by Kaia, and she reached out and grabbed the dolphin's dorsal fin. Nani pulled her quickly to the top, and Kaia took a deep breath, sucking air into her oxygen-starved lungs. Glancing behind, she saw the sea beginning to boil with sharks as they zoomed in to scavenge the fish the dolphins had attacked.

She had to get out of here. Grabbing Nani's fin again, she let the dolphin pull her toward the *Porpoise II.* She saw Jesse standing on deck with the ship-to-shore phone in his hand. Moments later, she grasped the side of the boat, almost too exhausted to pull herself up. She found the last vestiges of her strength and got to the ladder. She climbed aboard and fell onto the deck.

Jesse bent over her. "Are you all right?"

"Shark," she gasped. "Nani saved me, she and her friends."

Jesse helped her up. "I've got to get through to the captain. It's almost nine." He listened. "He's not answering his phone." He dialed another number and spoke to an SP. "Interrupt him," he shouted in the phone. "You can't let that missile launch! Tell him to call me before he gives the order." He clicked off the phone and went to the helm. "We've got to find Duncan just in case we can't reach Lawton."

She dropped into the seat beside him. "Where do we look?"

"I have no idea." His face betrayed unutterable weariness.

"I'll ask Nani." She grabbed DALE from the deck and dropped it over the side. "I'll punch in *shark* and put a man's face on the screen. Nani used *shark* when she wanted me to know Heidi was in danger. Maybe she'll get it."

Nani chattered and rose on her tail in the waves. She plunged into the sea and zoomed off toward shore. "Follow her, Jesse!"

Jesse revved the motor, and the boat zoomed into the wake left by the dolphin's fin. She veered toward shore just past Makaha Point. Jesse slowed the boat and strained to see into the valleys and crevices of the Na Pali coastline. There was no sign of Duncan's motorboat.

Nani stopped and danced through the waves. She chattered and whistled.

Kaia touched Jesse's forearm. "She's saying 'shark' again. You think Duncan is here somewhere?"

Jesse grabbed binoculars and focused them. "I think I see something."

Kaia waited, barely daring to breathe.

"There he is!"

"Where?" Kaia asked. He pointed, and Kaia made out a speck of movement on the slope of the mountain.

"Let's get in there." Jesse steered the boat to the shore until the bow touched sand. He dropped the anchor overboard. The radio crackled to life. "Finally," he said. He picked it up. "Matthews."

The captain's voice came on. "What's wrong, Jesse? Over."

"I think we've located the terrorist, sir," Jesse said. He gave his commander a brief report.

The radio crackled again. "I just launched the missile. You'd better stop that man now. Reinforcements are on their way."

Too late. They were too late. Kaia clenched her fists in her lap.

"Understood. Over and out." Jesse tossed the radio mic down. "I'm going ashore."

Kaia dropped the anchor overboard. "Let's go."

They hopped over the side and waded ashore. A steep path led straight up into a small valley. Jesse took Kaia's hand, and they raced to the path. Kaia's breath came hard as she climbed.

She glanced at her watch. Two minutes had already elapsed. The seconds were ticking by. They broke through the vegetation into a small valley. The remains of a *heiau*, an ancient Hawaiian temple, lay in front of them. On it was a portable satellite. Jesse, ahead of her, raced for it. Duncan was reaching for it.

"No!" Jesse tackled his friend as Duncan swung around with the satellite contraption in his hands. It went flying through the air to shatter against the stone of the crumbling temple structure. Both men rolled over and over on the ground.

Duncan's face reddened. "Arrghh!" He grabbed Jesse by the shoulders and tried to roll him off, but Jesse outweighed him by forty pounds. He beat ineffectually at Jesse's grip on his biceps.

Jesse rolled him over onto his stomach and pulled Duncan's hands behind his back, then dragged him to his feet while still keeping hold of Duncan's wrists.

Kaia rushed to his side, her breath coming in gasps. "You got him!"

"Take your hands off me!" Duncan twisted vainly in Jesse's grip then went limp. He began to sob. He sank to the ground, and Jesse let him. Duncan was a beaten figure with his head bowed and tears streaking his face.

"Let's go get Heidi and Faye," Kaia said.

The navy came and took Duncan away. He seemed smaller somehow. Shrunken and defeated. Captain Lawton congratulated Kaia and Jesse on a job well done and told them the missile test had been a complete success. With the Akis in custody as well, the munitions were safe too.

Kaia waded back to the *Porpoise II* with Jesse. Nani chattered her greeting, and Kaia studied the dolphin with tears in her eyes. "She did it. She talked to me. We communicated with *words*. I don't know what we would have done without her."

Jesse patted the dolphin's nostrum. "She was wonderful. So were you." He put his arm around her and helped her board the boat. They sat down in facing chairs.

Kaia's face grew hot at the love in his eyes. They now had time to explore that uncharted territory. The thought left her both terrified and elated.

Jesse leaned forward and took her hands in his. "Seeing what bitterness did to Duncan made me realize something, Kaia. We can't go forward, either of us, until we can forgive the people who hurt us and let go of the past. I'm willing to do that if you are. When we get back to the boat, can you tell your mother you forgive her?"

She stared at him. "I don't think I can," she whispered. "Not yet."

The elation in his eyes faded. "Try," he said.

She closed her eyes against the plea in his face. "Let's go get Heidi," she said.

He gave her a quick look then turned the key and fired the engine. They said nothing as they headed out to the boat where they'd left Faye and Heidi. Heidi waved to them as they pulled alongside.

Jesse gave Kaia a quick glance as he helped her mother aboard, but she avoided his gaze. Heidi rushed to hug her. Kaia clung to the little girl. Tears stung her eyes at the feel of Heidi's arms around her neck. They were all safe. She could hardly believe it.

Clenching her hands together, Faye stood off to one side. When Kaia released Heidi, Faye took a step toward Kaia. Kaia reflexively took a step back, and Faye's smile faltered. "I prayed and prayed you'd be all right," she whispered.

"We're fine. Duncan was caught in time. Ready to go home?" She tried to sound friendly, but when she saw Faye flinch, she knew her words had come out cold. So be it. Bridging this gap was going to take more strength than she could muster right now.

She caught the disappointment in Jesse's face and turned away from it. If forgiving her mother was a necessary prerequisite to a relationship with him, she might have to keep her distance for now.

THIRTY

Kaia hadn't seen or talked to Jesse for two days. He'd called, but she'd seen his name on the caller ID and not answered. She didn't know what to say. He'd made it clear he didn't want a relationship unless she got rid of her baggage. She wanted to do that, but she didn't know how.

Sitting on her garden bench with her cat in her lap, she could see the blue expanse of the Pacific over the cliff where her house perched. When she'd looked down on *Tûtû kâne's* cottage earlier, she'd seen her mother's Volvo parked in front. The feelings the sight evoked had not been worthy of a Christian, but she couldn't help herself. All her mother had to do was come back, and she was suddenly the family darling again.

Hiwa was licking her paws with relish. Kaia ran her hand over the cat's silky fur. She knew what she should do. The right thing would be to march down the stone steps and see her mother face-to-face. Talk to her.

Kaia rubbed her forehead and put the cat on the ground. Hiwa yowled and shot off toward the palm tree by the fountain. Kaia wished her grandmother were here. Her presence had been as calming as jasmine. Almost lonelier than she could bear, Kaia wished she could lay her head in *Tûtû's* lap and feel her grandmother's fingers in her hair.

A shadow blocked out the sun, and Kaia looked up to see her brother. Bane wasn't smiling.

"We need to talk," he said.

She scooted over on the bench. "So talk."

"I probably should have shown this to you before, but the time never seemed right." He held out an envelope. Kaia stared at it, not sure she wanted to know what it contained. "Read it," he urged.

"What is it?" He laid the envelope in her lap, and she stared at it. She recognized the writing. Bane's name was slashed boldly across the paper in her grandmother's familiar script.

"Read it and see."

Her hands trembled and her fingers felt clumsy as she pulled the paper inside free of the envelope. She unfolded it and began to read.

Bane,

I leave you this letter as the eldest. When I'm gone, I pray you will choose the right time to give this to your sister. Your wisdom is great in spite of your youth. You will know when.

My Kaia, though you are dearer to me than I can say, there is a cancer eating up the joy in your heart more ravenous than the disease devouring my body. I fear this bitterness I see growing in you will strangle the joy from your heart as seaweed chokes the lagoon. You have brought us much joy in your grow-ing years. Now you are a wahine, *a woman. The Bible says to put away childish things, and I hope as you read this letter, you can do that very thing. Forgiveness is an adult response, and you must take hold of it with the same zest with which you embraced your studies. Do not blame your mother for her mistakes. God says to forgive as He has forgiven us. Let go of it, my Kaia. Let go and let God heal your heart.*

Tûtû

Kaia dropped the letter, and it drifted to nest in a bed of mimosa. For a few moments, she was a little girl again, and her tûtû the woman with all the answers. If only her grandmother were here to guide her through these treacherous waters. She didn't know how to forgive her mother. If only she could forget the past and forge a new future. But it was easier said than done.

"You have to forgive her, Kaia," Bane said. He squeezed her shoulder and left her.

"Help me, *Tûtû*," she whispered. But the only answer was the wind in the palms.

JESSE SAT IN HIS JEEP AND LOOKED AT OKE KOHALA'S COTTAGE. From the vehicles parked around the sandy road and in the driveway, it looked like Kaia's brothers were here. Though Jesse wasn't enamored at the thought of baring his heart to the world, it was now or never.

If he had to fight for Kaia, so be it. She hadn't answered his calls, so this was the next step.

"Are we just going to sit here?" Heidi asked. "I want to go look for Nani. Will you come with me?"

Jesse glanced at his niece. Her blue eyes darted around in fear. He couldn't blame her for being scared. She'd been through things no child should witness.

"Let's go." He got out. Heidi scooted over the seat to get out on his side. She held his hand in a death grip.

"When is Mom coming?"

"As soon as she can get a flight." Jesse would miss Heidi. Now that the tests were over and he could spend more time with her, he was about to lose her.

"That's what you said yesterday." She watched the koa tree grove with suspicious eyes.

Her mother would have been home by now except for her canceled flight. There had been a terrorist scare, and Jillian had been stuck in Italy, much to her dismay. She hoped to get a flight out within a day or two, though Jesse didn't dare tell Heidi the reason for the delay. She would just worry all the more.

He stopped on the path and squatted to look her in the eye. "You don't have to be afraid anymore, monkey. The bad guys are locked up. You're safe."

Her face contorted. "It was scary, Uncle Jesse."

"I know. And I'm sorry I wasn't there to keep you from getting scared. But God was with you. You know that, right? And he kept you safe."

"I know." Her face relaxed. "I prayed and prayed for you to find me. And he sent Nani."

"That's right." Jesse smiled.

"Where is Kaia?" Heidi's voice was plaintive.

"I'm not sure. I'm going to go find her later." Maybe she was at the lab. She had plenty to keep her busy there now that Curtis had heard the story of how Nani helped rescue his wife. Jesse stood up and took Heidi's hand. His steps lagged. Man, he didn't want to have to enlist Kaia's family's help, but he didn't know what else to do. He felt like a kid going to his dad over a problem at school.

The imu pit was heating, and Mano was layering the hot coals with ti leaves. He waved at Jesse and went back to his work.

"Can I watch?" Heidi whispered.

Jesse nodded. "I'll come get you later and we'll go to the beach."

"Okay." She ran to join Mano, who handed ti leaves to her so she could help him.

Pressing his lips together, Jesse strode to the cottage door and knocked.

"Be right there," Bane called.

Wonderful scents came through the screen door, and Jesse's mouth watered. He hadn't eaten breakfast yet, and the aroma of baking coconut made his stomach rumble. He stepped away from the door as Bane joined him.

"Where have you been hiding?" Bane asked, holding open the screen for Jesse.

"I've been busy."

He followed Bane inside. "It's about time you showed your face." He studied Jesse's face. "You look a little haggard, *brah*."

If there was one thing a man hated, it was to let his emotions show on his face. Jesse had thought he was doing a good job of masking his pain. "Kaia isn't speaking to me. And Faye says she won't take her calls either. I made the stupid mistake of telling her she needed to forgive her mother before we could pursue our own relationship."

Bane gave Jesse a good-natured slap on the shoulder. "Smart man. You can't build anything on rotten ground. My sister can be stubborn. She's been hurt too many times, but she needs to learn to let it go. I've prayed about it, and I'm going to call a *ho'oponopono*."

Jesse was familiar with the family therapy session, though he'd never personally attended one. It meant literally "to make things right," though he suspected even a radical intervention like that would fail to reach Kaia. Still, it was worth a try. She at least had to listen out of respect for her family.

"When?" Jesse asked.

"Tomorrow at sundown. I'll send our grandfather to fetch her. She can't refuse the command of the *kahuna*." Bane grinned.

NANI WHISTLED AND CLICKED TO KAIA AS SHE SAT AT THE PIER with her feet hung over the side. "Good girl," she said. The dolphin had said "swim." Kaia still couldn't believe they'd breached the wall between the species. Real communication. It was a dream come true.

If only her other dreams would stop hounding her. Every night she went to bed vowing to forget Jesse: the sound of his voice, the scent of his skin, the touch of his hand. And every morning she awoke with a vivid dream of him: the sparks that had flown between them the first time they met, his gentleness with his niece, his commitment to those he loved.

Kaia had fought the dreams by throwing herself into her research. She wanted no time to think or feel. So far she hadn't succeeded. She felt like she'd been tossed around in the water by a humpback whale. And she couldn't get her grandmother's letter out of her mind.

Jenny hurried along the wooden dock. "Reporters are due in about an hour."

The other woman had been subdued the last few days. At least Jenny hadn't been involved in the plot to blow up the munitions storage area. And Kaia hoped her heart hadn't been too badly damaged by the discovery that Kim had murdered Jonah Kapolei. Kim and Nahele weren't getting out of jail anytime soon.

Was her own bitterness taking her in the same direction Duncan and Nahele had gone? She wanted to be rid of this. She glanced up at Jenny. "Is Curtis handling the interview?"

"He wants you to do it. He thinks the reporters would rather ask him about Duncan than the communication with Nani."

Kaia winced. Curtis had been hit hard by his younger brother's arrest and attempt to kill Faye. "I'll do my best," she said.

"I'll stall them until you're ready." Jenny touched her on the head and went back to the office.

Kaia glanced up as she left. Her grandfather was here. He stopped to speak to Jenny then continued on toward where Kaia sat on the dock.

"Curtis said you'd be out here," *Tûtû kâne* said.

She scrambled to her feet. "Is something wrong?"

Her grandfather was somber, a state she seldom saw him in. "Bane has asked me to call a *ho'oponopono* for tonight. I want you to be there."

Kaia brushed the debris from her shorts. "It's been ten years since you've called one of those." The last time, Bane and Mano had been fighting over the same girl and had refused to speak to one another for two weeks. Kaia gulped. If she had talked to her grandfather about how she was feeling, he might not have resorted to such a drastic measure. Refusal wasn't an option, though she wanted to ignore the summons.

"Is our mother coming?" she asked cautiously.

"Of course."

Great. Just great. The ho'oponopono was all about forgiveness and healing breaches. But in spite of her dismay, a thrill ran along her spine. Part of her longed to see her mother again. Her mother—*Faye*, she corrected herself—had caused too much pain and suffering. She had no idea of the damage she'd left in her wake. How could she? Her parents had never left her. They'd always been around to love and support her. Faye had no frame of reference to even understand what she'd done.

"I can see the wheels turning," her grandfather said, laughing. "You think too much sometimes, Kaia. You'll be there." It was a command, not a question.

"I'll be there. Even if I don't want to be."

"I think I already knew that." Her grandfather dropped a kiss on her head, then left her by the water.

Kaia glanced down at Nani. She had rolled to her side, and one eye peered up at Kaia as if to judge her temper. "You should be very afraid," Kaia told the dolphin. "I'm mad enough to bite lava in two."

Nani bumped against her, and Kaia remembered how lethal her head butt had been to the shark. It was hard to reconcile the loving sea mammal nudging against her with the deadly torpedo that had saved Kaia's life.

Later, Kaia introduced the reporters to Nani then answered their questions. They snapped what seemed like hundreds of pictures of her with Nani and the other two dolphins. Jenny joined her for several group photos as well. It had all seemed so important once upon a time, but now her personal problems outweighed her joy. By the time the crowd was gone, she was exhausted. How could she face the evening ahead?

She'd wear her new red mu'umu'u, she decided. It would give her courage. She hurried home to shower and change. Hiwa met her at the front door. The cat wore a satisfied expression as she sat on the rug and licked her whiskers.

"What have you been into?" Kaia asked, stepping over her pet.

She glanced around. The cat had knocked the picture of her grand-mother from the coffee table to the floor. Kaia picked it up and scolded Hiwa, who continued to groom herself without concern.

Kaia left off berating the cat and hurried to change her clothes. Was tonight going to be the beginning of a new phase of her life? She felt on the cusp of something momentous, and part of her wanted to crawl in her closet and hide. Her life had been going along just fine so far. Why did everything have to change? She scrubbed her teeth with particular care.

Hiwa followed her down the stone steps to her grandfather's cottage. The evening breakers were rolling to shore, the white foam they left soaking into the sand. Her mother's Volvo was parked in the driveway, and Jesse's Jeep was just behind it. Why had he been invited to gang up on her? Kaia wanted to turn tail and run back up the steps to the safety of her house. She was about to be bombarded from all sides.

Everyone looked up when she entered the living room. She didn't know which pair of eyes to gaze back into. She focused on her grandfather's face. He was safest. She found a seat across from Jesse.

Her grandfather stood. "Let us open with prayer." Bowing his head, he lifted his hands. "Father God, we your children ask your divine intervention. The power of forgiveness lies in you alone. Give us your love and wisdom today and guide us this day. In Jesus' holy name. Amen." He dropped his hands and folded his arms across his chest. "Today, at the request of my grandson, I have called this *ho'oponopono* to settle a dispute between Paie and her children. Which of you will begin?"

Not her. Kaia couldn't look at her mother or Jesse.

"I will." Her mother stood. "I beg the forgiveness of my family for the wrongs I've done to them. I offer no excuses for what I did. I was wrong."

"I give you aloha, *Makuahine*," Bane said after a slight pause. "I release any anger and bitterness to God."

"Same here," Mano said.

"Say the words of forgiveness, Mano," their grandfather said.

"I give you aloha, *Makuahine*." Mano looked up and met Faye's gaze.

Her brothers turned to look at Kaia with an expectant expression. If she said the words, would it make them true? She stood and clasped her hands in front of her. "I want to forgive." Kaia tipped her chin up and stared into Faye's sorrowful face. "You have no way of knowing what your desertion did to me. How it made me afraid to let a loved one out of my sight. How I seek everyone's approval and can never seem to have enough of it."

Kaia's voice rose until she was almost shouting.

Her mother closed her eyes and sank back against the cushion. "I'm so sorry, Kaia."

"Calmness, *lei aloha*," her grandfather said softly. "Sit down. Breathe deeply and ask God to heal your heart as we talk."

Kaia sank to her chair and buried her head in her hands. She would like to be rid of this load she carried, she suddenly realized.

"I want to ask you something," Bane said. "When you sin against God, what do you do?"

"I ask forgiveness." She thought she knew where he was going with this. "But He's God. I don't have His infinite grace and mercy."

Her brother stared at her a moment, his weathered face impassive. "Do you know how God feels when you hurt Him, Kaia? Do you fully understand what your sin does to Him? And what about Nani? Does she understand what you mean when you pat her and tell her you love her? Do you know if she feels betrayal or pain when you leave her?"

She was beginning to get a glimmer of what he was trying to say. He was right. She had no idea if her sin truly hurt God. Kaia bit her lip. "We are two different species."

"Exactly. There is no way for her to fully understand you or your emotions. And no way for you to understand her. All you can hope for is a distant echo of meaning and intent to come through. Just as your mother doesn't know how you felt when she left, so you can't really understand the pressures that drove her to do what she did. You say you would never do what she did, but we are all human and share a common frailty, Kaia. We all have a weakness, an area where we are most prone to sin. Hers is no worse than yours or mine. As God forgives us, we are to forgive others. Free aloha. No strings attached."

Kaia shut her eyes as her brother's words penetrated her heart. Did her willful sin affect God the way her mother's had hurt her? She'd never considered the fact that God could feel pain. It was so easy to forget Him, so easy to get caught up in life.

"Can you forgive, *lei aloha?*" her grandfather whispered. "Forgive as God would have us to do?"

"I want to." Fresh tears leaked from Kaia's face. She opened her eyes and looked at her mother. She vaguely remembered a somber time in the house when she'd been told her daddy was never coming home again. She'd found her mother looking through a photo album with black streaks of mascara running down her face. Kaia had crawled into her mother's lap and demanded a story. Her mother had wiped her eyes with a tissue and gotten out a Dr. Seuss book. She'd swallowed back her tears, but Kaia knew now the pain had still been there.

In that moment, Kaia realized how utterly solitary every person is. Who knew what went on in her heart except for God? Like her brother said, all she could grasp were distant echoes of the reality experienced by those she loved.

Her mother's eyes glistened with tears, and her soft, pink mouth trembled. "Forgive me, Kaia," she whispered.

Kaia nodded. "I give you aloha, *Makuahine.* I release the anger I feel to God and ask Him to heal it." Saying the words brought a rush of tears to her eyes. She was free. The heady knowledge sapped the strength from her knees as she rose.

Her mother stood at her approach. She started to raise her arms then faltered. Kaia opened her own arms, and her mother's face lit with joy. She rushed to embrace Kaia.

The scent of her mother's perfume wafted over her in a welcoming rush. She'd never been close enough to Faye to notice the perfume before, but its scent was familiar. Kaia felt the weight she'd carried for years melt away.

She released her mother and stepped back. Her grandfather beamed at her. The approval in his dark eyes lifted Kaia's spirits even more. Her gaze sought Jesse's.

"Do you have something to say to me?" he asked.

She nodded. "In private though." She finally dared to glance into his eyes and look away. The love shining there deepened the blue of his eyes.

"I don't know. I think I'd like to hear it too," Bane said. "What about you, Mano?"

She stuck out her tongue at her brothers. "Want me to sing a love song?"

Bane backed away with his hands held out. "Anything but that!"

Oke grinned. "Perhaps my granddaughter should grovel in front of all of us for putting Jesse through so much worry."

"Not a chance, *brahs*." She held out her hand to Jesse. "Let's go check on Nani." Jesse grinned. He rose and took her hand. They walked to the lagoon hand in hand.

He stopped by the lagoon and took her in his arms. "I love you, my beautiful mermaid, even if you're too young for me, even if you can't carry a tune in a water bucket, even if I have to put boots on to walk through your house. I'd adore you even if you smiled at me with raspberry seeds stuck in your teeth."

"Eww!" She smiled up at him. Happiness bubbled inside her like a hot lava spring. The unconditional love shining out of his eyes enveloped her in a warm glow. "I love you," she said softly. "You were right. We couldn't build a future with so much of the past holding us down. We've got time to build it with the right foundation now."

"But not too much time," he whispered. "I want to marry you. Soon."

The endless blue of the sea matched the eternal aloha in Jesse's eyes. As Nani rose on her tail and danced through the waves, Jesse took her in his arms, and her heart danced with her dolphin.

HAWAIIAN LANGUAGE
PRONUNCIATION GUIDE

Although Hawaiian words may look challenging to pronounce, they're typically easy to say when sounded out by each syllable. The Hawaiian language utilizes five vowels (a, e, i, o, u) and seven consonants (h, k, l, m, n, p, w). Please note that sometimes the *w* is pronounced the same as *v*, as in Hawai'i.

> a - ah, as in car: *aloha*
> e - a, as in may: *nene*
> i - ee, as in bee: *honi*
> o - oh, as in so: *mahalo*
> u - oo, as in spoon: *kapu*

Dipthongs: Generally, vowels are pronounced separately except when they appear together:

> ai, ae - sounds like *I* or *eye*
> ao - sounds like *ow* in *how*, but without a nasal twang
> au - sounds like the *ou* in *house* or *out*, but without a nasal twang
> ei - sounds like *ei* in *chow mein* or in *eight*
> eu - has no equivalent in English, but sounds like *eh-oo* run together as a single syllable
> iu - sounds like the *ew* in *few*
> oi - sounds like the *oi* in *voice*
> ou - sounds like the *ow* in *bowl*
> ui - an unusual sound for speakers of English, sort of like the *ooey* in *gooey*, but pronounced as a single syllable.

Characters:
  Anaki (ah-NAH-kee)
  Bane (BAH-AH-nay)
  Kaia (KIGH-yah)
  Liko (LEE-ko)
  Mahina (MAH-HEE-nah)
  Mano (m-AH-no)
  Nahele (nah-HAY-lay)
  Oke (OH-kay)
  Paie (PIE-ay)

Words used in this series:
  aloha (ah-LOW-hah): a warm Hawaiian greeting or parting;
      love, grace, sentiment, compassion, sympathy, kindness,
      affection, friendship; to show kindness or to remember
      with affection.
  aloha nô (ah-LOW-ha-NO): expression of sympathy
  auê (au-(W)EH): uh-oh, or oops
  brah (bra): brother
  haole (ha-OH-lay): white person. Can be a slur depending on tone.
  he aha ke 'no (HAY-ah-ha-KAY-ah-no): What is the kind?
Meaning, what kind of nonsense is this?
  ho'oponopono (HO-oh-PO-no-PO-no): ritual of family therapy.
      Literally means "to make things right."
  imu pit (EE-moo): pit for roasting a pig at a lu'au
  keiki (KAY-kee): child
  keikikane (KAY-kee-KAH-nay): son
  lei aloha (lay ah-LOW-hah) beloved child
  mahalo (mah-HAH-low): thank you. Heard everywhere in the
      islands, even when something is announced on the loud
      speaker in Kmart.
  makuahine (mah-koo-ah-HEE-nay): mother
  makuahini (ma-koo-ah-HEE-nee): mother

makuakane (mah-koo-ah-KAH-nay): father
'ono (OH-no): a popular fish for eating
tûtû (too-too): grandma.
tûtû kâne (too-too-KAH-nay): grandpa

READING GROUP GUIDE

1. Kaia's view of herself was tainted because of her mother's desertion. What events in your life have altered your view of yourself? How do you deal with them? How should you deal with them?

2. How did you feel about Jesse's sister leaving her daughter, Heidi, with Jesse? Women today are pulled in many different directions. Have you ever felt you should be able to do it all but had to neglect something important to you?

3. Jesse had to deal with a demanding boss who sometimes made stupid decisions, but he obeyed anyway. Why are we told to obey those in authority over us? Is that hard for you?

4. The spirit of aloha in Hawaii is unconditional love. As Christians we are told to show love to others. What does this mean to you?

5. Why do you think Bane was so hard on Mano? Was he justified?

6. Kaia's grandfather had trouble facing trouble when it came. Humor was his way of coping. How do you cope?

7. Kaia couldn't sing, though she had other talents. Do you recognize your talents or do you wish for those you don't have?

8. Sometimes we can think longingly of past loves, like Duncan did of Jillian, and it can affect how we interact with the people in our lives today. Have you been able to let go of the past?

9. The Pele group was trying to get the government to address past grievances. We humans often find it impossible to let go of past hurts. Is there something in your past that you find hard to put behind you?

10. Faye agreed to care for Heidi although she feared it would be too much for her. Do you have trouble saying no or do you fear saying yes to something that you think God would have you do? How do you find that balance?

11. Kaia was terrified of spiders. The Bible says we are not to have a spirit of fear but of power and a sound mind. (II Tim 1:7) What fears do you have? What are you doing about them?

12. Kaia was violently opposed to the idea of looking for her mother when Bane suggested it. What do you think her primary reaction really was at the first?

13. Jesse was accused of something he didn't do. Has that ever happened to you? What did you do? What should we do?

14. Jesse blamed himself for his wife's death, and he actually was to blame for taking his attention from the road while driving. Have you ever done something that harmed someone else, even if it was unintentional? How did you handle it?

15. Kaia was determined not to forgive her mother. What finally convinced her to forgive and allow the healing to come?

Acknowledgments

Sometimes I have to pinch myself to believe I'm fortunate enough to work with the fabulous WestBow Press team: Allen Arnold, Ami McConnell, Jenny Baumgartner, Amanda Corn Bostic, Lisa Young, Scott Harris, and Rebeca Seitz. God is so good to allow me to partner with you. Being a member of the family has been a dream come true. You all are the best!

No book is all it can be without great editing, and I get the best that's out there. Ami McConnell has a laser-sharp mind that sees to the heart of any character I create. You have made my work shine and made me better than I am. Your friendship has made my life sing.

My thanks to Erin Healy, freelance editor. You deserve the highest praise in the editing world: I can't tell where my words leave off and yours begin. Thanks for your wonderful attention to detail.

What can I say about my agent, Karen Solem? Without you, I'd be nowhere. You're more than a great agent; you're a wonderful person whose friendship I treasure. Thanks for keeping me calm, making me stay focused, and delivering a swift kick when needed.

My first line of help and encouragement is my critique partners: Kristin Billerbeck, Diann Hunt, and Denise Hunter. Your e-mails keep me sane, make me laugh, and make me better. Thanks for praying and for telling me when my scenes need more work.

A special thanks to Dolphin Quest at the Hilton Waikoloa on the Big Island. I actually got to touch their own Nani. The Hilton was a fabulous place to stay as well and I thank them for the aloha they extended.

Not many wives are fortunate enough to have a husband like mine. Dave prays for me, carts me to book signings, reads every word before it goes to the editors, and supports my career in every way he can. I love you for all those things, but even more for being a man who loves and follows God.

And all my love and thanks to God, who opened the doors and has held my hand every step of the way.

The *USA Today* Best-Selling Hope Beach Series

"Atmospheric and suspenseful"
—*Library Journal*

Available July 2014

Available in print and e-book

THE ALOHA REEF SERIES

About the Author

RITA finalist Colleen Coble is the author of several best-selling romantic suspense novels, including *Tidewater Inn*, and the Mercy Falls, Lonestar, and Rock Harbor series.